THE BEWITCHING MINUTE

MARK MOORE

The Bewitching Minute

Mark Moore

Copyright © 2022 Mark Moore
All Rights Reserved

Cover Design by Julia Midgley

for CDK

Does the silkworm expend her yellow labours
For thee? For thee does she undo herself?
Are lordships sold to maintain ladyships
For the poor benefit of a bewitching minute?...
Surely we're all mad people, and they
Whom we think are, are not...

From The Revenger's Tragedy by Thomas Middleton

PART 1
1 Tunnel
2 Noises
3 STC
4 Plan
5 Trail
6 π
7 Talk
8 Rochdale
9 Merci
10 Ranch
11 Sheep
12 Andromeda
13 Police
14 Ride
15 Arms
16 Koggs
17 Mask
18 Extract
19 Koggs
20 Rochdale
21 Drone
22 Wish
23 Doc
24 Bozon
25 2π

PART 2
26 Trail
27 Call
28 Perfect
29 Ricochet
30 Benefit
31 3π
32 Book
33 Slip
34 Tunnel
35 Shoes
36 Talk
37 Defile
38 Magda
39 Inside
40 Novice
41 Welcome
42 Ribbon
43 Feet
44 Eye
45 Gone
46 Ledge
47 Way
48 Road
EPILOGUE
49 Trail
50 Steel

PART 1

1

THERE WERE TUNNELS TO COME. He wasn't sure about tunnels. They were strange. Especially ones hacked out of the rock with no means of support. He couldn't see why the mountain didn't just collapse in on the cut and squash it, to heal the deadly intruding sore and seal it.

Tunnels seemed to be more than just providing quick ways through the mountain. They seemed more like wormholes to its hidden heart. The rock seemed to permit the incursion only reluctantly and would deny access without warning.

More than anything they were dark. To pass through you had to bring your own light. Your torch was your passport to the dark realm. Not a realm, he thought, more a republic, the rock republic.

There were tunnels ahead in the gorge, aside from the hidden forbidden one, that the walker is obliged to use. He knew some tunnels were voluntary, some compulsory. There were tunnels which could be avoided where the trail splits and provides an option to go through the obstruction in the dark or go round it and stay in the light. But there were others where there was no other way. There was no choice on those stretches of the trail. The cliffs are too steep and there is no other path.

First thing he checked before setting off was to dig out his headtorch from his pack and make sure it was working and that he had spare batteries.

Camo Lylly came down from the Pointe Sublime to the banks of the Verdon river and entered the gorge. He stepped into the water and wet his boots in the shallow edge of an eddying pool as a symbolic gesture. For him every hike along every trail needed a baptism at its start or a libation at its end. Then he went up the ramp and the eleven steps cut into the rock to the first tunnel. It was early and the morning was fresh and the amber rock on the cliffs on the far side of the river was sharp in the clear light of May in Provence.

Apart from the conversation over dinner, he'd read about the tunnels in the guidebook before he set out from Spain. It said they had been dug in the 1930s when there was a plan to dam the Verdon at the western end of the gorge and completely flood it for a reservoir. The artificial lake so created would have held a vast amount of fresh water. The mass of water retained by the dam would have created the largest reservoir by volume in Europe. The civil engineers pinpointed the spot where they would create the dam. It was then realised they would need to dig tunnels and carry a narrow gauge rail line through them and through the length of gorge to bring men and materials to the dam site in what was one of the most isolated and least populated parts of the continent. They got as far as digging the tunnels before better sense prevailed. They had second thoughts about destroying the gorge. In the end they left Europe's greatest gorge intact and built dams elsewhere to create two large reservoirs north and south, above and below the gorge instead. The tunnels were all that was left of the grand plan that in the end turned out to be a grand folly. But at least the presence of the tunnels did allow the long-distance footpath to make its way unimpeded all the way through the gorge.

As someone with civil engineering training himself Lylly wasn't at all surprised that the original engineers had put the provision of power and water ahead of maintaining the beauty of the landscape when it came to the decision to drown Europe's greatest gorge. It might be one of the very few occasions when politicians had stepped in to improve the decision and had created a better outcome for all concerned.

The path was mostly flat and stayed on the same contour all the way through to the ascent out of it at the far end. It was about thirty metres above the Verdon river. Occasionally the path descended to the river bank. In parts the sheer sides of the gorge reached vertically another fifteen hundred feet higher, and more.

The tunnels, both optional and compulsory, had been excavated in the first half of the gorge, before the river went through its right-angle bend halfway through, where it switched ninety degrees back to the north, before turning westerly again. After the big bend there were no more tunnels. One of the obligatory tunnels was over six hundred metres long and two of them were four hundred metres long. There were other tunnels too, but these were shorter. None of them were as long as Kellner's hidden tunnel, but Lylly thought he wouldn't want to have to go through any of them without a torch. Nor his walking poles.

The first tunnel came right at the gorge entrance. It had been dug four hundred metres long, cutting through a vertical cliff on the northern side at the start of the gorge.

Lylly dug out his headtorch and entered the tunnel. Far ahead he could see the light at the end. The tunnel was straight. His footsteps echoed along the passage. He caught up with a few picnickers who were feeling their way tentatively in the dark along the tunnel side wall because they had forgotten their torch, or didn't know one was needed. Lylly helped them out by slowing down and showing the way with his light. They emerged from the tunnel and the picnickers descended through the scrubby trees to the river. He wondered how the picnickers would find their way back through the tunnel after their picnic. Maybe they would latch on to someone else with a torch. He imagined the first tunnel and the picnic spots by the river would be quite crowded on a hot day. But he guessed that only someone walking the long-distance trail, armed with a torch, would proceed any further into the gorge. Lylly carried on along the trail. He was now completely alone.

Round the next bend in the path came the second tunnel. The first two tunnels were close together on the trail. This was also a four hundred metre one. Lylly switched on his headtorch. He carried it in his hand and didn't bother wearing it on his head. It didn't seem worth it in such a relatively short and straight tunnel, where the light from behind and beyond streamed a long way inside. This tunnel was also lighter because a window to the outside had been cut in the rock about halfway along on the left side above the river that let in a broad wash of light. It allowed a view of the river below.

Without being slowed down to help the untorched he strode on at a rapid pace through the dead straight tunnel. His boots felt good and the pack was comfortable on his back. The stiffness he had felt on the rest day in Castellane had now completely gone. He kicked the occasional loose stone with his boots and the stone skittered away into the dark with a tinny slither and clatter. Apart from his own footsteps there was dead silence. This tunnel still had a few sections of the original light rail tracks left abandoned on the rock of the tunnel floor. The railway sections incorporated their own iron sleepers fixed between the rails so no ballast was required to level and stabilise the rails in the ground and bed them in. The gauge seemed to be about half a metre or even as much as six hundred millimetres as far as Lylly could judge.

Later as he left the tunnels behind and walked in the open Lylly heard some deep rumbling explosive crump sounds in the distance coming from up and beyond the southern edge of the gorge. A helicopter chuntered ahead of him high in the sky above the gorge and occasional military jets screamed low overhead.

He thought the bangs and thumps were distant thunder at first, which was strange because the day was hot with a broad blue sky. But then as another jet screamed overhead followed by two more helicopters, he realised what he was hearing was distant gunfire. He thought more on it and eventually decided he was hearing military manoeuvres. A big all-arms exercise was taking place in the vast military reserve on the Plaine de Canjuers, which he knew was sited in the empty land somewhere south of the gorge. He knew about it, as it was after all western Europe's largest military playground, in comparison to which the army range on Salisbury Plain was a tiny relation, a mere grassy knoll. Lylly and his unit had actually been on NATO and joint-EU exercises on the Canjuers. He just hadn't realised he would be able to hear all the military bangs and whistles inside the gorge.

They were pulling out all the stops today he thought as another pair of jets screamed overhead barely sixty feet above the lip of the gorge. Everyone's here but the navy. But he checked that for confirmation by examining the torrent below to his left for a periscope. He marvelled at the universal ability of all armed forces everywhere to wreck and ruin even the wildest and most beautiful places.

But as he ventured further into the gorge he left the sound of gunfire behind and was troubled no more by screaming jets or thumping clattering helicopter gunships.

Now there came a long spell of a few hours when the gorge opened out a little and the were no tunnels because there were no riverside cliffs, bluffs or rocky shoulders which the trail couldn't pass and where it would need help from a tunnel to make further progress. Down to his left the river ran with a great noise between huge boulders and over unseen humps in the stream that caused the water to swell up and gush and swarm over them, sometimes creating a back-wave as it flowed. Above the river the land rose in angled shoulders thickly covered with small trees and shrubs until the shoulders met the bare vertical sides of the gorge. The vertical sides formed vast cliffs that rose up and up, for over two thousand feet in the deepest parts to the high plateau above. In places the high vertical sides cut out the sun. If a landscape could ever be described as dramatic, this was it. Though the path was well made and quite worn and well-trodden, Lylly felt he was venturing into the unknown, alone, like an intrepid navigator in a trusty caravel following nothing but a compass bearing into the void.

Then around midday Lylly came to the next tunnel. He knew this was the six hundred metre one. By that stage he hadn't see anyone since passing through the first two tunnels. The day trippers and picnickers didn't venture this far. After those first tunnels Lylly had packed away his headtorch. Now he took off the pack and retrieved the torch. He tightened the torch's elastic straps round his head. He wanted to have his hands free in the long tunnel. Overhead there was the majestic sight of a couple of European vultures circling, peeling and wheeling on the warm air currents rising out of the gorge.

This tunnel was not only different to the ones at the beginning of the gorge because Lylly was on his own in it, it was different because it had noises in it. The noises were strong enough and strange enough for Lylly to consider his options for defence.

Lylly had two options for defending himself. One was a fighting knife, the other was a pair of walking poles. He'd had the two items combined into one by his contact in the specialist workshop in Zaragoza.

Lylly had a pair of walking poles. Every hiker used walking poles. They were said to relieve the strain on the legs of walking all day by as much as fifteen per cent. But Lylly's poles were different. He'd had them not so much modified as copied and remade in the specialist engineering workshop in Zaragoza run by John the Lithuanian. Members of the Legion often used it for private and extracurricular commissions. The Lithuanian was a former member of the Legion himself and he'd set up the Zaragoza workshop partly to cater to the demand from current and former caballeros for licit and illicit items that involved a certain amount of metalwork and engineering. The workshop was known strictly through word of mouth only. The ostensible business of the workshop was in specialist engineering for machining, supplying and repairing parts for cars and foundry work making municipal spares such as manhole lids, gully grids and the like. But the Lithuanian was always ready to help fellow current and former caballeros with their engineering requests, for a price.

The other option Lylly had was a 1944-vintage Fairbairn-Sykes fighting knife with a blade just short of seven inches. It was said the seven inches was the minimum necessary to allow three inches to pass through the thickest clothing imaginable, such as a Soviet greatcoat, and still leave four inches for the kill. Though this was a relic from the Second World War which he'd come across on a forgotten shelf in a dusty cabinet in a militaria junkshop in Liege, in Lylly's view it had never been bettered as a close quarters stabbing weapon. Though he hadn't spent the ten thousand hours needed to fully master the lethal close combat skills, it couldn't be far off from that number, and what he'd learnt from the Dog Island combat instructor in the barracks basement in Melilla he'd expanded on and adapted to suit his own capabilities. He kept it in its leather sheath in a side pocket of the backpack.

The original walking poles which Lylly took to the workshop were three sections of telescopic aluminium tube. They could be fitted to the right usable length by twisting them and sliding the lengths inside each other. The necessary rigidity was achieved by loosening and tightening an internal rubber mechanism that expanded and contracted by rotation, pushing against the inside of the tube to create a tight and usable friction fit against the interior of the tubes. Good and steady for assisting your walking but not rigid enough for stabbing and thrusting. Lylly had the aluminium tubes replaced with still slender but much stronger thick walled stainless steel sections, and instead of the expansive friction rubber mechanisms the sections were linked by precision screw threads, with the overall length of the poles cut to Lylly's walking height. In practice they still served as collapsible walking poles, and Lylly even had the original paint and logos replicated on the steel tubes.

John the Lithuanian's workshop made a final adaptation to the walking poles and knife. They made a series of modified lugs on the knife and ring sockets on the poles at the bottom ends where he could fix and attach the F-S knife like a bayonet. The idea was that Lylly could attach the knife to either of the poles, whichever he grabbed first. Once in place the knife was fixed firm and converted the walking pole to a five foot spear with a bayonet at the tip. Not only were the bayonet anchors strong, rigid and firm they were also quick-release. The knife could be rapidly clicked into place at the and of the pole and equally rapidly removed.

It was a question of preference. The vintage knife was a deadly enough weapon when held in the hand. When fixed to the end of a strong and rigid pole it was even more deadly. Despite his training in knife combat in the Legion Lylly preferred to be deadly at a distance rather than close up. To a certain extent being able to fight at a bigger distance away eliminated some of the uncertainties that were inevitably involved in close-quarters knife fighting. A singular advantage among the others was that when attached to the end of the pole the knife could be wielded in two hands instead of one, thereby much increasing the penetrative power of the weapon. These attributes suited Lylly's fighting methodologies better. The modified hiking poles gave him a pair of two-handed weapons he could use to keep an opponent further away than arm's reach.

John also added a bonus. He made two extra screw-in sections for each pole so the stabbing spears could be increased in length to two metres and more should Lylly require the added length.

Like every soldier he hoped he would never have to use these assets but was glad he had them.

2

NOW AS HE HEARD the strange noises in the distance coming from the far end of the tunnel he unscrewed and collapsed one pole and stowed it, attaching it to the exterior of his backpack. He dug out the fighting knife from the backpack. By the light of his headtorch he clipped the knife to the bayonet sockets at the end of the pole. He looped one hand through the nylon strap at the top of the pole in a ski-pole grip and held the shaft with the other. Then he advanced holding the pole in two hands with the deadly knife tip facing forwards.

As well as the clinking sound of stones being shifted and disturbed he could see movement silhouetted in the distant tilted D at the end of the tunnel. But he was too far away to make out what the movement, human or animal, belonged to.

He realised that if he could see and hear whatever was making the noise, they could see and hear him. It was impossible in the small light of the headtorch to choose a route where there were no loose stones and so step quietly along the loose shingly floor of the tunnel. He knew that just as the figures in front were silhouetted against the distant tunnel mouth, so he too would be silhouetted against the distant tunnel entrance behind him. If he didn't want to just stand and stay where he was for an unknown length of time till whatever was moving ahead disappeared then he had no choice but to keep advancing.

Then at one point as he came closer he could clearly see silhouetted in the tunnel exit that whatever was waiting for him at the end of the tunnel had four legs. It was only goats. Or it was sheep. Lylly knew there were certain mountain species where it was difficult to tell the difference. He relaxed and unclipped the F-S knife from the end of the pole and stowed it in the pack. He extended the other pole and advanced again along the bare tunnel floor using both poles as walking aids. As he approached the end of the tunnel the small flock of sheep or herd of goats – he had no idea which – fled away from the approaching human out of the tunnel and down the woody mountain side out of sight towards the river below.

Lylly came out of the tunnel and pushed on. He was into a good rhythm. His boots still felt good. The pack was comfortable. It was fixed, still and steady on his back and didn't slosh about or waggle from side to side with each step, which he knew would tire him out if it did. The chest strap kept the shoulder straps in the right place and stopped them slipping. He was full of energy. The going was good. The scenery was breathtaking. He was glad to be there, then; everything seemed to fit. He felt good in the landscape. But he didn't try to push too fast. He knew the key to walking well all day every day was to pace himself. In a way that meant always walk a little slower than you think you could. Good marching was one of the things he'd learnt in the Legion.

High above to his right where the slope changed and the tree-covered gradient altered its angle from wooded shoulder to vertical cliff he could see a pair of rock climbers roped together, one leading, one following. They were attacking the rockface, searching for a way up. It seemed from Lylly's distance they were standing on nothing, hanging in the air as though supported on nothing but their own hidden super-powers.

He knew why they were there. The Verdon river had dug down and created the gorge through deep beds of limestone. Limestone being friable tended to cleave away from the cliff under the stress of the winter freeze-thaw cycle. Large parts of the cliff could fall away under the expansive pressure of the winter frosts. The big clumps of boulders and shattered rock, many as big as cars and some as big as a house, dropped and rolled among the trees and often all the way down into the river. It meant come spring there could be sections of the cliff which were bright pink new rock, that had never been climbed by humans before, ever. It was these newly exposed unclimbed sections the climbers came looking for.

He nearly stumbled as he watched the two climbers, one male the other female. A pair of vultures wheeled away above and beyond the climbers. Perhaps it was the same pair he'd seen earlier. Lylly wondered if the climbers were approaching a nest site in the cliff face.

He stopped to take a drink several times. And once where the path descended to the side of the river he went down to it and crossed to the middle of the stream by jumping and stepping from rock to rock and perched on a boulder as big as a truck that stood well above the water surface. There he ate a section of a cheese and ham baguette, a pain au chocolat and an apple for his lunch. He threw the core into the river and watched it bob away downstream. Later he rock-hopped back to the bank and continued the trek. The path left the river level and ascended gradually through trees to its more normal position thirty metres above the water.

Now came the decision point. Should he take Kellner's tunnel or not? He knew he must be getting close to it. Lylly knew that if he took this supposedly closed giant twelve hundred metre tunnel it would cut a sizeable chunk out of his itinerary for the day. It would cut off a large section of the trail where it zigzagged, climbed and dropped, and almost doubled back on itself in a ninety-degree bend round a high bluff, where a smaller tributary the Artuby joined the Verdon river from the southeast.

Taking the tunnel would put him well ahead of the clock and would mean he wouldn't have to camp for the supposedly risky night stop in the gorge down by the river. Kellner said he would find the entrance to the tunnel when he saw a very large scree originating on his right hand side which went all the way across the trail down to the water.

Kellner was right. Lylly followed the path round a rocky buttress and suddenly he was on the scree. The trail crossed the scree well below its halfway point. The bulk of the scree lay up on the slope on the right hand side. Lylly stopped. He decided he would climb the scree and check the tunnel out.

Lylly knew the scree was actually the rocky debris and outfall from cutting the tunnel. Kellner had told him that. He was now at the point where he had to make a decision. Should he stay with the trail or head up to the top of the scree to find the hidden tunnel? He stepped off the trail and began to ascend the loose rock of the scree. The first thing to do was have a look.

After twenty minutes of foot-slipping and knee-banging scramble, where with every step he went three feet forwards to lose two feet backwards, he reached the top of the scree. There was a flat area above it and at the back of the flat area almost hidden under trees loomed the dark tilted D-shaped entrance to the forbidden tunnel. Lylly pushed the foliage aside and stood in the entrance and peered into the dark. Unlike the previous ones this one was not straight and he could see no light in the distance. This one had a bend in it.

He knew that this happened in the old days with pre-electronic linear surveying techniques, when teams of navvies started hacking into the rock at both ends of the tunnel with much of the direction to be taken down to guesswork. They headed towards each other through the blind rock taking their best guess as to the direction to follow. But then they often missed each other near the halfway stage before they realised it, and overshot each other, and had to backtrack, and then a kink had to be dug to make the tunnel sections meet up. Lylly wondered if the first inkling the diggers had that they'd missed each other would be the boom of primitive quick-burning non-detonating explosives or the sound of pickaxes striking the rock somewhere at the side instead of ahead. The longer the tunnel the more likelihood of a miss. There was a famous rail tunnel under the Pennines that had just such a kink for the same primitive surveying reason.

Lylly decided to take the tunnel.

Strange how these things went, he thought. Purely because he literally could see no light at the end of the tunnel, and because he was now off the map, he felt far more wary in this tunnel than he had done in the previous straight ones. If he twisted an ankle or broke a leg, or was struck by falling debris, or was in any way immobilised there would be no walkers coming along afterwards to help him and raise the alarm. He was on his own.

Again he collapsed one pole and secured it to his pack. He took the remaining pole and attached the knife to the end. He held the pole lightly balanced in one hand, ready to instantly grip it with both hands if need be and point the tip forward. He fixed the torch on his head so to free both hands. Now he felt armed and ready as he advanced into the dark.

He was familiar with fear. As a soldier fear was good. It had been a constant companion on several occasions in Sarajevo and among the poppy fields in Helmand on the plains of Afghanistan. You could use it and make it work for you. You didn't evade it or try to overcome it. You used it. While it wasn't fear he now felt he did feel something, a hesitation and wariness. He thought it probably was ancient, genetic, generations old, from a time when his human ancestors would know that advancing into a dark cave could be a very dangerous thing. Who knew what powerful and deadly animal called the dark hole home? Having a modified spear disguised as a walking pole in his hand allowed him to overcome this ancestral caution and relax as he moved into the darkness. His headtorch threw an oval of light on the ground ahead.

This tunnel had low piles of rock cluttering the ground in places where bits and pieces of the roof had collapsed. They had never been cleared and instead the tunnel had been closed. Lylly made his way round the rubble with the light from his headtorch.

The tunnel had pools of water underfoot and there came constantly the sound of dripping water, plinking as drops fell into the clear shallow pools of standing water on the tunnel floor. The sounds always seemed to come from beyond the range of his torch.

There were other noises in this tunnel too. But they were different. It sounded like something was breathing deeply but with difficulty. The rock face was breathing to itself.

Lylly knew that didn't make any sense. But he also knew that there were many strange noises in long tunnels. The actual cause of the noise might not even be in the tunnel. It might be outside, and the sound projected into the tunnel mouth, and then the walls amplified and distorted it and carried it along. And the audible outcome was then nothing like the original source. And often much more mysterious.

So he knew very well that the rock walls of the tunnels were not breathing. It just seemed a little like they were.

He had flicked on the headtorch as soon he entered the tunnel. For a good few metres the ambient light streaming in from the tunnel entrance behind him was far stronger than the beam of the torch. He couldn't even tell if he had the torch switched on or not. Then came a time when he began to notice the beam, but the light around was still dominated by the light behind from the entrance. And then there came a stage when the light from the entrance behind reached no further and the only light ahead was the oval on the ground thrown by the torch. And if he looked over his shoulder the tunnel entrance was only a d-shaped ring of light in the distance from where no light reached his position.

And then the d-shaped light was gone as the tunnel bent quite sharply to the right and the tunnel entrance was cut off by the curve. Even though he was expecting it, Lylly felt a little bereft and uncomfortable that he could no longer see the light behind nor the light ahead. For what seemed to Lylly like nearly a hundred metres there was no light behind and no light ahead. Then the tunnel curved again to the left and in the far distance for the first time the light at the end of the tunnel loomed faintly. He'd lost the light behind for good but now had found the light ahead.

The sound of the walls breathing was stronger now.

The sound began to unnerve Lylly. He stopped and listened. The breathing seemed to come from a point ahead and to his right.

And for the first time the breathing sounded like it was coming from an animal. Or a person.

He advanced again. But there was no question, he was wary now. He didn't think France had any bears, but were there wolves here, he wondered? He knew they were increasingly being seen in the high Alps, gradually repopulating the mountains from their longterm home and last redoubt in Italy. They were welcomed and protected. But had they reached this far south yet? He wouldn't have thought so. Instead, much more likely he thought, it was an exotic pet that had escaped.

A billionaire's playground like the Cote d'Azur was bound to have sufficient egotistic idiots that kept big cats as pets. A puma or leopard or cheetah could possibly have escaped and made it this far north from the coast, especially if it was drawn to wilder country. He thought also it could be a wild boar. He had heard they could be very dangerous if they were protecting their young. They were solid and heavy and had tusks. He changed his grip on the pole and now held it pointing forward with both hands. Ready to attack or defend.

The breathing came louder. And then suddenly the thin light of the torch caught on something ahead on the side wall on his right that was a lighter shade than the rock, and the source of the shallow breathing became clearer. He moved on slowly and carefully, throwing the beam of his torch ahead and to the right to try to make out more clearly what it was that was there on the tunnel wall.

He thought a bear or a wolf or a puma would be more aggressive somehow and make its presence known with greater noise as a human approached. Especially if it was enjoying its dinner by gorging on a dead sheep. Yet there was no increased noise as he came nearer. Just the sound of breathing. So he expected to find the shape was a dead sheep or goat, and the apparent breathing in reality turn out to be the drone of a swarm of carrion flies. Then if it really was breathing he was hearing and it was then more likely to be alive, perhaps it was an injured animal with a broken leg.

He didn't know what he would do if he found an injured animal unable to move, slowly starving to death. He knew that whatever he did or didn't do the action and the thought would stay with him afterwards for a very long time. He knew from the previous tunnel that the wild sheep – or goats – liked to enter the tunnels. Perhaps they sought shelter from sun and rain.

He came closer and stopped in surprise in mid-stride. He stood still. He played the torch beam on the wall.

Lylly was shocked and horrified. The shape was human.

There was a woman chained to the rock. She was breathing but seemed to be unconscious. He quickly approached her. He could see in the light of his headtorch that four expansion bolts had been driven into the tunnel wall to act as anchor points. The woman's arms and legs had been spread and held apart like Leonardo's Vitruvian Man, and her wrists and ankles were tied to large rings on the heads of the anchor bolts with bright yellow and blue speckled nylon climbing rope.

She was naked and spreadeagled like a starfish and pinned against the tunnel wall. The ropes attached to the rock anchors pinning her ankles were of sufficient length to allow her feet to rest on the ground, so were taking her weight though still spread far apart to complete the starfish shape. Her head was hanging down forward, and her dark hair was shrouding her face.

There was something marked in white strokes round the woman. Lylly shone his torch round to check them out. There were two vertical strokes painted on the rock on either side of the woman, outside the line of the anchor bolts. And a horizontal line ran along the wall above her head and outstretched arms. The horizontal line touched the top of both vertical strokes but carried on some way past them. The entire shape seemed to be executed in white paint.

Lylly could make no sense of it, but it looked as if it had been deliberately daubed to include the pinned woman inside its strokes, as though the lines now defined and limited her world.

Lylly threw off his pack and dug out his multi-tool and opened up the longest cutting blade. He carefully cut the rope at her wrists and ankles. It occurred to him that the police might want to examine the knots on the rope so he steered clear of those. They looked to have been done with some kind of professional expertise or knowledge.

Even in the torch light he could see that the woman's skin was a darker shade than his own. She had a Mediterranean hue and complexion. That could place her anywhere in the countries of southern Europe and Turkey or in a broad sweep ranging from the western edge of north Africa to the eastern edge of the Mediterranean and beyond to Iraq and Iran. She could even be local French from Provence.

Though Lylly was hurrying to release the woman, he refused to apologise to himself, or to anyone, for taking a good look at the woman's body. She looked to be aged in her mid thirties, perhaps younger. She had the modern counter-evolutionary twenty-first century female body shape of a slim slender form, very athletic, with narrow almost boyish hips and medium-to-large breasts.

Lylly caught the unconscious woman as she sagged away when released from the wall. It was cool in the tunnel and Lylly had no way of knowing how long she had been held there. He felt her hands. They were freezing cold. He took out his camping insulation mat and laid her gently on it on the tunnel floor. He also reached into his pack and brought out his aluminium backed groundsheet and wrapped it over her body. He thought she would need to be kept warm.

But then thinking further on it he considered she might need greater warmth. He wondered if he should carry her out into the sunlight beyond the tunnel.

Without further thought he reached down and picked the woman up, still wrapped in the aluminium groundsheet, lifted and placed her gently as he could over his right shoulder and advanced with her out of the tunnel.

There was a wide flat open space at the tunnel mouth surrounded by trees. He laid her down sitting propped up against a tree in bright sunlight and went back in for his pack and the insulation mat. He unscrewed his poles and packed them away in his pack.

Only then did he think about contacting the emergency services.

And the police.

Already he was calling her Andromeda in his mind. But whatever was going to happen next, Lylly knew his gentle life-affirming birthday-marking hike through the Alps of Provence was over.

He sat down on a rock next to the woman and thought back on how it had come to this.

3

LIKE SAMUEL TAYLOR COLERIDGE, Camo Lylly very rapidly came to dislike his decision to join the army.

Unlike Coleridge Camo Lylly didn't need his friends to get together to buy him out or have him extracted on the grounds of insanity. He had enough money to do that himself, and while many considered him crazy they didn't think he was insane. Except he didn't want to get out anyway. He didn't like it but he he'd signed up for the three-year stretch so the three year stretch he did. He didn't like it but didn't regret it.

Coleridge joined a unit of the national army, whereas Lylly joined a mercenary unit. And while Coleridge left the Light Division pretty quickly when his friends and brother found out where he was, with Camo Lylly no one really cared where he was or what he was doing. He stayed for training. Then he stayed afterwards for action. Quite a bit of action as it turned out. And a lot of marching. Then he got out when his contract was over.

Of the two Coleridge joining the Army was probably more inappropriate than Camo Lylly joining the Legion. Samuel Taylor Coleridge was a book-loaded, unfit and podgy poet, a dreamer and while not yet a fully-fledged opium addict, he was very much someone who's interior life was far more real and vibrant to him than the exterior world around him. Coleridge joining the Army was like Billy Bunter or Frank Spencer joining the SAS.

Lylly on the other hand was healthy and in his mid-twenties. He was young and fit. He was also ruthless. Shortly after gaining his university degree Lylly had caused the death of three people. He did it because they tried to kill him. They probably thought they had killed him. Lylly took his revenge by unleashing the most unstable one against the other two. He pointed one killer in the direction of two other killers and wasn't shocked or surprised or remorseful when all three ended up dead.

But there was also a similarity between C Lylly and ST Coleridge. They both had the ability to do the unexpected.

The unexpected in Coleridge's case was joining the Army. In Lylly's case it was the Foreign Legion, but the unexpected thing was it wasn't the French Foreign Legion he joined, it was the Spanish Foreign Legion. Or to give it its modern name the Spanish Legion.

Foreign Legions are sometimes compared with the SAS. They're both elite units requiring the most fit, the most able, the most ruthless and the most deadly recruits. But there are only around 300 members of the SAS whereas the foreign legions are almost divisional in size. The French Foreign Legion has 9,000 men. And the Spanish Legion 8,000.

They're first in last out anywhere in the world. And unlike domestically-recruited national units, being a mercenary unit a Foreign Legion is totally expendable. Basically recruits to the Legion don't vote and they don't have mothers. Which in the French case goes some way to explain why they've been wiped out to the last man three times in the unit's history.

There's a lot of antiquated mystique about Foreign Legions. They're not romantic. They're not a hideaway for spurned lovers. They're not really anymore an anonymous haven for criminals and runaways. They're just elite mercenary fighting forces, on a par in capability with any special forces unit in the world but twenty to thirty times bigger. And they do a lot of marching.

Lylly was a caballero – trooper - in the Legion's Gonzalo de Cordoba tercio for three years. That's the minimum length of contract. Recruits join one of the four tercios – roughly equivalent to regiments, and named after some of the giants of Spanish military history - which make up the Legion. After that first three years the recruits either renewed the contract or they left. Most caballeros renew. Camo Lylly left.

He left for a number of reasons. He was tired of killing. He was tired of being in situations where he might have to kill. He was also tired of being in situations where he might be killed. He was tired of being in situations where he could be shot at but couldn't shoot back. He was tired of being a peacekeeper in other people's wars. He was utterly tired of taking orders. And above all he was tired of marching.

But more than that. After three years he was a different person than when he joined. When Camo Lylly joined the Spanish Legion he was a drifting aimless kid with no idea of what to do with his life. Three years later at the end of his contract in the Legion he was an adult. He was now a drifting aimless adult with no idea of what to do with his life. But he didn't care. He knew now it didn't matter. Aiming was for people who had targets. He'd just had three years of that. Being aimless meant you had no targets, and that was good enough for Lylly.

Samuel Taylor Coleridge left the Army and quite soon afterwards wrote one of the greatest poems in the English language. When Lylly left the Legion he knew that he would never do anything as magnificent or as significant as that. He was no Romantic poet or literary revolutionary. But he didn't care. He would treat each day the same and see what came up. A bit like the Wedding Guest before he met the Ancient Mariner.

He'd learnt a lot in the Legion. He'd learnt what he could do and what he couldn't do. He'd learned how to fight and to use a variety of weapons. He'd learned how to fight with projectile weapons and with bladed weapons. He'd learned how to fight without a weapon. He'd discovered he was stronger than he thought. He'd made some lifelong friends, and a few enemies.

Lylly could join the Spanish Legion because he had been a Spanish resident. Unlike its French competitor which took recruits from anywhere, the Spanish Legion was only open to Spanish citizens or citizens of the former Spanish colonies, or to residents of Spain. That included Camo Lylly.

Of course his real name wasn't Camo, it was Archer. But he'd been known as Camo from an early age at school after his habit of hiding and not getting involved in anything. In fact Camo was beginning to worry a little. For the first time in his life over the last few years he'd been getting involved in things.

First he took an English degree. Then he and some student friends found and lost a fortune in gold coins, only then to benefit from the sale of some valuable books they found instead. Then he went back to university and came out with a degree in Civil Engineering. He was a man with two degrees, plenty of money, and no job. So he went to live in Spain. Then he joined the Spanish Legion. He was hardly "Camo" any more at all.

Three years later he was out of the Legion. Three days after he left he was driving across Spain.

4

LYLLY DROVE NORTH. He was heading towards the French Alps across the great hot heart of Spain, arid and bare as a concrete runway. The high driving position gave him a good view of the countryside. The lack of traffic combined with Spain's long interstate-style dual-carriageways gave him plenty of opportunity to gaze around.

He used to own a Porsche 911, very low and very fast and no good for viewing the surroundings, making him concentrate on the road ahead. Just as well given the speed he used to drive it. That was in his old life, "before" as he now thought of it, in the innocent but careless and adventurous time before he joined the Legion. He sold the Porsche when he joined the Legion. And when he left it he bought a left hand drive Mazda SUV.

One of the plans he had after leaving the Legion was to drive all over Europe while that was still possible. He realised that this was the last golden age of driving, the last golden age of personal transport. The last possible time before road police, drones, cab spies and self-driving goody-goody vehicles stifled the fun out of the road. The last time before wall-to-wall radar traps and fast-breeding speed cameras over-regimented the rules of the road. The last free time before driving became a rigidised procession. While the open road was still possible and not just a fading dream he wanted to drive from Lisbon to Istanbul and from Bordeaux to Moscow and from Naples to Narvik. He knew he wouldn't have long.

But that was next. First he wanted a walking holiday in the Alps. He thought he might go on an Alpine walk for his thirtieth birthday. He thought a big trek might be a good way to put his military life behind him. He wanted to trek the mercenary soldier out of his system. He'd marched for three years with the Legion's very distinctive and idiosyncratic marching style under other peoples' orders. Now he would march at his own pace in his own way under his own command.

And though he knew that being a soldier was something you never really left behind he also knew that when he finished he thought he wouldn't be a soldier on the surface any more. It would be buried deep inside him. It was said that people could always tell when someone had been a soldier. Camo Lylly hoped that when his trek was over no one would be able to tell that about him.

He was heading for France and Cannes and the start of GR4. France is full of long distance hiking trails. They're all named according to the formula GR plus a number. GR stood for *Grande Randonnee*, big trail. There's one trail, GR5 the mother of all trails, which runs the full cross section of France from the North Sea to the Mediterranean via nearly every mountain range there is on France's eastern side.

But Lylly wasn't heading for GR5. He was heading for another one, GR4. This one began on the coastal mountain plateau above the Mediterranean town of Cannes and headed west and northwest. It eventually ended up in Bordeaux on the Atlantic coast, but Lylly wasn't going that far. He was going to hike the section through the coastal mountains, two hundred miles through the Alpes de Provence. Lylly reckoned it would take him two weeks. He knew he could do it much faster than that, at Legion speed, but that wasn't the point. He wanted it to take two weeks. Two weeks was good.

He'd start from Cannes and head north up into the mountains, then cut due west, heading eventually for the Rhone river. First there would be lavender fields. Then after following the Roman packhorse trail out of Castellane would come a two day stretch dropping through the stupendous Gorge du Verdon. Then there'd be an empty time through some wild and desolate country high above Lac Sainte-Croix and south of the crusader village of Moustiers, untravelled and unvisited; then he'd be back in civilisation and more lavender fields as he neared the Rhone. And finally before hitting the river there would be a two day up and over of Mont Ventoux, the giant of Provence, that overlooked the river; the first and last Alp, the gleaming white-topped monster famous for its deadly presence in the Tour de France.

Camo Lylly didn't care so much for the lavender fields, although he had to admit that part of him was even looking forward to that. What interested him more was the prospect of the plunge through the great gorge followed by the climb up and over the great mountain.

Lylly's plan was to leave the car in the care of a hotel he knew on the banks of the Rhone in Avignon, then make his way with his boots and his backpack by train to Cannes. There he'd get a bus up the mountain to the start of the trail near the Cote d'Azur Observatory. Then he'd trek west for two weeks till he reached the big river. He would be literally walking two hundred miles back to his car.

He took a big pack, a tent and a sleeping bag. He also took a map but he didn't think he'd need it. For a compass he'd use the app on his phone. But just in case he also had a military compass buried deep in his pack.

He didn't think he'd need the map because the trail was so well signposted. But one thing he'd learnt all his time marching in the Legion was you never went anywhere without a map. If you didn't have a map yourself you were always in the company of someone who did. Signposts could be altered and tampered with. Maps couldn't. Nor did you put your entire trust in map apps. You never knew when you wouldn't be able to charge your phone or link up to a signal. Like the military compass in the side pocket of his pack, a printed map was the ultra reliable backup.

He'd got himself ready and geared up. Lylly knew there were two schools of thought about the shades of clothing worn when trekking. The older school said you wear things very bright but not that beautiful, mainly so you can be seen clearly and easily should rescuers need to find you. The more modern school says you wear duller greener more rustic colours to blend in with nature better and don't shout your presence to the landscape; fitting in not alienating. Lylly didn't do either of those. He didn't care about either school of thought. He just wanted to be comfortable when walking all day up and down mountains with a heavy backpack. So for trousers he just took a couple of pairs of his old lightweight army ones from the Legion, hot weather issue in desert camouflage, plus a couple of state-of-the-art modern-material wicking shirts in light olive green and sky blue with chest pockets. He also had a cotton multi-pocketed sleeveless tan-coloured gilet over the shirt, mainly to increase the padding thickness on the tops of his shoulders under the straps of the backpack. He knew a shirt on its own would never be enough padding for two hundred miles. But he didn't wear his army boots. He bought a pair of expensive lightweight walking boots and wore those instead.

It was spring, late April and early May, so he was expecting it to be mainly warm in the Alps, but he might catch the end of the rainy season too. And given that he'd be walking through the Alpes de Provence in the south not far from the sea it was likely to be hot and sunny too.

He marvelled as he drove how parched and dry and arid the interior of Spain was. There was nothing but scrub growing for miles and miles. No wonder the conquistadors felt at home in Mexico and the southern USA he thought. Admittedly, never having been there, his idea of Mexico was derived straight from cowboy films. But there was the same aridity and parched landscape, the same dusty horizons, and similar bare sculpted rocky landscapes with mesas and buttes, arroyos and canyons. The Spanish words had become universal usage for desert landforms. It didn't feel like lush green Europe at all.

5

LYLLY CAUGHT THE MOUNTAIN BUS at Cannes railway station. It was a single-decker and passengers filed past the driver to pay. As he waited in the queue to get on Lylly looked through the windows and counted the seats from the front, identifying the seat midway between the axles. Then once on board he moved down through the aisle and found the seat was unoccupied. He knew the seat midway between the two axles was the most comfortable place to sit.

The bus went north through the town and its suburbs heading away from the sea and chugged up the mountain. It stopped at various places, some obvious others less so, and eventually came to a halt on an expanse of gravel exposed under trees on the outside of a hairpin bend.

The driver called out "Autostop." Lylly realised he thought he was getting off to start hitching. Maybe he didn't know a big walking trail started at this point. From inside the bus Lylly could see the red and white rectangles, the flashes of paint on a tree trunk by the side of the gravel, that were the route markers for the long-distance footpaths. There was also a wooden signpost with the red and white flash painted on it and the letters GR4. It was pointing into the trees. The door gave out its hydraulic snake hiss as it opened and Lylly stepped down. He lugged his pack one-handed by his side.

The bus turned back on to the road as Lylly hefted the big pack onto his shoulders. He oriented himself and peered about him in the bright hazy sunshine of a Provençal spring. He could see the path emerged from the far end of the gravel tract then disappeared under the trees. Far up above to the north and slightly to the east on the flatter almost-top of the mountain plateau he could see the big twin hemispherical domes of the observatory. A long way to the south he caught the glint of the sun shining on the sea.

He knew that before heading west the first part of the trail headed north into the interior to the walled town of Entrevaux on the Var river. This was a fortified citadel town, a strongpoint designed to block an invader coming over the mountains into France and looking to head down the Var valley to the jewels of the Mediterranean coast. After Entrevaux the path headed west.

Lylly and the trail turned north. He made his way into the woods. It was two o'clock in the afternoon in the last week of April as Lylly began his two week two hundred mile trek.

His first action was to check his walking gear. Boots first. He had done up the laces when he put them on in the morning at the hotel in Avignon. He had them loose and comfortable for the taxi ride to the station, the train journey to Cannes and the bus hop up the mountain. He intended to walk twenty minutes then tighten them. Thirty minutes after that they might or might not need tightening again. They felt good, light but sturdy. He would see how they felt after two hours walking.

Next he monitored his pack, how the shoulder straps felt and how much the weight was being spread between the shoulder straps and the hip belt. Lylly knew there was a wisdom that said you took the weight mainly on your shoulders going up a mountain and mostly on your hips coming down. But he didn't think it really mattered. He would find what was most comfortable for him on this terrain. He suspected a lot of it depended on the time of day. He'd marched with so much weight in the giant army packs in the Legion that the medium capacity forty-litre backpack now on his back felt no more onerous than a silk scarf.

One thing he had which he wouldn't have been without was his large bandanna. Some of the lads in the Legion called it a keffiyeh, others a shemagh. Lylly always called it a bandanna because it made him feel like an outlaw, a desperado, a Mexican bandido, a baddie from a cowboy film or a spaghetti western. Lylly's blue loose-weave cotton bandanna was worn anywhere round the head or neck to give protection from the sun and dust. Now he had it wound lightly round his neck, but bunched and raised more so at the back than the front to maximise protection from the sun on the back of his neck. He also sometimes wore a plain tan baseball cap with no logo, but as often as not walked bareheaded.

It was hot and sunny, as he'd expected. He pulled out his sunglasses from a chest pocket and slid them on.

The path was a rocky gravel-strewn trail, well-worn and in good condition, about a metre and half wide. Occasional bigger lumps of rock protruded from the ground like the back-coils of the Loch Ness Monster. Lylly could either step on those or go round them. He did both for a while. Generally the path was hugging the contour but also gradually and imperceptibly was breaking the contours and making its way higher, up the mountain shoulder. It was easy going. Sometimes the path cut through open treeless patches in the woods. This gave Lylly a view to the south to the flat blue sea. Then the trail turned away and took a route through a small dry valley in its northwards vector. The view of the sea was cut off by the mountainside and never came again.

He'd studied the map and knew that each day at first would be an up and over hike. Up a valley side to a col, then along the plateau edge for a while, then down the other side into another river valley. He would find a place to camp when he'd had enough for the day. If he was still on the heights among the plateau and the peaks when he'd had enough, then so be it. He didn't need to descend to a valley.

He had a tent and a sleeping bag, an insulation mat, a small gas cooker, a nest of light aluminium pans, a multitool that converted into a knife, fork and spoon and some supplies. Enough for a night stop. He had two one-litre bottles of water in the pack's side pockets. There were plenty of towns and villages on the route where he could find water, buy supplies and stock up for the day. He also had some silver-based water purification tablets in case he had no choice but to drink from the local streams. And he knew occasionally he would stay in a hotel if he fancied a comfortable bed and a good meal, and perhaps some company too. After three years in the Legion his Spanish was fluent. His French was pretty good too.

That first night Lylly put up his tent on a flat piece of ground under Mediterranean pines some way below and not far from the small ski resort of Greolieres les Neiges. He heated a can of cassoulet and mopped it up with chunks of baguette. Even after three years in the military, food outdoors still tasted good to Lylly. He slept well. It was the day after that he began to walk through lavender.

The lavender fields came in waves. It looked like the ground was carpeted with line after line of purple corduroy. He knew there was both lavender and lavandin in the purple lines but he didn't know the difference between them. He couldn't say he cared really, it was just something he'd picked up over the years living in Europe. He also knew the oil from the plants was the historical base of the European perfume industry.

Then as he moved further west he left the lavender fields behind. Over the next three days the ground became more arid, the terrain more rocky, the plants spikier and the villages fewer and further between. From Entrevaux he turned west and went up and over the high ground above the treeline for a while then came down again to the town of Castellane. Lylly booked into a hotel for two nights and took a rest day in Castellane.

Apart from taking a break after four days walking, he wanted a rest day because he didn't want to be going anywhere on the first of May, the bank holiday. He knew the minor roads everywhere would be heaving and crawling with cyclists and the hill trails flooded with day-walkers and mountain-bikers.

He had been four days on the trail. It was easy going. He was getting in to the swing of it, but was in no hurry. He had seen no one else on the trail in either direction. He thought that was either because GR4 was not a popular trail, or more likely it was not a popular trail in spring and early May.

There was a six hundred foot cliff almost in the middle of Castellane, overlooking the town square, and a small chapel was perched on top of it. Lylly learnt the chapel was built to celebrate the town's deliverance from a particularly nasty occurrence of the regular and periodic bouts of cholera that used to ravage Europe. Lylly strolled up the path round the back of the cliff to have a look both at the chapel and the view from the top.

The winding path up the back of the cliff had the fourteen stations of the cross marked out at intervals. He guessed a stalwart Castellane citizen had been pressganged in to carrying a cross up the cliff in a civic procession to deposit the cross in the chapel in thanks to Jesus for the town's deliverance from the cholera plague.

Lylly took a day's rest in Castellane. He pottered round the town. He admired the vertical cliff from below. He sat in cafes drinking coffee and beer and reading the English, Spanish and French newspapers. He perched for hours on a big rock by the Verdon river which passed by the town, thinking mainly about cholera. He also played Poohsticks by himself with pairs of Mediterranean pine cones, throwing them simultaneously into the river from his vantage point on the rock and watching which one would be first to reach the buttresses of the arched road bridge downstream. Then after the day's rest he hit the trail again early on the sixth day.

The path out of Castellane followed an ancient Roman packhorse trail. Not as celebrated as Roman roads, the packhorse trail was still a wondrous thing, graded and engineered. The old engineers knew that the most tiring thing for animals and man were undulations with incessant ups and downs in the trail. So they cut them out. They created a trail with a constant gradient. Where the path would naturally have descended following the natural fall of the landscape, they artificially built the trail up on elevated ramps of stones. The ramp was continued until the ground naturally rose up again to meet it. In this way the trail kept a constant gradient.

Lylly marvelled at such precise and large scale engineering in the service of such a relatively minor trail. Then perhaps it wasn't so minor a route in its day he wondered. Maybe in Roman times it was the main trade highway across the coastal mountains. Even in the remotest middle of nowhere crossing an insignificant minor mountain range the Roman engineers had engineered the path so that it kept a constant gradient. It must have mattered to them in a way we couldn't see now, he thought. On the other hand maybe they did it purely because they could. They had the time, the money and the expertise.

The Roman packhorse trail went all the way to the top of the pass threequarters of the way to his next destination, the entrance to the Gorge du Verdon, before being lost to modern eyes in the stretches of bare rock on top of the col. Lylly knew the packhorse trail separated from the long-distance footpath at the top of the col. The packhorses avoided the gorge and headed further north to places with better trading prospects, where the reasons for the way things were done in the past were lost now in the incommunicable black hole of time. As he turned away from the packhorse trail he could see that the Roman engineers were still modifying the gradient. But Lylly stayed with the modern ad hoc lolloping footpath and descended down from the col.

There at the isolated hotel that had been built on the belvedere known as the Pointe Sublime overlooking the cleft's entrance, Lylly planned to stay for the night.

6

LYLLY CHECKED IN, had a shower, and lay on the bed for a while snoozing and wiggling his toes. They were slightly sore but that was only to be expected after walking for five days out of the last six over hard unforgiving rock under the load of a heavy pack. The boots had done their job well.

Later he came down to the hotel restaurant for dinner. It was surprisingly busy, the restaurant looked full, but casting his eyes around he suspected he might be the only walker staying in the hotel. The rest of the guests were probably sightseers taking the spectacular circular tourist drive on the roads round the top edges of the gorge. He was shown to the last table, set for two in the large window at the far side of the restaurant. The window had a view over the approach to the Pointe Sublime.

Ten minutes later as Lylly was still looking at the menu and sipping his second beer a man approached accompanied by a waitress. The waitress asked Lylly if he minded another person sitting at the other space at the table? He said that would be fine.

He stood up to shake the man's hand and give his name. Another thing Lylly had gained in the Legion was some European manners.

The man was dressed in blue jeans, a black tee-shirt, a short blue denim jacket, and black elastic-sided boots. Lylly didn't recognise the maker's name on the tab on the jacket's right breast pocket. He looked to be some years older than Lylly which would put him around forty, perhaps forty-two. He was tall and thin. His black hair was swept straight back from his forehead and fell over the top of his ears. Lylly thought he looked distinguished and well-groomed. The studied casualness of the designer denim accentuated that.

Lylly had introduced himself in French, this being France and his language skills good. The man extended his hand.

"My name's Louis," he said in fluent English, pronouncing it Loo-iss. "Louis Kellner. I'm German. May I assume you are English?"

They both sat down. It turned out they got on very well. Lylly thought Louis was an unusual first name for a German, but he didn't ask and anyway his knowledge of such things was slender. Louis Kellner was good company, full of anecdotes and witty stories. He was, he said, a doctor.

Lylly realised that this was exactly one of the reasons he had come on this long walk: to meet interesting people.

An hour later eating his steak-frites Lylly asked, "How did you know I was English?"

Kellner laughed and sat back in his chair. He reached for his glass and took a sip of the white wine he was drinking before replying.

"Don't you think all nationalities have a certain look?" Kellner went on to back this claim up with a story about how all the British prisoners of war who tried to escape from the German camps in the Second World War were all rapidly recaptured.

"Breaking out of camp wasn't the problem. That was easy enough, and many did it, many times. But they were all recaptured in days, sometimes in hours. Why do you think that was?"

Lylly smiled and said he didn't know. "They couldn't speak German?"

"Actually many of them could. No that wasn't the problem. The absolute giveaway was they never thought to change their hairstyles to copy the cut and styles of the locals. They stood out like haystacks in a corn field."

Lylly laughed. It was an excellent story. And probably true.

"So you looked at my hairstyle and thought I was English?"

"In part, yes," Kellner said. "But also, you're drinking beer. No self-respecting French person does that with dinner, even though your French is good. You were slouching in your chair. In my experience British people never sit straight or properly upright. Your mouth looks like you speak English. How we speak and pronounce vowel sounds tends to govern the shape of our mouths. And to be perfectly honest I just guessed."

"You're very observant."

Kellner shrugged but looked pleased with the compliment.

They talked about themselves a little more. Louis Kellner was more than a doctor. He was what he called a "reconstructive surgeon" in practice at a number of private clinics in the French Alps and in his native Germany. Lylly wondered if that was a fancy self-aggrandising way of describing being a plastic surgeon

"You think that's a fancy way of saying plastic surgeon?" Kellner asked with a smile.

It was uncanny, Lylly thought. He'd almost read his mind.

"Well you would be right. I am a plastic surgeon. My work is a time machine. Breast lifts, tummy tucks, lipo, necks, botox, lips, gastric ties, the complete package. I turn back time. Sure that's the work in private clinics. But I also spend a lot my time using my expertise in public hospitals, with infants and children. I repair things. I do a better job than nature did. I mend cleft palates and remedy plenty of other birth defects. I'm good at it. There, in those cases it isn't so much turning back time as creating it. I give kids time. Time to be normal."

It was a good speech and it sounded pretty impressive to Lylly. Both the private and the public work. Lylly wasn't put off by the boasting. This was a man who knew he was good at what he did, and that what he did was important. But he also thought there would be more money in turning back time than there was in repairing nature. Far more.

Lylly outlined his situation and what he was doing. Kellner was fascinated. He asked a lot of questions about Lylly's time in the Spanish Legion, where he'd been and if he'd seen any action. That was after saying he had no idea that Spain had a foreign legion.

Lylly tried to move the conversation away a little from his army career and mentioned he was in the hotel because he was on the long-distance trail.

"You're going through the gorge tomorrow?" Kellner said. He sounded familiar with it.

"Yes. I gather it'll take at least a day and a half plus a night stop to go all the way through."

"Well you must take the hidden tunnel. You don't really want to camp out down by the river. It's too dangerous. You might be lucky and find a level spot near the trail on the slopes to sleep, but I doubt it. You'd waste so much time and energy looking. Most people descend and camp on the flat shingle on the banks and even on sandbanks in the river. It's beautiful but dangerous."

"But why's it dangerous?"

"Yes it is. Very. We've had the occasional catastrophe over the decades. Young adults mostly camping wild who think they're immortal. It's dangerous because the spillway on the dam on the lake upstream can overflow after rain and the flash flood rushes down the gorge. The dam authorities also periodically open the spillway gates to release large volumes of water too every now and then. They do that at night. People drown. And it's more dangerous at night because you can't see the water coming. You can hear it but you can't see it. Their last moments must be quite horrific."

"But what if it hasn't rained recently?"

"I still wouldn't recommend it. Yes it would be perfectly safe down by the river if there is no rain, I agree, and if you're there on a day that's not on the big flood release schedules. But we've had thunderstorms at night after perfect blue-sky days. Seriously I wouldn't do it. But there is a way you can avoid having to stay the night in the gorge. By taking the hidden tunnel."

Lylly thought that was good to know. "Do you know this area?"

Kellner said he did because he practised at clinics in Digne and Draguignan, which he said were the main two towns north and south of the gorge, which was why he was staying the night at the hotel – "It's a very favourite stop of mine" - because he was driving between the two. "But I do know the gorge. I know it well. If you'll take my advice do not camp on the river bed. I can tell you about the hidden tunnel if you like?"

Kellner told him about the long but supposedly closed tunnel that cut off a big corner of the trail. "By taking the hidden tunnel you can easily walk the entire length of the gorge in a day. You wouldn't have to camp out."

Kellner explained that the long tunnel was rarely travelled. "To tell you the truth it's supposed to be closed and forbidden to walkers. But don't let that bother you. There's nothing stopping you taking it once you know where it is. In fact I know that rock climbers use it regularly for quicker access to the cliffs."

"What does closed and forbidden mean?"

Kellner explained that the unused tunnel was considered dangerous and had been removed from the trail and forbidden to walkers after a couple of rockfalls from the tunnel roof and fragments of rock had struck and badly hurt members of a hiking party. The tunnel was supposedly closed, he said, but in practical terms that just meant it had been removed from some of the trail maps and guidebooks or had a serious warning about it in others. There was no actual barrier at the entrances. "Nothing stops you taking it."

"So I've either got a dangerous river if I stay or a dangerous tunnel if I don't?"

Kellner smiled, "You would be seriously unlucky to get harmed by a rockfall in the tunnel. I gather it's been stable for a while now. But you would have to be seriously lucky to escape drowning if you're down on the river in a flood. I can show you on a map. After dinner."

After they'd eaten they left the restaurant and Kellner took a coffee and Camo Lylly a beer to the hotel's lounge room. There was a television on the wall there and a number of board games laid out on tables. Some young kids were watching a French TV programme. In Lylly's view French television programmes were the worst he'd ever seen. They were full of philosophical talking heads spouting seeming profundities that were actually total vacuities in front of an admiring audience. The programme they were watching looked like it was shot in a holiday resort with games contestants and celebrities and pop singers. There was even the standard French standby, a mime artist doing Charlie Chaplin standing perfectly still. The kids were mesmerised.

Kellner led Lylly to a map on the wall. As they closed on it Lylly could see it wasn't actually a flat map it was a relief map in three dimensions. The contours were physically raised and realised on the map. He looked closer and saw it was made of plastic. It was a real large scale map of the area but in three dimensions.

Kellner showed where the deep gash of the gorge was situated on the map. He pointed to the area about halfway along the trail where the Artuby river joined the Verdon. At that point the gorge underwent a big turn, a dogleg well over ninety degrees, cutting halfway back on itself. Lylly looked closer and could see the scale of the relief map was large enough to show the GR4 trail which was marked by a dashed line running the length of the gorge. It too cut back and followed the big dogleg in the gorge.

"Look closer," Kellner said, and pointed with his finger to a spot away from the cutback.

Lylly followed his finger. Another line dotted and dashed in a different way was shown cutting off the big loop.

"That's the tunnel," Kellner said. "It's big, over twelve hundred metres long, but if you take it you can save half a day's walk and do the whole gorge in a day. You'd be in and out in daylight. You wouldn't have to camp anywhere."

Lylly memorised the position of the tunnel on the map.

"Good to know," he said.

Late the next day Camo Lylly sat on a convenient boulder by the woman's side under the base of the trees as he waited for the rescue helicopter to arrive. From his experience in the Legion he thought there would be enough room for the helicopter to land in the flat area that had been excavated out of the shoulder of the slope in front of the tunnel portal.

It was while he was sitting on the boulder by the side of the woman that he noticed something had been painted on the rock at the side of the tunnel entrance. It had been daubed or spray-painted on the bare rockface. It was white and consisted of three lines, with two verticals and a horizontal cross-piece. The horizontal line extended beyond the verticals to give the impression of horns. The marks were fresh and clean. The white paint glinted in the sun. He could see it clearly now. This was very obviously a version of the Greek letter pi.

He wondered if that's what the lines painted around the woman in the tunnel were too? A bigger version of a pi sign. But he didn't have time to go back inside and check. The helicopter could arrive at any moment.

He stood up and cast around on the ground. He found four stones each the size of his spread hand and balanced one on top of the other in a stack by the tunnel mouth. He went back and sat down again ten metres away on his boulder by the woman. He started chucking small pebbles at the stack of stones.

His pebbles often missed the stones and skittered and skipped away across the portal. Others hit the stack but did not topple them. It was a small, sturdy and difficult target. But he also knocked the small stack over four times before he heard the thump and clatter of the helicopter engine coming in from the east.

7

"WE'D LIKE TO TAKE a blood sample," the capitaine said, after complementing Lylly on his French. The police capitaine said his name was Camus.

Lylly didn't think this was because they wanted to see if he was over the alcohol limit or had malaria. It would be to check and keep a record of his DNA for comparative purposes. Lylly knew there was no point in refusing. And in any case he knew his DNA was on file somewhere in Spain. Under the confraternity rules of the EU he was sure it would be an easy option for the French authorities to request it. He also knew his DNA was all over the woman, Andromeda as he thought of her. He'd held her, carried her, wrapped her in his groundsheet, checked to see if she was dead or alive or injured or harmed in any way.

"Can't you get it from Spain?" His reply told the capitaine he knew it was his DNA they were after.

The police capitaine nodded, and said "Of course but easier and quicker to have our own sample." Then he changed tack. "You are British? You are a resident of Spain?" He was looking at his computer screen. "And you were a soldier. A mercenary?"

Lylly didn't verbally agree. He didn't say anything. But the capitaine was right. He had a townhouse apartment in Antequera down in Andalusia in the south, and he had just spent three years in the Spanish mercenary force, the Spanish Legion. He wondered how they knew. Confraternity again.

While he never minded being called a mercenary, as nor did most of his fellow members in the Legion, he also knew there were some who were desperate to avoid the name. To them it had too many unpleasant connotations, as though somehow they were less than serious soldiers. As though there was a scale of these things with fighting for your country at the top and fighting for someone else's country, or even worse fighting for money, way down at the bottom. They often hunted for other terms to avoid the m-word. But in the end no matter how hard they searched for alternatives such as the ludicrous genteelism "soldiers of fortune" or the even-worse faux-romantic "wild geese", or the absurd "contractors", mercenary soldiers were what they were. Those American flyers known as the Eagle Squadron who volunteered and came over to fight for Britain in the early years of the Second World War, before America joined the war, they were mercenaries, and had never been seen as anything but brave and admirable. It depended on where you were looking from, he guessed.

Anyway the capitaine was only trying to get a rise out of him, he knew, by seeing what his reaction to the m-word was. Perhaps the capitaine thought, too, that members of the French Foreign Legion were brave and admirable, while members of the Spanish Foreign Legion were just "mercenaries". It was an age-old almost universal crappy police technique: shake the tree and see what falls out.

"It's an EU thing," the capitaine said gesturing to the computer screen. "We like to keep a high awareness of people who fight for money. They tend to be, how shall I put this, more adventurous."

Lylly suspected "adventurous" was a euphemism for "dangerous" or "unpredictable".

"I've always thought that fighting for money was a lot more humane than fighting for your country. And far less prone to committing atrocities."

The capitaine gave a kind of dipping nod as though that was something he hadn't considered before but neither agreed nor disagreed with.

"Another serious advantage of a mercenary outfit is it's totally expendable," Lylly said. "You can see that from the history of your own Foreign Legion. How many times has it been wiped out to the last man? Twice? Three times? You can't do that with regular soldiers."

The policeman looked up, indicating he would be pleased to hear if Lylly had anything else to say on this topic. Lylly knew he wanted to get him talking, to see if would let something slip and damn himself out of his own mouth. But Lylly rushed on. It was like he'd uncovered a verbal well and was falling down it.

"Yes," Lylly went on. "No one's there to count the body bags. So effectively a mercenary unit hasn't got any mothers, and doesn't vote. Expendable. They've been around for a long time too."

"Oh yes? Expendable and long-standing? A contradiction, no? Quite an accomplishment, surely?"

"There's a lot of crap about prostitution being 'the world's oldest profession,'" Lylly continued. "Well that's a load of crap because the world's oldest profession is being a mercenary soldier." Lylly stopped. He realised he was talking too much. The capitaine had got his rise after all.

"Is that what you are? A worker in the world's oldest profession?"

"Yes. Something like that. Was," he stressed the past tense. "I left." Lylly was trying to talk less. The police capitaine was skilled at this. Lylly knew he wasn't.

"Ah yes," the capitaine peered at the screen. "You've just come out now?"

"Yes."

"The other legion. The Spanish one." He didn't try to hide his disdain. "Did you enjoy it?"

"It's not something you enjoy or not enjoy. You just do it."

"So why did you do it?"

Did he really want to know, Lylly wondered? But I guess he wouldn't ask if he didn't want to know. He wasn't making conversation to pass the time of day. He was aware that it wouldn't be a good idea to try and second guess the police. The capitaine clearly suspected him of something. But Lylly didn't know what. He resolved to keep his answers truthful and straightforward.

"I thought it would do me good."

"In what way?"

"I thought it would give me purpose and perspective." It was lame, he knew but it was also the truth. Or at least one of the truths. Another truth was he did it because it was there. It seemed a good idea at the time.

"And did it?"

Lylly smiled. "Not really."

The capitaine refocused. To Lylly he seemed now to accept Lylly for what he was, and accept his story for what it was. The truth.

"We need to account for and eliminate your DNA from any DNA evidence we find on madame Stahl."

"Did you look at the knots on her wrists and ankles?" Lylly tried to move the interview away from its current focus on him.

"How? Yes?"

Lylly explained they looked to him to have been tied by someone who had knowledge of climbing, or fishing. Perhaps even the military. They were good knots.

The capitaine tilted his head and sucked in air through his upper teeth, indicating they had thought about that then rejected it as unworthy of further study. Many people knew about knots, the head tilt said. Climbers for one.

"You realise that tunnel is closed? Dangerous?" The capitaine made it into an accusation. "Yes I can see that you know it was closed. Why were you walking in a forbidden tunnel?"

Lylly was becoming annoyed by the line of questioning. "It's a good thing I was, don't you think? How long had she been there?"

The capitaine said nothing. He looked at Lylly sharply but didn't answer his question.

Lylly sighed. "I wanted to cut off the big corner at that point where the river turns over ninety degrees almost back on itself, where it's joined by the Artuby stream. Save some time. Avoid camping by the river. I looked at the map and saw the tunnel. Sure I knew it was supposed to be closed. I know the story." He shrugged.

"I was in it at my own risk."

The capitaine nodded again.

"So you had no idea there would be someone else in that tunnel?"

"How is she?" Lylly asked, ignoring the policeman's question. That was the most important thing, Lylly thought. Not whether he was walking illegally.

There was silence as the capitaine's question hung in the air.

"No. Of course not," Lylly said eventually. "Has she regained consciousness? You said she was drugged?" he added quickly. "Has she told you who did it? How did she get into the tunnel? Was it a helicopter? Kayak? Quadbikes?" He added, "One person couldn't do it on their own. Surely?" This was to move the questioning away from him. If the police agreed it couldn't have been done by one person on their own then that would put Camo in the clear. "Have you removed the expansion bolts? Any fingerprints?"

But the capitaine didn't reply.

Lylly was being interviewed in a windowless room in the sub-regional police municipale headquarters in Draguignan.

At the start of the interview capitaine Camus had told him that the woman – who Lylly now learned was madame Mercedes Stahl – had been kidnapped. Early on the same day Lylly had found her in the tunnel she had been to the shops in her car. She had been on her way to her riding school, capitaine Camus said.

"It seems she wanted to buy some apples for the horses."

She had parked in the busy carpark of the big out-of-town Casino supermarket outside Castellane. As soon as she got out of the car and before she entered the supermarket she had heard rapid footsteps approaching from behind, but before she could turn round a black cloth bag had been thrust over her head, she felt a sharp prick in her arm and she fell rapidly unconscious.

She didn't wake up until she was wrapped in Lylly's groundsheet outside the tunnel in the Gorge du Verdon over half a day later. And she didn't become fully conscious until halfway through the helicopter flight to the hospital. She was unable to give a description of her kidnappers. She was unable to say how many there were. She hadn't noticed if they were in a car or a van.

"Was there a ransom? Any demands? Was she followed to the supermarket? Or was it an opportune ambush? Who knew she was going riding? Who knew she would stop at the supermarket?" Lylly threw his questions at the police capitaine hoping he might answer some of them.

It would be weirdly opportune if you were just carrying around the requisite knock-out drops, just in case, Lylly thought. So that was too much of a coincidence. Which meant the attack was probably pre-planned and she was most likely followed to the supermarket. And the unscheduled stop in the supermarket car park presented the attackers with the best opportunity.

But again the capitaine didn't reply. Then after a while he said, "No no demands." He looked sternly across the table at Lylly.

If she wasn't kidnapped for ransom, did that make it attempted murder then, Lylly wondered? He thought it highly likely she would have died, pinned to the wall, probably quite rapidly, if he hadn't come through the unvisited off-route tunnel when he did. So how likely was it that someone else would have come through in time? There were very few walkers hiking the full length of the trail at this time of year. Lylly hadn't seen anyone in either direction. And anyway none of them would be likely to know about the lost tunnel. There probably wouldn't have been anyone else in the tunnel that day or for untold days.

Perhaps the rock climbers he saw had come that way earlier in the day to their favoured pitch on the cliff? And would they have returned that way at the end of the day anyway? But instead they could of course have planned to stay the night hanging from the cliff face and wouldn't have returned through the tunnel in time to rescue her. He knew that was possible with certain bivouacs. He also knew they used strong expansion bolts and climbing rope to anchor their bivouacs to the cliff. There was another thing, it was likely they wouldn't descend the cliff once they'd gone all the way up and would have made their way out of the gorge from the top of the cliff. So he thought it very likely they wouldn't have come back through the tunnel.

It hit him with a full and sudden realisation. If he hadn't decided at the last minute to take the hidden tunnel she would be dead. He didn't think the human body could stand being fixed in that spreadeagled position for long. It was a kind of crucifixion.

He wondered if the climbers had seen anything from their vantage point on the cliff? If the kidnappers came by quad bike or helicopter the rock-climbers must have heard them. And perhaps seen them. Had the police talked to them?

"There were some rock-climbers on the cliffs," he said to capitaine Camus. "They may have come through the tunnel to get to the base of the cliff there. They might have seen or heard something. Have you talked to them? There were two of them. A man and a woman."

Capitaine Camus made no response. Instead he shuffled some papers into a stack and banged the bottom edge of the stack on the desk.

"What about the white paint lines? What do you make of those?" Lylly thought they must mean something, otherwise why bother? "I thought they might represent pi. God knows why or what for."

Capitaine Camus made no response.

"You know, the Greek letter? The mathematical ratio?"

This time the capitaine just shrugged before straightening the edges of the papers in the stack.

Lylly thought back to his rescue of the woman.

Outside the tunnel mouth he'd checked the woman for a pulse. She was breathing but seemed to be unconscious. He found the pulse and held it for a minute according to his watch, counting the beats. It was faint but steady and slow. He tried to make her as comfortable as possible. Her skin seemed a little warmer than it had done in the tunnel, but it was difficult to tell. She still seemed dangerously cold.

Lylly couldn't tell if she was showing signs of hypothermia, but he assumed it would be indicated by violent shivering, and there were no signs of that, but he didn't know. He was more familiar with hyperthermia, overheating, from some of the punishing route marches in the Legion, than its opposite.

Her head hung forward over the groundsheet over her chest and the bright brown hair almost entirely hid her face. She was lying fully in broad sunlight wrapped in the cocoon of Lylly's insulated and reflective aluminium groundsheet. He lifted her head, then dug out his pullover from his pack, rolled it into a sausage and placed it behind her head against the tree trunk.

Then he'd dug out his phone and checked for a signal. There was nothing. So he headed up to higher ground, scrambling up through the trees for a quarter of a mile until the steep but scalable woody shoulder ended abruptly at the base of the vertical cliff. He got a faint signal there, just one bar, but it was enough. He made the call.

Forty-five minutes after his emergency phonecall he heard the deep throaty clatter of a bright yellow helicopter coming in low, searching like a bumble bee, following the course of the river through the gorge, heading downstream from the east. The noise was magnified as it was contained by the gorge walls, bouncing off them and echoing multiple times. Far above, two vultures soared upwards climbing as quick as they could to get away from this deafening intrusive mechanical alien invading their space.

Lylly stood in the flat open clearing at the entrance to the tunnel and waved his arms over his head. His phone rang. It was one of the medics in the helicopter. They'd taken his number when he called emergency services on 112. He guided them in to the open space in front of the tunnel. Lylly backed up and stood away in the tunnel entrance to give the helicopter as much space as possible in the small clearing to land. He took out his phone and took a photo of the chopper as it landed.

Two medics rushed out of a rear door of the chopper carrying a folding stretcher. Lylly pointed to the woman lying against a tree trunk. The man and woman examined her. One of them injected her with something. They placed her on the stretcher and carried it back inside the helicopter. She was still wrapped in Camo's groundsheet. Lylly took another shot of the woman and stretcher being loaded into the helicopter. Then the passenger door opened and a man in police uniform leaned out. He told Lylly to get in the helicopter, pointing to the door behind him where the medics had climbed in. It didn't seem to be a polite request. It was an order. Lylly hesitated. Then he lifted up his backpack and ran to get in the chopper.

They took off, tearing the air, lifting seeming effortlessly but with huge energy expenditure out of the gorge, then headed south. One of the medics told him they were heading for the hospital in Draguignan. South of the gorge it was the nearest sizeable town.

But now here in the sub-regional police station in Draguignan, there was one thing that Lylly was still thinking and wondering about.

Just before the rescue helicopter arrived the woman woke. Drowsily she stirred and peered around, seemingly not knowing where she was. She tried to speak. Lylly bent his ear down to her mouth. She tried again. He held a water bottle to her lips and she gulped thirstily. She stared at him, unfocused and unseeing with deep brown eyes. She tried to speak again. Lylly bent down and placed an ear to her lips again. She whispered something faintly in French before she fainted and passed out again. Her accent seemed more American rather than French. But Lylly couldn't easily pin it down. Lylly struggled to make sense of what he thought she had whispered.

"Ne me quittez pas. Il va réessayer."

A police medic arrived to take a blood sample.

When the medic left with a vial of Lylly's blood, capitaine Camus opened a drawer in his desk and brought out something shiny folded into a clear plastic wrapper. Lylly recognised it as his aluminium groundsheet.

"I presume you would like this back." It wasn't a question. The capitaine slid it across the desk. "And there is one more thing…"

Lylly waited for the capitaine to continue.

"I must ask you not to mention to anyone the situation, the position, in which you found madame Stahl. Oh certainly you are most welcome to mention your part in her rescue—" Lylly thought he was being damned with faint praise here "—but please do not mention the, ah, crucifixion."

Was that what it was, Lylly thought? A crucifixion? It felt like something else, but he didn't know what. "Oh? Why's that?"

"We think the perpetrators seek publicity. This is clearly a publicity seeking demonstration. We seek to deny them that. We consider that if their stunt is not publicised they will attempt something else and they will make mistakes. In fact monsieur Lylly we insist you keep silent on this."

Lylly said he would abide by the capitaine's wishes.

Then the police capitaine waved his hand dismissively, as though shooing a stray animal.

Finally it seemed that police capitaine Camus had heard enough. He said that Lylly was free to go.

As he left the interview room Lylly was still mulling over in his mind the words the woman had struggled to whisper as she lay on the ground under Lylly's aluminium sheet. He turned the original French into English, but it didn't make it any less ominous and sombre.

"Don't leave me," she'd said. "He will try again."

8

LYLLY KNEW THE FIRST place he was going to go after leaving the police station was the hospital. He wanted to check on madame "Andromeda" Stahl and to see if and how she was progressing successfully from her ordeal.

He walked across town. He could have taken a taxi but he wanted to walk to move the furniture round in his head.

Draguignan is the city of the dragon. That's what its name means. A local bishop who was also a saint but who wasn't St George had killed a dragon in the vicinity and so saved the area from pillage and destruction. It calls itself the gateway to the Verdon. Not surprisingly being so close to the massive Canjuers military manoeuvres area, the town hosts the national artillery and infantry schools.

Lylly found the large hospital on the northern side of town. But disappointingly he wasn't allowed in to see madame Stahl. Perhaps he should have expected that. The nurse receptionist, backed up by a couple of gendarmes, refused to let him past them nor anywhere near her room. But she told him that she was doing better. The drugs that were in her system had been flushed out. She was tired but on the way to recovery. Looking over the nurse's shoulder as she read out the details from her clipboard, Lylly noticed it confirmed that madame Stahl's first name was Mercedes. He left his name and phone number with the nurse then he returned to his hotel.

Lylly had been very surprised by the police capitaine's obvious reluctance to take seriously his questions about the rock climbers. The police's clear disdain for that line of investigation both annoyed and piqued Lylly and spurred him into action. He had been wondering what he might do next. Now if the police weren't going to talk to the rock climbers then he would. The two climbers he saw might still be working the cliffs of the gorge. And if they were no longer around, there might be other climbers there who knew them. Serious rockclimbing was a relatively small world.

But first he wanted to fetch his car. He thought he might need it. It would give him options and a certain freedom of movement. He also thought it was beginning to look as though he didn't want to be too far away from what was hidden in the spare wheel too.

Camo's micro-compact LW Seecamp .32 semi-automatic pistol was hidden in a special secret compartment inside his spare tyre and wheel. The clever thing was it still functioned as a workable spare wheel.

It was a soldier thing, especially perhaps a mercenary soldier thing. Once you'd been armed by licence of the state you didn't want to be without a weapon after your licence was taken away. Camo expected he'd grow out of the feeling of nakedness without a weapon – or more accurately without knowledge of access to a weapon. But that wasn't yet.

Again John the Lithuanian's specialist workshop in Zaragoza had been instrumental in creating the hiding place in the spare tyre accessible through the rim of the spare wheel. Camo had the workshop smear the whole of the sides and rim of the wheel with a mixture of road dirt, dust and dirty old black worn-out sump oil. This ensured that any telltale visible cracks indicating the hiding place were well hidden and covered. The workshop also supplied a special key, a tool that was necessary to unlock the covering plate and open up the hiding place. Only the special tool would do it, as the plate was under pressure from the inflated tyre. You also had to let all the air out of the tyre first before you could remove the plate. But Camo saw that as a helpful delaying precaution rather than a hindrance. Anyone who tried to access the gun by trying to remove the plate before deflating the tyre would have the plate blown into his hands or even his face with all the incapacitating power and shock of a small explosion.

There was a TGV station just out of town to the south and Lylly caught a cab to take him there. From there it took three and a half hours by train to get to Avignon. The line went down to the coast then went lolloping along the sea front via Toulon and Marseille. The trouble with the supposed "fast" TGV travelling along the coast wasn't the slowness of the train it was the slowness of the line. This wasn't a new high-speed dedicated TGV line. It was a nineteenth century line with not enough viaducts and not enough tunnels, so essentially the high-speed trains had to insinuate their way delicately along every tight curve round every headland at a snail's pace. There weren't even that many fine panoramas of the seafronts or the coastal towns to compensate for the slowness of the journey because a multitude of scrappy mini-cuttings blocked the view.

He picked up his car in Avignon and was back in Draguignan only two hours later. People said trains were far faster than cars, but Lylly could tell them for this journey it was over three and a half hours one way by train, and two hours back the other by car. Trains didn't like mountains. Whereas roads were happy with them. With stops, breaks, and waits it was a six hour round trip.

He booked a room back in the hotel on the bluff overlooking the gorge entrance. He drove up from Draguignan via Castellane and parked in the hotel car park. Next day he would make his way into the Gorge du Verdon again. There was something he thought he might be able to check before he did anything else. It was to do with helicopters.

He knew there had been plenty of helicopters in the sky the morning of the day he found the woman in the tunnel. The big military manoeuvres had been taking place on the Plaine de Canjuers south of the gorge. He'd seen plenty of them buzzing back and to before he left them and their noise behind. It was conceivable that a civilian chopper could have sneaked into the gorge while all the aerial activity was going on. No one would have noticed.

For the second time in two days it was early morning when

Lylly left the hotel with his walking boots on his feet and his pack on his back and descended from the panoramic viewpoint of the Point Sublime down to the river level to enter the gorge. This time there were no picnickers at the start of the trail. And as before, after he had walked through the first two tunnels, the trail was deserted.

This time he didn't dawdle or descend to the river to eat a sandwich. He pressed on along the trail. He stopped occasionally to swig some water out of one of his bottles. It was another hot day in the bathymetric depths of the gorge. A few hours later he came to the base of the big scree, which was the outfall debris from the tunnel which had been dumped when they were digging the tunnel. As he did before he scrambled laboriously up the side of the scree to find the tunnel entrance.

He stopped at the entrance, half-hidden by tree branches. He looked up and saw in the far distance on his right a pair of climbers on the high cliff. They were perhaps a third of the way up to the top. He stood for a while on the trail looking up at them, wondering how best to intercept them. He had only rudimentary climbing skills, more importantly he had no climbing equipment. He could go through this long hidden tunnel, like they must have done, then clamber up the wooded shoulder above the tunnel exit to get to the base of the cliff. But then what? He would be standing below them way out of conversation range. He doubted they would be willing to descend to the base of the cliff just to talk to a stranger who was shouting unintelligibly up at them.

The way Lylly looked at it the only way he could get close to talk to them was to intercept them as they finished the climb and came out onto the road some way beyond the top of the cliff. He resolved to meet them there. By the rate they were progressing up the vertical rock he judged that that might be sometime towards the end of the day. He had plenty of time to do what he wanted to do first.

He dug out his torch and switched it on. He advanced into the long tunnel. There were no breathing sounds this time. The rock was silent now. There was just the constant but erratic plinking of water droplets as they fell from the roof into the many pools and puddles along the tunnel floor.

He reached the dark chicane where the tunnellers had missed each other and had had to backtrack and dig out a kink in the route to meet up with each other. Then as he came round the second bend of the chicane he saw the distant sideways-tilted D of light in the distance. He marvelled at how much better it felt when you could actually see the light at the end of the tunnel.

He came to the point where the woman had been pinned to the rock, as far as he could judge. He carried on to the end of the tunnel, and came out into the light, then went back in and returned to the scene, counting his steps. The place was about fifty metres in from the tunnel mouth. Lylly counted sixty-six paces.

He slowed and played his torch along the side wall to locate the spot. The beam threw strange shapes and shadows along the rock. He found the place. He was glad but a little surprised that the expansion bolts and the lengths of rope had not yet been removed from the rock. He assumed a forensic team would be coming very soon before the scene became too contaminated. The white paint lines were still there too.

The cut lengths of climbing rope hung listlessly from the rings on the bolt heads. From what he could see of the bolts they were stainless steel and looked expensive. These were specialist equipment, perhaps used in climbing, rather than the galvanised type used for construction, he thought. Though he had a feeling that modern climbers took a dim view of any equipment that irreversibly damaged the rock. Maybe these bolts dated from a time when the climbing fraternity was less fastidious.

The holes for the bolts had been driven deep into the rock, the bolts pushed in, then the rotating heads had been screwed clockwise to expand the mechanism inside the shafts and push the jackets on the bolts outwards to grip tightly against the wall of the holes in an inviolable friction fit. Lylly knew it would be impossible to pull them out by force. They would need to be rotated anticlockwise to shrink them back to their original size so they no longer fitted rigidly into the holes. He also knew you would need a good heavy-duty battery-powered drill with a couple of back-up batteries to drill the four holes here with no power source. It wouldn't have been done quickly.

He stepped further back against the other tunnel wall to see the white lines in full better and shone his torch on the markings. There were definitely two verticals and a horizontal. The horizontal formed short horns past the verticals. It was a bigger version of the markings at the tunnel exit. It seemed odd but to Lylly both markings more than anything did seem to represent the Greek letter π, pi; the symbol used to express the ratio of the diameter of a circle to its circumference, among other things.

He tried to abandon the idea. Why would anyone do that? What was the point of daubing pi on the rock? Instead he pushed the idea to himself that the marker had just made a mistake. They'd drawn the horizontal line first, then when it came to painting the verticals had decided they should go a shade closer to the woman than the ends of the horizontal line allowed, resulting in redundant lines extending past the verticals. The fact that the resultant markings resembled pi was purely accidental. What they actually represented was another matter. But the more he pushed it away the more he kept coming back to the certainty that both images did in fact represent pi. It seemed unlikely the dauber would make the same mistake twice. So the symbols, both of them, were images of pi. But he had no idea why.

He stood a while looking at the four bolts. If he hadn't passed this way the woman would be dead. If he had found her only just now she would already be shrinking with decay and undergoing the anti-life revenge of microbial processes and biological activity. He shook his head slightly at the mystery and the serendipity of chance events and carried on.

Eventually the light streaming in from the tunnel end was greater than the beam of his torch and he switched it off. Then he stepped out into the small flat area by the tunnel mouth where he had laid the woman down in his groundsheet and where he had waited for the rescue helicopter to land.

He still had a sharp image on his mind of where the big yellow helicopter had landed in the flat open space in front of the tunnel entrance. He had watched it intently as he stood in the tunnel mouth. In a way he had guided it in to land.

While he had a rough idea where the rescue helicopter had landed, he also knew he could do better than that. He took his phone out of a pocket and searched out the photos app. He found the picture he'd take of the helicopter landing. He oriented himself relative to the evidence in the photograph. He knelt on his haunches and examined the ground. The big landing bars of the chopper had made a pair of grooves in the loose stones and scattered rock shards that covered the ground surface. A straight line of crushed pine cones was another indication of where the chopper had landed. The middle of the open space in front of the tunnel entrance was the only safe and logical place to land. He examined the ground more closely. There was something else there. There was another fainter groove dug into the bed of rock splinters, at a different angle. He could see a second barely discernible groove parallel to the faint one. It too contained several squashed pine cones.

The evidence was clear. Another smaller helicopter with its landing bars closer together than the rescue helicopter had landed here. It had landed earlier than the rescue helicopter because the bigger grooves of the medical rescue chopper overlaid the smaller ones in places. It seemed conclusive to Lylly. A smaller helicopter had landed in the open space some time before the rescue helicopter. But there was no telling when or how long before. It could be the same day. It could have been a week before. But it was suspicious nonetheless. There was no reason why any helicopter that wasn't a rescue machine would land here.

Had the woman been brought in by helicopter? Then bundled out of the chopper and bolted to the tunnel wall? Certainly coming in to the gorge by chopper would be the quickest way, as long as you knew there would be a usable landing area. It beat walking in carrying a reluctant load. And coming in on the river, though a possibility, looked to require too much knowledge and skill in the rapids. It might also be that in places you would have to land and portage your kayak or canoe round impassable obstacles in the river. Helicopter was the obvious and most practical method. It hovered in Lylly's mind somewhere between a possibility and a probability. But it wasn't yet a certainty because the use of a helicopter implied a whole bunch of money, wealth, organisation and sophistication.

There was one thing he could check. Had the climbers seen or heard it? Now he needed to talk to them.

There was another thing, apart from all the implications of a helicopter. And that was, why bother? Why go to all that trouble of pinning your victim on the side wall of an abandoned untravelled tunnel in the – presumed – hope that she would die of exposure before she was seen and rescued? If you were going to kill someone, why not just do it and bury her? Come to that, if you did possess a helicopter why not kill her and drop her body way out at sea? Why the tunnel?

There was an element of showmanship and drama about it. It seemed like someone was telling a story. To Lylly also there was the clear reference to the story of Andromeda. Could that possibly be part of what was going on here? If so, that was weird. Again, why would someone bother? There was a series of imponderables here that Lylly knew he was missing the key to understanding.

Lylly turned round and retraced his steps through the long tunnel. As before he didn't dally but kept striding on along the trail. He stopped only to access his water bottles from the backpack. By early afternoon he was out of the gorge and making his way up the path through the trees to the hotel on its bluff overlooking the gorge entrance where his car was parked. He chucked his backpack in the car boot, changed out of his boots into a pair of trainers and set off in the car on the road along the northern lip of the gorge.

He had no local area map and the satnav didn't show enough detail surrounding the road to help locate the point where the climbers might be ascending the cliff face. But there were a series of "belvederes" along the road. These were lay-bys and parking areas which afforded spectacular views of the gorge below. So he road-hopped from belvedere to belvedere, examining the rockface through his binoculars, searching for the spot where the climbers might climb out of the gorge.

In a way he got lucky. The sixth belvedere he stopped in had a small yellow and green campervan based on a VW mini-bus also parked there. The van had a UK numberplate. On an instinct he parked next to it. He got out and inspected the campervan. It had stickers and transfers over most of the windows apart for the windscreen. The rear window was almost completely obscured by stickers. They were all mementoes of mountains and climbs. One said "El Capitan". Another said "West Crack". Lylly had a feeling El Capitan was a famous climb in Yosemite national park in California. He guessed that West Crack could be there as well. Another sticker said "Do it in winter" superimposed on a vertical mountainside, which Lylly thought might be the North Wall of the Eiger. Whether he was right or wrong in his surmises, it looked like he'd found a campervan that belonged to some climbers.

He wandered to the edge of the belvedere's parking area. He carried one of his water bottles with him in his hand. There was a wide foliage-free path running out of the parking area down at an angle towards the edge of the gorge. He followed it. The path ran for a hundred metres then petered out in a bare rocky landscape with an abrupt drop at its far side.

Lylly approached the drop and peered over. He was standing on top of one of the big cliffs on the north side of the gorge.

About three hundred feet below him he saw the bright red tops of a pair of climbing helmets. He could see arms and legs and a lot of rope and climbing equipment. He could also hear the two climbers calling out to each other. They were coming up.

Lylly looked round. There was a rock formation some way back from the edge which had a flattish area at a comfortable height. Lylly went over to it and sat down. He waited.

An hour and more later a red-helmeted head poked up above the edge of the cliff. The climber turned to look down and shouted, "Fuckin' topped it" down the cliff. Then he noticed Lylly sitting on the rock. "Oops," he said, "Pardon my French," then cackled hysterically at his own ironic wit. He climbed up and stood on the edge of the cliff handling a rope down to his companion who was still out of sight.

To Lylly the man definitely sounded English, and if Lylly was any judge he had a Lancashire accent. Oldham, Bolton, Bury or Rochdale? Lylly wondered, his knowledge of Lancashire towns exhausted. He chose Rochdale, arbitrarily. Lylly grinned at him.

A few minutes later the two "Rochdale" climbers were standing out on top of the cliff.

"Fancy some water?" Lylly said. He got up from his perch and approached the climbers, offering his bottle as came closer.

"Eh-up ta," the man said, taking it.

"That is nice, thank you," the woman said. She didn't sound English. Possibly French, Lylly thought. Not at all Rochdale then.

They were both young, in their early twenties. Lylly guessed they might be students. They both wore bright blue sleeveless tops and the man wore black shorts and the woman brilliant red and yellow tight lightweight stretchy climbing trousers.

"I know this might sound strange," Lylly said. "But were you two climbing here three days ago?"

They both looked at him silently as if to say what business was that of his?

"And if you did, did you get to the cliff base through the big hidden tunnel down there?"

Still neither of the climbers said anything. The man handed the water bottle back to Lylly.

"I'm asking because I rescued someone who was trapped in the tunnel down there." He pointed towards the cliff edge.

He decided to give them the full story. It seemed best. It looked like it might be the only way to allay their suspicions and get them to talk freely. He laid it all out. His walk along the long trail. The decision to enter the hidden tunnel. The discovery of the chained woman. Her rescue by helicopter. The need to find out whether anyone might have seen a helicopter in the gorge earlier that day aside from the military ones.

"Is the person all right?" The woman asked when Lylly had finished his story.

"Jesus Christ," the man said.

"Yes we were here that day," the woman said. "There was very much noise from the army."

"And we did come through that tunnel. But there was no one there," the man said.

"But we did that very early in the morning. So it is not surprising."

They explained to Lylly their climbing routine was to leave their campervan in the same belvedere every day; then phone for a taxi to take them to the gorge entrance; then walk through to the base of the cliff, using the hidden tunnel. They'd heard about the cliffs with fresh rock exposed after the winter and the hidden tunnel to access the base of the cliffs from other members of the climbing fraternity. Then they would climb out of the gorge up the cliffs back to their van. They took a different route up the series of cliffs each day.

"Did you see or hear any helicopters that day?"

"Christ there were like tons of em. Yeah but there was one…"

The climbers said they heard plenty of helicopters that day but did notice one – a small blue and white one, maybe a four or six seater – that seemed to be running along the course of the river rather than clattering over the far rim to the military area beyond to join in the manoeuvres. But they hadn't seen it land. The steepness of the gorge had cut off their view.

"We didn't think it was any different to the others to be honest," the man said. "But Chris heard something else. A bit later." He looked at the woman to confirm it.

"I thought I heard drilling," the woman said. "And banging. Like hammering. But I couldn't have here, it is ridiculous. So I dismissed it in my mind. I do not know what it was. Perhaps it was a bird."

"Some birds are right clever," her companion said with a grin at her. She punched him on the upper arm in response.

Lylly was pretty sure he hadn't heard of a bird that made a sound like a drill boring into rock, but let it go. He thought she had very well heard drilling. That was because someone had been drilling.

"Could you tell where this drilling, this bird, came from?"

"No, not really. Somewhere below us it was," she said. "Not higher and not in the sky. But it was hidden. I couldn't see. In the trees I think. Or hidden by the trees."

Good to know, Lylly thought. So it was very possible there had been a strange helicopter in the gorge that day.

He thanked them as they began packing away their climbing kit ready for the same cliff the next day. Lylly walked back to his car.

There was another question that was intriguing Lylly. Had the small helicopter used the day of the military exercise deliberately, to disguise its intrusion into the gorge? Did they know there was a big military exercise happening that day? But how had they known? Were these things publicised? Lylly thought that if they were it would be within a very small circle of manly military and political personnel. All the military in the area would know about it. But maybe some local politicians would too, such as the mayors of the nearest towns? Maybe the military would have to give notice of road closures? Or perhaps the administrators of the nearest large hospital would have to be informed in case of accidents? That was a possibility. But Lylly doubted if the date of the exercise was actually published anywhere. It was extremely unlikely that residents of the area would know anything about it until the heard the bangs and booms of the gunfire and the whistle and clatter of the planes and helicopters overhead.

As he clicked the remote to unlock his car he heard the sound of his phone receiving a text. He dug it out of his pocket and looked at the screen.

<Hi! Is that Camo Lylly? This is Merci Stahl. Can I buy you a drink?>

9

THEY MET IN A café-bar in Draguignan.

It was early evening. Camo had driven back down south to Dragon town from the gorge. He realised he was looking forward to meeting Merci Stahl in a situation where she could actually talk to him.

Stahl said she had been released from hospital that afternoon.

"They didn't want to let me go. But jeez I reckon I'd had enough after two and a half days." She had a wide grin that lit up her face.

She said she wanted to meet Lylly before her husband came to pick her up. She sounded American and confirmed that she was, and was married to a Frenchman. Her bright brown eyes seemed to accentuate the golden tan of her face. Her brown hair reached down and curled under her jaw in a bob on both sides. She looked a lot better healthwise but not necessarily prettier than when Lylly saw her last. Even tied up, drugged and exhausted she had been stunning to look at. Now she was wearing a white tank top which came down only as far as her stomach leaving her midriff bare. The thin white straps exposed much of her upper arms and shoulders. Below the tank top she was wearing black skin-tight stretchy jeans and on her feet she had leather sandals with a heel. She entered the bar with a white linen jacket draped across her shoulders. She took that off when she sat down. She looked good in the clothes; they were casual but enhancing. They made another interesting change from when he had last seen her.

She must have known that Lylly had seen her without any clothes on, but she didn't seem the slightest bit embarrassed by it.

She also looked a good deal more comfortable than when Lylly had last seen her, and he told her so.

"You feel ok? Better?"

"Sure. Pretty much. They said it was dehydration mainly. They fixed me a drip and stoked me up on fluids and electrolytes and I'm good to go."

"Did the police talk to you? Do they have any idea what's going on?"

"Oh sure yeah," she drew out the phrase to emphasise the irony. "Capitaine Sherlock's on the case." Then she grinned and shrugged, "They're right out of ideas. So what can I get you?"

Lylly thought she didn't seem to be taking it very seriously, but he smiled and said he'd have a beer. Stahl raised an arm in the air and waved the waiter over. He couldn't get over to their table quick enough when he saw her. She ordered a vodka and tonic for herself.

While they were waiting Stahl asked Lylly to tell her what happened. How did he find her?

"They told me I was pinned up like a butt-naked butterfly in that tunnel. And they told me you got me out. But I don't know anything else. They said I would have died if you hadn't been there. What can you tell me? What's your side of the story?"

Lylly went back to the beginning. He gave her the whole thing. At the end she toasted him with her drink.

"Well Mr Lylly I'm mighty grateful." She took a sip.

To Lylly she seemed to be talking too much and too brightly. She was taking it all far too lightly. As though it was some kind of game of hide and seek or i-erky or kickstone-one-two-three, and when you closed your eyes and counted to forty you got another go and everything was all right.

"You don't remember any of it?"

"Nope. Not a thing. I was in the supermarket car park. I just popped the trunk of my SUV. Someone jumped me. They came up behind and put a bag over my head. I felt a sharp prick in the side of my neck which I guess was a needle. The next thing I know I'm in a chopper heading for hospital. They said I'd been drugged with something. I must have been out for hours."

Lylly thought the way it had been done seemed the most sensible thing to do. If you've got the knowledge, the raw material and the expertise then knocking the victim out with a rapid acting drug as soon as you could would keep her quiet and malleable. It would be the best thing to do in a public environment. And clearly had been skilfully done. But it also meant it would turn her from a mobile human into a sack of potatoes, which you'd probably need more than one person to lug.

"When were the police involved? Did your husband call them when he realised you were missing?"

"No that's just it. No one knew I was gone. No one knew I wasn't anywhere I was supposed to be. My husband – Alain – was on a business trip. After the shops and the riding school I was going to the tennis club. Alain thought I was still there, in the mixed doubles quarters, when he got back. The quarter-finals," she added when she saw that Lylly didn't know what "quarters" meant. "The first he knew I wasn't was a call from the police sometime while I was in the air in the chopper. He went straight to the hospital."

"When I cut you down and brought you out of the tunnel, you asked me not to leave because 'il va réessayer - he will try again'. Who were you thinking of? Someone specific? Your husband?" Lylly wasn't sure he hadn't said too much.

But Stahl just laughed.

"Jeez no. Are you sure I said that?"

"Definitely."

"Well I got no idea. A bad dream I guess. Drug talk."

She tilted her drink back and finished it. She stood up.

"Well I gotta go. Being picked up at the hospital. Real nice to meet you and thanks for everything."

She dug out a purse from her shoulder bag and laid a twenty euro note on the table. She did a kind of salute with two fingers to her forehead, turned and headed for the door. Then she stopped. She was frozen in the doorway.

She came back to the table. She stood opposite him and

leaned forward, and laid her hands down flat on the table top. She took a big breath.

"Look. It's all an act. I'm scared shitless. Someone tried to kill me. I don't know why. Or maybe it was a kidnap that went wrong. I don't know what it was. I don't know who it was. I don't know if they'll try again, or what the hell's going on." Her voice was quieter, less bouncy, more earnest, more real.

"Why not sit down," Lylly said. "Let's try again. What do the police say? Have you talked to them?"

"They don't say much."

If she was a member of a wealthy family the obvious conclusion was kidnap for money. But it didn't seem anything like a kidnapping for ransom that Lylly had ever heard of. There was a possible kidnap to start with, but that was it. She'd been taken then abandoned. It did seem more likely it was a murder attempt. But then hanging someone up and leaving them to die of dehydration was an uncertain methodology. Or maybe they changed their minds? Was it a warning? They probably saw the climbers on the cliffs when they came in on the helicopter, if that's what they did. Maybe they knew the climbers might come back that way and release the woman? Or they expected them or some other climbers to come through the tunnel the next day on the way to their pitch on the cliff. But it was a risky move.

Lylly didn't think she would have survived the night pinned against the wall. It was still absolutely fortunate that Lylly had come along when he did. Lylly just couldn't get a handle on it. He didn't see it. Kidnap for ransom which was then abandoned? Or attempted murder? Or a warning? Which was it? And whichever it was, did the failure mean they would try again soon? And if it was a warning, who was it aimed at?

It suddenly hit Lylly that if the kidnap was a warning not a murder attempt then the kidnappers had to be watching the tunnel. They'd watch all day to see if anyone progressed through the tunnel. If no one did then they would have planned to phone the husband – or someone – to tell him where she was. Otherwise she'd die. A warning was a warning. It wasn't so good and didn't work so well if it was also a murder. And because the husband didn't know about the kidnapping until he was told by the police after his wife was released that meant he had not been phoned by the kidnappers. And that in turn meant that they must have seen Lylly rescue her from the tunnel. They knew.

Lylly felt things were getting a little too warm. Lylly changed direction and tried to relax her a little.

"How do you get your name?"

"Merci from Mercedes?" She smiled a more natural smaller smile. "Yeah it's a French joke of my husband's. Sure, I don't mind it. Makes it feel like I'm being thanked for something every time people talk to me or call my name."

"Your graciousness in even talking to them perhaps?"

"You got it."

"What about Stahl? You said your husband's French? But that sounds like a German name?"

"He's from Alsace. Lotta German names there. Alain says Alsace has been German twice since 1870 before the French got it back each time. Anyhow where do you get your name from?"

Lylly explained that his real name was Archer. Camo was a nickname. Short for Camouflage.

"I was always trying to hide and blend in at school."

"You and me both mister."

"You too? Funny I would have thought you were cheerleader commander-in-chief, the most popular girl in class, and The Girl Most Likely To…"

He nearly prefaced that with something like 'With your looks,' but guessed it was implied. And it was too familiar too. Rescuing someone didn't mean you knew them. Nor give you a right to assume you knew them. She probably had a bucket load of cheesy comments like that throughout her life.

"But funny back on you," Merci Stahl batted the word back. "It kinda suits you. But more ironic, like because you do the opposite of blending in. You stand out."

"Do you remember asking me to stay close because you feared 'he' would try again?" He wasn't trying to trick her exactly but he thought it would give her less time to prepare an answer.

If she was thrown by the abrupt change of tack she didn't show it.

"No I don't. And I can't think why I'd say that. But that doesn't mean I'm not worried. I am."

"Do you include your husband in that worry?"

"No!" she was emphatic. "No way. Of course not."

Lylly wondered if she was protesting too much. He had definitely heard her right as she murmured in her stupor at the tunnel mouth as they waited for rescue. She had definitely said what she said. Now she was saying she didn't know of any direct threat by anyone specific. It was inconsistent. And Lylly didn't know why. Did she really think there was no threat from someone she knew or was she dissembling? Was she denying it because she was too scared to admit it? Lylly couldn't tell.

She stood up again, ready to leave. "I really gotta go." But then she hesitated. "But look what're you doing right now? You looking for a job? You look like you can handle yourself. Are you for hire?"

She fell silent. She rotated her head, peering round the interior of the bar, as though her attackers might be dodging the Dubonnet or lurking behind the Noilly Prat and Pernod bottles. "I'd feel happier with some kinda protection." Her voice was small and quiet. This was the real Merci, Lylly thought.

"What? I'd be some kind of bodyguard? Is that what you want?"

"Pretty much," she said. Her nonchalance had returned momentarily. But then she became serious again, "Yeah I do. As I said, you look like you know what you're doing. You look like army?"

He nodded. She was sharp, Lylly thought. Behind the wide grin and the slightly dipsy manner there was a keen mind. She was unlikely to have seen the army trousers he'd worn in the tunnel, and she wouldn't have had a chance to see them since. He'd packed them away once off the trail and bought a pair of lightweight walking trousers in one of the camping and outdoor shops in town. On the other hand, the police might have told her.

"But my husband's not going to go for that, not one little bit," she said.

Lylly thought he probably agreed with that assessment. Some husbands would take it as a personal affront to their self-esteem if their wife had a bodyguard that wasn't them.

"How about as a shepherd?" She looked like she'd hit on a solution. Her eyes were bright, communicating the wisdom of need.

Lylly cocked his head to one side. "How would that work?"

Merci Stahl explained that she and her husband owned a big farm. "It's kinda more of a ranch." She said their big flocks of sheep were driven up into the high meadows for the summer. "They call it transhumance over here. It's a bit like the old cattle drives back home. Except the shepherds go up with the flocks on quadbikes. The dogs ride on the bikes too." She smiled, again it was more natural than the big professional beam she'd used earlier. It was good to see her with the real smile, Lylly thought.

Lylly didn't think he fancied living up in the peaks in a fallen-down roofless stone hut, and told her. "And anyway I won't be any good to you as a covert bodyguard if I'm up in the high slopes with the quadbikes and quadrupeds and you're down on the ranch."

"No that ain't it. It's not like that. Once the shepherds have taken the sheep up high they leave em there. You'd come straight back down. You just go up and check up on the flocks every now and then. Most of the time you'd be doing stuff on the farm. You'd live in the annex." She also explained that she'd be able to persuade her husband to let her have Lylly accompany her for trips, "Like when I go shopping. Stuff like that." She hesitated and exhaled. "I don't wanna go on my own," she said, very quietly.

Lylly knew she ought to get the police involved in some way. But he also knew they couldn't protect her all the time, especially as she went about her normal life. He thought what she suggested might work.

"I think it might work," he said. "But I don't really know. Sure I've got army experience, but I'm no professional bodyguard." But maybe I can get in people's way if necessary, he thought, acting more as a visual deterrent than an actual protector. "Maybe more disruptor than bodyguard." That might be enough. It was likely to be sufficiently effective just to have her no longer be on her own when she was out. But for how long?

"Can we try it and see? I'd sleep a lot easier. Don't worry 'bout the money. We're generous. What d'you say?"

The money wasn't one of Lylly's main concerns. "What will your husband say? Don't you have to get this shepherd idea past him?"

"Sure. But if I tell him you're looking for work he'll be glad to offer you the job. He knows what you did. He'd be pleased to take you on."

Lylly suggested she put the idea to him and see what he said.
"Let me know."
"When can you start?"
"Tomorrow."

10

NINETY MINUTES AFTER Merci Stahl left the bar Lylly's phone pinged with a text from her. It said Alain Stahl liked the idea. He'd like to meet Lylly straightaway. There was an invitation to dinner. She added the address to the text and directions.

Lylly was wondering what was next when the text came. He knew he needed to think more about what he might have agreed to undertake. Acting as Merci Stahl's bodyguard wasn't something he was fully equipped to do. There were plenty of outfits out there who would do a better and more professional job. And if the Stahl family had plenty of cash, which was Lylly's impression, then spending a chunk of it on protection would be no big deal.

He wasn't worried about any personal danger. He knew he could look after himself. And if necessary he could be armed. He was more worried about any harm coming to Merci Stahl through his own incompetence as a bodyguard.

The more he thought about the problem the more he realised it was a question of time. A professional protection consultancy could do many things but what it couldn't do was attend to Merci Stahl twenty-four hours a day seven days a week. Only someone living on the Stahl farm could do that. And he could fill that role. Lylly could see his role as a bodyguard as a bonus rather than a necessity. The necessities would be provided by professionals. He thought it was the only way that would work. The only safe way.

Lylly was still sitting in the bar. There was a half-finished glass of beer on the table. He finished the drink and left the bar. He knew now what he was going to recommend to the Stahls. Lylly would offer his services as an extra and an add-on to the professional protection services the Stahls should also employ. He would try not to get in their way but would keep an eye out and be around during those times when the professionals were not available. If they didn't go for that then he would say goodbye and drive away.

He had a feeling that Merci Stahl knew that being tailed and monitored and cosseted by professional protection agents would irk and annoy her. It would involve too much of a step away from her normal lifestyle. Lylly thought Merci Stahl already suspected that which was way she seemed to be insisting on having Lylly around as a closer and less disruptive bodyguard. That may or may not work, Lylly suspected. But they would just have to try it and see how it went.

At the same time Lylly thought it remarkable that Merci Stahl wasn't crying out for as much protection as she could get, from whatever source. The ordeal she had been through was life threatening. More than that, it was life-terminating if Lylly hadn't arrived as a deus ex machina to save her. Yet she seemed almost reluctant to seek help. Asking Lylly to provide bodyguard services seemed a token at best. There was something about her behaviour that Lylly couldn't put his finger on. It was as though she knew somehow there wouldn't be a second attack. But how could she know that? Lylly was searching for patterns he knew might be there but which he couldn't see.

He found his car and headed out of town. To find the place Lylly headed north out of Draguignan back to Castellane. While passing through there he booked into a hotel for the night stay. Then he went west. He took the road to La Palud. Once there he turned right on the D123 heading north. The road took him into a wild, deserted and uncultivated region. Mediterranean pines grew tightly together on red and white rocky bluffs, with mimosa, witches fingers and the occasional agave providing the underbrush. It was hard and unforgiving country to walk through without a dedicated path, Lylly knew. And Lylly recognised a grove of cork oak close to the road as he drove slowly past. The trunks still showed the mark just below first bough level, the upper limit from where the bark had been stripped in days gone by. Now the oaks were untended and were no longer husbanded. Fungus-free plastic stoppers and aluminium screwtops were killing the cork industry.

Merci Stahl's directions said while on the D123 heading north Lylly should climb straight up and down the Col de la Croix de Chateauneuf, which was nearly three thousand feet high but really not much more than the first ridge in a series of ridges in the folding tree-covered landscape. Descending from the col down to the valley bottom on the other side, still heading north, Lylly was to look out for a bridge over a dried-up river bed. Immediately after that on right there was a kilometre marker stone which was white with a yellow top, and had no numbers nor directions on it, and just beyond that he should look on the left hand side for a pair of stone pillars opening on to a red tarmac track disappearing over a brow under a canopy of scrubby wiry Mediterranean conifers. He should take the track between the pillars and then keep going, the text said. The red road only led to one destination. Her place.

Lylly followed the directions. He had a rough idea he was in the wild and empty country north of the Gorge du Verdon, in a vast triangle of territory between the town of Castellane in the east and the big village of Moustiers to the west and La Palud between them further south. For some reason he was reminded of the Roman packhorse trail. When he'd looked at the map he seemed to remember it came this way after he'd veered away from it on top of the col above the descent to the Pointe Sublime and the gorge entrance. He reminded himself to buy a better map.

He found the relevant landmarks as described in Merci Stahl's text. He went up and over the col and dropped down the other side. He crossed a tidy parapeted bridge over a dried up riverbed, something he well recognised from his time in Spain, which was known there as an arroyo. He spotted the blank yellow-topped kilometre marker. He came to the gateway pillars on the left. The pillars looked like identical Roman columns, made of gleaming marble with flutes cut in the circumference of the drums, but without capitals on top. He wondered if maybe they were ancient, the real thing, and thought again on the packhorse trail. He turned in between them and continued along the red tarmac drive road. The satnav said he was now heading north-northwest. He was in the bottom of a broad valley following the course of the arroyo.

After four miles along the red drive Lylly came out of the trees and was surprised to see ahead of him not the isolated cluster of farm buildings he was expecting but a chateau, facing south and sited just at the point where the relatively flat land began to curl and buckle and twist up into higher ground that marked the beginning of the lower mountain slopes to the north and east. The approach drive ended in a vast smooth gravel parking area in front of the chateau bordered by lawns. A series of sprinklers set in the lawns kept the grass green and luscious in the teeth of the natural aridity and horticultural unfriendliness of the Provençal climate where everything that grows has thorns and an attitude problem.

So when Merci Stahl described her abode as not only a "farm" but more of a "ranch" she really ought to have added that it was also a chateau. There was a farm certainly, but it was a collection of impressive russet brick and cream stone buildings set round a courtyard down a cypress tree-lined avenue some way away from the main building, the chateau. There was a broad brick archway carrying the first floor above which gave access to the courtyard beyond.

The chateau was a multistorey building with two four-storey wings either side of a three-storey square central section. The four-storey wings had oriel-style bay windows on the first three floors, while the three-storey central section had rectilinear flush windows. On the wings there were three floors of bright-white rendered stone under a fourth floor set into the steep curved and sloping roofs of grey tiles and zinc flashing. Tall blue brick chimney stacks stood at each end of the rooflines. The wing roofs had a line of protruding circular windows set all along the eaves. The central section was lower, with two storeys set in the white stone under a squarer and sharper roof in the shape of a truncated pyramid, which also contained the third floor. The third floor line of dormer windows in the central section's roof were rectilinear. The flashings round the windows and chimneys on the central roof were copper, bright green with verdigris.

Lylly drove past a pair of tennis courts behind a three metre high wire fence on the right hand side as he approached the front of the chateau. They were both surfaced with red shale which made them look like a continuation of the drive, complete with white lines. He stopped the car on the edge of the gravel by the tennis courts and saw the building's main door open. Merci Stahl, who must have been alerted by the sound of the car engine, came out and stood on top of the steps to welcome him.

Merci Stahl was joined on the steps by a tall lean man. He draped a long arm around Merci Stahl's shoulders in what Lylly considered to be an old-fashioned and unnecessarily proprietorial gesture. But maybe it was a necessary proprietorial gesture for Alain Stahl's peace of mind. Maybe having your wife kidnapped and then rescued by someone else was somehow a threat to the man's ownership of his wife, but Lylly didn't know. Lylly assumed this must be him. He was wearing a blue blazer, smart grey trousers with a sharp crease, and to Lylly's bewilderment, a cravat. Lylly was glad he hadn't continued to wear the army trousers and had changed into the only alternative he had with him, the pair he'd bought in Draguignan. But he still felt underdressed in his navy-blue ultra lightweight walking trousers. He knew he'd have to explain at some point that he'd been on a walking holiday. But then maybe not, Merci would have made that clear.

They made rapid introductions as Lylly mounted the flight of steps to the chateau's central front double doors. Alain Stahl shook his hand and thanked him for Merci's rescue. Stahl was tall and thin and reminded Lylly strongly of Kellner the German surgeon he'd met in the hotel before tackling the gorge. He also had long black hair swept back from his forehead. He had long delicate fingers and an easy confident manner.

Now there came one of those linguistic ping-pong matches where each party attempted to show their knowledge of the other person's language was better than the other person's knowledge of theirs. Camo Lylly had introduced himself in French. Alain Stahl answered in English. His English was good with a slight French accent. He carried on in the same language with his thanks for Merci's rescue. Lylly responded in French. Merci Stahl chipped in in English. Lylly gave it up and changed to English himself.

Alain Stahl clapped Lylly on the back and ushered him through the door into the main hall leaving Merci to shut the door behind them.

Stahl led them to a reception room the other side of the large hall. It looked to Lylly as though there'd be a drink before dinner. The fine and ancient wooden floor creaked slightly under their footsteps. He heard noises emanating from another direction from the hall and realised the chateau had some staff. For some reason that hadn't occurred to him. But now he assumed you couldn't run a building this size without assistance. He guessed the sounds he had heard were coming from the kitchen. Maybe the cook was beheading a chicken.

In response to Stahl's query Lylly asked for a beer and carried it with him shortly afterwards as they trooped in another direction through to the dining room.

The three of them sat at the end of a large dining table that Lylly judged could easily sit sixteen people. Alain Stahl sat at the head with Merci on his right and Lylly on his left. The conversation was formal at first, following the formulaic norms of what do you do, and where do you live, and what do your parents do, what are you doing in this neck of the woods, how old was the chateau, and similar strands. And of course Camo Lylly was asked to go into great detail about his time in the Spanish Legion.

It turned out that Alain Stahl was an angel. He was an investor. That is, he invested in promising start-up companies, particularly in the high-tech and medical sectors. In return he took a big chunk of the profits or a share in the companies, or both. That was now. But he'd gained his first millions as he put it purely by the luck of geography.

"My family was in building materials and we owned a quarry just where they wanted to dig the portal for the French end of the Channel Tunnel. My father knew they couldn't change the line of the Tunnel at that stage and refused to sell. He held out till the last minute. Then he made a deal for three times what it was worth just before it would have been compulsorily purchased. That put us on our way."

It was over large glasses of marc in Merci and Alain Stahl's case and a small cup of coffee in Lylly's case at the end of dinner that Alain Stahl said he was a breeder.

"I breed cattle."

Specifically the cow and bull steers in question were the two ancient Savoie mountain breeds, the Abondance and the Tarentaise.

"I'm not trying to improve the stock. I'm just trying to stop them dying out." Stahl said it was important to contribute in any way you could to the region you lived in.

"I thought this was Provence still?" Lylly thought Savoie was further north. Where the high mountains were.

"In modern France, that's true," Alain Stahl agreed. "But not historically. Historically much of this area didn't become French until the Revolution. Savoie was an independent country, and France was its main concern, even its main enemy. Many of the mountain passes were fortified by Savoie against French incursion. My home area of Alsace didn't finally become French until 1945. France wasn't always as large as it is now. And what does 'finally' mean anyway?"

Lylly smiled to himself that his mythological premise was still intact: you couldn't find a French person who didn't resort to cod-philosophical questions sooner or later.

Alain and Merci Stahl between them explained the workings of the "farm". As well as the breeding herds of Abondance and Tarentaise cattle there was a small herd of goats, a hundred or so, and a large flock of sheep, perhaps twelve hundred strong.

"You say 'perhaps'. Don't you know the number?" Lylly was surprised. It seemed casual and economically naïve.

"I know exactly how many," Alain Stahl said. "But the number is always fluctuating. You always lose some. You lose some in the trek up to the high meadows. You lose some up there to predators and scavengers and accidents. You lose a few more on the way back down. Some just get lost. Some are stolen. Stopping that is part of the shepherds' job. And some of the older ones just die. Last summer we started out with twelve hundred and forty two. We got twelve hundred and thirty-six back down from the mountain in the autumn."

"Losing only net six head was a pretty good year," Merci Stahl said. "We think they were all stolen too. That's one reason we need another guardian shepherd up there. Then of course the numbers go up dramatically in the lambing season."

"What happens to those?"

There was a silence round the table. Eventually Alain Stahl pointed to Lylly's empty dinner plate and raised his eyebrows in an interrogative gesture.

Lylly nodded. He was beginning to see things more clearly.

Finally as the evening grew late they began to talk about the events in the hidden tunnel and how Merci Stahl now needed some kind of protection.

"I was reluctant, naturally," Alain Stahl said. "But I can see the wisdom. Merci convinced me. Anything to keep my wife happy." He laid is hand over hers on the table top.

"We have to do something," Merci Stahl said. She sounded earnest and not a little frightened. "Who knows if they will try again."

Lylly noticed that Merci withdrew her hand from under her husband's as she spoke. She also sounded more concerned than she had in the café in Draguignan. Was that for her husband's benefit?

"If you want it, you have the job." Stahl said. If he was piqued that his wife withdrew from overt physical contact with him, he didn't show it. He put out his hand. Lylly shook it. Lylly reckoned it was the fiction that he was being hired as a shepherd rather than a bodyguard that allowed Alain Stahl to run with the idea. It allowed him to convince himself that his wife's protection wasn't really in the hands of someone else.

Lylly now brought up the question of hiring professionals. He could see that neither of the Stahls were keen. Alain perhaps even less so than Merci. Alain did seem to take the attack on his wife even more personally than she did.

But Lylly insisted. He explained how it might work, with him and the professional protection working together, seamlessly and unofficially, combining their strengths and their timing with him on the inside and the professionals on the outside. Camo Lylly wanted to make clear it was non-negotiable.

Eventually Merci Stahl agreed. Once his wife had agreed, Alain Stahl could see that it was illogical for him to continue insisting against it. Finally he too agreed and said he would set about immediately contacting various companies for a quote.

"Is that the best way?" Lylly asked.

Alain Stahl didn't follow what Lylly meant.

"I would have thought a better way of appointing something as serious and as personal as bodyguard services is to do it by recommendation, by word of mouth. Do you have any friends or colleagues that have hired bodyguards? Or are you aware of any companies that have used protection services?"

Lylly knew it wasn't uncommon at the higher levels of industry to have fulltime bodyguard services. There was the fear of kidnapping for ransom. Not just of the principal, but of their family members. What had happened to Merci Stahl could be part of a scenario like that. It was also not unheard of for company bosses to be assassinated. Business rivalry could be deadly. In a way Lylly thought it was surprising if the Stahls were as wealthy as their property seemed to indicate that they hadn't had recourse to protection services already. The world is an envious place. And for some people the easiest way of making money was to steal it. By any means.

Alain Stahl agreed. He said he would ask around his business contacts.

"Protection is a growth industry," Lylly said. "Maybe one of these outfits might be worth investing in."

Alain Stahl smiled and tilted his head in acknowledgment

that he might already be thinking that. Merci Stahl laughed out loud.

But both of them insisted they wanted Lylly to be on hand as an unofficial bodyguard too.

"When can you start?" Alain Stahl asked him.

"Tomorrow morning. I just need to nip back into town and stock up with some clothes," Lylly said. "Then I'm good to go. Show me the sheep."

11

SO CAMO LYLLY GOT a job operating as Merci Stahl's in-house bodyguard under the guise of working as a shepherd and farmhand on the Stahl farm. He still couldn't tell the difference between the sheep and the goats. But it didn't matter. Merci told him that anything either sheep or goat that had a blue painted S somewhere on its fleece was theirs to look after. It didn't matter and wouldn't make any difference to his primary role of protection, but it seemed that Alain Stahl was involved with the cattle and Merci Stahl was involved with the sheep.

The morning after the dinner Lylly returned to the chateau. He'd bought a few more outfits in Castellane but for the outdoor shepherding work he wore his walking gear and boots.

Merci Stahl introduced him to the head of the chateau's farm operations Robert Garnier.

"The farm works in two directions," Garnier said. He spoke in French and either assumed Lylly would understand or didn't care if he didn't. "Below the chateau is cattle. Above the chateau is sheep. You'll work above the chateau."

Lylly was initially concerned about the hierarchy. It sounded like Garnier thought Lylly was working for him. But Merci assured him that Garnier knew the score. "He knows your primary job is to look after me." He presumably didn't know that the shepherding job was a piece of face-saving cosmetic surgery to keep Alain Stahl's ego intact. Though Lylly wouldn't hesitate to tell Garnier that if necessary.

At the moment Garnier was friendly enough as he showed Lylly to his room in the large complex of farm buildings, stables, workshops and barns centred round the courtyard. Lylly dumped his stuff then Garnier took him beyond the farm courtyard further up the slope to an area of stone barns, stables, shippons, dutch barns, sheep pens, garages and shed outbuildings. Garnier opened a pair of double doors in a stone-built shed and showed Lylly a quadbike, asked him if he knew how to handle one, and handed Lylly the keys and a hand-held GPS tracker when he said he did. Garnier didn't call it a quadbike, instead he referred to it as an "ATV," Which Lylly extrapolated as "all terrain vehicle." He guessed there was no French equivalent acronym.

The bright red quadbike felt more than anything like a wheeled version of a snowmobile. There were wheels at the four corners, set as far apart as possible for stability, riding on broad chunky tyres. The central drive section was the bit that looked most like a motorbike, with steering handlebars, brake levers and a large headlamp. There were load carrying basket frames set fore and aft.

Camo's first job was to get on his quadbike and catch up the flock that was already on the trail on its way up to the higher ground for the summer.

"This is transhumance," Merci Stahl told him again. "The animals go up north and east to the high level pastures for the summer. Here in Provence we don't need to go up to the real high peaks, we just have to go high enough to where it's cooler, and wetter, that's where the grass grows. In the autumn they are rounded up and brought down to spend the winter round the buildings here or under cover on the farm. You wouldn't believe it but grass actually grows down here in the winter."

There were two other farm hands – a father and daughter team named Pierre and Veronique - on quadbikes with five sheepdogs already on the trail, she said. Lylly assumed they knew the deal too and wouldn't object if and when Lylly descended abruptly from the high pastures and returned to the chateau. On the other hand Lylly couldn't say he gave a damn if they did object. He wasn't their workmate, he just had to work with them for a while.

The ground inside the courtyard and all round the exterior, between the farm and the shippons and stables, as well as on the drive between the chateau and the farm, was paved with blue brick pavers. Each paver had five spherical half-domes on top taking up most of the upper surface.

Merci Stahl explained that the pavers were much older than they looked. "They're original," she said. "Laid down when the original farm was built in the eighteenth century. They're special pavers for horses. The farm buildings were mostly stables in those days. There were many more horses on farms then than there are now. Horses for riding and for working. And these pavers are designed to stop horses slipping. The five round caps on the surface of each paver allow the horseshoes to grip and not slip. It's a real shame we don't have horses no more now so you could see how they work."

Beyond the paved area a gravelled track headed uphill through a gate above the farm. Lylly mounted the quadbike and headed up through the gate up to the higher ground. The stony track, wide enough for off-road vehicles, followed the edge of a valley by a tired and insipid stream which looked like a poor relation to what it might be in a different season. The remnant was falling down the slope in a hurry like it had an appointment to keep. He imagined the stream was fuller higher up. He stayed with the track for several miles before coming to a second gate. The engineered track stopped at this point. Beyond the gate was wild country. There were still tracks and some of them were wide enough for vehicles, but as often as not Lylly went off-road and followed the grassland adjacent to the valley stream. He marvelled at the speed with which the four-wheeled bike covered the ground. He was climbing in minutes distances that would have taken him hours on foot. He was gaining on the flock.

It could take as long as a week to get all the flock up to the destination high meadows. It could be quicker. Pierre and Veronique said it depended on how many animals had done the trek before. They would then lead the entire flock at a faster pace.

"They want to taste the good grass," Pierre said in French. "So they hurry up."

However long it took, a week or only four days, to get up to the high ground, the advantage of a quadbike was that Lylly could be back down at the chateau in under an hour from getting the call, even from the uppermost of the high level pastures.

Lylly had long talks with the other two shepherds as they followed the flock. They formed a roving rearguard behind the five sheepdogs behind the sheep. The goats were there somewhere too, but Lylly didn't bother trying to differentiate them. It was the dogs which were doing the actual hard work of keeping the huge flock in the right shape and on the move and aiming in the right direction. Pierre or Veronique would whistle something and a dog or two or all of them would immediately set about doing to the flock what the whistle said they should.

Sometimes there was a fascinating floor show which involved a battle of wills between a sheep, invariably one of the rams, and a sheepdog. The ram would stand its ground, duck its head to threaten the dog with its headgear, and refuse to do what the dog wanted it to do.

The dogs never backed off. It was as though they realised instinctively if they showed any sign of weakness the sheep bossing game would be over. Perhaps also they took the refusal as a personal affront. The dog would crouch down on bent legs, showing its teeth and snarling and advancing towards the ram, trying to give the impression, Lylly thought, that it was only waiting for the right kind of whistle to leap upwards and take the ram by the throat or savage various delicate parts of its undercarriage.

The ram would hold its position until the advancing dog reached a certain threshold, which was its flight distance which varied with the ram, and then it would always retreat and begin to do what the dog wanted it to do.

Sometimes the confrontation would go on for minutes and an interested audience of other sheep would stop and watch. On those occasions another dog would often come in to help to speed things up and get the sheep moving again. The second dog would come at the ram from a different direction, in a predator's classic pincer movement that was millions of years old. Faced with two dogs outflanking it, where it was impossible to face off two dogs in two different directions simultaneously, the ram always backed down rapidly and turned tail.

Shepherd Pierre had gained his experience as a shepherd purely by doing the job. Shepherd Veronique came to it by passing exams. There was often friendly banter between them about how best to do something flock-related. Pierre would argue from a position of practice and tradition, while Veronique would take a more academic and science based approach. Lylly noticed that in the end it was usually Veronique who won the argument. Pierre might disdain qualifications but he deferred to them.

If Pierre and Veronique ever wondered why a complete novice such as Camo Lylly had been added to the sheep guarding team they didn't say. But with Lylly's frequent phone summons off the mountain back to the chateau, perhaps they understood what his primary function was.

Though Lylly was overtly assigned to shepherding the flocks, he had both his mobile phone and a walkie-talkie with him. He could be summoned down from the heights at a moment's notice if his bodyguard duties required it. Apart from the sheep there was also the shopping. Merci Stahl wanted Camo to accompany her on her shopping trips and other solo visits. She was scared of being kidnapped again, she said, finally admitting it. The way it worked was he'd be called back by phone or radio from the high meadows on his quadbike or round the farm buildings if he was down from the slopes.

He'd left the Seecamp .32 in its hiding place in the car. He had the fighting knife in his backpack. But he had the two modified walking poles with him at all times. He carried them with him on the quadbike and always made sure he brought at least one of them down with him when he got the call to escort Merci Stahl to wherever she was going by car.

Until the protection company was hired Lylly was doing all the bodyguard work. He knew once they were in place he would have to come to some arrangement with them. Or he could say nothing and operate completely unconnected as a shadow behind the scenes. He wasn't sure yet which way was the best option.

Most of the time when Merci left the chateau it was sometimes to go shopping, or visits to the gym, or to the riding school. It was sometimes other more social outings such as meeting friends or visiting their houses. Whenever Merci Stahl went out on her own Lylly went with her. When Alain and Merci Stahl went out together, Alain decided that Lylly wasn't needed. Lylly didn't argue, though he wasn't sure what good Alain Stahl would be if there was a determined attack on his wife. He looked too thin, too elegant and too well-dressed to engage in a fight. His centre of gravity was too high to achieve the necessary combat stability. Sometimes when the Stahls went out together at night Lylly followed them incognito in his car at a distance.

Some of the time Lylly could combine shepherding and bodyguarding simultaneously. That was because Merci Stahl often came up by quadbike to the trail to see how the transhumance was progressing. She seemed far more relaxed and natural, Lylly noted, as she chatted with the two professional shepherds. She noticed him looking.

"I'm an outdoor gal," she said by way of explanation. "The sheep and the slopes. You gotta love it."

Merci Stahl's riding school was just outside Castellane. When Merci Stahl went riding, Lylly thought at first it might be best if he rode with her as part of the same riding group. But then having scouted out by quadbike all the trek, trail and cross-country options available to the riders he reckoned an attack on her while out riding was no more than a remote possibility. To kill her on those occasions would require a professional sniper with a very good rifle. And if whoever wanted her dead was resorting to those extreme and organised lengths then there was nothing that Lylly nor anyone else could do about it. On those occasions he either waited for her at the stables or dropped her off and picked her up later after the ride.

12

THERE ONCE WAS A silly mother who claimed her daughter Andromeda was more beautiful than the Nereids, the sea nymphs. Really the gods should have laughed it off because she would say that wouldn't she? And in any case how would a mother know? But the god of the sea took offence on behalf his staff. A sea monster called Cetus was deputised to ravage the area, as sea monsters do. Merchant ships and fishing vessels were unmercifully harassed. The coast was ransacked. Harbours were tormented. People were drowned or eaten. The economy plummeted. The GDP was in freefall.

An oracle said, as oracles do, that the ravages could only be stopped if the girl was sacrificed to the monster. She was chained to the rocks by the sea and Cetus was scheduled to come by and snack on the girl. But a passing superhero wearing flying sandals, armed with a vorpal blade and a petrifying head in a magic bag, spotted the damsel and glided in to the rescue. He killed the sea monster, or according to images on an old urn threw stones at it which scared it away. But there was consanguineous marriage trouble with an amorous uncle and more killing before the aerial hero and the rocky damsel were happily wed.

Lylly exited Wikipedia. The thing about the old gods was they weren't nice. Where and when did the notion of a nice god start he wondered? If none of them are real you might as well characterise and personify them as nice, surely. What was the point of making them nasty? But he knew the likeliest reason gods were made capricious and daunting was because the surrounding environment was unpredictable and frightening. The world was a scary place when you didn't know anything about anything. Your gods mirrored both your knowledge and your environment. Shame though, he thought, not to have nice gods in those mythological days. And also what happened to ravenous rampaging sea monsters? Where did they all go? Those mythological monsters thought they ruled the world, they had everything, they were friends with the gods, they could ravage and rampage and wreck and ruin anything they wanted to. But they never knew they were in fact an endangered species.

The question for Camo Lylly was, if the woman Merci Stahl pinned to the tunnel wall was like Andromeda chained to the rocks, was he then her rescuer Perseus with his flying sandals? But more important who had placed her there in sacrifice? The myth said it was her father Cepheus after her mother Cassiopeia's foolish boast that Andromeda was more beautiful than the Nereids. And who was Cetus the monster that would come to devour her? And where was Medusa's head in the magic bag when you needed it?

Lylly went back to Wikipedia. He clicked through a series of images and paintings depicting the climactic scene of the myth. These showed Andromeda chained to the rocks on the seashore and Perseus's flying sandals giving him an aerial advantage in his battle with the monster Cetus.

He noticed the earliest images had Andromeda fully clothed when she was chained to the rocks. But the clothes were strange and exotic. That was because Andromeda was supposed to come from Ethiopia. She didn't look black but she had strange clothes. Maybe the Greeks didn't think or know that the inhabitants of "Ethiopia" were black? Despite her American lineage Merci Stahl was decidedly of a Mediterranean hue, accentuated and augmented by her golden tan.

Later images, especially in Renaissance paintings, showed Andromeda completely naked. That was much more titillating, Lylly thought, but then you didn't have the benefit of strange clothes to show the woman was from foreign parts. He guessed that by Renaissance times no one cared where the girl came from, it was the myth and its central drama that mattered.

Lylly's favourite in all the images was the one from an ancient Grecian urn which showed Perseus throwing stones at Cetus to drive him off. Why hadn't anyone else tried that? You didn't have to be a hero with flying sandals to be able to do that. And why would anyone depicting or relating the myth suppose that such a course of action would be effective? Maybe they were big stones, thrown hard. They must have stung a bit. Maybe Cetus didn't think throwing stones was fair, like biting and scratching, or pulling hair, and refused to play any more and skulked off in a huff?

Lylly was becoming convinced that someone had deliberately created echoes of the Andromeda myth in the curtailed kidnap or attempted murder of Merci Stahl. He always thought one of the weirdest aspects of the myth was the aftermath in that the trouble didn't immediately cease with killing the monster. There was the amorous uncle to deal with and the scheduled consanguineous marriage. What was that about? And did it have any relevance now?

But the key to all this was why would anyone bother? If it had been a re-enactment, if there was a connection to the Greek myth, then why? What for? It suggested a strange kind of mind behind it where history and myth were interchangeable and where the ancient ramifications were still important or were still being felt.

Lylly was resting in his room in the dormitory part of the group of farm buildings. He had a meeting scheduled with the representative of the security firm that Alain Stahl planned to hire. He'd come down from a two-day stint with the sheep. He'd spent the night in surprising comfort in a wooden cabin on the mountain. The cabin had a kitchen, an eating area and a sleeping area. Shepherd Pierre was the cook.

The advance groups of the flock were now approaching the lush and well-watered grass of the high pastures. In two more days the entire twelve hundred sheep would be enjoying their summer holiday camp. Then Lylly's job as a shepherd would be largely over for the summer. He would be able to concentrate on being a bodyguard more full time. As well as learning on the job.

As he rested his mind constantly returned to the strange

events of recent days. His mind swam with images of dark tunnels and a half-seen human form pinned against the wall. Constantly and always he returned to that central question: if he hadn't come that way would Merci Stahl have died?

And then for the first time he asked himself the subsidiary question: why had he walked that way? Why had he taken the route through the hidden tunnel?

The only answer to that question was he decided at the last minute that he would take the tunnel because it represented a short-cut. If he went that way he could be through the entire gorge in a day and wouldn't have to find somewhere to spend the night, especially as he'd learnt that the banks of the river were dangerous. So he'd headed that way. But he hadn't decided until he parted the vegetation and looked in. It was a last minute decision. It seemed that Merci Stahl's life depended on nothing more solid than that.

The final subsidiary question was perhaps the biggest question of all. Was he Lylly a pawn in someone's game? Was he the innocent third party sent through the tunnel to rescue Merci Stahl, or at least raise the alarm before she died? Did whoever planned all this want Merci Stahl to be rescued? Scared but rescued?

It was all exceedingly tenuous. What if Lylly, staring into the long dark of the hidden tunnel had decided at the last possible second not to take it, but instead had turned aside and taken the conventional path? What did that mean for Merci Stahl? Was there a contingency plan? Did it mean also that Lylly was being watched somehow, so the watchers would know and report back that Lylly had in fact taken the tunnel, or had not?

Lylly felt his mind becoming numb with unanswered questions. Some of the questions were unanswerable, certainly. But a few of the unanswered ones could be answered. But for the moment he didn't know where to start looking for answers.

His mind returned to the day he'd walked through the hidden tunnel and checked out the helicopter landing ground and the place where he'd found Merci Stahl. He was beginning to conclude that pinning her to the tunnel wall wasn't a kidnap for ransom, and it wasn't a murder attempt. It was some kind of warning. Merci Stahl wasn't supposed to die. And that meant movement through the tunnel had to be monitored by the kidnappers. If no one came through to find her and raise the alarm they would have to go back into the tunnel and release her themselves. Otherwise she'd die. And if they wanted to remain anonymous they'd have to do that before Merci Stahl became conscious enough to identify them. But Camo Lylly had in fact come through. He felt it was certain now that his rescue had been seen. It had to be. But seen by who? And where from?

He was tying the laces on his boots when the obvious answer hit him. Who better to monitor the tunnel activities but a pair of rock-climbers perched all day on the cliffs above it? Lylly realised he needed to find the climbers and talk to them again.

Temporarily Lylly put the questions aside, he had some meetings to attend.

13

POLICE CAPITAINE CAMUS didn't want to know.

Lylly went into Draguignan to talk to the capitaine at the police municipale. The climbers had disappeared.

Lylly had ventured along the northern rim of the gorge to the point where he had intercepted the climbers previously. The camper-van was not parked in the belvedere. He checked they weren't climbing there anyway, thinking perhaps it was possible they'd been dropped off. He followed the wide stony track through the undergrowth to the clearing along the edge and leaned as far as he dared over the lip of the cliff. To be certain he walked along the edge to where the cliff changed angle and a section protruded like a re-entrant on a fortification and he could look forward and back from there along the cliff face. He could see there was nobody on the face below.

He motored slowly along the rim road checking every belvedere and parking place and the cliff faces below. The VW camper-van with the adventurous stickers was nowhere to be seen. He briefly considered driving round to the southern rim and checking the cliffs, belvederes and climbing sites on that side but rejected the idea as a fool's errand. The police could do it better.

"It would be a good idea to find a pair of British and French climbers," Lylly told the capitaine.

He outlined his theory that his movements on the day he had penetrated into the long forbidden tunnel had been monitored by the climbers. That they had been placed there – paid? – to watch for any activities in the tunnel the whole day. It was, he claimed, the only way the kidnappers could make sure that Merci Stahl was not left there to die.

Lylly's current thinking was the climbers were unconnected to the kidnappers in any other way apart from being paid to watch the tunnel during their cliff-scaling activities. It must have been made worth their while. He reckoned it would have to have been a substantial cash sum, to ensure they remained climbing constantly in sight of the tunnel exit below.

Lylly was certain they'd lied to him about being out of sight of the tunnel during their climbing on the day. As well as the money they would also have been given a phone number to call in the event that no one came through the tunnel or if someone did – either way the kidnappers would need to know. Merci Stahl would not have survived the night pinned to the tunnel wall.

Then again, Lylly tracking them down and interviewing them three days after the tunnel incident must have spooked them. They'd run. But had they run all the way back home to Rochdale? Or just run to the next climbing area? Lylly's instinct said they'd want to get away with the big money prize they'd earned for basically doing nothing but just being themselves, but want to carry on with their climbing activities as well. That meant they moved to a safe distance, to more cliffs somewhere else. Lylly had no idea where that might be.

"A big black Mercedes saloon with blacked out windows carrying men in black suits, black ties, black hats, and shiny black shoes wearing black sunglasses and shoulder holsters would be a little conspicuous lurking in the relevant observational belvedere all day, wouldn't you say?" Lylly's list put together all the bad-hat instant cliches he could think of from a hundred years of films.

But the capitaine didn't do irony. He was clearly less than impressed with Lylly's generic description of potential kidnappers. He shot Lylly a scornful glance, a look reserved for professionals obliged to listen to amateurs.

"So what better way to monitor the activities in the tunnel than a pair of totally innocent looking rock-climbers?" Lylly said. He didn't add – you need to find them – but it was implicit.

But the capitaine was having none of it.

Lylly was free to drive along the gorge rim then seek out the police captain in Draguignan because the security company was looking after Merci Stahl's protection during the day. The meeting between the Stahls and the security company representative, plus Lylly as a kind of unspecified observer, had led to the company being appointed.

Lylly and the Stahls decided that the security firm would handle protection duties during the day. They would follow Merci Stahl closely in a separate car wherever she went when leaving home. They would have a constant daytime presence on the chateau-farm complex. They would patrol the grounds at night. They were informed of Lylly's unofficial security activities and seemed happy with that.

To avoid any problems Lylly might run into with the security around the chateau at night, the Stahls thought it best if Lylly now slept in a room in the chateau. The Stahls asked him to dine with them too, whenever he wasn't away with the sheep in the high ground.

The company was American, SteadyState Secure, running out of a European head office in Paris with a subsidiary branch in Marseille. It had been recommended to Alain Stahl by a business colleague. Lylly was impressed with the four of the company's security guys he met, all US ex-pats, all out of either the Paris or Marseille offices. They were bilingual in English and French. They appeared to be well trained. They were also big. They were armed, not with guns but with Tasers and nightsticks. Carrying firearms as a private individual was probably illegal in France, Lylly suspected, and elsewhere in Europe.

He did wonder whether one or two of them might be carrying guns illegally, which was extremely risky so their paymaster Alain Stahl must be making it worth their while, or either Stahl or the company boss had sufficient clout in France to get a special dispensation. On the other hand it must be reasonably easy in France to apply for and receive licenses to own shotguns and hunting rifles.

Either way, Tasers, nightsticks and possibly long guns, it seemed they were taking the threat to Merci Stahl seriously.

Lylly's job was where and when the security company's people couldn't be. In the chateau at night. And up on the slopes with the sheep on the days when Merci wanted to be there, which was often. She'd also decided she wanted Lylly to go with her when she went riding next time.

Riding was something Lylly wasn't sure about. But he found he rather looked forward to the idea.

It was over a week since Lylly had moved into the Stahl's world as a farm hand and bodyguard. He was a bodyguard moving on interior lines but accepted and known to the security company moving in the Stahl's world on exterior lines.

The security guys had set up twin cameras on the Roman columns at the beginning of the red drive to monitor any vehicles – or anyone on foot for that matter – entering the four mile red road. Two of the guys – Lylly learned their names were Todd and Brad - had apps on their phones which warned of, and showed, any activity passing the cameras and entering the drive. Todd and Brad were big blonde beefy and indistinguishable apart from one of them having a beard, but Lylly didn't know if that was Todd or Brad.

The company had installed a command post consisting of a pair of portacabins and a portaloo chemical closet on the gravel expanse next to the tennis courts. The portacabins sprouted aircon units on a sidewall. They enabled the security team to operate independently of the big house, providing a food and accommodation base.

Lylly was beginning to wonder what the endgame or exit strategy was going to look like. How long would Alain Stahl pay for this level of security? How long would they want Lylly himself around? A month? Six months? Lylly thought neither. He doubted whether this intensity could be kept up for much more than a couple of weeks. Then it had to be scaled down. The cost must be astronomical.

He guessed if there were no more alarms the team would disband, the portacabins and loo would be taken away. Perhaps only the twin cameras and phone app would remain. If things remained quiet then he too would move on. He wasn't sure if what he did next would involve driving or walking, but he'd decide when the time came.

Meanwhile there was some riding to do.

Unlike Lylly, who had thought it unlikely that Merci would be attacked anywhere in the inaccessible terrain in the uplands when only feet, horses and quadbikes could go, Merci Stahl herself wasn't so sure. And to a certain extent Lylly now tended to bend from his previous opinion. This was because he had seen after a week of use exactly where quadbikes could go and what they could do. A sniper on a quadbike could hit Merci and be off the mountain before any police presence could be organised or even summoned.

At the same time he wasn't convinced he wanted to be with Merci every time she wanted to go riding. She didn't yet seem to realise that for the time being she had to modify her behaviour. No one really knew by how much or for how long. But Lylly suspected that from now on her life was going to be different whether she liked it or not.

14

LYLLY HAD NO IDEA WHAT to wear for riding. He asked Merci who said his sheep herding clothes would do.

"You're gonna look more like a cowhand than a member of the Royal Hoity-Toity Fancyshire Hunt, that's for sure. But if I say it's ok no one at the club will say different."

Normal rules of etiquette and appropriate attire didn't apply when big money spoke, Lylly had come to realise.

At the riding school after some discussion about Lylly's capabilities he was given a mare that was described as being the quietest calmest least excitable and most biddable horse they had. In fact Lylly had done a short riding course in the Legion. Most of the time being a soldier life is so utterly boring you sign up for almost anything either to just to have something to do or to get out of doing something else even more boring. So he was a novice but not a total ingénue.

Merci Stahl decided that she and Lylly wouldn't join the nine other riders in rest of the school on their outing but would go off by themselves. She knew all the rides in the area. This particular ride trailed along a mountain stream in the woods, then came out above the treeline, rose up to a col on the ridge line, then down to woods again on the other side, then eventually out of the trees up to another col further along the ridge and so followed a circuit back down to the riding school. It would be a day's ride. They were carrying all the food and drink they needed.

Lylly's inappropriate riding outfit raised no comment at the school. It was just accepted that Merci Stahl made the rules. Something else possibly inappropriate that Lylly brought along was one of his hiking poles. He stashed it and his small backpack containing the Fairbairn-Sykes knife in the saddlebags along with the rest of their supplies. Merci herself wore twill riding trousers tucked into riding boots with a white polo shirt on top under a short tweed riding jacket.

The school insisted they both wore riding helmets. Even Merci's authority didn't run to gainsaying that, Lylly thought. That is until they turned out of sight of the school complex, when Merci immediately removed her helmet and suggested Lylly do the same. Lylly went bareheaded while Merci replaced her helmet with a turquoise headscarf.

Sometimes the trail was wide enough to allow them to ride side by side. They could talk then. Other times the trail narrowed and the horses went one behind the other as Lylly followed Merci as she led the way.

Lylly found it fascinating. He realised this was the normal way of travel for thousands of years, if you were wealthy enough to own a horse. In this region there were no ancillary costs. There was plenty of water and free food for the horses was growing all around. Perhaps the biggest revelation for Lylly was that this way of travelling saved human energy. Sure enough, controlling a horse was not necessarily easy and you had to concentrate, and that in itself was tiring. But not as tiring as travelling on your own feet carrying your own supplies. And most of all, with this mode of travel through the centuries you always had enough energy to fight at any moment if necessary. Maybe that was the key to its success.

They made good progress, though as Merci said they didn't have to be anywhere and they would be back at the school well before dark even if they dawdled. In single file they followed the stream uphill through the woods as the stream jumped and bobbed and slid from boulder to boulder. The noise it made wasn't a roar, and it wasn't a murmur, it was somewhere in between, like a distant clapping sound heard close to.

They emerged from the woods and headed uphill on grassland interspersed with rocky crags and vast isolated boulders left there by glaciers in ice ages long gone. At the foot of the climb to the ridge the trail zigzagged up the steeper slope towards the col above. They dismounted at the high point of the col and had a drink while admiring the view. They weren't talking much, but it was a companionable silence.

There were no signs of life anywhere. To Lylly it seemed they were Adam and Eve making their way out of Paradise. He began to realise something else too. What they were doing was sensual as well. To imagine and play with the idea in your mind that they were both the first and last people in the world was a seductive and amorous notion. If this carried on Merci Stahl was going to need bodyguards and chaperones up on the mountain tops too. He wondered if Merci Stahl was feeling the same way.

They remounted and descended into the next valley. As on the first side the path zigzagged across the mountainside on the steeper sections. Then it bottomed out and followed the contours down to where it entered the treeline again. They followed the course of the stream as it leaped and humped downhill. Eventually they came to a junction of streams. Another stream came in from the right hand side. Ahead their track turned and followed the new stream uphill through the trees towards a second col and a second crossing of the ridgeline before a final descent to the riding school.

But where the streams joined there was a wide pool at the confluence under the trees with a wide flat space round it and the banks and open space were covered in thick grass. Slower eddies in the streams had formed several large grey sandbanks near the water's edge.

"This is a great place to stop and eat," Merci said. "Let's take a break."

They dismounted and began to unpack the food and drink. Lilly looked at the pool and had an idea. He took a large bottle of mineral water and two bottles of beer and stepped into the shallow water round the nearest sandbank. He laid the water bottle flat on its side and pushed into a dent in the sand until it was all underwater. He wedged the two beer bottles upright in the sand until only the tops were above water. Twenty minutes later he was drinking a cold beer.

They ate and drank, and talked sitting side by side on grass leaning back against the trunk of a fallen tree at the edge of the open space.

They finished eating and packed everything away. They sat again on the ground, drinking and talking. This time Lylly noticed that Merci sat down much closer to him than she had before.

Suddenly Merci Stahl stood up. "Yeah," she said. She untied her headscarf, took it off and walked to the water's edge. She dunked the scarf in the water, wrung it out, then rolled it and tied it round her neck. She approached Lylly and stood in front of him. She looked down at him. He looked up at her. Nothing was said. She grinned and pulled the polo shirt out of the riding trousers. She unbuttoned it and pulled it off over her head. She threw it to one side. Then she reached behind her back and undid her bra and removed it. She threw it on top of the polo shirt.

She stood in front of Lylly wearing nothing but the damp scarf on her top half, with riding trousers and boots below.

"That there's the easy bit," she said. "Now I'm gonna need your help."

She sat down again and pointed her riding boots at Lylly. He grabbed one and tugged. She was right. But eventually he got both boots off. Now she stood up again and began to remove the riding trousers which required a lot of wriggling and wiggling. She stood up again in front of Lylly wearing only white panties and a pair of white socks and the scarf. She stood on one leg and removed a sock. She repeated the move with the other sock. She stood straight again, then bent and removed her panties. All she wore was the scarf.

"Well I guess you had the benefit one time of seeing me like this, when I couldn't do anything about it. Different now I'd say," she said and laughed.

As Lylly had already seen, she had a tight honed slender athletic body with large breasts.

She came forward and kneeled down on him straddling his legs. She pushed her breasts towards him. He put his arms round her.

"Now you," she said and stood up.

He rapidly removed his boots then all his clothes.

They embraced tightly by the water's edge, their hands hungry for each other.

Merci stopped and said, "This way."

She took Lylly's hand and they stepped into the water to the nearest and largest sandbank. It was freezing, but Lylly didn't care. In fact he hardly noticed.

Merci lay down on the sandbank. Her legs were open.

"Now this," she said.

Afterwards they washed sand off each other then lay on the bank together in a jumbled pile of clothes in the dappled sun on the grass.

It didn't need saying there would be no consequences, Lylly knew. They weren't starting a relationship. Nothing had changed. They just wanted sex with each other at a certain time in a certain place. There might be other times and other places but it didn't matter if there were and it didn't matter if there weren't.

It was early afternoon when they remounted the horses and hit the trail again, Merci leading, Lylly alongside. They followed the stream uphill to the point where it emerged from the trees and the trail turned away from the stream valley up towards the col. They could ride side by side in this section. They kept looking at each other, saying nothing, just smiling.

It was where the trail turned through a hairpin bend on the first zigzag at the bottom of the steeper zigzagged section that Lylly saw Merci's horse's head explode in a cloud of blood an instant before he heard the gunshot.

While her horse was still collapsing and as Merci inhaled deeply to begin to scream Lylly leapt across from his own horse and threw Merci to the ground with himself lying on top of her. Her horse folded in a heap a few feet away. Still lying prone, Lylly shoved Merci right up to the line of the dead horse's back. There she was fully hidden from the ridge above.

They lay there against the horse's back without moving for a full twenty minutes. Merci was crying and heaving and having trouble catching her breath. Lylly held her and did his best to calm her. He wrapped his arms around her and stroked her hair. He whispered to her and gradually the heaving sobs diminished.

There were no more gunshots after the first one. Very soon after the gunshot Lylly thought he heard the sound of a petrol engine, and assumed it must be a trail bike or a quadbike. He hoped it was the sound of the gunman leaving the area. After twenty minutes Lylly poked his head up above the horse's back. He was certain the sound of the shot had come from up on the ridgeline, perhaps from the col. He looked up towards the col. Nothing happened. After a while he stood up, gesturing to Merci to stay down hidden behind the horse's back.

His own horse was standing placidly nearby eating grass. Lylly went over to it and brought it over and placed it between the col and the dead horse. He stood behind it. From there he reached into one of the saddlebags it was carrying and dug out his hiking pole. and the F-S knife. He screwed the sections together and clipped the knife to the end.

"Can you stand?" he asked her. "If you can, stand directly behind me."

They stood there for thirty more minutes, with Lylly's horse standing sideways on to the ridgeline, with Lylly standing behind it and Merci behind him.

"OK," Lylly said after thirty minutes. "Let's move."

Lylly decided it was still unwise to mount the horses. He took the reins and walked alongside the horse's head, with Merci behind him sheltered to a degree by the body bulk of the horse. They were using the horse as much as they could to cover them from a shooter up on the col. When the track zigged or zagged they changed sides to keep the horse constantly between them and the top of the ridge.

They walked, climbing slowly and warily up to the col. As

they neared the top Lylly left Merci and the horse twenty metres below the ridge and advanced on his own, carrying his walking pole like a halberd. He reached the level ground of the col and looked around. The area was deserted. The ground was too rocky to see any vehicle tracks. But there was a jumbled collection of rocks and boulders on the right where a spotter could hide and observe the ground below and be hidden from anyone down there looking up. If you were going to shoot from the col, this was the best place to do it from.

Out of interest Lylly went over to the rocks. He cast his eyes around and was slightly amazed to see something glinting in the sun in a crevice in the rocks. He bent down to examine what it might be. It was a spent rifle cartridge casing. He thought about fishing it out, but then thought better of it. He pulled out his phone and took several photos of the casing in situ as well as several close-ups of the markings on the base.

"Careless," he said.

He called Merci to bring up the horse. She did and he told her about the cartridge casing. Now they both mounted Lylly's horse. At first Merci wanted to be the one in front, since she was the better rider. But Lylly convinced her it was wiser for her to stay behind him, as far as was possible.

And so Merci Stahl and Camo Lylly descended from the col back to the riding school and back to safety.

And there they called the police.

15

LYLLY KNEW THAT AFTER the dead horse incident he wouldn't be returning to quadbike shepherding nor trailing the flocks up the mountainside to the high pastures. Protecting Merci Stahl had instantly become a full time operation for everyone involved.

Later on he would look back at that shepherding time as one of the highlights of his life. He came to see that time as a special quiet island, an almost idyllic interlude before things jumped to a new dimension and began to accelerate and fall apart.

The shepherds. The sheep. The mountains. A trinity of work and calm and quiet where his only focus was the shape of the fluid movement of the dogs, and his prime target the health and wellbeing of the flock. He often thought back to the dark nights of absolute stillness where the pressing pinhole canopy of stars was bounded and defined by the looming blackness of the ridgelines. And to the grey head-down days in weather unique to the mountains where the wind was so strong the only direction the rain didn't come was downwards.

The only differences Lylly knew between what they were doing now and how it had gone for shepherds for centuries before them were GPS, Gore-Tex and quadbikes. And Lylly didn't regret their intrusion. It meant you could combine two worlds, retooling the methodology of the old with the mechanisms of the new. That was how he liked it. Maybe today can be better than yesterday.

A few days after the shooting incident with the dead horse on the mountain, the head of the European arm of the security company SteadyState Secure flew down from Paris. It was essentially a business meeting, a conference about what to do next; to step up security in some way, or better still get Merci Stahl to adapt her lifestyle to the new reality.

Alain Stahl decided the meeting should take place over dinner. Merci would be present obviously. But less obviously he also asked Lylly to attend. He was after all the one whose quick reactions had prevented any further shots being aimed at Merci, if there were or had been any.

The head of SteadyState Secure was American. Frank Koggs had flown in from Paris in the company chopper. He had piloted it himself. It had landed on the tennis courts.

Koggs introduced himself to Lylly as they went in for dinner.

"Good thing you were there."

Koggs had thick white hair pulled back from his forehead, flopping over his ears, and a white gunslinger's moustache drooping down past the sides of his mouth. He wore a sharp Italian fawn-coloured linen suit with the jacket sleeves so carefully and precisely rolled up to the elbow they looked ironed in place. Under the suit he wore a white shirt with buttoned-down collar and a deep navy blue tie dotted with some kind of regimental monogram. His face and his forearms were deeply tanned.

Lylly smiled. Koggs clearly didn't waste words. It left a lot to be desired in the way of saying who he was, but Lylly assumed he was talking about the horse ride. He could also see that Koggs was apologising in a way for the fact his own men hadn't been there.

While it was obvious to Lylly that Merci Stahl had changed the rules about him riding with her purely so she could have sex with him on the mountainside, it was a good thing she had. He didn't want to exaggerate the heroics of his own actions during the shooting, but if he hadn't leapt off his horse and pushed Merci behind the dead form of her own horse, the shooter might have had a second shot at a static and easier target.

"I was lucky. We both were."

Koggs looked at him, appraisingly. Then nodded.

Alain Stahl made the formal introductions as they sat down for dinner. There was another American present at the dinner table, a business associate of Stahl's. He was introduced to Lylly as Walton Holber. It was clear he already knew the rest of the people round the table, Koggs included. But Lylly had no idea who he was or why he was there.

Not sure himself how Lylly fitted in to the deal, Holber took an instant dislike to him. Particularly so when he discovered very quickly that Camo had been in the Spanish Legion. And was English. He attacked Lylly with such dogged relish it was as though he felt a constant necessity to fight and re-win the Revolutionary War.

"Why didn't you join a proper army?" Holber said.

He was being designer-aggressive, Lylly knew, with an affectation of belligerence. But what the hell, he might as well rise to it.

"Like the French Foreign Legion?"

"Yeah you got it. Spain's got no military capability. France not much neither. But maybe both are better than you Brits. You can't take anyone's military seriously that puts an F into lootenant."

"Spain has or had? Well if you're talking about the past, you're completely wrong," Lylly said. Examining Spain's exceptional military history was part of the deal in the Legion. "Spain is the reason why for four hundred years Europeans could go anywhere in the world and kick the shit out of the locals. I guess you've never heard of Gonzalo de Cordoba?"

"No of course not! Why the hell should I know about some dago?"

"If you think you know military history and you've never heard of Gonzalo de Cordoba then you don't know your arse from your elbow and you know sod-all about the military. At one stage Spain was the only Christian power capable of taking on the Ottoman Turks. And they didn't hesitate to do so. And Gonzalo de Cordoba is the man who created the army of Castile for Isabella and her successors that was capable of doing that."

"I 'spect they kinda just got lucky."

"Get real. Without the bulwark of the Spanish army we'd all be speaking Turkish now. Why do you think all the words for all the military ranks in English and French come from Spanish?"

That stumped him, Lylly could see. It was something he'd never known nor considered.

"General. Colonel. Major. Captain. Lieutenant. Corporal. Private. All Spanish words. Only sergeant doesn't come from Spanish, it comes from French. And it's not even a military rank, it's civilian. And it's why we say "cur-nel" not "coll-o-nel" and "lef-tenant" not "loo-tenant" in English. We took the spelling from French but retained an echo of the Spanish pronunciation. Which has an R in coronel and an F in lefteniento in Spanish. And that's why we put the effing F in lieutenant."

The American was silent now. Lylly had the advantage. He carried on.

"It's the Thirty Years' War that's the key to European domination of the world. In that war Spain took on the rest of Europe. For twenty of those thirty years Spain was winning. It took another ten years for the rest of Europe put together to force the Spanish to give up. They weren't beaten, they were just forced to give up. And during those thirty years Spain's enemies only won in the end because they modelled themselves on the Spanish army.

"That's when the words for the military ranks came into English, with the Spanish model. Historians call it the Military Revolution. After it a European army modelled on the Spanish system could go anywhere in the world and beat anybody. And thrash the Turks. That's why Spain is the most important military power in modern history. And that's why I joined the Spanish Legion."

It sounded good. But it wasn't the reason.

After dinner Holber and Alain Stahl left the dining room together and went through to Stahl's study to "discuss our business" as Stahl put it. He invited the others to move into the lounge where he would join them shortly. But Merci Stahl excused herself. That left Frank Koggs and Camo Lylly who walked together into the huge lounge. They were both drinking beer.

"I was a *coronel* in the US Army," Koggs said, using the Spanish version of the word. "A col-o-nel," he repeated, stressing the three syllables ironically.

He smiled and held up a hand to say he wasn't criticising Lylly's outburst and carried on.

"Retired. Fact I kinda liked what you said. Walton's always had a tendency to be a pain in the ass. I always did reckon the worst kind of people are loud ignorant people who think they know something. They should never spout off. They got to learn to keep their mouths in line. Otherwise sooner or later they're going to take a hammering. You sure did that. He took a real dislike to you though."

Lylly shrugged. He didn't mind having enemies.

"It didn't seem to be personal. I think it was because of what I represented on two counts, England and Spain, as opposed to what I am. I don't mind him wanting to re-fight the American Revolution, nothing I can do about losing that one, but it was the total ignorance about Spain that annoyed me."

"I guess you don't know what Walton does?"

Lylly said he didn't.

"He sells weapons, silent spies in the sky, and things that go whizzbang. He's an armaments salesman. A factor, a middleman and agent for more than a few US manufacturers."

Lylly raised both eyebrows in surprise.

"You didn't know?"

Lylly shook his head. He seemed to be at a loss for words.

"Then I guess you don't know what Alain Stahl does neither, do you?"

"No not really. I gathered he was some sort of investor, a financial angel."

"Yeah. Right. Angel my ass. Well Walton Holber as well as being an a-hole is Stahl's main supplier of US weapons. You think breeding a bunch of crappy old steers pays for all this?" He waved his hand around to include the chateau. "No way Jose. Alain Stahl might spend his cash in assisting start-ups and suchlike. But where he gets his cash is as an arms dealer."

16

"I BEEN TELLING PEOPLE LIKE HIM for years they've got to take security seriously. They do nothing until it hits close to home. Think they're immune somehow and it'll never happen to them. It takes stringing up his wife on the rocks in a deserted tunnel for Alain to give me a call." Koggs took a swig of his beer bottle.

Lylly was stunned. He felt like the ugly monochrome swan at the duckling beauty pageant. He felt the whole world knew more than he did. He felt he was the last person to know what was common knowledge to everyone else.

Koggs excused himself. "They'll want me to lean into that meeting as well," he said, for some bizarre reason tapping the side of his nose with a forefinger. He went off in the direction of Stahl's study.

Lylly wondered what tapping the side of your nose meant. Or rather he knew what it meant, but why did it mean "I got secrets I got to keep"?

Lylly took his beer and his padded down vest and wandered through a set of French windows outside to the back terrace, which was a broad sweep of stone on three levels following the full width of the chateau.

He found Merci Stahl already there. She was sitting back in a lounger. She was wrapped in a knee-length thick wool cardigan against the chill. The horn buttons seemed to Lylly to be the size of ashtrays. A tumbler with a drink and ice cubes stood on the small white iron table beside her.

"Hi there," she said patting the seat beside her. "You love the night sounds too?"

Lylly took the lounger next to hers. The night was full of

a thousand sounds. There was the sound of birds, of insects, of mooing cows, and all the strange indeterminate noise of the night. Somewhere up in the woods an owl called. An answering call came from what seemed to be right over their heads. Overhead the night sky was lit with stars like an end-of-war fireworks display. The stars were so seeming close it was almost spooky, and Lylly felt he could reach up and grab one.

He heard a voice and followed the sound to the far edge of the terrace where he recognised Todd or Brad talking quietly into a walkie-talkie with the glow from the handset lighting up his face. Todd or Brad then disappeared along the path into the woods at the back of the big house.

"I just learnt your husband is an arms dealer," Lylly said by way of idle chit-chat.

Merci shrugged.

He half expected her to use the great evasive phrase of the first decades of the 21st century: *it is what it is.*

"He doesn't advertise," she said instead.

Lylly tried to resist his feeling of being lied to. Righteous indignation was a bottomless pit. Of course they hadn't lied to him. He doubted he would readily admit to strangers he was an arms dealer either.

Did it make a difference, Lylly wondered, that Alain Stahl dealt in weapons? He now resisted his first instinct that said of course it did, because why should it? Just because a man had a business selling dangerous items didn't in itself mean his job was dangerous. He needed necessarily have any more disgruntled customers than someone who sold insurance. Assuming disgruntled clients would kidnap or take shots at your wife in any case.

Unless of course it was just another warning. The gunman hadn't missed, Lylly realised. He had deliberately aimed at the horse. Then if in fact it was a series of two warnings then what Alain Stahl did for a living could add to the significance of that. The warning could be saying: stop what you're doing, or else. Might it really come down to one party not wanting Stahl to sell guns to another party?

Even though his mind was reeling and he still felt he was going round in aimless circles, like the universal worm Ourobouros circling round to devour its own tail, Lylly did feel that this at last did begin to make more sense. Hey Stahl stop what you're doing or else your wife gets it.

"The cops called," Merci said. "They found the spent cartridge case up on the ridge where you told them to look."

For some reason Lylly was thinking what happened to the dead horse?

"That's good. They say anything else?"

Merci didn't respond. After a while she said, "I got to go see someone tomorrow. Will you come?"

Lylly told her he didn't think it was a good idea for her to do anything or go anywhere other than stay on the farm.

Merci both nodded her head and rocked and tilted it in a way like a seesaw that suggested "I know but I have to."

"Who is it? Who do you have to see?"

"It's my little girl." She looked at him. The look said I don't care how dangerous it is for me out there, this I have to do. "Sylvie."

She carried on, "She's living with religious nuts. She's a religious nut. They live in a commune on the other side. Over Moustiers way." She pointed in the dark towards the mountain side. "I'm her mom," she added with great sadness and a degree of desolation.

Lylly told her they should only go if Todd or Brad or both came along too in a separate car. She saw the sense in that and agreed.

"I had her when I was sixteen. She came over here with me. It looked good for a while. She did well at school. Took Alain's surname when we got married. She was a great lively loving kid. Then she met *him*. Bad people. Though she did real well in her Bacc, after it kept bunking off school, suddenly didn't want to go to college. When she hit seventeen she lit out and left. She lives with them. A year now. In a commune."

"What happened to the father? I assume it's not Alain."

"No. Back home. A boy I knew. He died while I was pregnant. Accident on the farm. We would've wed I guess."

They were silent. Lylly reached out and touched her arm.

"Of course I'll come," he said.

One thing he hadn't asked was who *him* was. But he knew she would tell him more.

17

BOTH KOGGS AND HOLBER were staying at the chateau for a few days. Lylly saw the helicopter was still standing in the middle of the tennis courts and Holber's black faux-utilitarian G-Class Mercedes was parked on the gravel as he joined Merci next morning at her silver Porsche 911 in front of the building.

Both Todd and Brad were already waiting in one of SteadyState's Mercedes windowless white vans. Lylly surmised a black van would have looked too obviously villainous. Frank Koggs was talking to them through a front side window.

Lylly had asked if he could get a set of the SteadyState company uniform. He thought it would look better, more official, and might make the company operatives accept him more. He was wearing the black shirt and combat trousers in readiness for the visit to Sylvie's commune.

"If you're coming with me there's something else you need to know, need to do," Merci said. She sounded apologetic as though there was something she was ashamed of, but was in the rules. "You have to wear this."

She opened her bag and pulled out a full face mask in the form of a devil. It was red, had little horns and seemed to be made out of stiff plastic. Velcro fastening straps dangled from its edges.

Lylly laughed. "You're kidding."

"I'm afraid not. Look, it's really silly, I know, but everyone who enters the compound who isn't a member of the commune has to wear one."

"Kind of all outsiders are devils?"

"Yeah that's it." She sounded tired. "Look if you'd rather not come I understand."

"No I'll wear it." He reached out and took the mask and placed it on his face and velcroed the straps in place behind his head.

"What about them?" He pointed to the white van where Todd and Brad waited to follow Merci's Porsche.

"There's a stash by the gates. Everyone who enters, every visitor has to put one on before entering. You put the mask on then ring the bell."

"But you don't have to?"

"No. Sylvie arranged that."

What is this place? Lylly wondered. He followed Merci towards her car.

Merci Stahl seemed to change her mind. She opened then closed the driver's door on the 911.

"Can we go in yours?" she said.

"Sure, fine by me." He didn't ask the reason. "I can see well enough to drive in this mask."

"You don't have to wear it till we get there."

"May as well get used to it. The devil you know…" he added.

Sylvie grimaced at his attempt at humour.

"Sylvie hates it." She pointed to her car. "Hates me in it. Says I love running the money too much, flashing the cash."

"Just a sec," Lylly said. He walked over to Brad and Todd in the van.

"What do you fucking look like?" Todd said as Lylly approached his side window. He explained the mask deal.

Brad swore, "No fucking way."

But Todd laughed. "Get with the program son," he said to Brad.

They set off in Lylly's Mazda with Todd and Brad following in the white van. Brad was the one with a beard, he'd learnt, and Brad was driving. Lylly had stashed one of his walking poles on the back seat together with the F-S knife hidden in his small backpack..

Merci was giving directions and Lylly had checked out

Google Maps on his phone before they set off. It seemed the commune was situated in a valley on one of the hillsides above the small town of Moustiers-Sainte-Marie a few miles to the west.

To reach the road Merci directed Lylly along a track different to the red tarmacked main approach road. This track ran north, snaking and switchbacking up and through the hills rather than running along the arroyo and was unmetalled, though still in excellent and well-maintained condition. Merci explained it was an unofficial route, not on any maps, and never used by any visitors, tradesmen or deliveries to the chateau but was known and used only by the Stahls and the farm workers, should they so wish.

"It's a quicker way of heading north or west," Merci said. "Shorter to the main road too."

For some reason Lylly was glad and relieved in a way there was a second route in and out of the chateau estate. Maybe he was becoming a proper bodyguard after all, conscious at all times of his environment and possible escape routes.

While directing them Merci also explained to Lylly what the deal was.

"I can only see Sylvie on a certain day at a certain time for a certain length of time. Once a month. I don't like it but I have no choice. It's either that or have no contact at all. It's today. At midday. For one hour."

"Jesus," Lylly said. "Who makes these rules?"

He was already jumping to the conclusion there must be some Stockholm Syndrome going on with Sylvie Stahl. As far as he was concerned any "commune" was like the army but far worse. At least the rules in the army were there for a reason; to make you a better soldier, also known as making you a better killer, but no one mentioned that. But what were the "rules" in a commune for? Who did they benefit? And who was better off with them? He was beginning to dislike this commune.

"She does. They do. He does," She stressed the *he*. "Bruno."

"Do you want to tell me about Bruno?"

"Bruno Ludo. You'll be able to judge for yourself when you

see him. He's a religious asshole. I think he's a fake." She hesitated, "No perhaps not fake. Something else. But Sylvie believes him."

Merci said that when Sylvie first met Bruno she just visited the commune.

"Seemed kind of ok. Well he was an older man, sure. But he didn't do anything, far as I knew. And it made her seem maturer. Oh I don't know, better able to meet the world and get through it on a level footing, I guess. I thought he was doing her good. Kind of letting her find her platform. So for six months it wasn't so bad. Kept doing well at school and kept visiting the commune, seeing – and listening – to Bruno. But then it all changed. After six months she moved in there. Dropped out of school. Just seventeen. New rules I had to keep if I wanted to see her." She sighed. "That's how it is. Nearly a year now."

They approached then passed by the small town of Moustiers-Sainte-Marie. Lylly read somewhere the town was a pretty hillside tourist town. A tourist town known not just for its inherent prettiness but also partly because some local crusader in the Middle Ages had come home from Outremer and strung a big gold star on a chain two hundred metres long across part of the town. The chain was still there.

"Let me tell you the legend," Merci said. "Some local crusader knight called Bozon de Blacas swore he'd hang up the star on the chain if he managed to escape from the Saracens and ever made it back home. He did. And there it is. Bruno's assholes call themselves the Bozonians. It kind of suits them: Bozo-nians."

Lylly was sure there was some name in the study of linguistics for a word that was innocent in one language but absurd in another. But he didn't know what it was. But he was beginning to reckon that "Bozo" and "Bozo-nians" was just right for this Bruno and his gang.

They carried on up the gently receding hillside beyond the town. A dusty turn off appeared on the right of the road. A large boulder at one side of the turn off had the words Le Maison de Bozon daubed on it in white paint in two lines. Dribbles from the upper line had interfered with the lettering on the lower line. Dribbles from the lower line disappeared downwards into the grass at the base of the rock. Beyond it a track disappeared downhill under Mediterranean conifers.

"Down there," Merci said. The way Merci said "there" and not the more obvious "here" told Lylly that Merci viewed the turn-off with distance and distaste, as though it were the entrance to hell, or worse.

Lylly turned into the stony track. Immediately they crossed a sturdy stone arched bridge over a stream. Then he had to slow down immediately after the bridge and weave about because the track was full of potholes. He also had to be wary of and dodge large stones left lying on the track surface. Lylly had a feeling both were deliberate. The white van followed.

The track they turned into soon ran adjacent to the stream which was on their left. They continued on under trees following the stream until the trees thinned and cleared. Ahead was a pair of open ramshackle wooden gates hanging loosely from a pair of short but thick red terracotta tiled walls. The walls were three metres high and three metres wide, topped with red Roman half-pipe tiles, semicircular in section. The wall on the left as they viewed it terminated at the edge of the stream. Wire fencing the same height as the gate walls ran off from the walls in both directions, one way disappearing back over the stream into the trees, the other way disappearing over a brow.

"They should be expecting me," Merci said. She looked at her watch. Lylly glanced at the car clock. It was ten minutes to midday.

The track now split. Ahead on the left on the far side of the stream was a big two-storey stone barn structure with a red Roman half-pipe tiled roof. A turning to the left ran over a sturdy wooden bridge giving vehicle access over the stream to the barn. The track straight ahead of them led to a second wall blocking the way. This was a whitewashed wall centred on a pair of wooden gates attached to replica terracotta tiled stone pillars exactly as had been seen at the main entrance. The difference was these gates were closed.

Another difference was one of the gate walls had a bell in it. A square hole had been built into – or was punched through later - the left hand gate wall all the way through the half-metre-thick brickwork. And hanging in the hole was a large bronze bell. Next to the bell was a large wicker basket.

"Go straight," Merci said. "You gotta ring the bell," she added. "And the devil masks are in the basket."

She grabbed the door handle.

"Let me," Lylly said. "Stay put."

He got out of the car. As he approached the bell he saw that a short thick rope was attached below the clapper. You were supposed to use the rope to wave the clapper back and to against the interior of the bell. But then he noticed some big stones lying along the base of the wall. He picked one up and banged it hard against the side of the bell six times. It clanged reluctantly but loudly and the sound seemed to run off into the distance.

He hadn't done that for any particular reason, except only to not do what you were supposed to. Sometimes they taught you that in the army too. He delved into the basket and retrieved a pair of devil masks. He took them to the white van and handed them through the window.

"Get with the program," he said.

They dutifully put on the masks. He came back to the car.

A pair of women approached the gates from the commune side. They wore plain cotton-print dresses and headscarves. One of the women unlocked a padlock on their side of the gates then loosened a restraining chain through a pair of eyebolts. Then each of them pulled open a gate. Lylly drove the Mazda through. The woman on Merci's side of the car smiled. The one on Lylly's side frowned and scowled at him.

Lylly wondered if the women would try to shut the gates before the van with Todd and Brad came through. But Brad driving gave them no opportunity to do that. Brad floored the accelerator in the van and came into the compound on the Mazda's tail. Both women shouted at the van but it didn't stop. They left the gates open.

A large cleared area opened up ahead with what was clearly the main building also on the left, backing on to the stream with a series of ancillary buildings of various sizes grouped opposite, adjacent or round it. On that right hand side too was a bank of mobile homes and caravans with a vehicle park behind. Lylly saw there was also another building close to the stream on the left which was a kind of ancient but still sturdy open port with a red half-pipe tiled roof, and four brick piers holding up the corners but with no walls. A series of strangely shaped stone basins and troughs stood under the roof.

With something between shock and surprise Lylly recognised it as a place where clothes washing was done by hand in the old days. In the old days before electricity and machines. Why wouldn't he be further shocked and surprised if the washing area was still in use? Were they actually using water from the stream to wash clothes? Looks like we're going back to the Middle Ages here, he thought.

Merci directed him to a parking area by the side of the main building. He pulled in and the white van parked nearby, but further back so Todd and Brad could still see the front door of the building from the van.

As they got out of the car Lylly took his walking pole from the back seat. He screwed it together. He didn't want to attach the knife at this stage, so the pole was indistinguishable in looks and usage from any other hiking pole. But he shouldered the small pack containing the knife onto his back. He also affected a slight limp and used the pole as a crutch, support and walking aid as they approached the main building which he could see now was some kind of dilapidated farmhouse.

Merci stopped in front of and ten metres away from the front door of the farmhouse. Lylly stood alongside her. Todd and Brad wound their side windows down but stayed in the white van and watched. They were wearing the devil masks.

Nothing happened. But he realised only Merci among them had any idea of what was likely to happen here. He noticed the two women who had opened the gates were standing in a growing crowd on the other sight of the compound, watching them.

He focused on the front door of the farmhouse again for a while. Then he turned and walked over to the white van. He stood at the open passenger window. Both Brad and Todd were also in the black company combat gear. The company name and the SSS logo gleamed in red and white on the left breast pocket.

"Hi guys," he said. "What d'you make of this place?"

"Jesus," Brad at the wheel with the beard sticking out below the mask said. "Not good."

"Christ," Todd in the passenger seat said. "Bad."

Lylly noticed on the seat between them was a shotgun and a Remington bolt-action hunting rifle.

"Yeah," Lylly said. "This is a bad place.

The door to the farmhouse opened. A man and a young woman came out of the house. Lylly left the van and strode purposefully back to Merci's side and watched the two figures approach.

Bruno Ludo was rake thin. Tall. He was supremely good-looking in a French hippie-philosopher kind of way and knew it. His long luscious absolutely white hair was pulled back and held behind his head by a leather band in a ponytail. The hair was bright white, Lylly specifically noted. Not grey, white. He wore a short kaftan over blue jeans. The frayed bottoms of the jeans spread out over the oiled leather open-toed sandals on his feet. The kaftan had a black background with multi-coloured whirls and motifs embroidered over it in broad swathes like a psychedelic Michelin road map to the soul hand drawn by an ultra-intelligent Caledonian crow. The top two bunched-string buttons of the kaftan were undone and a small gold indeterminate gold pendant dangled on a gold neck chain lurking among the visible black body hair on his chest. He looked to be about forty years old.

In his right hand Bruno walked with what looked to Lylly like a bishop's crook. It was made of very light almost white wood with a small silver cross set above an orb fixed to the top. The only wood that white naturally that Lylly had seen was holly. Something about that struck a discord in Lylly's mind. Could it be he wondered? If it was then that was very interesting. It was interesting because holly was associated not with Christianity but more than anything with the Druids. Did Bruno know that? Lylly had a sudden feeling that Bruno knew it very well. So what looked like a bishop's crook was actually a Druid wizard's staff? Was that why the cross on top was so small – so it wouldn't interfere with the inherent 'magic' in the wood? If there was any mistletoe around that would clinch it. Bruno was a druid masquerading as a Christian. But why? Lylly would keep his eyes open for mistletoe.

The seventeen year old girl walking slightly behind Bruno and to his left was Sylvie Stahl. She walked with downcast eyes. She was already a beauty and soon in a very few more years would become beautiful. She had darker hair than her mother, almost black. She had huge almond shaped eyes that shone like mysterious pools. Her eyes were angled up slightly at the outside corners. Like the women at the gates she wore a plain cotton-print dress plus a headscarf. In Sylvie's case the dress was a very light shade of pink with a darker strip of red bordering every edge. The pink headscarf also had strong red edging. The dress buttoned up to a top red border at the neck.

"Welcome sister Stahl," Bruno said. He spoke English with a French accent. His voice was not pleasant. It was high and thin and wavered like an old man's. The way he said 'sister' put Lylly's teeth on edge. The word in itself implies some kind of equality but the way Bruno said it carried a strong undercurrent of implied servility.

"May the Lord of Earth shine on you and keep you. May he bless his light upon you."

He waved two fingers of his left hand in Merci's direction in some kind of manual benediction. Lylly wondered if he'd seen the stretched two-finger gesture on religious paintings such as Byzantine icons, and run with it.

"And on time too sister. Time as the Lord of Water knows

finds its own level."

Jesus, Lylly thought, cod-Christianity and cod-philosophy, that's a seriously bad combination.

Bruno waved the two-fingered benediction in the direction of the white van, then homed the fingers in on Lylly. His voice became shrill and mean.

"Only the Lord of Fire is secure. Is this protection you trespass with? It is not needed here."

Suddenly he raised both hands to the skies. His right hand carried the staff while with the left he made the benediction gesture to the air. His eyes went wide, then wider still.

"Be gone!" he shrieked in a high-pitched scream.

At the sound of the command the crowd moved forward and surrounded the white van. There were at least twenty people placing their hands on both sides of the van with another twenty or so thronging behind. They began rocking it from one side to the other, getting into a rhythm and building up momentum.

Lylly realised, at the same time as did Todd and Brad inside it, that the crowd fully intended to topple the van over on its side.

Through the windscreen he could see Brad ducking down and coming up with the shotgun.

"No!" Merci Stahl cried as a plea to Bruno to stop the rocking.

Lylly frantically waved and signalled to Brad not to use the shotgun.

"Stop. They'll leave." Merci pleaded. "Please Bruno. Stop it. Sylvie! Sylvie! I had no choice. They're protection. I've been attacked. I don't want to be attacked again."

"You will be safe before the Lord of Air here. They should not have come into this place," Bruno uttered the words in a monotone.

Bruno raised his arms and the staff again. He waved the benediction with his left hand towards the white van.

"Cease!" he called, in English.

Instantly the crowd stopped rocking the van and backed

away.

Lylly ran over to the van. He suggested they should retreat in it to the pair of gates at the inner compound entrance and keep an eye on proceedings from there.

"Block the track at the gates with the van. So no one can leave. Turn it round so you can see in," he suggested.

"Assholes. Jesus X,Y, and fucking Zee Christ," Todd said.

As Brad fired up the van and began to back out Lylly ran back to Merci's side.

Bruno now turned his bright blue wide-eyed stare in Lylly's direction. His eyes were opened so wide Lylly could see white all round the iris like the eyes of a ring-tailed lemur. There were tiny black pupils set into the blue surround.

My what big eyes you have grandma, Lylly murmured to himself. The big bad wolf was here. And he was hungry.

"And you brother? Who under the Lord of Air's skies are you?"

Lylly now realised it was Bruno's eyes that were the most arresting thing about him. They were glacier blue. But then he looked again and they seemed to have no colour at all. And only then did he notice the bright but faded blue. Like a husky's eyes, you'd think their shade of arresting wasted blue was an eye colour dogs didn't or couldn't have; then you saw the dog's eyes and were amazed they did. So with Bruno. It wasn't a human blue. Lylly could feel him using his eyes like augers, delving down, screwing deep into his existence, seeing if he could bend him to his will.

He realised what was going on. Bruno was trying to hypnotise him.

Lylly already had had enough if this place. The devil masks, the locked gates, the bell, the ritual of standing ten metres from the door, and above all Merci Stahl's evident fright that unless things were done just so she would be unable to see her daughter. And now there was this chilling clown with the husky eyes with total command over his flock trying to hypnotise him.

Having to wear the devil mask so they couldn't see his face, he decided there was absolutely no reason at all why Bruno or anyone else in this place should hear his real voice either. On an instant whim he decided he would be Eli Wallach's character in The Magnificent Seven, the devious nasty over-the-top Mexican bandit leader.

He also reckoned the act was well in keeping with the big blue bandanna he wore round his neck. Lylly leaned forward, resting both forearms comfortably on the top of his hiking pole.

"I ham thee dee-vil you know. I'm the seester's how-you-say disceepline, noh I meen disceeple," he replied.

It certainly sounded the most ludicrous sub-Hollywood or Spaghetti Western version of a desperado Mexican bandit he had ever heard. Certainly enough to get him referred to any racial equality or cultural appropriation watchdog. He had no idea what Bruno would make of it, but Merci had shot him a horrified look. He knew it was provocative but didn't care.

"Where thee seester goes I follow thee seester."

He looked over Bruno's head, as though the building behind held more interest.

Bruno said nothing. But he shot Lylly a very careful look. The circles of his widened eyes closed slightly and the attempt at hypnotism seemed to end.

Bruno turned and gestured to Merci that she should come forward and enter the farmhouse with him and Sylvie.

"I have to go in on my own," she whispered to Lylly.

"No way. Sorry."

Instantly concerned she placed an arresting hand on Lylly's upper arm.

"Please. I mean it. I'm safe here. I think. There's been no problems before. We just sit at the kitchen table…"

"You and Sylvie? Just you and Sylvie?"

"No. Me on one side and Sylvie and Bruno on the other."

"Jesus Christ." This was bad, he thought, and getting worse with everything he heard. "OK," he said. "I'll wait out here. I'll hear you if you call."

"It's one hour exactly. Sylvie won't let them harm me."

Lylly wasn't so sure about that.

He stood still watching as Merci joined Bruno and Sylvie until they passed out of sight through the door. He stood for a while longer, staring at the door, leaning on his pole.

He was angry. It took him a while to pin it down. It came from Merci's fear. She was scared rigid at the power this man had over her daughter. It dehumanised her and reduced her to a gibbering cipher. He realised Merci would do everything, anything, this troll commanded as long as she could still see her daughter. And what kind of 'seeing' was it anyway? With her on one side of the table with Sylvie and Bruno on the other? She hadn't said but Lylly could well imagine that Bruno didn't allow Sylvie to speak and spoke for her.

He stilled his anger and gazed round the compound. He saw there was now a bigger group of people watching him and the white van. Between forty and fifty people of all ages from running children to men and women in their thirties, but no older and more women than men, were standing some way back, forty yards from the farmhouse. All the women wore plain cotton dresses with headscarves. The men wore kaftans of different colours over blue jeans and sandals. No one spoke. They just stood watching.

Somewhere nearby he heard the sound of a chainsaw. There was another engine sound too, which he took to be a diesel. There was some kind of work going on somewhere. He looked around. There were electricity cables passing overhead and several of the buildings were linked to the wires.

So there was electricity here, he realised. He hoped they had mains running water as well and weren't entirely dependent on the stream. Then further back under the nearest trees he spotted some small modern-looking brick and metal buildings. Generator housings he thought. So they have back-up generators too. Lylly guessed what they had here was a convenient mix of apparent Spartan puritanism plus all mod-cons.

So maybe they weren't totally going back to the Middle Ages

after all.

Lylly walked over to the white van which was now parked just outside the inner compound gates, facing in. He approached the side window.

"He's called Bruno Ludo, who runs this shithouse, the bloke with the bishop's stick, the two-fingered salute and the verbal bollocks. He's full of shit."

"You tell that already?" Todd said with a grin. "What's with the Speedy Gonzales shit?"

Lylly grinned and changed the subject.

"You guys ever get involved with pulling people out of communes and deprogramming?"

"Not us personally," Todd said. "But talk to the boss. He's done it a few times."

"Ran the extraction and called in a specialist outfit he knows for the Stockholm," Brad said.

"US or here?"

"Definitely US," Todd said. "More of this kind of shit over there."

They were silent, the three of them looking towards the farmhouse. After a while Todd spoke.

"What's with the steel pole?" he said. "You ain't lame?"

"No," Lylly said. He lifted it up to show them the end which looked exactly like what it was, a standard hiking steel ferrule. They watched as Lylly pulled out the fighting knife from his backpack and clipped it on to the end of the stick. The pole was revealed for what it was. It was now a five foot long stabbing spear with a razor sharp seven inch hardened steel, pointed two-sided blade at the end. He lifted up the pole again and showed them.

Todd whistled and Brad behind the wheel laughed.

"Man I got to get me one of those," Todd said. "Hide in plain sight."

"Keep watching the farmhouse, ears too," Lylly said as he unclipped the knife.

He developed the limp again and used the pole as he approached the big silent group of people on the far side of the compound. They kept retreating as he tried to close with them.

It was becoming tiresome, so he stopped and leaned on his pole and stared at them. He was still twenty yards from them.

Eventually a man and women broke from the crowd and advanced towards him. They stopped five yards away, within speaking distance but wary. They wore what Lylly had come to realise was the uniform here: kaftan, jeans, sandals, cotton dress, headscarf.

"What do you want with us Satan?" The woman spoke.

She was the scowling one of the pair that had unlocked and opened the inner gates. It seemed making visitors wear devil masks allowed them to call everyone Satan, Lylly understood.

"Be gone," she said.

It seemed to be the standby command here. If Lylly was any judge she had a German accent. The man said nothing. He stood by her side. He was huge, shaggy-haired and broad.

"Watch him, Dieter," the woman said. There was a vacant look in his eyes.

Still keeping to his Eli Wallach persona, Lylly replied.

"What would Satan warnt with hanyone hanywhere?" Lylly said, but that seemed to confuse her. "How about a leetle conversation? Maybe we pass the time of day? You maybe tell mee some more about thees place."

"That is not so," the woman said. Her accent seemed definitely German. "You only seek to trick us Satan."

French, German, American if you included Sylvie; well if nothing else it was a broad church Lylly thought.

"Can I not treeck you and learn a beet more about thees place at thee same time?"

"We do not play games Satan," the woman said.

"That ees a pity. Thee keeds here might love eet." Then tiring of the whole thing: "Oh you peeple fuck yourselves. Rejoin thee human race. You are fuckin hoke." He turned and began to head towards the white van which was still parked outside the open gates, blocking the way.

"Do not judge!" the woman screamed at his back. "Who are you to dare to judge us Satan? You shall be judged!"

Lylly ignored her and carried on towards the van.

"Apparently there's a judge shortage," he said to Todd and Brad. "Call me Satan."

"That bad huh?" Todd said. "What d'ya expect? Tea at the Savoy?"

Lylly went back to stand ten metres in front of the farmhouse door at the place where he and Merci had stood earlier. He leaned on his pole. After a while he advanced and stood five metres in front of the door. He wanted to be able to hear a scream. He stayed still. He leaned on his pole and waited.

Exactly an hour after she went in Merci Stahl came out of the farmhouse. She seemed to be wiping tears from her eyes with a tissue.

She got into Lylly's car. But she refused to speak. She sat there silent as he drove out of the place with tears streaming down her cheeks, which she occasionally dabbed with the tissue.

Finally Merci Stahl spoke.

"She says she's Sylvie Ludo now. They got married she said."

She cried again.

As soon as they left the compound Lylly took the devil mask off and chucked it onto the back seat. At one point on the drive back Lylly asked Merci whether what Sylvie was doing was surely illegal?

"Isn't she still a minor?" he said. "Can't you legally force her to leave Bozo-Bruno's circus and come home?"

Merci was silent for a long time. She looked left out of the passenger side window. Eventually she sighed.

"I was scared to, before" she said. "I reckoned I'd lose her for good if we did that." She sobbed again.

And now of course if she's married it was a different story, Lylly thought. If she was really married, that is. Looked like old Bruno had every angle covered. Pulling out a young probably brainwashed girl from a commune was one thing, pulling out a woman married to the commune's leader was another thing altogether.

Lylly didn't reply. But he was beginning to wonder if he might research Stockholm Syndrome a little more. He'd also read of occasions where brainwashed Stockholmed individuals, usually young women but not exclusively, had been kidnapped out of their communes by special activists commissioned by the families.

Clearly Frank Koggs had some experience of that. Then they'd been taken to safe environments and deprogrammed. Sometimes it took months.

And of course they needed to find out if Sylvie really was married to Bruno. They might have gone through some sort of Bible-bashing backwoods mistletoe-and-holly ceremony, but did that make it legal?

Surely here in mega-centralised bureaucratic France there had to be some sort of documentation? You could only be married by a person authorised to do so, either by the state or a recognised church? If they could prove that Sylvie was not legally married to Bruno then she became a young Stockholmed girl again. And they could get her out.

There was another angle here too. How did this relate to the attacks on Merci Stahl? Was this just a tragic sideshow? Was this circus of Bruno Ludo's irrelevant to the attacks and/or threats against the Stahl family? Was it completely unconnected? Had Lylly found himself in a random nest of vipers or was everything connected?

Another thing was whirling round Lylly's head.

As they had driven back – retreated really, he knew – out of the commune gates back down the dusty track to the road, with Todd and Brad in the white van behind, Lylly glanced to his right and saw there was a line of vehicles parked along the long back wall of the big stone barn.

He couldn't see all of them, but among the ones he could see one stood out. It was a dull green and yellow campervan. A campervan based on a VW mini-bus. And for a moment as they passed through the gates and Lylly looked back in his side mirror to inspect the camper-van again before the perimeter parasol pines blocked the view, it seemed to him that the back window of the van was almost completely covered with climbing stickers.

And then as the last image in the review mirror before the pines closed off the view, Lylly saw a ball of something green hanging from the roof ridgeplate timber high up at the gable end of the barn.

Lylly wasn't sure, but he would bet that what he had just seen was a ball of mistletoe.

18

LYLLY NEEDED AN URGENT conference with Frank Koggs. He wanted to go back to the commune to check out the campervan he had seen. He was sure it was the same one. Then he needed to talk to the two climbers, Rochdale and his friend. And he wanted Todd and Brad and maybe the other two members of the SteadyState team to go with him. Ideally they would go at night. And ideally they would be able to take advantage of any state-of-the-art night-seeing equipment that SteadyState Secure might have.

He also wanted to check out the possible mistletoe. Could that really be true? Holly and mistletoe? Druids? Or was Lylly's imagination running up all sorts of blind alleys?

He also wanted to pick Koggs' brains about his experience of possible commune rescue and deprogramming.

One thing he knew. He might at last know where the Rochdale climbers were and he was going to talk them. Whether they liked it or not.

Alain Stahl couldn't see any connection between the attacks on his wife and the regrettable presence of her daughter Sylvie in the Bruno commune. He didn't say it but it was clear to Lylly from his demeanour that he fully expected the attacks to be part and parcel of his situation as an arms salesman. Lylly could see that in a way he'd always half expected something like this would eventually come to pass.

Lylly didn't expect that Alain Stahl would suddenly start talking realities with him. He had after all avoided saying anything resembling the truth in their brief relationship. But surely he must be talking real turkey with Frank Koggs? And he had a feeling that

Koggs might be prepared to pass anything vital on to him. He was beginning to feel like one of Koggs's team.

If both Stahl and Koggs decided that one or other of Stahl's customers, rivals or potential customers or rivals wanted him to stop pushing through a particular sale, then would he do it? Lylly guessed that would depend on how easy it was to spot the risky sale. Logically it seemed to Lylly that the problem must have arisen over a recent sale or a newly proposed sale, otherwise the attacks would surely have manifested themselves before?

There were thus two things to consider, the daughter problem and the arms sales problem. Lylly would assume for the moment they were not related. He also felt he couldn't do much about the sales problem, but he definitely could do something about the daughter problem.

On the way into dinner Lylly had almost literally bumped into Walton Holber. It seemed Holber had deliberately intercepted him.

"Say what soldier, we kinda got off on the wrong paw back there somehow. Can we start from the get-go again?" He extended a hand.

"Of course. No problem." Lylly shook his hand. At least that meant there would now be a more comfortable atmosphere at the dinner table.

Over dinner Lylly asked Merci something particular about the commune that had been troubling him. He couldn't imagine the rockclimbers were part of the commune. They'd seemed more natural and down to earth. But why were they there? He couldn't put it together

"What do you know about that big barn on the other side of the stream as you enter the compound? There were some cars parked behind it?"

"That's their guest accommodation," Merci said. "That's where it gets its income, from tourists. How it survives, well, apart from everyone who joins contributing all the money they got and their savings." There was deep sarcasm in her voice. "They take in paying guests there. It's their B&B. It's actually in guidebooks can you believe it? It's deliberately set well away from the rest of the community, so they're not contaminated by non-believers I guess. Take their money but keep the ungodly at a distance. So much so I think the staff who work there aren't part of the commune. They're hired to run the B&B."

"Rendering unto Caesar on the one hand in the B&B and rendering unto God on the other in the commune?"

Merci smiled for the first time in two days. "I guess," she said quietly.

Then maybe rendering unto Caesar might be the way in, Lylly thought.

Lylly also wondered what Alain Stahl made of his step-daughter being permanently lost to a commune.

"Have you met Bruno?" Lylly asked him.

"Unfortunately not," Alain Stahl replied. To have met him would have given him a better idea of his worth, his calibre as a human being, he said. "If he is to be an adversary then I would have liked to have met him, to better understand him."

But it turned out that Alain Stahl was not allowed to enter the commune.

"That's what Sylvie told us. And I accepted that rule for her sake."

Stahl also said a little incongruously that Bruno Ludo had a brother.

"Or a half-brother. We are not sure. It's just something Sylvie said when she was just visiting the place. She had an idea he wasn't even French. Apparently even Bruno thinks the brother is a better version of himself, Sylvie said. But we have no idea what she meant by that. She said the brother is not a member of the commune and does not live there." He shrugged. "That's all we know. I don't think it is particularly useful to know. Interesting but not useful."

Also interesting but not useful was whether Bruno was being truthful about a better brother, or just ironic. Which was more likely, Lylly suspected. And what did the word "brother" mean to

Bruno anyway?

"Colonel have you had any history of doing a sect extraction?"

Lylly wanted to outline his plan to Koggs. But would Alain Stahl pay for it? And would Merci Stahl agree to it?

They were standing on the back terrace after dinner taking in the evening view. Both with a beer.

He was trying to find out what Koggs's experience of commune extractions was. He was trying to put a plan together in his mind. But he knew nothing would happen unless both the Stahls went for it. Alain Stahl to fund not just the extraction but the deprogramming as well; and Merci Stahl to realise that it was the only way to get her daughter clear. And he hadn't talked to either of them yet.

"Yes I've had cause to do two extractions," Frank Koggs said. "You got to know that's the easy part. But I know an outfit that does the hard bit. Exorcising the Stockholm."

"But not in Europe?

"Don't matter where it is. Same problem. Same solution."

"I want to hold a meeting with you and the Stahls. If they go for it, can you carry out the extraction?"

"Sure. The daughter? Glad to."

"What about the deprogramming? Would the people you worked with before come over?"

"Oh I think they will. Woman who runs it is a zealot. College pysch prof and doctor. Takes it personally when younger minds are controlled and closed down and their lives stymied by evil men." He sighed, "It's usually men. And I've got to tell you. It's usually sexual."

"Hiding under the religious mumbo-jumbo and gobshite there's a sexual predator?"

"That's for sure."

Lylly thought that Merci Stahl knew that already.

"You ever see older women in these crap-hole communes?" Koggs asked.

Lylly guessed not. Certainly none of the women he'd seen in the silently aggressive crowd at the Bruno compound had appeared to be over thirty-five.

"It's usually one man with a bunch of crap-dealing scrap-stealing back-up stoolies and lootenants acting as muscle and enforcers, and a lot of young women and girls. Amateurs when it comes to real muscle though."

"But they'll know their ground. They could be armed to the teeth? They'll have been prepared against the world for years, and they'll be ruthless I imagine?"

"Amen to that. But still no match."

"I also imagine the top man won't have any qualms if any of his 'disciples' get caught in the crossfire."

"Sure. All expendable. But I seen it all before. We can do it. Takes time. We take care. Watch them. Get an idea of their patterns. Make a plan."

Lylly admired his certainty. But he didn't think they should underestimate Bruno Ludo nor the desperate and fanatical support he could count on among his Bozonian flock. Instantly attempting to topple the van at his single word of command was evidence of that.

19

IT WAS TIME TO TALK. Alain Stahl chose to hold the meeting in the dining room. There were more chairs there. Present were Alain and Merci Stahl, Colonel Frank Koggs and Camo Lylly.

First on the agenda was Lylly's request to take a team to track down the climbers. He didn't think he could do it on his own. He'd already tried that.

"Best idea is to catch them in some isolated spot where they're climbing," he said. "I'm sure they can link us to the people responsible for the attacks on Merci."

He also explained his view that it looked like they'd been hiding out in the commune B&B while the police might be searching for them in relation to the kidnapping.

"I think now after two and a half weeks they'll come out of hiding and resume their rock-climbing. I don't think they'll abandon it and go home. I think they love it too much. They'll think now or very soon it's all blown over and it's safe to come out. Either way I'd like to find out what they know, or eliminate them from suspicion."

Frank Koggs responded and said in his view the best way to deal with the climbers was to watch the B&B.

"Then if and when they leave the B&B we tail them to the right spot. Then we talk to them."

He said he could put Todd and Brad and the other two members of his on-site team Dex and Donna on a rota up in the woods watching the exit to the commune. He thought they only needed to watch the place during the day. "I don't reckon they'll want to go climbing at night."

Lylly knew that everything he, or they, suggested had to be

passed by Alain Stahl for continued funding. Stahl rapidly agreed to this part of the plan.

Next Lylly brought up the most sensitive item.

"We need to find out if Sylvie is really married or not. Legally married."

"What difference does it make now?" Merci Stahl said. "If Sylvie says she's married, she's married. She won't come back."

Koggs stepped in. "It matters a whole lot, Merci. If she's not married we can get her out."

"What do you mean? If she doesn't want to leave there, leave him, she won't. I've tried." She angrily wiped a stray tear away with her hand.

Alain Stahl laid his hand on hers.

"I think the colonel means we don't give her a choice."

Merci Stahl stared at her husband. She stared with disbelief round the table.

"Is that kinda possible?" she said. "What do you mean?"

Alain Stahl stood up.

"I think my wife and I need to talk about this is private. Will you give us a moment?"

Lylly and Koggs left the room. Koggs closed the door behind him as they left.

The midday sun was high overhead. Lylly and Koggs walked in circles around the huge terrace. Koggs was fascinated by the Spanish Legion.

"When I retire, finally retire I guess, I got me a plan to write a history of mercenaries."

Lylly laughed. "About time someone did. When you're ready to write, pick my brains about the Legion."

He told Koggs he'd had a run-in with the police chief in Draguignan.

"Didn't like my definition of the oldest profession."

Koggs laughed. "You got that right."

"For your book, start with Xenophon, go via Hawkwood

and the White Company, and the Italian proverb from those mercenary days: 'The devil is an Englishman,' and on to Robert Knollys, Swiss guards and Danjou's wooden hand and finish with the private contractors and put me and the Legion in the middle somewhere! I like that."

They carried on walking and talking for another forty minutes. Eventually Alain Stahl joined them on the terrace.

"We do it," he said.

"Climbers first," Koggs said. "We get that one out the way."

Koggs said he also had to contact "the doc" in the USA to make sure she could bring over a team to do "the hard part".

"And you need to hire somewhere quiet private self-contained and pretty isolated. You realise it could take a while?"

Stahl said he understood. "How about my mountain lodge?"

He said this was a large chalet, a former hiking gite in the wooded slopes above the French Alpine town of Gap.

"It's pretty quiet up there in summer. Pretty big too. I can have it stocked up."

"Sounds good," Koggs said. "But I'll need to check it out myself. Maybe the doc will too. I'll talk to her."

"Meanwhile I will myself contact the local authorities and have the marriage license checked out. If there is one. I hope there is not."

"Likewise," Koggs said.

They all knew they could do nothing about Sylvie Stahl until her legal married status was known.

"You good to tag along?" Koggs asked. "When we do it?"

Lylly said he was. "Can I get some of your company gear too?"

Koggs laughed. Lylly asked him if they had enough people to "talk to" the climbers?

"Yeah, I reckon. I'll oversee it all from here. Radios, cell phones, W-Ts, what we need we get. We use two cars – one of my vans and we get an SUV off Alain."

Koggs explained they needed two cars to check the likely

climbing places more quickly, once Rochdale was on the move.

"But after that's done I'm gonna bring in more people for the extraction," Koggs said. "Then soon as we know about the marriage papers I talk to the doc."

Frank Koggs said he'd start the ball rolling.

"Need to set up the stake out."

He moved on towards the end of the terrace then round the end of the chateau to the gravel expanse at the front where the company portacabins were squatting on the ground like giant shoeboxes.

20

TWO EVENTS HAPPENED almost simultaneously. Camo Lylly was peering through a monocular lying prone deep in the undergrowth on the hillside above the Bruno commune's B&B barn when word came through on his silenced mobile phone that Alain Stahl had been in contact with the authorities in the marie, the town hall in the departmental prefecture in Digne. This was the equivalent of the county town in England.

There were no records anywhere of any legal marriage between Bruno Ludo and Sylvie Stahl in the Alpes-Provencale department. To be certain, Stahl had his secretary and admin team in the company HQ in Geneva contact the town halls in four of the surrounding departments.

It was sham. A biblical-druidic combo possibly under a mistletoe festooned oak tree, where the two principals swore to be true to the "Lord of Earth, Air, Fire and Water," as well as being true to nature and each other, or some such, Lylly suspected. Long lean mean machine Bruno probably gave her the two-fingered salute to finish off. He also thought news of the event had been timed to cause maximum grief to Sylvie's mother.

The second thing was Rochdale was on the move. The green and yellow campervan reversed out of its parking slot behind the barn and filled the field of view of Lylly's lens.

"Hey Todd," he called to the blond giant resting up the slope under a parasol pine with his ball cap over his eyes. "We're on."

Both Lylly and Todd were wearing the full black combat gear uniform and black boots of SteadyState Secure. A clever detail about the combat shirts which impressed Lylly was the chest pocket flaps. These were usually doubled up and velcroed in place above the company name and logo. But they could be unfolded and doubled in length and velcroed down to another strip further down the pocket, so the name and logo were covered. They both were now wearing the shirts with the company information obscured. They got up and began to move fast up the hill to the white van parked under trees on a track on the crown of the hill.

They'd been watching the barn for three days. It was now fully three weeks since the attempted kidnapping of Merci Stahl. Clearly Rochdale finally thought it was safe to return to the rock.

In the white van Lylly drove while Todd got on his mobile phone to call to Dex and Donna in the Stahl SUV. Brad the final member of the team was staying back at the chateau after a long stint on the stake out. His job was to act as main back up to Koggs in providing protection to Merci while the full team was out. This was part of the rotation. Their SUV was waiting hidden in a farm entrance by the first crossroads out of the commune. They would be able to see which choice of route the campervan took.

A few minutes later Donna called back. The climbers were heading for the gorge, it seemed. Lylly pressed the pedal to close the gap.

He knew there would come a point, if Rochdale was headed for the gorge to resume their climbing stints on the gorge cliffs, where their two chasing vehicles would have to choose which direction to go in. He decided he and Todd should travel east along the northern rim of the gorge and Dex and Donna in the SUV should head west. They should check every possible parking place and belvedere, keeping in phone touch all the time. And if necessary this time they would take both vehicles all the way round the southern rim too, to complete a full circuit. He got Todd to pass the message on.

They came to the junction. He knew Dex and Donna ahead of them had gone right, to the west. He turned the van left, east.

He drove as fast as he dared along the twisting road. As they slowed to drive into and examine the first belvedere they came to Todd said, "You got to leave this to me."

Lylly looked across to his right to the passenger seat.

"You know how to do this? You've done it before?"

"Sure have. You've got to let me do it."

"You can't harm them. You know that?"

Todd smiled.

"Yeah I know. I won't have to harm them. I'll just scare the living shit out of them. They'll talk. Good?"

"Good."

They examined three more belvederes with no sign of the campervan among the vehicles parked there. As he slowed and entered the parking area in the fifth belvedere Lylly realised it was the same one he had met the climbers in before, when he'd come from the other direction.

There were no vehicles in the parking area. Lylly was disappointed. He had a feeling this was Rochdale's favourite pitch. He began to swing the van round to rejoin the road, but as he did so something yellow seen through foliage flashed into the corner of his eye. He stopped and looked. Through the trees bordering the track down to the edge of the cliff he saw a yellow and green VW campervan in the distance. There were climbing stickers pasted on to most of the windows except the windscreen. Perhaps still cautious and wanting to hide, Rochdale had driven the campervan all the way down the stony track from the belvedere to the clearing at the edge of the cliff.

Lylly stopped and parked the van.

Todd called up the other car.

"Got 'em," he said. "Come east. Fifth belvedere from the junction. Down the track to the end by the cliff."

Todd reached down and grabbed the shotgun from under the seat. He held a finger to his lips in case Lylly was about to object. He cracked it open to show it was not loaded. But he also took four cartridges and put them in a breast pocket of his combat shirt. Lylly took one of his walking poles. He screwed the three sections together and clipped the knife to the walking tip.

They stepped like black ghosts down the stony track to

the cliff edge, keeping under the bordering trees all the way. They emerged silently into the shallow clearing. The French climber was standing at the very edge of the cliff in loud conversation with Rochdale who was out of sight below the cliff. She was wearing her full rockclimbing gear including webbing harness and seemed to Lylly to be preparing to rappel down the cliff face to join her companion.

Lylly realised this was a much quicker way for them of reaching the section of cliff they intended to climb than laboriously walking all the way along the trail through the gorge every time to reach the foot of the same section.

"Hold it there," Todd said. "Don't jump lady." He pointed the shotgun straight at her.

"Tell your mate to come up," Lylly said. He repeated it in French to make sure.

Lylly could see she recognised him. There was something else as well. Was it a realisation they weren't going to get away with it? Lylly didn't know. She called down to Rochdale to come up. There was a problem, she said. Her voice gave away her plight.

While they waited for Rochdale to appear, Todd asked Lylly to hold the shotgun.

"Cover the edge, and her," he said.

Then he bound her tightly hand and foot. Then did something strange, and Lylly couldn't follow the logic. He took a section of their climbing rope. Then doubled it. He cut it to a required length. He tied one end of the doubled rope to the hefty carabiner on her climbing harness. The other double end he tied round the bumper of the campervan. There was about three metres of slack rope on the ground behind the woman. When he'd finished he took the shotgun back from Lylly. He then made the woman stand on the edge of the cliff just as Rochdale's head poked up above the cliff edge.

"What the fook," he said as he took in the scene.

"Join us. Now." Todd said, threatening him with the shotgun.

Rochdale came up.

"Sit with your legs over the edge," Todd said.

Rochdale did so. He looked to his right where his friend was tightly bound, tied up, standing perched on the edge. They exchanged a panicked and defeated look. Their grand plans had not worked out the look said.

"Over to you," Todd said to Lylly.

Lylly walked over and stood beside Rochdale, between him and the French woman.

"I want to know more about the day I talked to you about before. The strange incident of the woman in the tunnel and the climbers who didn't bark." He gestured over the edge of the cliff. "You saw the whole thing didn't you?"

"Fook off," Rochdale said. "I'm not saying nowt." He glanced over again towards his friend, but Lylly was standing in the way. "We're not saying nothin'."

"How much were you paid to watch the tunnel?"

Rochdale shook his head and looked away, over the drop. His body language said I can climb cliffs that would freeze your blood. I'm not scared of you.

"Let's speed it up," Todd said.

He had been covering both Rochdale and the French woman with the shotgun. Now he came forward and placed a boot against the middle of her backside. Then he kicked her off the cliff. She screamed and fell forward over the cliff edge. Rochdale also scream-shouted as she disappeared from sight, shocked, all defiance done. The doubled rope running back to the campervan bumper gave out a vibrant thrum sound as it took the woman's weight and was now stretched taut. To Lylly it looked barely strong enough to hold her.

Lylly held his breath. He almost didn't dare look. But he came forward and peered over the edge of the cliff. The woman was dangling in space unhurt but shocked into silence, about three metres below the top. There was a slight but bloody graze on her right shoulder where she had glanced off the rock, but otherwise she was unhurt. Her chest was heaving. She was breathing rapidly and trying to catch her breath. Then she calmed down as she realised she was safe. For the time being. She was after all used to hanging in space.

"That's just the beginning, son," Todd said.

He came over and handed the shotgun to Lylly.

"Watch him," he said.

Then he began to cast around among the stones and shards on the cliff edge. Lylly wondered what was going on. But then Todd reached down and came up with a sharp-edged stone the size of a cobble that fit nicely in his hand like a Stone Age hand-axe. He sat apparently comfortably on the campervan bumper next to the rope knot.

"Such a gol-darn tragedy," Todd said. "And you only got yourself to blame. Sure the coroner will reach a verdict of accidental death. But you won't get away with it in the court of public opinion. No sirree. No one'll ever climb with you again. Social media's going to kick up a shit-storm. The family'll always blame you for not checking the state of your ropes when you went out climbing this morning. Who knows, they may even bring a civil suit against you. Could get very nasty. Could get very costly."

And with that he began cutting through the first rope of the double strand with the edge of the rock in his hand. Astonishing quickly to Lylly the first rope split open and frayed and rapidly snapped apart. Even from the distance where he was standing the rope ends looked not smoothly cut but naturally frayed. Lylly could also see the tension in the remaining rope dramatically increase.

"Nooo!" Rochdale screamed. "Please. 'Kin'ell. Please." His voice broke. He was in tears.

Todd reached across and held the stone edge against the last strand of the double rope. He looked across at Rochdale as though seeking permission to carry on cutting.

"No. No. Enough. Stop," Rochdale shouted. "Five thousand euros."

"You were paid five thousand euros to watch the tunnel?"

"Yes. Yes. In cash. We did that."

"How were you contacted?"

"Phone." Rochdale gestured to a pocket. "A man. Bloke with an accent. Dunno how he knew."

"What exactly were your instructions?"

"We had to watch the tunnel all day. If someone came through we had to call a number. And at the end of the day if no one had come through all day we had to phone the same number and report that too. That was all. For five thousand. Watch the tunnel. Then report summat or report nowt."

"So you saw me didn't you? And the rescue helicopter? All that?"

Rochdale hesitated. "Yeah," he said eventually. "So we phoned and said so."

"What about the small blue and white helicopter you said you saw?"

Rochdale shrugged.

"There wasn't one was there? You could tell that's what I wanted to hear so you invented one to tell me about."

Rochdale shrugged again.

Todd interrupted. "What's the number kid?"

He took the shotgun back from Lylly.

Rochdale reached for his pocket.

"Careful," Todd raised the shotgun.

"Just me phone," he said.

He dug the phone out of a pocket, flicked it live, searched for something on it, then handed it to Lylly.

"There," he said.

Lylly took a photo of the number with his phone. It was a French mobile phone number. He nodded at Todd and gave the phone back to the climber.

"How did you get the money? How did you actually get your hands on it?"

"The voice on the phone told us it would be waiting in our room at the B&B. We were already staying there. It's cheap. It was there when we got back. Like creepy."

"And then you thought you'd lay low for a couple of weeks. Just in case. Five thousand is a lot of money. Let it blow over?"

Rochdale shrugged and said nothing.

Lylly looked at Todd again and nodded again.

"Ok," he said. "Thanks. That's all I want to know. Enjoy the money. You've earned it."

Rochdale looked amazed, as though he'd expected much worse.

"Right son," Todd said. "Pull her up. Best way is reverse the bus ten feet. That should do it. Rope's good."

They left them there. As they emerged from the track back into the belvedere the SUV with Dex and Donna aboard entered the area from the road. Todd circled a finger and thumb and grinned success in their direction.

21

"NICE CAVEMAN ACT with the stone," Lylly said. They were driving back to the Stahl chateau.

"Men always talk if you threaten the woman. Other way round, not so much," Todd said.

He looked pleased with this insight into the workings of the world. Lylly wasn't so sure it was a valid philosophical tenet or an accurate view of human nature, but it was better than the gibberish Bruno Ludo spouted.

"That right?"

"Sure is. Needed to double the rope to make it believable, like increases the tension," he said with a grin. "Whole show don't work with just one strand of rope. Are you calling the number?"

"I'm going to talk to the colonel first."

Colonel Frank and Lylly had something of a disagreement. Koggs wasn't convinced there was anything to be gained by chasing the number Lylly had been given and following where it led.

"Waste of resources," Koggs said. "We need to concentrate on the extraction."

Lylly pointed out that though he was wearing a SteadyState Secure outfit he wasn't actually working for the company.

"You're not paying me in any case."

"I can do that," Koggs said. "I need you for this."

In the end they compromised. The extraction was nowhere near ready for action. It would be two weeks, maybe more before they were ready. Alain Stahl had gone north to the high Alps to get the chalet at Gap ready. Koggs's "psych doc" had not yet arrived to assess the situation, though she had agreed to come. Koggs and the "doc" would inspect the commune from a safe distance, then travel together to Gap so the doc could meet Alain and assess the effectiveness and aptitude of the chalet for the deprogramming operation. And if the extraction was carried out successfully the doc would bring over a team at a moment's notice straight to Gap to pursue the next phase with Sylvie Stahl. She had worked with Frank Koggs before.

So until the extraction was imminent, Lylly pointed out he was free and had all the time he wanted to follow up the phone number. Koggs still frowned to the last but finally said it was ok with him. Eventually Koggs even agreed that Lylly could "borrow" Todd if he needed back up at any time when chasing the number.

The rest of Kogg's team was set to monitor discreetly the comings and goings at the commune and get an idea of any set routines, if there were any. They also wanted to know as much as they could about the numbers and geography of the commune. They needed to know how many people were there, and the rough population split between men, women and children. They needed a plan of the site. They'd need to know what was where, who slept where, what each building was for.

And there was also the question of defences. Was the place patrolled? What armaments did they have? Were there any tripwires or booby traps in the woods above the commune? Did any of the communards look to have military or police experience? Above all they needed to have a very accurate idea of where Sylvie Stahl was at all times of day and night.

Koggs had several drones brought up from Marseille. They had night-sight and infra-red cameras and would be used exclusively at night. They couldn't afford anyone in the commune spotting them during the day and wondering and thus being forewarned.

The monitoring team was in place on rotation already, but Koggs knew finding all this information could take the best part of two weeks even with full time observation. He'd brought two more men, one down from Paris and one up from Marseille, to augment the team. If Lylly was included then Koggs now had seven members of the extraction team on site, plus himself.

"Good thing Alain's got plenty of dough," he said.

They agreed between them that the extraction would begin at the earliest in two weeks time.

Two days later Lylly called the number.

It rang for thirty seconds without being picked up. Lylly broke off then immediately tried again. This time it was answered after a single ring.

"What?" a neutral female voice said in English. The accent was a strange one and Lylly couldn't place it. For some reason the single word sounded Australian, but there was something else, another more native accent underneath. But what really threw him was the fact the voice was a woman. Rochdale had said it was a "bloke".

Lylly had been working on his script.

"I've been talking to two rockclimbers."

"So?"

"I'm the one that rescued Merci Stahl from the tunnel that you paid the climbers to watch."

Silence. The quiet went on for over half a minute but the voice didn't break the contact.

"We can meet," the voice said.

Lylly wasn't going to meet anywhere that wasn't a public place. So he was mightily relieved when the voice named a café-bar in Castellane as the venue for the meeting. At noon the next day.

"I have red hair," the voice said. Lylly thought that was a nice homely snippet. "I will have a copy of The Economist."

The connection ended.

Lylly wondered if Todd would be free to come with him.

Both Todd and Lylly had jettisoned their company outfits for nondescript casual but loose clothes for the meeting in Castellane.

"Never wear jeans on the job," Todd said. "Can't run in jeans. Can't fight in jeans. Too tight."

The plan was for Lylly to enter the café with Todd remaining in the white van parked nearby or across the street. Lylly would have his phone connected to Todd's and would leave it on while he was in the meeting.

In the middle of Castellane the town square lies directly below the six hundred foot cliff with the smallpox chapel on top. The central section of the square doubles as a boules court and parking for cars. Lining both long sides of the square are rows of shops, restaurants and cafes.

Thirty minutes ahead of midday, Todd drove into the parking area adjacent to the boules court where the old men were already throwing the solid steel balls at the jack in the dusty densely packed gravel. He parked the white van in a bay right in front of the café where the meeting would take place. All the cafes along that side of the square had external seating areas under parasols or cane rattan shading. Todd and Lylly sat back and watched the café intently through the van windscreen.

Though they would have a phone connection open when Lylly left the van they also agreed on a code word if Lylly was obliged at some point to break the connection. If Lylly said the word 'football' then he was safe and comfortable closing the call, and Todd would not come charging into the café.

When Lylly entered the café from the square there was a red-haired woman sitting at a table with three empty chairs round it on the right hand edge of the external seating area well away from any of the other occupied tables. Lylly was slightly mystified. They hadn't seen her from the van and they hadn't seen her come in. Where had she come from? He noticed she was reading a magazine. As he came into the seating area she looked up and raised the cover of the magazine in his direction. It showed the red and white title of The Economist.

The woman appeared to be in her late-thirties. Her red hair was folded into an intricate bun design at the back of her head. She was wearing Oakley sports sunglasses with a bright blue tint.

Lylly approached her table and sat down opposite the woman.

"Hello there," he said. "Do we need names or not?"

"I don't think *you* do," she said, stressing the you. Her intonation went up at the end of the sentence, making it sound like she was asking a question. The usage again sounded strongly Australian to Lylly, but her accent didn't go with the dialect.

She took off her sunglasses and smiled at him. Her eyes were coloured bright bottle green contrasting sweetly with her flawless olive complexion and red hair.

"But we know you are Archer Lylly known as Camo. English. Recently released – or demobbed is it? - from the Spanish Legion."

A man in his forties in fawn chinos and a fawn lightweight jacket over a blue polo shirt with blue Nike trainers came into the café and rapidly joined them at the table. He looked more weather-beaten than suntanned as though he'd spent much of his life on the farm or the construction site rather than by the pool or on the beach. He had grey streaks in his short black hair which was cut close to the skin above and round his ears and longer on top.

Lylly pushed his chair back and was about to stand up. He hadn't agreed to this. The woman placed a gentle hand on his arm.

"No worries mate. Please calm down," she said. "I think we may have similar interests."

Lylly sat back in the chair again. He was reeling slightly because he was getting a bunch of mixed messages from the way the woman spoke. She had this strange indeterminate possibly Middle East accent but the idiom she'd just used was pure Australian. 'No worries mate' was straight out of the Oz playbook. So his original instinct had been right.

"Close your phone connection to the man in the van," the man said. "But tell him not to worry."

His English was good, accented in a very similar way to the accent underlying the red-haired woman's Australian. But Lylly still couldn't place it. His experience of foreign accented English was good and wide after his time in the Legion but this one he couldn't place.

"Todd," Lylly said to his phone. "Did you catch that? If you did or didn't, it's okay. Football. Wait there," Lylly said and closed the link.

"How did you get the number?" the man said. It wasn't an accusation, but more of a mild and polite enquiry.

Lylly told them about tracking down the climbers to their favourite pitch. He told them about his partner in the van booting the woman off the cliff. That got the number very quickly.

The man nodded and smiled very slightly.

"Not a problem," he said. "Loose ends are often unavoidable."

"Coffee? Beer?" the woman asked. She waved a long-fingered hand but with short fingernails, Lylly noticed, in the air to attract the waiter.

"Both please," Lylly responded. "What are these similar interests?"

"The safety of Merci Stahl," the man said.

Lylly was astonished. This was something else he hadn't expected.

"I think you want to tell me things," Camo said.

They did.

For reasons they didn't specify they had been sent by "their government" to keep a watch on the Stahls. He was, they knew, one of the relatively few large-scale arms dealers in the world.

"Why watch him? Or is it them?" Lylly asked. It seemed a strange thing to do.

It turned out they didn't really know. But it was probably some kind of mixed message about a threat to Stahl from one of their informants.

"We have quite a few. But they sometimes don't tell us the full story. They often don't have the full story themselves. But we always act on the information."

So the man and woman team had been sent to seek out and watch the Stahls a month and more earlier. And if there was a direct threat, then they should intervene to protect him.

Suddenly Lylly had a thought he might have an idea what their accent was; at least in the woman's case the one underlying the Australian. He hadn't heard it before, but he thought it might be Israeli.

If so, there was something here immediately troubling Lylly.

"I'm not making any judgments, or naming names, but say Stahl was selling armaments to the Palestinians, or to some Iranian element, wouldn't "your government" want you to interfere with that? In other words, wouldn't it be in your interests to eliminate Stahl not protect him?"

The man and woman exchanged a look which said Lylly now understood something that he hadn't understood before: the fact that they were agents of a subsidiary of the Israeli defence department.

"It's not who that matters but what," the woman said.

But Lylly didn't understand what she meant.

"We don't care who he sells to as long as we know what he's selling." The man said.

"Well how do you know what he sells?" Lylly couldn't see how they could know.

"Alain Stahl tells us."

He really was a devious bugger, Alain Stahl, Lylly thought. Both ends against the middle. But he almost whistled in admiration. Among his presumably other customers, Stahl makes a packet by selling arms to Israel's enemies. But then tells the Israelis exactly what he's selling, and to whom. But then wouldn't Israel's enemies be a little short with Stahl if they found out what he was doing? They surely would. But then he got it. Ah, he thought, hence the Israelis sending "protection" to make sure Stahl was unharmed.

"The problem for us when it comes to the supply of weapons to our enemies is it's better with the devil you know than the devil you don't. Alain Stahl is a devil we know," the man said.

"Despite the fact he sells weapons to our enemies," the woman said. "We consider him a friend."

It's a complicated world, Lylly thought.

"Ok, I see the logic," Lylly said. "I see where you're coming from. But what about Merci? And the climbers? The tunnel?"

"She is also under our protection," the man said. "Unfortunately we were stretched with some false alarms on the day she was kidnapped. I have to say that at that time we were not concentrating so much on the wife. We were more concerned with the husband."

"So we were not able to interfere with the attack on her. We witnessed it," the woman said. "And what happened after, what they did subsequently."

"Wait a minute," Lylly said. "But did you actually see the kidnap?"

"No we didn't," the woman said. "But because we were not able to observe her directly we had a drone up monitoring her movements. We saw the recording later. There were five attackers. The drone was able to follow their progress after the kidnap. We could see they went into the gorge. They actually carried her down into the gorge and into the hidden tunnel on the back of a donkey."

Lylly had never thought of that option. So much then for his helicopter theory. Doesn't pay to be too clever sometimes.

"Then after a while the five people came out of the other end of the tunnel with their donkey, we could see all that with the drone recording. But without Merci Stahl. She was no longer on the back of the donkey. We considered that they had left her in the tunnel for some reason."

"They did," Lylly said.

He told them how he had found her naked and spreadeagled, pinned against the tunnel wall.

"I think she would have died."

The man swore in a language Lylly didn't recognise.

"That is evil. We do not know why they did this."

"We didn't know what it was all about," the woman said. "I don't think either of us have seen anything like it."

"So it seemed certain to us that Merci had been left in the tunnel," the man said. "So I contacted the climbers – we knew who they were and had discounted them as a threat - and I paid them to watch the tunnel. They were in a good position to do that, and we could not leave our drone in the air all day. We did not want to take the risk of being seen ourselves. We were not sure if the kidnappers had finished with her, or whether they might come back. If the climbers told us at the end of the day the kidnappers had not returned, yet Merci Stahl was still in the tunnel, we would have gone down there and brought her out."

"But gladly you came through," the woman said.

She lifted her glass of beer in a silent toast."

"There was another attack, did you know?" Lylly asked them. "They killed her horse."

"The horse?" The man asked. "Oh yes. The second attempt. You were there. We know about it but we didn't see it."

It seemed the details were news to him, so Lylly told them about the dead horse.

"This is very strange," the man said. "But at least you have some good protection there now."

"Frank Koggs?"

"Yes, the colonel is one of the best of the private operators. The man in the van is one of his."

That was good to know Lylly thought. Good to know that Koggs's outfit was respected to a certain extent by these professionals.

"I think our work is done now Koggs is there," the man said. "And anyway our assignment is coming to an end. We have ascertained there is no threat, nor has been any threat, to Alain Stahl. It is time to go home."

He got up and left the table without saying anything further.

The woman too stood up a few moments later. She smiled across the table at Lylly.

"Good work with the horse, I think," she said mysteriously.

So she had been watching after all, presumably via a drone, even if her colleague hadn't. He wondered whether she'd also been watching the action before the horse was killed as well, but hoped the tree canopy by the stream pool had been too thick for the drone cameras to see through.

"Other things too. Before the horse," she said. "Sandbank. Interesting, but a little cold surely?" her smile was wider. "No worries mate," she said with a final smile. "Maybe see you again. My name is Viv."

Lylly didn't know quite what to do. So he smiled back. They both stood up to leave, to go their separate ways.

"These drones you use," Camo said, changing the subject. "You're talking about small hand-controlled items? Or something bigger?" And more military, he thought but didn't say.

"Something bigger," the woman said. "We have friends who help with that," she added mysteriously.

That made sense Camo thought. A small commercial drone didn't have much range or time in the air. What they'd described must have much bigger capabilities.

"But what is most strangest thing," the woman said, turning back to speak to him again. "I'm referring to the kidnap. The kidnappers, at the supermarket, they did not look professionals. These are not the usual semi-competent adversaries we are used to dealing with."

"Oh, how so?" Lylly asked, not sure what she meant.

"Well for one thing there is a woman among them who appears to be the leader, and she wears just a simple cotton dress with a headscarf. Very old-fashioned. She applies the hypodermic knockout when they bag her head. And the four men with her are all dressed alike. Like they attend a fancy dress party. Like your silly morris dancers. They wear black gaily decorated kaftans and blue jeans."

22

KAFTANS AND BLUE JEANS. Dresses and headscarves. Lylly was amazed yet again as the revelations kept coming. Was it finally all coming together?

"I know where these people came from," Viv said. "These amateurs."

"So do I." Camo replied, saying that he too had seen and been to the commune where Sylvie Stahl lived, and had seen what they wore there.

"So you've visited the commune too?"

Viv walked away without replying.

None of it was anything to do with Alain Stahl nor his operations as an arms dealer. There was no disgruntled customer. Nor someone making sure an undesirable deal didn't go through. Instead it was all about Merci Stahl. It was all about the Bozonian commune. It was all about the relationship between Bruno Ludo, Sylvie Stahl and her mother. There hadn't been any warnings to Alain Stahl to do, or not to do, something by attacking his wife twice. There'd been instead two real attempts on his wife's life. One had been foiled by Camo Lylly in the tunnel. The other had been a bad shot. The shooter had simply missed her and hit the horse's head. But the intention in both instances had been her death. And it looked to Lylly that the man behind the attempts was Bruno Ludo. For some reason he wanted Sylvie's mother dead.

There was something else nagging at Lylly's mind. Tunnels. Caves. Dark underground places. He couldn't get a hold on it though. He cast it aside in his mind. He'd try to grind his way into it another time.

He talked through his conclusions with Todd as they drove

back to the chateau.

"Maybe the cops have some info on the casing now?" Todd said. "The casing you found on the col where the shooter hid."

He tapped his phone which was bluetooth connected to the van's communications system, and rang ahead to his boss the colonel. He asked him to ask Alain Stahl to ask the police in Draguignan if they had any information about the likely gun used in the horse shooting?

"Alain Stahl can probably get more cooperation from the feds than any of us," Todd said.

Half an hour later Frank Koggs called Todd back. He was clearly being given some information.

"OK," Todd said, "Got it boss."

He closed the call and turned to Lylly.

"Turns out it was a round fired from most likely a Savage Arms Axis II XP in a Remington .223 calibre. US-made of course, we use 'em ourselves, but it's a pretty common Frenchie hunting rifle too."

So definitely not a professional sniper's weapon then, Lylly thought. But more widespread and easier to get hold of than a more apposite weapon. Good but not good enough. It wasn't surprising then, perhaps, he missed. Or she, he realised, remembering what the Israeli agent had said about the woman seeming to be the leader of the group of kidnappers.

Lylly lay back on his bed, his arms in a triangle with his hands under the back of his head. He blamed his education. It was all too classical. It had made him jump to so many wrong conclusions. Andromeda. Helicopters. He constantly followed the wrong strands when he should have been less hasty and tried to judge the information more dispassionately. It wasn't just the phantom prior helicopter outside the tunnel he'd been convinced about. It was a kidnapper's phantom helicopter that turned out to be a donkey. He had forced the non-existent evidence to fit a fanciful theory. But it wasn't just that. It was also Merci Stahl pinned like a sacrificial victim on the tunnel wall, waiting for the monster. He had been almost certain it was all an elaborate staging of the Andromeda myth. When in fact a different reality now seemed much more certain. It wasn't Andromeda it was Druids. It showed the bias of your education and experience when you tried to make deductions from what you thought was the evidence. Trouble was, even in the light of this knowledge he didn't think he would be able to change and do any better.

And then as soon as he'd learnt that Alain Stahl was an arms dealer he'd assumed the attacks on his wife were indirect attacks on him. He'd never thought the attacks were actually direct attacks on Merci. It was because you just expected an arms dealer to be wading in murky waters and dealing with dodgy ruthless people. He'd kind of assumed Stahl would be the target of any attacks exactly because he was an arms dealer.

Well, to be fair, it wasn't just him, Lylly thought, giving himself a bit of wiggle room. They'd all assumed the attacks on Merci Stahl weren't actually attacks on Merci Stahl at all. They all refused to believe the evidence. And to be fair to Lylly, he was the one that first realised the attacks on Merci were real, and she was the target.

Later, in the ensuite bathroom in his room at the chateau Lylly was showering off the dust of the day. He was half-singing half-humming the Joni Mitchell song Big Yellow Taxi. Just at the point where she goes "and they charged the people a dollar and a half just to see 'em," he stopped in mid-hum. He sagged against the shower wall. He was struck so hard by a thought he had to sit down on the shower floor. The water bounced and drummed on his head. He'd just remembered what Merci Stahl had murmured in her delirious semi-conscious state when he carried her out of the tunnel.

"Don't leave me," she'd said. "He will try again."

At the time Lylly was mightily suspicious she was referring to her husband, even though she strenuously denied it. As though part of her brain knew it but the conscious part wouldn't allow her to acknowledge it or even think it.

But what if in fact she was referring to Bruno Ludo?

And did that mean that Merci Stahl knew a lot more than she had been letting on?

Camo Lylly realised that like her husband Merci Stahl did not give away the truth easily.

It was just three of them at dinner. Merci Stahl, Koggs and Lylly. Alain Stahl was still in Gap preparing the chalet. Walton Holber had left, his business with Alain Stahl done. The revelation that Alain Stahl was not the target, neither directly nor indirectly, and nothing about the attacks were in any way related to his activities, had changed the equation. Instead they now all acknowledged that it was Merci Stahl's relations with the Bruno's Bozonian commune that lay at the heart of the matter.

"Now we know who we got to protect and why," Koggs said. "Makes it easier all round when you can see the trees for the wood."

Lylly was still trying to pin down what it was about dark places, tunnels, caves and the perceived realm under the earth that he had thought on earlier. Then he got it. It was another thing that was associated with Druidic beliefs. The magic and inherent holiness of the sub-earth, the underground. That caves were connected to the spirit world, the world of the ancestors. And what better cave to reach the spirit world from than the long hidden tunnel in the gorge?

His mind leapt. The Romans claimed the Druids carried out human sacrifice. No one these days really believed that because the Romans would say that wouldn't they? Seeing as how the Romans wiped them out they naturally had to justify it. And the modern idiom was to take whatever the Romans did or said with a bucket of salt. But what if it were true? More importantly, what if someone believed it were true? And then….

What if pinning Merci Stahl against the tunnel wall had been an attempted human sacrifice to the hidden underground world of the ancestors?

He was now convinced that Bruno Ludo was a real live hard-driving hard-believing Druid ultra. The semi-Christian trappings he affected were hocus-pocus, mumbo-jumbo designed to throw people off the scent. Lylly guessed this might be because people, outsiders and even the authorities, were relatively comfortable with the notion of a Christian sect or commune – up to a point at least – but would probably be much more wary if they knew the commune was actually a hardcase Druidic sect. And so Bruno adopted the overt sub-Christian mumbo-jumbo to indicate to the world that his commune and its beliefs were far less dangerous than they actually were. But now it seemed there was a more serious and much more dangerous and deadly mumbo-jumbo lurking underneath.

For the moment Lylly thought he would keep his conclusions to himself. But there was one thing which was imperative. He needed a private talk with Merci Stahl at the earliest opportunity.

"You know Bruno Ludo is a real live Druid don't you? A believer. A Roman-style Druid. And highly dangerous? You've always known it? Or always suspected it? You said 'Don't leave me. He'll try again' Do you remember? You whispered it to me just outside the tunnel when I found you and brought you out. You were talking about Bruno."

They were standing on the terrace, under the spangled leaping dome of stars. They were alone. Frank Koggs had taken some beers, wine and a bottle of whisky to the portacabins to drink with his team.

"It would be a lot easier for us all if you – and Alain – told us the truth a bit more often. You know more about Bruno Ludo than you've told us don't you?"

Merci Stahl looked stricken. Then she roused herself. It reminded Lylly that this was not a defenceless decorative flower. This was a woman who had survived two attempts on her life and the prospect of the permanent loss of her daughter with a surprising degree of strength, resolve and equanimity. Now he knew she was lifted by the prospect of getting her daughter back.

She linked her arm through Lylly's and leaned in close to

him. He felt the swell of her breast pressing in to his upper arm. Of course it was sexual, and he was aware of that. But there was more to it. It seemed to comfort her.

"I remember what I said," she said quietly. "I was so grateful to you. But I didn't know where I was or what was happening. I'd got so used to keeping my worries hidden. It just came out." She switched tangent, "Sure I suspected. Things Sylvie told me. Before. Before she went to live there. I thought I better read what Julius Caesar and the others wrote about them. Horrible. Horrible and totally gross. I think Bruno believes what the Romans said. He doesn't believe it was all Roman propaganda. He believes it was all true.

"But he's also into something else, deeper somehow, something to do with the way the universe works, or how he thinks it does, but I don't know what it is. Magic ratios or something. Sylvie couldn't tell me. But she also told me he has a thing for Artemis. Sylvie could talk to me for a while – she just visited them in the early days. And she'd tell me things. But it stopped when she moved in with them."

"Artemis? As in Diana the huntress?"

"Yes. But no I guess not. Older and darker, she told me. Ephesus is important, she said. Artemis. The goddess at Ephesus. Called Diana, sure as in the Bible, but older, deeper, darker and far nastier. Babylonian. In reality she's not Artemis or Diana but Wish-Heart or some such. Something to do with bulls."

Jesus, Lylly thought, where's all this going? He'd never heard of a goddess called Wish-Heart. In fact he thought Wish-Heart might have been a character in a John Wayne film, or a cowboy cattle-drive film where he was running the chuck-wagon, or something, but it certainly didn't sound like a goddess. But, god knows, it could even be correct, but be a malapropism, where the original name was too difficult for English-speaking ears and the nearest sound-alike had been adopted.

"You sure it was Wish-Heart?"

"Jeez no. I didn't get a chance to get her to clarify before she disappeared off to live there."

Wish-Heart or not, once you start to study and delve into all this ancient gods shit, Lylly thought, it was jumping into a bottomless pit. And not very nice on the way down. But then he took a leap. He didn't know anything about Artemis or Wish-Heart or Ephesus or Babylonians or any of that. But he knew a bit about the Romans, you had to if you studied war.

"And for a while you've suspected Bruno might want you as a human sacrifice? The Romans said they did that."

"Yeah," she said. "I couldn't believe it. But I think that's right. I wouldn't bet against him trying anything like that."

"You should have said. It took me a long while to work it out. We –" he gestured towards Koggs's portacabins – "Could have protected you."

"How could I have said? To who?" Merci said, indignant "Who was gonna believe me? Some Roman-style Druids – like you say - were looking to sacrifice me? Yeah. Right." She paused, then surprisingly she smiled.

"But you know what? I thought you would work it out."

"Yes I got it in the end. Holly staff. Mistletoe. Tunnels. Underground. Ancestors. Horses. But I had help too."

He told her about the two Israeli agents.

There was one thing, though, Lylly thought. The shooting incident where they missed Merci and killed her horse didn't really tally with the human sacrifice theme. If the object was to sacrifice Merci, then shooting her seemed contrary to Bruno's world view. It seemed all wrong. The appropriate rites, rituals, magic ratios and deadly deities had been bypassed. It didn't fit the pattern that Lylly was learning to associate with Bruno. He shrugged mentally, perhaps Bruno was just trying to speed things up. But it still left an unfilled hole in his mind.

"You know what? I'm glad they were there," she said. Merci said she had suspected in the past that there might be undercover protectors looking out for her husband.

"They had a drone watching when you were kidnapped. They said they would have gone down and got you out of the tunnel if I hadn't been there."

"I'm glad it was you," she said. She pressed into his side again. "And I'm glad it's all coming to an end now," Merci said. "We're gonna get her out. We'll all be safe then."

Lylly didn't say that everyone he'd spoke to said the extraction was going to be the easy bit. Whatever happened, and however it turned out, Merci and Sylvie would never now go back to that comfortable loving happy mother-daughter relationship they'd known before.

23

THE PSYCH DOC FLEW in from Chicago O'Hare to Paris Charles De Gaulle then took a fast train down to Draguignan TGV station. Frank Koggs sent a car down from the chateau to meet the train.

Alain Stahl had arrived back from Gap. The chalet in the woods there above the town was ready.

The extraction was on. In less than a week's time if all went well.

Camo Lylly met the psych doc in the main lounge reception room at the chateau. Frank Koggs introduced them.

"Doc this is Camo Lylly. Yeah I know stupid name. He's been a big help. Saved the mom's life twice. Camo this is Tess Siding."

Professor Tessa Siding was in her mid-forties. She was small slight and birdlike with tiny wrists and collar bones like twigs and a big voice and big hair. She also had a broad smile. She had a mass of bubbling brown hair cascading to her shoulders. She wore circular black-rimmed glasses. She wore a grey two-piece suit with the skirt length tailored to mid-calf. She was a professor of applied psychology at Chicago university. Koggs outlined her CV.

"English?" Siding asked Lylly when Koggs finished. "Which are you? City or United? Arsenal or Chelsea?"

Camo laughed. "Actually I probably favour Real Madrid." He hadn't seen any live football for a long while.

"Figures," Siding said.

Without any further niceties the first thing Siding wanted was a long private talk with Alain and Merci Stahl. The three of them disappeared into Stahl's ground floor office. Last in, Siding closed the door firmly behind her.

Koggs told Lylly she would be laying out the realities.

"De-Stockholming don't always work. Sure it's maybe seventy to eighty percent successful. Sometimes even ninety. But the parents got to realise the woman they get back ain't going to be the girl that left them. That's sometimes harder for the ma and pa. Sure I reckon the subject comes to realise most times in time they were brainwashed and they'll be glad they were got out. But they don't necessarily thank their parents. It's hard for both sides. Takes time. Years sometime before they're comfortable with each other."

"Better than the Bruno alternative though," Lylly said. "Better than the status quo."

"That's for sure."

Especially better than the status quo, Lylly thought if in the status quo the commune was going to continue to attempt to sacrifice the "subject's" mother.

The plan now was for Frank Koggs to take professor Siding out on a surreptitious reconnaissance of the commune from a safe distance. This was purely for the professor to get an idea and a picture of the circumstances and environment of Sylvie Stahl's habitation.

Next Alain Stahl would drive Tess Siding the two-hour ninety mile journey up to Gap so she could give the chalet the once-over. Only if the place met with Siding's approval would she give the go-ahead for the extraction. If the chalet was approved, Alain Stahl would drive Siding onto Geneva airport where she would fly back to Paris and Chicago. She would await developments there.

If the extraction was successful, Siding would fly back to Marseille or Geneva with a team of three qualified assistants to begin the deprogramming at the chalet.

Koggs's company would provide full-time but discrete protection around the chalet while the deprogramming took place. This was not only to provide privacy and possible protection to the team in the chalet, it was also intended as a safeguard to thwart any attempt by the commune to retrieve Sylvie Stahl if they discovered her whereabouts. Kogg's team was also there to prevent Sylvie Stahl escaping at any time and would return her to the chalet if she tried to leave, willingly or unwillingly.

Camo Lylly had volunteered his services to be a member of the extraction squad. But Koggs wanted him to assist in the overview team rather than be in the strike team.

"You ain't familiar with this kind of thing. Never used night vision goggles in the Legion I'll bet?"

Lylly had to agree. He would partner up with Koggs in the command vehicle while the rest of the six-man team, in three mutually supporting pairs, penetrated the commune and brought Sylvie Stahl out. If that was successful Sylvie would be drugged and knocked out. Then Koggs with Merci Stahl in attendance – just in case - would fly Sylvie to Gap in the SteadyState helicopter. Sylvie would wake up there next morning in the care of professor Tess Siding and her team. The Stahls, mother and father, would keep their distance until invited to the chalet by Siding when she considered the time was right.

At that point Camo Lylly wondered what he might do. His connection to the Stahls would be ended. It was likely they would not welcome strangers to be around when the deprogramming was taking place. It was essentially a family affair assisted and steered by the professionals. He could, he supposed, ask Koggs if he could be part of the protection team at the chalet, but he couldn't see the point. It would also be boring and repetitive work.

He was beginning to wonder whether he might actually return to his long-interrupted walk along the GR4 trail, through the lavender fields of Provence heading for Mont Ventoux. He could restart the walk at the far western end of the Gorge du Verdon. But then he had a rethink. He thought one last time he would like to go through the long hidden forbidden tunnel. Perhaps he might be able to commune with his ancestors in there too. So he would rejoin his stymied walk at the eastern entrance to the gorge, at the Pointe Sublime and repeat his descent into the gorge, and the tunnel, from there. But all that future plan depended on getting Sylvie Stahl out of the commune successfully.

The Stahls and the professor emerged from the study. Alain Stahl looked shaken and Merci Stahl was biting her lip. But Alain nodded to Koggs. It was good so far.

Professor Siding stayed the night with them in the chateau.

After breakfast next day Koggs drove Siding out immediately in one of the Stahl SUVs to take in a perspective of the commune from the road on the hilltop above it, where it could be seen laid out below through the trees. Koggs also showed her the layout they'd worked out from eyeballing the place from a distance, and from the camera shots from drones.

"I needed to be able to see where she lives," Siding told Lylly when they returned. "What kind of accommodation she has. Basic or otherwise."

Lylly told her he suspected they washed their laundry by hand at the stream. And presumably though Sylvie Stahl lived some sort of privileged and elite existence with Bruno Ludo in the farmhouse, she would be expected to be among the washer-women.

"It's all women doing things like that," Lylly said. "I think it's a strict patriarchy. The men sit around all day pretending to be warriors sharpening their spears and munching mistletoe and magic mushrooms and the women do all the work."

"Jesus Christ in a handcart," Siding said. "That's not good."

Koggs agreed and took Siding to one of his portacabins to see the rotas they had worked up from their observations on who did what and when in the commune. She took a copy of the spreadsheets for use in the post-extraction period. Then she requested Koggs take her out on the road for another look to see more for herself.

When they came back they had lunch.

Over coffee on the terrace after lunch Lylly asked professor Siding how she thought it might go if they got Sylvie out successfully?

"The usual stuff. Starving herself, refusing to eat. Throwing things. Screaming till she's hoarse. Throwing the name of her lover at us like a weapon of mass destruction. She will have been raped, of course. But she won't see it as rape, not yet. She sees it only as Bruno favouring her and choosing her above all the others. She sees Bruno not as her raper but as her lover. She thinks his name has an intense magic that will somehow unsettle us. So it's Bruno this, Bruno that. Wait till Bruno gets here. Bruno wouldn't want me to do that. Bruno is cleverer than you. Bruno will come and get me. She'll go through a long phase where the only word she says will be Bruno. Will you have some breakfast? Bruno. Will you drink something? Bruno. How about a shower now? Bruno. Let's go outside for a walk. Bruno, and so on. There will be a dirty protest, smearing the walls of her room with excrement. She thinks she'll be able to shock us into letting her go. She hopes that if she's too much trouble we'll give up. What she never sees, what they never realise, there's nothing new. We've seen it all before. We just get the hazmat suits on and clean the walls. Every time. The thing we know that she doesn't is our patience is greater than her impatience. We've done this before; she hasn't. Time is on our side, not hers. The longer the time between her and Bruno the thinner the umbilical cord that connects them becomes. She doesn't see it, she thinks she still feels the same. But not so. She cries at first very much. Tears of anger and frustration, tears at being kept from Bruno, wailing and keening to be back with him. Then that stops. No tears for a while. Then suddenly she pretends she's cured, as though she's had a brush with a nasty disease but is better now. She sees it now. She was deluded. Her mind was fogged. She is glad to be out of that place. She hates this Bruno, she says. She doesn't recognise who she was. She never wants to see him again. She's clever she thinks, pretends to try to make us let her go. But we see it. We see through to the real person. We have seen it before. We can tell the difference between the pretence and the person. So we don't let her go. She continues to pretend for a while. But she realises it's hopeless and she stops. Then later she cries again. But it's different. Now she cries for herself and what she was. This is the crux. Now is the difficult time. They can go on or they never go on. The crux. The watershed.

Sometimes they disassociate themselves. They refuse to acknowledge what happened to them, they were not there, it wasn't them. And so dangerously sometimes they never get past this stage. And if the care treatment stops now they will revert. They have not got clear. They must reach the stage where they acknowledge it all. It was me. I was there. I did bad things. They must begin to say that they were at fault, no one else. They were young and silly and angry and the world was big and frightening and they needed a guide and instructor. But now they can see they have a chance now to be silly no more and they do not need a guide. They must reach that stage of self-knowledge. For in the end it is only self-knowledge that saves them. They come to understand they are their own guide for always. And then if all goes well, slowly, slowly she changes. She mentions Bruno less. She listens when we tell her about the attacks on her mom and is shocked. We read her the extracts from the Roman writers and we can see they echo with her. She is shocked again. She's heard them before, but now she can see they're not good. And we're kind and careful and we wait. We get her to talk about her life in the commune, and we see there are things she doesn't want to tell us. They're bad things. And that's good because she's making a judgment, and we want her to get her judgment back. We don't force it, we let her brood on it. And we never ever judge. And gradually she gets it. She gets where she's been. And now she wants to come back from there. She sees she fell down a well, and she's been at the bottom of the well, rooting in the mud, chasing the Bruno phantasm of gold in the mud. She's not out yet, but now she's looking up from the bottom of the well. And now at last she begins the long climb out. It's precarious and she can slip back to the mud any time. And she talks more about the commune, but now it's distanced, it's not her, it's someone who was taken in, cheated, deluded, led astray, deliberately by a bad and evil man. A manipulator. A man-ipulator. Then if we get to that state we know we're on the road home. And maybe then we might bring in the parents. One then the other, then both together. Maybe, but that's a delicate moment. I think we may get her to the bottom of the well looking up in two months.

She may meet her parents again a month after that, as she climbs. And she might just be ready to come out in another month. So four months before she's ready. Sometimes it's longer. Six months. If it goes well. Of course with some who are already doubting their guide and instructor it's much quicker. Three months, or perhaps even two. We don't know where Sylvie's mind is yet. But when we meet her we will know. And we will know if it's two months or six months, or somewhere in between."

"Wow," Lylly said. He was amazed at the dedication and hard work Siding and her team had to put in just to bring one person back from the bottom of the well. Hard work they seemed very willing to do.

"How many have you done?"

"Six. Five successful."

"What happened with the one that wasn't?"

Siding was silent for a moment. She looked hard into Lylly's eyes, looking for something Lylly didn't know what.

"Hanged herself. In the first week. Dammit. Left a note saying she'd go on ahead and wait for her lover in Heaven. Gonna be a long wait."

"I'm sorry."

"And you know what?" Siding said, brightening. "Birdsong and trees and the sight and smell of flowers help too. They help a lot. The lodge place will be good if it's got those."

Then Alain Stahl and Tess Siding headed off for Gap by road. She planned to be on the Chicago flight from Geneva via Paris later that same night.

Later that evening word came back from Alain Stahl at Geneva airport. Professor Siding was very pleased with the setup at the Gap chalet. She had asked for a three metre high chain link fence to be put in place all round the property through the woods, and an intercom and a remotely-controlled electric gate at the entrance. This would all be done. She was happy with the birds and trees too.

"It'll do," she'd said.

"That means she thinks it's perfect," Koggs said.

Koggs decided. It was on. He told Lylly they were going to undertake the extraction on the night after the next new moon. That would be in six days time.

"Why the day after the new moon?" Lylly said. "Isn't the new moon the darkest night?"

"Cliché avoidance," Koggs said. Lylly shot him a look to say what the hell are you talking about?

"They might expect us on the night of the new moon." Koggs said. "I would."

"I get it," Lylly said. He was becoming more impressed with Frank Koggs all the time.

"Dark is good," Koggs said. "Darker is better. We go the night after the darkest."

24

WITH SIX DAYS TO GO to the night after the dark of the moon that meant there was time for the next monthly permitted meeting between Merci and her daughter before the extraction.

Lylly very much wanted to have another look at the commune from the inside. He volunteered to drive Merci to the commune again. Koggs agreed that Lylly was the best one to accompany Merci, as he had been seen in the commune already. He also decided that Todd and Brad should follow, as before, but they should park in the gateway, as before, and not first try to park the van in the commune.

Koggs said it had to be the same people as before. He didn't want any new faces in his team being seen by the communards. "Yet," he said.

Lylly had to insist to Merci that once he'd started it he now had to stick with the Eli Wallach-speak when they visited the commune. He knew she didn't like it. She was intensely worried that anything abnormal, or disrespectful or even just ironic would sent Bruno into some kind of righteous paroxysm and deny her access to her daughter.

"Please be careful," she said. "Don't antagonise him."

On the appointed day, as before, with Lylly again wearing the company combat outfit, they drove through the pair of gates standing open at the main entrance to the Bozonian commune in the valley beyond Moustiers-Sainte-Marie.

Lylly was driving his Mazda with Merci in the passenger seat. Brad and Todd were in the white van immediately behind. Lylly, Brad and Todd were all wearing the devil masks as before. As they passed through the gates he glanced over to the line of cars behind the B&B barn. The yellow and green campervan was still there. They must be rock mad, he thought.

They approached the locked gates of the inner entrance. Lylly stopped in front of the gates. He got out and swung the clapper multiple times to strike the bell.

"I was doing it ironically," he said to Merci as he got back in driving seat.

The same two women as before, the smiley one and the scowling German, approached the gates from the other side. They unlocked the padlock and slid the chain away. They pulled the gates open towards them and stood on each side.

Lylly drove almost all the way through then stopped. He slid his window down as though to talk to the German woman. But it was also a ploy to allow Brad to drive the van right up to his back bumper and prevent the gates being closed again in the face of the van. Brad and Todd had been instructed to wait in the entrance and surreptitiously take as many photos as they could of the layout of the inner compound. And take shots of any groups of people that might gather, as they had the previous time. This was intended to give them an idea of how many people, particularly adults, were living in the commune.

"He-lo lervlee," Lylly said in his best desperado banditese behind the devil mask. "How yoo do thees day?"

"You cannot trick me Satan," the woman hissed in response.

Merci put her hand on Lylly's arm.

"Please don't antagonise them," she said. "Don't stop."

Lylly nodded.

As he drove, a thought struck Lylly about the way the woman hissed the word Satan. She was doing it because Lylly was wearing a devil mask, sure. But was she fully with the programme, he wondered? Surely as far as old-style Druids were concerned, he didn't know but would hazard a guess that Satan wouldn't be considered a mortal enemy but some kind of ally or even a pal?

Which in turn made him wonder if the communards were actually unknowingly split between those who were quasi-Christian and the fully initiated insiders who played the game but were secret Druids? And would there be any advantage in letting the Christian elements know that the commune hierarchy weren't actually Christian? Discord, falling out and friction might be a bonus.

But then again, he thought, was it a double bluff? Was the German women calling him Satan exactly because that's what a sceptical outsider like Lylly would expect her to say? Lylly decided this was more likely. The woman was an insider after all. She was most likely the one that had injected Merci Stahl with the knockout drops and had been seen to be the leader of the kidnappers. She might even be the shooter on the ridge who had shot Merci's horse.

She was definitely an insider then, and was just keeping up appearances. In fact Lylly now reckoned she was the Bruno commune's Hyacinth Bucket.

Lylly drove on and parked in front of the farmhouse. Brad and Todd stayed back at the entrance. Their van was now fully blocking the entrance way.

The German woman shouted something in German at the white van as she tried to close the gates but the van was preventing it. Brad and Todd ignored her, staring at her unseen through the devil masks. She let go of the gate, then banged on the van bonnet in frustration with a clenched fist and dented it. She stood in front of the van daring Todd and Brad to challenge her about the dent.

They continued to ignore her, though Brad was muttering "Man, oh man, oh man, oh man," under his breath. Eventually she gave it up and walked away. She joined a large group of people standing on the far side of the compound opposite the front of the farmhouse.

Merci got out of the car. Lylly took his walking pole, affected the limp, and joined her waiting ten yards from the front door of the farmhouse. It was almost midday.

The door opened and Bruno Ludo and Sylvie Stahl came out. Sylvie was walking slightly behind Bruno, as though it was her place never to be forward of him, with her eyes downcast. Bruno and Sylvie advanced until they stopped five yards in front of Merci and Lylly.

"Sister Stahl," Bruno oozed. He planted the tip of the white staff firmly on the ground and waved the two-fingered benediction in her direction.

"Welcome."

Bruno turned round towards the door.

"Please join us sister," he called back over his shoulder. Merci followed them to the door.

Lylly rested his arms on the top of his pole and leaned on it. He couldn't help it, despite Merci not wanting him to antagonise them. He wanted to appear relaxed and carefree. But more than that, he wanted to appear insolent. He wanted his body language to show he despised them. He despised them all for being taken in by this hippie-philosopher charlatan.

Sylvie and Merci passed through the open door into the dark of the farmhouse beyond. But Bruno suddenly turned round and faced Lylly.

He raised his arms. His right hand held the holly staff. Lylly suddenly noticed the small orb and cross on top were no longer there. His left hand made the two-fingered benediction. Except this wasn't a benediction. It was a kind of finger curse.

"You are not welcome Satan." It wasn't a shout, but it was a kind of mantra or chant. "The Lord of Earth shall bury you in the cave. The Lord of Air shall hurl you to your doom. The Lord of Fire shall consume you in the flames. The Lord of Water shall drown you in the pool."

"Got eet," Lylly said. He leaned even more lazily on his pole. "Mee not yoor fren," he said.

Bruno gave Lylly his wide-eyed white-eyed stare. Lylly felt he was being remembered and marked. It really did feel like Bruno was trying to hypnotise him. For the first time he was actually glad we was wearing the devil mask and using the desperado speak. Bruno couldn't see his face nor hear his real voice. Then Bruno too disappeared into the farmhouse.

Afterwards Lylly reckoned it was fortunate that Bruno had

not said the words "Be gone!" That command was clearly the trigger. Had Bruno shouted those words the crowd standing silent on the other side of the space would have come forward and attacked him.

For an idle moment Lylly thought he might engage in another game of hide and seek with the large silent crowd that was still standing on the far side of the compound, watching. He knew if he advanced towards them they would retreat. Maybe eventually he would have the pleasure of talking to the German woman again and her hulking friend Dieter. But instead, bearing in mind Merci's pleas not to antagonise them, he went over to chat to Todd and Brad in the van. It also didn't make any sense, he knew, to make any moves that might put the commune on its guard.

"I sure hope he waves those two fingers at me when we come back," Brad said when Lylly approached the van window. "I'll fucking begone them."

"Break that asshole stick and toss it in the stream too," Todd said. "And ram this mask up his ass."

"See if the gate woman's head makes a bigger dent in the hood than her fist did," Brad said.

Ten minutes before the hour was up Lylly returned to the spot five yards in front of the farmhouse door. He listened hard, just in case. But on the hour Merci emerged from the house unhurt.

She looked sad and sombre and worn out. But at least she wasn't crying this time.

On the way back to the chateau, riding next to the silent Merci, Lylly had another partial insight.

When Bruno spoke of the Lord of Earth, of Air, of Fire and of Water, he wasn't thinking of a single deity in charge of those four elements. He was imagining four gods, each in charge of an element. His paganism was hiding in plain sight all along.

25

THEY WERE AS READY as they could be. For two days and two nights they'd motored to a hillside well out of the way and ten miles north of the commune. They tested all their equipment. They practised moving through thick woods in the dark. They got used to finding ways through waves of thick undergrowth without making any noise. They practised penetrating and attacking in the dark a ruined and abandoned shepherd's hut they found on the hillside. They came back and rested up.

Lylly had practised with them. He wanted to try the equipment he'd never used before, particularly the night goggles. He was amazed how much you could see, even if it was slightly two dimensional all in a ghostly green. But you got used to it. And it was way better than not having them.

Then the day before the extraction Charlie, who was scheduled to be in the six-man extraction team tripped on a root on the trail in the woods and fell while out jogging. He broke one of the metatarsals in his right foot.

Now Koggs had to solve a conundrum. Should he bring in a new man from Paris or Marseille?

"Or put me in the team," Lylly said. "You know I've been on the training. I'm familiar with the equipment now.

After some heated and less heated discussion Lylly persuaded Koggs that was the best option. In fact Lylly suspected Koggs intended to put him in as a substitute all along. He just didn't want to lose face by agreeing immediately.

On the night of the extraction Koggs was installed in the back of his command vehicle. This was a white van identical to the others but this one was outfitted with a specially equipped interior, to observe and monitor and communicate remotely. The van was parked in a layby on the hilltop road above the commune stream valley. Koggs was in live radio contact with all six members of the extraction team.

There was an observation drone up in the night sky. The six persons of Koggs's extraction team were under Donna's command. They sat lined up, waiting in the back of Koggs's white van on the road above the commune. They were armed with Tasers and nightsticks. They all wore night vision goggles over full face masks. Donna was the only one armed with a weapon. She carried a lever action hunting rifle.

"Just in case," Koggs said. "She's the best shot. She'll aim to maim. Not to kill."

Lylly had been allocated to partner Todd in the six-man team. Because of Lylly's relative inexperience both with the equipment and working with the team, he and Todd would act as backup to the other two leading pairs.

At exactly one o'clock in the morning the three pairs in the extraction team were dropped off by Koggs in the white van on the mountain slope in the trees above the commune.

According to the plan laid down by Koggs they would slowly make their way down the slope, with lack of sound a prerequisite over speed. They hoped to make it to the stream by 2am and to the back of the farmhouse and inside the back door by 2.30. They would spend no more than twenty minutes in the farmhouse. They would be back up the slope with Sylvie to the waiting white van by 4am.

It was a lot easier done than Lylly expected. Their aerial reconnaissance had indicated there was a private walled off paved area between the back of the farmhouse and the stream. A back door opened on to the paved area.

The plan was to steal down the hillside, cross the stream then go in through the back door after crossing the paved area. They would find and enter the room being used by Bruno and Sylvie Stahl as their bedroom. There had been some debate as to whether

Sylvie would have her own room. The final consensus was that Bruno would not allow that, and the team would find them together in the same room. In any case they would search every room in the building to make sure.

The babbling stream helped to mask any sounds they made as they approached and waded through the thigh deep water. There were irregular stepping stones crossing the flow but they avoided those automatically because of the slight chance of slipping into the water and making a noisy splash. They turned off their radios temporarily when they stood in the stream so no static or other unwanted sounds would alert the farmhouse. They would immediately turn their radios back on as they exited the commune and crossed back over the stream. At that stage they expected to have news to relate to Frank Koggs waiting in the white van up the hill.

But it turned out they didn't need to enter the farmhouse at all. An astonishing and arresting sight held them spellbound for a few seconds as the team rose up the shallow bank from the stream bed and stepped silently onto the paved patio area.

As they emerged silently, on time, up the slightly raised bank to the paved area from the stream they saw there was a large metal double bed, complete with mattress which had been wheeled out on the paved area under the stars. A la belle étoile as the French say. But it wasn't the bed that grabbed their attention, incongruous as that was.

Next to the bed a sturdy steel structure loomed out of the ground. It was shaped like a huge croquet hoop two metres high with a flat crosspiece held up by two upright poles inserted solidly into the ground. In fact Lylly realised it was more of a frame in the form of the Greek letter pi, complete with short horns where the horizontal piece extended half a metre beyond the uprights. The pi-shaped structure formed the centre focus for the actions of three people.

Sylvie Stahl was spread out in an X-shape, fixed to the pi-shape with her legs apart and her arms outstretched above her shoulders. Some soft fabric tied her wrists to the top corners of the pi, and her legs were stretched open and fixed to the base of the uprights. She was naked and blindfolded. Lyly was instantly struck by the similarities of this scene and the circumstances in which he had discovered Sylvie's mother. Pi there and pi here. Why?

Nor was Sylvie alone. She was the centre of attention of two other people. Both of these forms were naked too. One was Bruno, the other Lyly recognised as gate-woman. She had the same severely short mousy hair he had seen twice before. Bruno as raping Sylvie from the front while gate-woman was simultaneously raping her from behind, armed with a huge pink dildo glistening with lubricant strapped to her loins with broad black webbing and gleaming buckles. Gate-woman's right hand was reaching round to grasp Sylvie's right breast. Bruno's white hair was loosed and spread like a foaming wave round his head and shoulders. It shone like a lighthouse beam in the night sights.

It didn't look as though Sylvie was enjoying it. She was sobbing gently with her head bowed as Bruno drove into her like a human piledriver. He was probably hurting her, but he clearly didn't care.

Gate-woman had her back to the stream and Bruno was staring unfocused and empty-eyed at a point somewhere behind Sylvie, while Sylvie herself was blindfolded. Which was good because it meant that none of them was looking in the direction of the stream as the black-clad pair of Donna and Brad stepped forward stealthily and silently to take one each and Taser them both in the side of the neck.

Brad tasered gate-woman first. She made no sound and collapsed in a heap on the bed with her hand sliding seemingly reluctantly from its grip on Sylvie's right breast. Bruno didn't seem to notice anything in the exterior world at all such was his physical commitment to the task in hand. He grunted and drooled on the side of Sylvie's neck as he climaxed in ecstatic spasm and commanded her in a harsh guttural whisper to "receive and nurture the holy seed," and started to ejaculate just as Donna hit him in the neck with the Taser. He instantly jerked away sideways, paralysed, his eyes wide with the whites showing. He fell hard onto the stone paving, his now flaccid and shrinking member still spilling his seed, holy or otherwise, onto the stony ground.

Nor did Sylvie have time to react. As she tried to turn her head to try to see why the hurting had stopped and what had happened to Bruno and Heidi she was gagged, head-bagged, and injected while the bonds holding her to the pi-frame were severed. She was then wrapped in a sleeping bag as she sagged to the ground and thrown over a shoulder as two of the team took turns to carry her already unconscious form back across the stream up the hill to the nearest road and the waiting white van.

They left Bruno lying on the paving. All he would have seen as they left were black figures in full face coverings and masks. And that was only if he was looking in the right direction. He wouldn't be able to turn for a while yet. Nor cry out. All he would discern were black shapes moving indistinctly against the black of the night.

As they retreated across the paved patio back towards the stream Lylly noticed that there was large log or stump of wood standing upright on the far edge of the paved area. It seemed to have something carved into the surface on one side.

Intrigued, he ran rapidly over to have a look at it. It was a wood cylinder about three feet high and nearly the same in diameter. He couldn't tell what type of wood it was but clearly the tree it had been cut from had been a substantial one. It still had all the bark attached, except in one place. This was about half way up the log. And there an image had been cut and traced into the surface of the wood. It looked like a woman's face and head, larger than life-sized and to Lylly it looked unfinished. He guessed the image had been scratched into the wood by a chainsaw.

He looked more closely at the image. With a chill he thought it was a representation of Sylvie's face that had been cut into the wood. But then he rejected the idea. The light was not sufficient to tell.

He had no time to examine the effigy is more detail, but he wondered what it was and what it was doing there. What did it mean? Why carve Sylvie's face into a tree? And did that mean it was closely connected in some way to Bruno?

Lylly was the last to leave the paved area and the last to cross back over the stream. Though he looked back, he resisted the overwhelming urge to give Bruno a version of his favourite two fingered benediction.

The whole operation from first moving down the slope in the trees above the commune to placing Sylvie carefully in the back of the white van had taken less than two and a half hours.

At the Stahls' chateau Sylvie was transferred from the white van to Frank Koggs's helicopter which then flew the unconscious Sylvie to Gap where another of his white vans waited.

Tess Siding and her team had flown in to Geneva earlier that same day. Now they were already waiting at the chalet when the white van left Sylvie in their care around dawn. She was put straight to bed in her room on the first floor to sleep it off.

The difficult bit, the de-Stockholming, could now begin.

PART 2

26

LYLLY STOPPED ABOUT fifty metres from the exit of the long hidden forbidden tunnel.

He shone his headtorch on the wall. There were just four holes in the rock now. They were surprisingly difficult to spot. The expansion bolts and the remnants of the ropes that had pinned Merci Stahl to the tunnel wall had gone. The white pi-symbol – as he now thought of it - seemed to be fading too, as though the rock it was painted on was absorbing it.

It was now mid-summer. After what was nearly a two month break at the Stahl chateau he had restarted his long walk through Provence at the entrance to the Gorge du Verdon, at the Pointe Sublime, just as he intended. He wanted now to push on hard for Mont Ventoux and the descent to the Rhone. He would decide what to do next when he got to the river.

Merci had wanted him to stay a while longer. They all did. Alain Stahl even offered him a permanent job, either as a bodyguard or a shepherd.

"Take your pick, whichever you fancy," he'd said.

Lylly said he needed time to think about it. He would let them know in a couple of weeks, he said, when he finished the trek to the Rhone. In the meantime he would leave his car at the Stahl's place.

A week after the extraction of Sylvie Stahl, Merci Stahl had driven him to the restart point. They'd spent the night together at the hotel overlooking the gorge.

"Just because we've got Sylvie out doesn't mean Bruno will stop trying to kill you," Lylly said as they lay together. "You can be sure he'll be desperately searching for her. He may want to harm you in revenge, just because he can, to hurt Sylvie. It's a way of reaching her even if he doesn't know where she is."

And if by some horrible circumstance he does get Sylvie back, won't the whole sorry pagan-and-pi circus start again, Lylly thought but didn't say.

"There's a ritual element to this, and you're part of it. Just because it's hocus-pocus doesn't make the consequences of it any less real."

He was feeling guilty about leaving her, he knew. He felt she needed him, and he wouldn't be there, even though Koggs's men would remain at the chateau for the foreseeable future.

Merci didn't reply. But she stroked him and for a good while neither of them said anything.

"Go," she said, next morning.

Lylly shuffled his pack over his shoulders.

"You need this," she said. "I need you to do it. Walk it out of your system. I'll be all right. The colonel's good at his job."

They embraced among the rocks at the edge of the car park at the lead-in to the gorge. Then he held her at arm's length, nodded in kind of salute, disengaged and turned away towards the darkness of the first tunnel.

"Just come back," she called as he was almost lost to sight in the black entry. He raised a hand in acknowledgement.

"I'll be waiting," she added, but she knew that Lylly didn't hear.

Lylly went on past the expansion bolt holes and the painted pi symbol. He emerged into bright sunlight. All the tunnels were behind him now. For many miles the track ran alongside the Verdon river, through trees thirty metres above the water. And as time went on, Lylly's troubled mind began to ease.

It was perhaps the combination of hot sun, the sound of restless water, the remoteness of the place, together with the spectacular scenery that eased his mind. As well as the feeling of fullness and completion because what he had with him was all he needed. He was free and wanted for nothing.

But there was one factor that helped more than any other, and that was overhead. That was the European vultures. He knew they were indigenous to the area but had had to be reintroduced in recent years. The original birds had all been wiped out as soon as local farmers could afford shotguns and rifles, probably in the nineteenth century. Now numbers of the birds wheeled and circled overhead, riding on the updraughts as the heat built up and convected hot air upwards and channelled it into the sky. One pair particularly seemed to be shadowing him. He sat on a rock down by the water and drank and watched the vultures.

He was in no hurry and thought he might spend a night in the gorge rather than hurry through it. He knew it was dangerous to camp down by the river after a storm when they opened the spillways and a wave of water would cascade through the gorge. There were warning signs everywhere, and a while back the surgeon Louis Kellner had added his twopenn'orth on that too. But it hadn't rained for a good while and he was prepared to take the risk.

So that night Lylly descended to the river and found a large grey sandbank by the edge of the stream where he pitched his tent. The sandbank reminded of another grey sandbank. The one with Merci Stahl shortly before her horse's head exploded in a cloud of blood. It seemed you could never have just the good. It was always hand in hand with the bad. The river sounds lulled him to sleep and the river flow washed away the sense of doom.

Next morning he pressed on, refreshed. The pair of vultures still seemed to be trailing him. Do they know something I don't, he wondered?

One thing Lylly couldn't get out of his head was the steel frame erected on the back-patio of Bruno's house by the stream. The rape-frame as he thought of it. The more he thought on it the more he was convinced it was a shape in the form of π – pi - and not just a large human-size croquet hoop. Why go to the trouble, he wondered? Why bother to make a pi-shape when a trio of scaffold poles or timber baulks put together simply like the stones at Stonehenge would do just as well? Why go to the trouble of making sure the crosspiece extended past the uprights? You'd only bother if the shape meant something to you. The white paint marks in the tunnel and the rape-frame had to represent pi. But why? Was pi then special to Bruno in some way?

He knew π – pi - turned up in all sorts of unlikely places. It was even inherent in Planck's Constant which was to do with the change in frequencies electrons made when quantum-jumping from one cloud orbit to another, where h was multiplied by 2π to make h-bar. It seemed to be one of the necessary underlying realities of the universe.

Lylly's heart missed a beat. He thought he could see that the fixation on pi derived from an egotistical perception of the underlying realities of the universe. If you thought you and you alone had such perception then you would think you were pretty special, Lylly guessed. A prophet maybe. Divinely inspired. You might have to choose your gods carefully, but still divinely inspired.

He was beginning to realise Bruno was cleverer and far more knowledgeable than they'd thought. They all, Lylly not least, had dismissed him as a charlatan showman, nothing but a sexual predator who disguised his sexual aggression within a miasma of half-understood ancient folklore and preposterous quasi-Christian mumbo-jumbo. And when you thought someone was half-educated you tended to dismiss them as incompetent too. But that would be a dangerous mistake, Lylly now realised. For some reason the pi symbol was deeply important to Bruno, and Lylly felt he would be well aware of all its semi-magical manifestations, including its appearance in Planck's Constant at the heart of quantum dynamics. And while being cleverer and more knowledgeable than they thought he was didn't necessarily make Bruno any more competent or dangerous, but Lylly now knew it would not do just to dismiss him as a half-educated charlatan. He was an educated charlatan, very educated, and that in itself somehow made him more unknown as well as devious and dangerous.

Lylly realised that Bruno Ludo's belief system, and its raison d'etre as the belief system of his followers seemed to function on three levels. On the surface there was the cod-Christianity with the tiny cross and the two-fingered benediction. Below that was the pagan Druidism with the holly and the mistletoe and the lords of earth, air, water and fire, plus possibly the notion of human sacrifice. And then hidden again below that was the pi-symbol quantum mysticism, which also seemed to relate to the notion of sacrifice. This was the deep level that Sylvie had hinted to her mother about. And finally there was the rumoured connection to Ephesus and Artemis. But what it all meant Lylly had no idea.

When he next got a signal he sent a text to Koggs.

<Be specially vigilant. Bruno will not give up>

Koggs didn't reply. Guess he thinks I'm telling him how to do his job, Lylly thought. Grandmothers and egg-sucking.

By mid-morning Lylly emerged onto the road at the top of the gorge by the Chalet Martel. He hitched a ride along the road to the small town of La Palud and carried on up and beyond it into the wild high ground above the town. He spent a night in the wild country, disturbed only the by the sound of the hooves of a rapidly passing stag some time in the early hours. In the morning he looked for his friends the vulture pair, but they had stayed back in the safe haven of the gorge.

Next day he was not far south of Moustiers. He hurried on, not wanting to tangle with any of Bruno's acolytes he might meet in the area, but of course they wouldn't know who he was because he'd been obliged to wear the full face covering devil mask when visiting their compound. But even so it wasn't until he was halfway across the Plateau de Remoules that the wariness passed and he fully relaxed.

As the days went by he made his leisurely passage along the GR4 trail through Manosque, Cereste, Riez and Apt, all small and pleasant towns in the Luberon region. He took a rest day in Greoux-les-Bains and pottered about and relaxed in bars, catching up on the news and doing the crossword in several papers, English and Spanish, and sipping a beer. And the day after leaving Greoux he was in lavender fields again for the first time since leaving Grasse. He left the fields behind as he rose up to cross the humps and bumps of the Luberon ranges, and so came down to the hill town of Sault, south of Mont Ventoux.

The climb up the south side of Mont Ventoux started almost straight out of Sault. Though the slope was steep in places Lylly was well into his stride, as well as being residually super-fit from his time in the Legion, and he moved at a rapid pace up the slopes, through the trees, until he eventually emerged onto the treeless blinding white shingle field that caps the summit of Ventoux in all directions. The path followed the ridgeline towards the distant summit topped with a red and white painted meteorology tower. Lylly strode on.

A little way below the summit Lylly took a detour down to his left towards the road ascending the mountain from Sault. On a bend in the road, just above the tarmac there was something Lylly wanted to see. This was the monument to professional cyclist Tom Simpson, one of the best in his day and one of the few Britons able to compete with the best in the world on races such as the Tour de France. Simpson died during the Tour while cycling up the 23 kilometre long climb along the road up the south side of Ventoux.

Lylly stood by the stone monument. The granite plaque and plinth were festooned with tyres and water bottles, all left there in homage by other cyclists. It was fitting in a way, he thought, and didn't detract from the solemnity of the place. He turned and pushed on hard for the summit.

Ventoux is a two-day mountain for walkers. Lylly stopped for a beer at the summit café, then carried on down the north side. He took another small detour to drink from the Fonfiole spring which oozed out of a shoulder of the mountain above the treeline, then crossed the last of the shingle and was soon back into the trees, this time on the north side. He found a flat area near the ski resort of Montserein to pitch his tent and spend the night.

Next day he carried on down and booked in to a hotel in the

town of Malaucene. He had been eleven days on the trail and was looking forward to a long hot shower and had had enough of tents.

He knew after Malaucene the landscape changed and from now on all the way to the river and beyond it would no longer be rugged rocky spiny country but heavily cultivated land with vines, vines all the way in, up and along the Rhone valley.

After his shower he lay on the bed for a while wiggling his toes and resting his feet after the relentless pounding he'd given them on the descent from the mountain. No matter how fit you think you are and how good your equipment is and how accustomed to walking and marching you are, hard ground still takes a toll on your feet.

Later he went out wearing tee-shirt, shorts and sandals to explore the town. He found a place to eat under the plane trees. Then he went back to his room at the hotel where he had another shower. Then he slept.

It was during the night, just before four in the early hours of the morning, when he got the phonecall he had been dreading but feared would always come.

27

IT WAS MERCI STAHL on the phone. She was crying and screaming.

"They took her. Alain's dead."

Between her sobs he pieced the story together.

It was well planned. Bruno sent his acolytes to hit the chateau ranch. They surrounded the place and peppered the shuttered windows with shots from automatic weapons. Koggs and his men replied and a lengthy gun battle ensued. It was a kind of stalemate, and to break it Koggs ordered the guard at the Gap chalet to pile into the chopper and get to the ranch as fast as they could. His idea was that the chopper squad outside and his men inside the house would catch the acolytes in a cross fire. For the moment he held off calling the police for help. It was only after Alain Stahl had been killed by a stray bullet fired wildly from outside that Koggs called the police. His chopper meanwhile was approaching fast. No one at the chateau at that stage realised the attack there was a diversion.

Back in Gap as soon as the chopper had left the chalet, leaving only two guards behind, Bruno himself and his A team attacked the building. One guard was killed and the other badly wounded. One of Doc Siding's team was killed trying to protect Siding from an enraged and vengeful Bruno. The Doc herself was personally beaten, raped and pistol whipped by Bruno.

Sylvie Stahl was abducted. No one knew if she went willingly or unwillingly.

Camo Lylly said the only thing he could say.

"I'm on my way," he said.

Lylly got the hotel to rouse a taxi and persuaded the driver to drive him direct to the Stahl ranch. It cost a fortune but he didn't care. From further phone conversations on route both with Merci Stahl and Frank Koggs he gained more information.

Koggs himself was incandescent he'd been out-thought and out-generaled by Bruno Ludo.

"I underestimated the son of a bitch," he said.

"We all did," Lylly said. "I think that's sort of his game plan."

"We thought the son of a bitch didn't know about the Gap place. But of course Sylvie would've told him about it. We should've figured."

Lylly pointed out there was one good thing that emerged from the drubbing they'd all received at the hands of Bruno.

"At least the police will be after them now. They won't be able to hide."

Three murders and several badly wounded, and a band on the run armed with deadly weapons wouldn't be ignored by any police force.

"Their arrest will be a prime target for the French police."

"Them and me," Koggs said grimly. "He ain't going to beat me twice."

Though Lylly had said that Bruno and his band had nowhere to hide, he had no idea if that was true. And the more he thought about it the more he realised he was wrong, dead wrong. Would Bruno have abducted Sylvie if he had nowhere to take her? Unlikely, he thought. In which case he could be anywhere. He needn't even be in France anymore.

When Lylly arrived at the Stahl chateau he wasn't allowed through the police cordon at the gates until a message came up from the house to let him in. He found Frank Koggs, Donna and Todd in conference round the breakfast table. He learned from them that Merci Stahl was upstairs in her room. Koggs and Donna were about to take the chopper to Gap to check on the wounded operative in hospital and to arrange repatriation of their dead comrade. Todd would stay at the chateau.

"We'll be back tomorrow or day after," Koggs said as he,

Lylly and Donna approached the chopper. "Then we find them."

"One thing you can do," Lylly said. "You've got good contacts with the French police? Not here, not local, but in Paris?"

"Sure have. Need that to operate."

"Can you find out everything they know about Bruno? Is Ludo his real name? It just means 'game' in Latin—" he saw Koggs raise an eyebrow at that "—So getting all there is on him might be a start."

"Yeah. Can do. Probably should've done that before."

For the rest of the day Lylly rested. He avoided company, and spent most of the time by himself in the woods round the building, and when he heard Todd calling and searching for him he didn't reply. He wouldn't admit it to himself but he recognised he was in a state of shock. They all were, even Koggs, who must be more experienced in the ups and downs of martial chance than any of them.

They had seriously underestimated Bruno Ludo. They had assumed he was some kind of vicious buffoon, a non-professional vicious verbal bollocks-spouting buffoon who could be easily taken down and utterly vanquished by the professionals.

That wasn't the case. It's us who now look like the non-professionals, Lylly thought. Bruno had waited until the time was right. Though he must have been desperate to pay back the humiliation he'd received on the back terrace by the stream, and perhaps even more desperate to retrieve Sylvie Stahl, he had still waited. He'd waited for three weeks. Long enough for us to think we got clean away with it, and that Bruno wouldn't be coming after her, and would slink away, beaten and defeated, his tail between his legs, non-professional charlatan that he was.

But he hadn't slunk away. He'd waited and then struck when everyone had relaxed. He beat us, Lylly thought. Now we have to do everything we can to make sure he hasn't also defeated us. The war isn't over.

He remembered the story, not the story of Robert the Bruce hiding from the English in the cave and seeing the spider trying desperately six times to complete the web and failing each time, then succeeding on the seventh attempt, which inspired Robert to come out of hiding one more time and beat the English.

But that wasn't it. The story he remembered was a larger scale than that. It was of Joseph Radetzky, the Austrian marshal who had guided Austria's twenty-year war against Napoleon. Six times Radetzky put a coalition of nations together to fight Napoleon. And six times Napoleon smashed the coalition and made Austria sue for peace. But Radetzky's seventh coalition won the war.

Lylly came out of the woods ready to fight back.

28

NEXT MORNING LYLLY joined Todd at the breakfast table.

"We don't wait for the boss to come back," Lylly said. "We see if we can find anything out right away."

"Yay," Todd said. "Any ideas?"

"Well, the Bozonian compound is big, as you saw, maybe sixty or eighty people living there. Could be even a hundred. And my impression of the Bozonians is that there's an inner circle centred on Bruno and the German woman. Maybe twenty people, no more, the hard core. They'll be the ones involved in the two attacks, here and Gap. Maybe ten or a dozen here and six or eight at the chalet.

"It's my guess the remaining fifty, sixty, seventy of the sect don't know anything about the actions of Bruno and his inner circle. That means they're all still living there, wondering where the hell their leader and his mates have gone. And why the police are all over them this morning."

"You think they're worth talking to? Doubt it."

Lylly told Todd about his conviction that Bruno would not have taken Sylvie with violence, and so become an outlaw, unless he was certain of a place to run to. A safe place. A place to hide up.

"We need to know how far this is an itinerant sect, if they move about, if there are other places they lay up in regularly. How long they've been installed in Moustiers. Where they were before. Has Bruno ever talked about upping sticks and moving on? That kind of thing."

"I like it. Let's go."

There was another possibility, but Lylly kept it to himself for the time being. Which was, maybe Bruno had some kind of reciprocal agreement with other sects. In which case they wouldn't need a safe haven of their own, but could lay up as guests of another commune.

Either way, first thing was to talk to the remaining members of the Bozonians.

"We go in as soon as the police are done with them," Lylly said.

"So we set up an observation post on the hill above?"

"We do. And another thing—"

"Yeah what's that?"

"We go armed."

"I reckon so," Todd grinned. "We don't have time to be polite."

Lylly wondered whether he should go up and see Merci, but decided against it. Leave her be, he thought. He sent a text instead, saying he had arrived.

First thing Lylly and Todd saw from their position undercover on the hillside above the commune was a handful of police vehicles leaving the scene. It wasn't clear whether there had been any arrests.

They decided to wait another hour before entering the compound themselves.

"And when we go in," Todd said. "I ain't wearing no devil mask."

Before they drove to the commune and laid up on the hillside above it Lylly took one of his walking poles and screwed it together. He clipped the fighting knife on to the end. He also retrieved his Seecamp from its hiding place in the spare wheel. Todd brought along two hunting rifles, a Ruger and a Browning. There was a shotgun on the floor of the back seat of the black SteadyState SUV they travelled in.

They returned to the observation point they had established over the previous weeks as they watched the commune, prior to the night of the extraction.

An hour after the police left the compound Lylly nodded to

Todd. They both stood up and made their way down the slope of the hillside. It was exactly the same route they had both traversed before, on the night they had extracted Sylvie.

They crossed the stream by various irregularly spaced rocks piercing the surface, unlike on the night of the extraction when they had waded through the water.

Lylly saw with some surprise that the big log with what may have been Sylvie's face carved on it which he had seen standing on the patio on the night of the extraction was now lying on its side, dumped in the stream. It was over half submerged and caused a partial obstruction in the flow of the water. The side with the representation of Sylvie's face on it was on the underside, so could no longer be seen. He wondered if that orientation was deliberate. He tried to imagine what the story behind it was but thought no more of it. Bruno stuff, he supposed. Effigies and magic ratios.

They rose up the bank behind Bruno's house and crossed the paved area. The pi-frame and the bed had both been removed from the patio area, Lylly noticed. So the pi-frame, the bed, and the stump had all been removed or dumped. He assumed it was Bruno clearing up before he left. Did that indicate he wasn't intending to come back?

The duck-egg blue shutters on the rear windows and back door of the farmhouse were closed up. There was a mark of pi painted in white across the door shutters, but it was faded and faint in the aggressive sunlight. Or perhaps there'd been an attempt to remove it? There was another one on the shutters of a back window. The pi marks would be only visible when the shutters were closed. But then in Bruno's dark and closed-up world, maybe he had the shutters closed permanently? The place looked dead and shrunken. It seemed as if the building was desiccated. It had dried up and tightened in on itself with its occupants gone.

They followed the path round the end of the building and emerged into the open space in the middle of the compound. They stood by a tree growing in the middle of the area and waited. Lylly leaned on his walking pole. Todd held a thumb behind the strap to the Browning .300 calibre hunting rifle hanging from his right shoulder.

They didn't have to wait long. A woman emerged from one of the buildings on the far side of the open space. Lylly recognised her as the smiley one of the two women who had opened the gate twice to him when he visited with Merci. She was wearing the plain dress and headscarf that seemed to be the uniform.

She stood close to the two men under the tree.

"What do you want?"

She was English, Lylly realised from the way she spoke.

"We want you to talk to us, lady," Todd said. "Where's Bruno?"

"We don't know anything. Sod all," she replied. "All we know we learnt from the police." She gestured towards the compound gates.

Lylly raised his walking pole. The first inkling the woman had that the item wasn't a standard harmless walking pole was when Lylly placed the razor sharp knife tip against the front of her neck and pressed delicately on it. A drop of blood seeped out. The woman stared wide-eyed and motionless.

"Think again," Lylly said. "Oh yes. And don't move."

"Hold on, hold on," she said breathlessly. "Some, many, of us are glad Bruno's gone. He was--" she hesitated as though seeking the right word "—cruel."

Lylly didn't lower the pole but he pulled the knife tip back from her neck.

"How about a cuppa?" She asked.

It was so incongruous Lylly laughed. Todd looked bemused; he clearly had no idea what a 'cuppa' was.

"Sounds good," Lylly said. He lowered the pole. "Lead on."

He nodded to Todd.

The woman led them to the largest building on the other side of the compound. It had a series of large casement windows along the ground floor and a row of smaller windows under the eaves. They followed her round the left hand gable end to where two large barn doors stood open.

The interior was one large open space, with the roof timbers exposed. It looked like the building had been a barn originally. Now the stalls and hay racks were gone and the space was clean and tidy, and the floor paving slabs cleaned and polished.

Groups of people sat on benches at trestle tables and on chairs and stools at work benches talking or engaging in various activities such as mending tools and equipment, darning and sewing or playing with children. There was a loud hubbub of conversation which instantly ceased when Lylly and Todd entered the space. They were the centre of observation, but Lylly did not feel that the stares were particularly hostile. Interested and cautious but not hostile.

The woman led them to the side of the barn where a kitchen had been separated out from the general space. There were worktops and dresser-cupboards and several large gas bottles and a hefty cast iron cooker, a bit like an ancient Aga, Lylly thought. A sturdy table and spindle-backed chairs stood in front of the worktops. The woman placed a large kettle on a gas ring and invited them to sit at the table.

She made a pot of tea, then before joining them at the table called one of the men over. She didn't introduce him. The four of them sat at the table.

"We need to know everything you can tell us about Bruno," Lylly said.

"Are you the ones that took her?" The woman asked.

"Rescued her from this goddam shit-show? Yes lady you got that right." Todd was taking no prisoners, Lylly thought, playing the bad cop.

"Oh yeah? How long did your 'rescue' last?" the woman said fighting back.

"We work with them," Lylly said. So it was good-cop, bad-cop.

The woman and the man looked at each other. The man nodded and shrugged as if to say why not? Then both began to talk.

It was as Lylly had thought. The man and woman told them

that Bruno surrounded himself at the commune with an inner circle of twenty-one people. It always consisted of ten men and eleven women, the woman said.

"He called them the Perfects. And we had to call them that too," she said.

Why twenty-one Perfects, Lylly asked? It turned out it was because 22 was a near multiple of π. Pi was sometimes thought of in non-decimal terms as the fraction 22 over 7. Seven times pi was almost 22, just a shade under. So apparently Bruno saw himself as the twenty-second person with a band of twenty-one close followers. All nice as pi.

Todd asked if the commune was Christian? The man told them that the commune's central idea – until Bruno arrived – was that their beliefs combined Christianity and what he called the "Old Religion" – which Lylly took to mean Druidism.

Lylly wasn't sure if it was actually possible to combine the teachings of Christianity with the trappings of the Old Religion. Where for example did human sacrifice fit into that? But the woman informed him that Jesus was the original human sacrifice. So obviously if people believed that then it was possible to combine anything with anything.

"But obviously we don't carry it out," the woman insisted.

"What about Bruno?" Lylly countered.

The woman looked at the man and they both shrugged but said nothing. To Lylly this meant the activities of Bruno's inner circle were independent of the rest of the commune. But it looked like they suspected.

"They burnt cats," the man said. "Not us. Not us. Them."

Lylly knew it would be too easy to criticise the remnants of the commune for allowing Bruno's excesses, for not trying to prevent them. Too easy, because for all he knew they had tried to stop him. The instant reaction of the entire commune to topple the van at Bruno's words of command – *be gone* - was evidence of the total control that Bruno exerted. But maybe there'd been all sorts of friction, strife and infighting before Bruno reached that stage and wrenched full control and cowed the whole body.

"What about this pi stuff? What's all that?" he asked.

It seemed the pi stuff was purely the realm of Bruno and his inner circle. Neither the woman nor the man could say why pi was important to Bruno, or even what it meant to him. It was another thing that "they" did that the rest of the commune didn't.

Neither of the informers seemed to know much about Bruno. He'd just appeared one day about two years before. Within six months he was the acknowledged leader. He then set about surrounding himself with an inner circle of followers. Some of these were newcomers, others were identified and "elevated" from the rest of the commune. Increasingly the commune had become split into those carrying on in the same old way and those following Bruno's way. But if you stepped out of line you were punished.

Not only that, in the early days there had been one or two former leaders who had objected to Bruno's rise and had tried to resist. They had been "expelled" from the fellowship. Lylly wondered if "expelled" meant "disappeared". With the dissenters removed the rest of the members were cowed into going Bruno's way.

"What's with all the devil mask shit?" Todd asked them. "That Bruno again?"

"Yes," the woman said. "It's a year ago now. He decided every visitor should wear the mask. Everyone who comes through the inner gate. It was to show our moral superiority, he said. The devil is everywhere except here." She frowned.

Lylly picked up on the frown.

"But you thought it was silly?"

"Many of us did. We did not, we do not, want to antagonise the outside world. We sought harmony. Bruno sought and brought conflict."

"But you were too darn scared to do anything about it." Todd said. It was an accusation not a question.

Lylly laid a hand on Todd's arm to cool his unjust righteousness. He turned again to the man and woman across the table from him.

"What happened after Sylvie Stahl was taken? Did anything change?" It must have, Lylly thought.

The man said, "You say that was you? We thought her family must have sent someone."

"Bruno was certain it was her mother's doing" the woman said. "He announced that the Satanists had taken her. He vowed to us all that the 'sacrilege' as he called it would not stand."

But, strangely, that was the time when the non-inner-circle members of the sect had least strife and domineering from Bruno, she said.

"He was too focused on finding her, I think, and left us alone."

"What do you know of Bruno's last night? The night he and his followers left. What happened here?" Lylly said.

The man said the whole of the inner circle, all the 'Perfects', were summoned to a conference in Bruno's farmhouse. He didn't know anything about them after that.

"I kept out of the way. We all kept our distance when there was a meeting of the Perfects. Nothing good came out," the man said. He went to bed early he said.

"I heard them," the woman said. "I heard the first minibus and vans leaving about an hour before midnight. Then I heard another group of vans leaving about midnight."

And in the morning there was no Bruno and none of the Perfects.

"They had all gone," she said. "I didn't dare believe that they'd gone. I could not believe that they would not come back."

"His house was abandoned," the man said, pointing through the wall in the direction of the house on the stream side of the commune. "All his belongings gone." He looked directly at the woman. "I do not believe he means to return."

"We can hope," she said.

"This idea of 'Perfects', Lylly asked. "Did Bruno really think they were that? Perfect?"

"Oh yes. I think Bruno probably did," the woman said.

"But it is also what the members of the Cathars in the Middle Ages called themselves," the man said. "He stole the name. But also he liked the word very much, I think."

"Some of us called them the 'Prefects'," the woman said with half a smile. "They were always bossing us about. It's good they scarpered too. All of them."

Then after Bruno and the Perfects had gone, a while later the police arrived.

"And we learnt what Bruno had done. I think he was obsessed with her," the woman said. "She was the Perfect of the Perfects. He was different after she joined. More wilful. Erratic. Harsher. I don't know…"

"Don't know?"

"I don't know. After she came, Bruno was different. Maybe it was the real Bruno, finally. Yet somehow he was fulfilled. As though he had been searching for something all his life and had found it. Sorry, it was just a feeling."

Interesting all the same, Lylly thought. Maybe why he couldn't let Sylvie go.

It seemed neither of the communards thought Bruno would be back and Lylly tended to agree with them. The police would keep monitoring the place now.

"We will try to recover now," the man said. "We will remain here and try to return to how it was before Bruno came."

"You any idea where Bruno came from?" Todd asked them.

They hadn't. There were rumours about him in the commune. Some thought he was a college professor, others said he was a defrocked priest, others again said he'd been high in the civil service, or industry, or the church, but no one knew. One thing was certain, they said, was that he had military knowledge and expertise.

"Is he definitely French?" Lylly asked them. "Is Bruno Ludo his real name?"

They said yes he was French. But no one was sure about his name.

"He's French, I'm sure," the woman said. "He spoke French

and also English and German."

"His French has a Breton accent," the man said. "I'm from there, Concarneau in the west. I recognised it. And he once told us the standing stones at Carnac was a special place."

Later as they drove away from the commune Lylly and Todd reviewed what they now knew.

"What's the deal with these stones? Standing? What the hell's that mean?" Todd took an aggressive approach when he didn't know something or thought it was irrelevant.

"It's like Stonehenge," Lylly replied. "But different. Less dramatic but more substantial. Bigger. Older. Stones laid out in lines."

Lylly gave Todd a brief outline of what he knew of Carnac in southern Brittany.

"It's the largest collection of prehistoric standing stones in Europe. A thousand years older then Stonehenge. Rows and rows of big stones spaced out and planted end on in the ground. Called menhirs if I remember. Asterix's mate Obelix used to carve them –" He glanced over at Todd behind the wheel, but the references didn't register. "--The rows go on for miles. Maybe astronomical event markers, maybe calendar or seasonal markers, maybe not, who knows. But impressive. All the stones weigh well over a ton, some are ten tons. And they've all been shifted, shaped, brought there, planted in the ground in massive parallel rows. It's not surprising Bruno thinks it's a special place."

"Or he tells them what they expect him to say, what they want to hear from their boss?"

"Ay there is that. And he just plucks the first mystery stones place he can think of to keep them happy. Maybe the only one he knows."

So maybe Bruno's apparent reverence for Carnac was phony after all, Lylly realised. But it did seem the connection to Brittany was real.

"It's all kind of interesting," Todd said. "But it don't tell us where Bruno is now."

"Know your enemy," Lylly replied. But he tended to agree.

"What now?" Todd said. "The S.O.B could be anywhere."

Lylly started ticking items off his fingers.

"He's got probably twenty-one followers on the road with him. Plus Sylvie. So maybe twenty-three people in all. One group was here at the Stahl ranch. The other group – probably smaller – was up in Gap.

"What's that? A couple of minibuses? Four or half a dozen vans? The woman said she heard engines. Did the two groups meet up somewhere after the attacks? Somewhere between here and Gap? Then head in convoy to wherever they're going? Or did they all know where they're going and made their way there separately?

"One thing is absolutely certain: they've got to hide. They've got to keep their heads down now and for the foreseeable future. All the police forces in France are looking for them. Maybe the word's already gone out to forces in Spain and Italy. Germany even. And who knows, maybe England too."

Lylly outlined his conviction that Bruno must have a ready-made bolthole waiting where he thought he'd be safe. Otherwise the attacks and the abduction of Sylvie couldn't take place.

"They weren't suicide missions," he said. "They thought they could do it. They thought they could succeed. And they thought they could get away."

"So what do we do? How do we get on to them?"

"I don't know. But what we do have to do first is find out exactly who Bruno Ludo is. As well as maybe coming from Brittany and knowing all about the Carnac stones."

"The boss will be able to help with that."

29

AT THE STAHL CHATEAU Lylly sent a text to Merci asking if he could see her. She replied that she would come down from her room after dinner.

Lylly and Todd sat on the large terrace outside the lounge area of the ranch and each cradled a beer, watching the sun go down over the ridgeline. They were both wrestling with what little they knew about Bruno Ludo, but also knew it was idle in a way until Frank Koggs had gained what information there was on him from the French authorities.

Later Merci Stahl came out of the lounge onto the terrace. She was wearing blue jeans and a loose flowing white shirt. The was a black scarf round her neck.

The scarf looked good and right to Lylly. Wearing all black would have been over the top and inauthentic. Trying too hard. Protesting too much.

Her eyes looked puffy. She'd been crying. Both Lylly and Todd stood up as she emerged onto the paving.

"I'll get," Todd said, indicating the direction of the portacabin on the gravel beyond the end of the terrace.

"No, Todd please stay," Merci said. "I need company. Voices. Talk. A kind of normality."

At her request Lylly brought her a beer from the bar. She asked for it straight from the bottle. She asked for the ground lights along the terrace edge to be turned off, as well as all the wall lights. They sat down on the terrace in the near dark.

The only illumination came from out through the patio doors of the large lounge behind them and through the windows of whatever other rooms in the building were lit. Above them the night sky was bright, lit up by the breathtaking massed sparks of stars, but seeming cold, distant and unfriendly.

"He was right beside me when he was hit," she said. "The colonel told us to move to the back of the room and lay on the floor when they started shooting the windows up. We were all in there—" she gestured to the lounge behind the terrace "—The colonel wanted to use the brightly lit-up terrace as a fire zone he said. He thought it was too dangerous for us to stay in our rooms.

"So we lay down at the back of the room near the bar while he and his men started firing at anything that moved on or near the terrace and beyond. They had night sights, infra red viewers, they said, but they didn't think they hit anyone. Seems they were firing from a safe distance. Didn't know that then though. Sounded close to us to me."

She paused and looked out into the dark, then used the ends of the scarf to wipe her eyes.

"It was a ricochet, they said. One minute Alain had his arm round me with his head and upper body covering me, the next second he was dead. Hit in the side of the head by a slug that came off the stone of the side wall. If it hadn't hit him it would have hit me."

Lylly on one side of her and Todd on the other both touched her shoulder. She smiled tiredly, tilted her head back and took a plug of beer.

"So they were just firing blind?" Lylly asked. "Not aiming?"

"So the colonel said. I couldn't tell," Merci replied. She looked at Todd for conformation. He nodded.

"Afterwards the colonel said they were just pinning us down, keeping us busy. It seemed to go on a long time. Then it stopped. Then a while later the police came. And ambulances."

"What time did they start?" Lylly asked.

"I think around one-thirty, maybe two am. I called you when the police came. That was four o'clock."

Lylly tried to imagine the scene. The whole house roused by wild shooting in the early hours. The scary sound of gunshots heard close to, then the even scarier realisation the gunshots are aimed at you, so you assume, windows smashed to smithereens, mullions splintered, curtains shredded, shards of flying glass, bits of plaster exploding in clouds. Koggs trying to get a grip on things, does a good job of organising everyone, keeping them together in one place under his eye and initiating the counter-attack. Then makes the fatal mistake of calling for reinforcements from the team at Gap. But by then Alain Stahl was dead. And soon after that Sylvie Stahl gets taken.

"What about you guys?" Merci said. "What's your story?"

Lylly recognised she no longer wanted to talk about the attack on the chateau. So he told her everything that he and Todd had been doing in the search for Bruno.

"And the search for information about Bruno." She added.

"Yes," Lylly said. "We need to know who he is. That would be a start."

It turned out there was a longstanding warrant out for Bruno's arrest. He had been an officer in the French army. And before that a university academic. And his real name was Bruno Ludovico. And he came from Brittany.

Koggs and Donna returned next morning in the helicopter from Gap, with information.

"I got contact with one of my sources at the interior ministry," Koggs said. "They owe me," he added mysteriously, "And let me have everything they got on him. He is from Brittany as you sussed. But took his Italian mom's surname for some reason."

Bruno Ludovico had been a professor of comparative religion at Brest university, the youngest professor there and one of the youngest in France. His area of expertise within comparative religion was the pre-Christian religions of Celtic Europe.

"Wrote papers on it," Koggs said. "Then something happened. Nobody seems to know what. Not clear whether he was dismissed or resigned. Or threatened with dismissal if he didn't resign. Ministry seems to think the college covered something up. Something bad.

"Any road he gave it all up and joined the army. Went in right at the bottom as a goddam private and rapidly rose to major. Was kind of old to be a major of course at thirty-five, but his rise from private to major was rapid."

Lylly made a silent whistle. That was impressive.

"Then something happened again. Could have been the same shit as happened when he was teaching, nobody knows. Maybe he got up to doing in the army what he'd been doing at college. The bad stuff. Just a thought.

"Anyhow he just up and left the army. Deserted. On the lam. AWOL. And that time he dropped right off the radar. That was seven years ago. My man at the ministry said there was good reason to think he spent time in Germany, since it was in Germany – on joint EU Franco-German manoeuvres - he deserted from his unit."

The moment he deserted the army there would be an arrest warrant issued. Professor-major Bruno Ludovico had disappeared and been successfully on the run for seven years. That was impressive in itself, Lylly thought. The last two years of the seven had been spent in the Bozonian commune, they knew that.

Maybe living in an off-the-grid commune was one certain way you could evade the authorities, Lylly thought. If you wanted to remain anonymous and unfound, and you don't care about owning things, nor credit cards, nor bank accounts, nor paying taxes, nor interacting with society to the extent of having appointments with doctors and dentists, nor registering things like deaths and births and marriages, and everything you needed could be either bought for cash or made or mended on site, then living in a commune was the place to be.

"The authorities some while ago assumed he was dead," Koggs said. "After five years of no sign of him they closed the book."

Lylly wondered instinctively if the "bad things" Bruno had been rumoured to be up to at college and possibly in the army had derived from his interest in human sacrifice which in turn might have arisen out of his deep study of the 'old religion'. But he didn't say anything.

"So we know who he is. And we know what he was. We don't know where he is, but we know more about him than we did. But it don't necessarily help," Koggs concluded.

30

LYLLY WANTED A TALK with the two Israeli agents. It was a long shot but they might know something arising from their time "observing" Alain and Merci Stahl. They might even have seen something and not known its significance. He decided he would call the number.

The woman, Viv, answered.

"Mr Sandbank, interesting to hear you."

"Can we meet? Need to pick your brains."

"Sure, mate," she said. "But it will just be me. Art's gone back."

They arranged to meet at lunchtime next day in the same bar in Castellane as before. It did strike Lylly that she never asked what it was he wanted to pick her brains about. Maybe she wants to see me anyway, he thought, ever hopeful.

First, next morning, Merci and Lylly and Koggs, Donna and Todd had a conference over breakfast. The only topic on the agenda: how to find Bruno Ludovico.

Koggs as the senior man laid out the next moves. He said that they should try to back track Bruno Ludovico's career.

"To see if anything jumps out like a rabbit out of a hat."

So Donna would go to Brest to talk to the college people there. Her French was good, Koggs said.

"A darn sight better than mine and I lived here five years."

Donna dipped her head in acknowledgment.

Koggs himself would track back through Bruno's army career.

"I got me some army contacts." Via them he would go and

talk to members of Bruno's old units in Lyon and Marseille. "With both of us shaking the tree maybe something'll drop out."

He pointed out that although he would get to see, eventually, everything that was in the interior ministry's reports on the case, there may be useful items in people's memories not included in the official reports.

The remaining members of Koggs's team, Todd and the rest, would remain at the Stahl chateau, which would act as the base for collating information. With Sylvie Stahl gone Koggs decided there was no point in continuing to guard the Gap chalet.

Koggs said his contact in the interior ministry would let him know immediately if the French police discovered any leads as to Bruno's whereabouts.

"What about me?" Lylly said.

"You're the loose cannon. Either cool your ass here till we find something, or go back on your little hike, sharpen your spear, or do whatever you like. I'll contact you if we hear anything."

Koggs flew off, and returned from, Lyon quite rapidly.

"They wouldn't talk," he said. "Closed ranks."

Koggs said there was just one thing. The officer he talked to had made Koggs follow him into the middle of the parade ground outside his office.

"Bastard didn't want anyone to hear what he said, I guess."

The officer said that all he knew was that something had happened to Bruno Ludovico while he was stationed with the French army in Iraq, as peacekeepers. He wasn't the same when he came back.

"Something in Iraq, diddly squat else." Either the officer didn't know any more or wouldn't say for the sake of the unit's reputation. "That's all we got. Eye-raq."

Lylly also wanted to talk to psych doc Siding. She was in hospital in Gap. He knew Koggs had seen her a couple of times and had reported that she was in astonishingly good spirits considering the ordeal she'd been through, but he wanted to talk to her himself.

Koggs was intending to fly up to Gap immediately that morning and settle all his business there before returning to the chateau the same day, before heading for Marseille to talk to Bruno Ludovico's old comrades and superiors. Lylly asked if he could go with him to Gap.

Donna had already driven down to Draguignan to get a fast train to Paris and then Brest when Lylly joined Koggs on the tennis courts at the helicopter. They flew in companionable silence as Koggs flew the chopper the fifty minute flight to Gap.

The chopper landed in the flat sheep pasture by the side of the Stahl's mountain retreat. It had followed the road into the mountains and had not attempted to cross any of the mountain ridges to reach Gap.

"Easier to find your way following the roads," Koggs said in explanation. He said they'd only gain five minutes by heading direct over the mountains, so it didn't make much of a difference. But Lylly had a feeling there was more too it. Maybe it was because if there was a problem with the helicopter it would be better to emergency land it by a road than on a mountain crag or in some high deserted valley. He realised that Frank Koggs was a careful man. Maybe in his line of work he had to be.

There were two SteadyState company white Mercedes vans in the lodge parking area. Koggs offered him one rather take a taxi and Lylly took it up. He set the satnav and followed its recommendations to Gap hospital.

He found Tess Siding in a private room. He assumed Koggs was paying. Lylly hadn't wanted to criticise but it had been a serious blunder by Koggs to withdraw most of the guards from the mountain lodge. That left Siding and her team almost completely exposed when the attack came.

But as Koggs had previously reported, Siding was in good spirits. He found her sitting up in bed reading some documents. She welcomed Lylly with a grin.

"It's Real Madrid isn't it?"

"That's right."

Siding had bandages round most of her head and face. Her left eye had a huge black surround. Her right hand and wrist were heavily bandaged.

"Student papers, depositions, and theses, ugh," she said as she lifted up the papers from the wheeled table-platform-cum-desk that crossed the bed and threw them on the floor.

"Did I really think I knew everything too at that age? Have a seat."

"Good to see you," Lylly said.

"It's good to see you too," Siding said. "But you want something don't you?" she grinned. "And I reckon I know what it is."

Lylly laughed. "Got me," he said.

"I think she's come much further out than I thought she would."

"In only three weeks or less?"

"Oh yes. I think she was already trying to climb up the walls of the well before we got to her. I think she was trying to get out but didn't know how."

"But will she revert?" That was the big question. "Now he's got her back."

"You know what? I don't know. When we had her at the lodge there was none of the Bruno this and Bruno that, Bruno is cleverer than you, Bruno will come and get me. She was already at the silent stage. She was already trying to think her way out. And I reckon she's been doing that for quite a while. She knows Bruno did unspeakable things to her, and I think she realises that – she wasn't just telling me all that because she knows that's what I want to hear from her. In my opinion Bruno was already not her guide and lodestar. And is no longer. And maybe, just maybe, never will be again." She held up her unbandaged left hand and crossed the first two fingers.

"And that's good?"

"Oh yes that's good. If you asked me with anyone else I've cared for whether they would revert after only three weeks out of the well, I'd say yes, absolutely definitely they'd revert. We just wouldn't have had long enough with them to counter the damage. But with this one, I'm not so sure. To be honest I just don't know." Siding paused. "But there was one thing she said. I didn't get it. Didn't understand. Then it struck me it might be a quote and I looked it up."

"What did she say?"

"She whispered to the wall. For some time she wouldn't look at me and would talk only to the wall. But I heard it. She whispered: 'He was the poor benefit of a bewitching minute'"

"She said that? He meaning Bruno? She said 'Bruno was the poor benefit of a bewitching minute?' Isn't that good? It sounds dismissive?"

"It's from a Jacobean tragedy. Full of dark and danger where nobody's good. So maybe good, yes. It's also good that she didn't want me to hear. She's not ready to admit anything to outsiders yet. But she is internalising it all. I think she's moving towards perspective. That's where we need her to be."

"So there is hope?"

It sounded to Lylly that Sylvie might, just, be seeing Bruno for what he was. His bewitching had only one outcome, a poor benefit.

Siding opened both hands to show the palms, one damaged.

"Hope yes. That quote shows she's aware of where she's been. She's seeing herself there and realises to a degree what was happening. Whether the hope is real or actual, I've no idea." She stopped. "But…"

"Yes?"

"This is only a guess, based on no more than my paltry instinct – and I hate doing that – but I think—" she put a stress on the word "—that she may be able to pretend. She may pretend, may try to convince Bruno that she's his again. But that's just a hope, and anyway the real danger is if it doesn't fool Bruno."

"What if he isn't fooled?"

"Then I fear the worst."

"Which is?"

"Bruno will transfer his need for human sacrifice from the mother to the daughter."

"You think that's the root to Bruno? Human sacrifice?" Lylly had come to the same conclusion himself.

"I do. I talked to Sylvie for as many hours as she could stand. Meaning, I got her to talk to me for as many hours as she could stand. I got a real feel for Bruno."

"You think he's fascinated by the idea – and possibly the actuality – of human sacrifice, isn't he?"

"Yes I think that's the key. I think he sees it as some kind of key to the universe. Along with old forgotten gods and certain mathematical constants and symbols. Pi especially."

That was a rum old combo, Lylly thought, human sacrifice, long-gone gods, and the ratio between a circle's circumference and its diameter. It was a bit more than that, he recognised. It was the way pi kept popping up in unlikely places – in Planck's Constant for one – that made it so mysterious and attractive for Bruno. Maybe for Bruno pi was the conductor of the orchestra that played the music of the spheres.

"So unless we get her out quick, she's either going to spend months and years pretending to be whatever Bruno thinks she is and wants her to be, or she's going to get burnt at the stake." Harsh but true, he thought.

"Harsh but true," professor Siding said. "And probably the sacrificing will come inevitably sooner or later as Bruno tires of her, even if he's still convinced she's not pretending."

Professor Siding also told Lylly she'd learnt from Sylvie that Bruno's most trusted disciple, his main lieutenant, was the blonde crop-haired German woman. She was known as Heidi.

"She's despicable," Siding said. "What she did to Sylvie."

But she wouldn't tell Lylly any more.

Siding sighed and looked away from Lylly through the window. Not far away the mountains loomed like a wall of the world. It seemed a metaphor for their situation: surrounded and no way out.

"You have to find her," she said over her shoulder. "You don't have much time."

Lylly was silent for most of the helicopter trip back to the Stahl chateau.

31

MERCI STAHL HAD TOLD Lylly he could stay at the chateau as long as he liked. She had given him a suite of rooms on the first floor in the left side wing. He had dinner with Koggs and Merci then went to bed early.

He didn't think they'd find out anything useful about Bruno, neither in Brest nor Marseille or Lyon. And if not, what then? He was beginning to wonder if the only realistic chance of finding Bruno was through the French police. And they hadn't found him in seven years so why should they suddenly do better? He slept badly.

It was the day of Alain Stahl's funeral. Merci knew he had wished for a small family affair. He was being buried next to his parents' graves in the village church not far from the Maginot Line fort of Fermont near Longuyon in Alsace. Merci told Lylly the fort was well-known to Alain.

"He used to explore the fort as a kid," she said, finding lost and secret ways in to the massive underground complex long before the place was opened as a tourist attraction. "It was maybe his favourite place in the whole world."

Lylly wondered why Stahl wasn't being buried in a plot in the chateau grounds. But then, who knew how long the chateau would stay in the family?

Koggs had offered to fly her up to Alsace and she had accepted the offer. Merci hadn't asked Lylly if he wanted to attend the service too, and he thought that was good, because he would have felt obliged to decline. He would have stood out like a hawthorn tree in a fig forest at an event intended for the Stahl family and close business associates of Alain Stahl. The use of Koggs's chopper meant

Merci could be back the day after, and Lylly knew that until Koggs's offer she had fretted about being away from the chateau for too long and missing any potential developments in the search for Sylvie.

In the later morning Lylly drove to Castellane to meet up with Viv, as arranged. Though neither she nor her partner had admitted they worked in some capacity for one or other of Israel's security or information-gathering services, Lylly was convinced they did. And anyway they'd more-or-less admitted that the knowledge of who Alain Stahl sold arms to, and what kind of arms, was of considerable importance to the well-being of their country.

She was before him at the café, sitting at the same table as when he'd first met her. She took off her sunglasses as he approached her table. The bottle green eyes and red hair was an arresting combination. She was wearing a mid-length black cotton skirt, sandals, and a khaki tee-shirt. A black denim jacket with the arms cut off was draped over the back of her chair.

"G'day mate," she said.

They didn't shake hands. Lilly sat down. Even more arresting for Lylly was the odd combination of broad Australianisms said with her Israeli accent.

"Have you spent time there?" he asked. "Oz," he added when he realised she had no idea which country in the world, or which part of which country in the world, he was referring to.

She laughed. "No, mate, and I couldn't tell you if I did. I learned my English by watching TV. I preferred very much the Australian soaps to American ones. I tried the English ones but there were too many strange ways of talking, you have too many dialects. I didn't know whether I should say garaaage or garridge."

"Nobody does," Lylly said and grinned. "It's odd, but nice."

Lylly could think of no reason why he shouldn't tell the Israeli agent more-or-less everything he knew. He was after all looking to get information out of her too.

"You know Alain Stahl is dead?"

"Of course." She gestured towards the TV attached to the

wall over the bar. "But we don't have any information about the circumstances nor who was responsible. So you can't 'pick my brains' about that if that was your intention mate."

"Then on this I know a lot more than you do. And it's nothing to do with weapons or arms dealing at all."

In a way it was far nastier.

She listened while he talked. The green eyes looked hard at him, assessing what he was saying. Some of what he told her she knew. Other bits were new to her. He told her about Merci Stahl and Sylvie Stahl. He told her about the Bozonian commune. He told her about Bruno Ludo, now known to be Bruno Ludovico. He told her in full about the extraction of Sylvie Stahl. He even told her about the simultaneous double rape and the pi-shaped rape scaffold. If that shocked her she didn't show it, though she did tilt her head slightly as though a thought had struck her. He ended by telling her all the details about the diversionary attack on the chateau and the storming of the mountain retreat and the recapture of Sylvie Stahl.

Of course she knew about Bruno and the commune.

"We did watch that place on several occasions. Part of learning about their lifestyle and the possible threats."

"But you didn't see the set-up we came across on the back patio of the farmhouse?"

"No. We did of course look at that place on our visits. But this structure was not there, although, strange--" she stopped as if unsure of where the sentence would take her. "Nor the bed," she finished, without following the sidetrack.

Lylly wondered why she hadn't followed the sidetrack her 'although, strange' seemed to indicate.

Maybe Bruno only set it up on particular nights, Lylly surmised, maybe at certain times of the month, such as the dark of the moon, according to whichever quasi-religion he was pulling eclectic chunks out of at the time.

"What did you make of the commune's fighting capabilities?"

"We dismissed them quite rapidly as non-professional." She shrugged as if they were insignificant and irrelevant.

"Yeah, we thought Bruno and his outfit were non-professional too, much to our cost. So you know nothing more about Bruno than I do?"

"I'm afraid not much mate. But maybe a little more. Because there is something. Have you brought your hiking clothes?" She asked.

It was so unconnected Lylly wondered if she was back on the sidetrack.

"My boots are in the car."

He was wearing lightweight fawn-coloured baggy trousers, a white polo shirt and a light jacket. They'd do as long as he had decent footwear to match the terrain.

"What do you have in mind?"

"What you said. The pi shape on the patio. There's something you should see. Strange. First I need to change."

She picked up a medium sized backpack that had been standing on the floor by her chair.

"Give me five minutes."

Lylly finished his beer while he waited. When she came back she was still wearing the khaki tee-shirt and the black denim sleeveless vest, but now wore olive-coloured combat trousers and hiking boots.

"We go in your ute please."

She got in the passenger seat and began to direct him to the Bozonian compound.

"Interesting," he said. But she just smiled at him.

Three-quarters of an hour later when they arrived at the compound she told him to go left at the first pair of gates, which were open, then go left again and go over the bridge over the stream and park in the public parking area next to the big stone barn-style B & B building outside the commune proper. He switched the engine off and looked at her with a questioning face.

"We can leave the ute here," she said. "It's not too far."

Viv took her pack and led Lylly to the far end of the parking area, which also coincided with the far end of the building. A narrow overgrown path led out of the car park under the trees. They followed the path which ran alongside the stream.

After a quarter of a mile Lylly reckoned they were directly below the point on the hillside on their left where Koggs's teams had set up their observation point, and from where they had descended on the night of the extraction. In confirmation he could see the roof and back of Bruno's building on the right on the other side of the stream.

But Viv didn't stop. She kept going for perhaps another threequarters of a mile. Lylly thought they were well past the end of the commune area, into wilder and untravelled country. She stopped and offered Lylly a drink from her pack. Then they carried on for Lylly what thought was around another quarter mile.

The path now ran right alongside the bank of the stream. Soon they came to a point where the path seemed to go no further and the way ahead was blocked by trees and unbroken undergrowth. But to their right a set of regular steppingstones had been placed in the bed of the stream. Viv stopped.

"When we started looking at this place we searched it from all angles and all sides."

More than we did, Lylly thought.

"It is standard practice. We needed to know their escape routes and any secret entry routes if it should come to it and they were more dangerous than we first thought."

She started stepping across the stream with long confident strides. Lylly followed.

"And we found this," she said.

They both rose up to the top of the shallow bank on the other side of the stream. They were in a small clearing in the thick woods. It looked like the clearing was man-made and had been cut out of the woods. A much fainter path disappeared into the trees on the far side of the clearing, seeming to turn back in the direction of the commune before it was lost to sight, obscured by trees. Some tree trunk bases were still visible, sawn off close to the ground to fashion the clearing. Some of the cut tree trunks and branches had been formed and fashioned into benches which lined the edges of the clearing.

And set in the middle of the clearing were three copies of the pi-rape-frame that Lylly had seen before behind Bruno's house at the commune. They were laid out to form three sides of a triangle right in the centre of the clearing.

The only difference as far as Lylly could see between these pi-frames and the one on Bruno's patio was these three frames were made of wood. They looked solid and sturdy. Perhaps these were intended to be permanent and the one on Bruno's patio a personal and temporary one, for his use only.

There was something else. In the centre space formed by the loose triangle of pi-frames was a wooden statue. It was larger than life-size, over two metres high, and Lylly thought it was one of the strangest and most disconcerting effigies he'd ever seen. It was a woman. Perhaps even a deity. She was carved out of wood and it seemed to have been done in a hurry. She was covered in chisel marks, nor had the wood been smoothed or sanded. But the woody roughness seemed deliberate as it augmented her immediacy. The spirit and essence, the life force, of the deity seemed to be caught in the act of emerging from the wood. She was new and fresh and urgent. Her arms were outstretched and in each hand she held a snake. The holes where her eyes were cut were staring blanks, which made her seem manic and obsessed. But the most arresting and startling thing about her was the fact that her whole body front and back, chest to shin, neck to ankle, seemed to be covered in small breasts. It was as though she was wearing a coat made of small breasts.

Perhaps an even greater shock for Lylly was the fact that the face of the statue was most definitely a representation of Sylvie's face. Just like the face on the big wood block he'd seen on the patio the night they brought Sylvie safely out of the commune.

"Any idea what this is supposed to be?" Lylly pointed to the statue.

Viv grinned at him. "I don't think you know your Bible, do you? Acts 19:28. 'Great is Diana of the Ephesians'," she quoted. "This is Diana of Ephesus. Also known as Artemis. This is how she is portrayed. But the Romans and Greeks put a civilised cloak on a much more ancient and much more evil and hungry deity. This is really Ishtar of the Babylonians."

"Ishtar?" He queried. Then he got it. Was this Merci's 'Wish-Heart'? Malapropisms are us.

"Yes Ishtar, a nasty piece of work. You don't want to be crossing her, mate."

"But evil?" Lylly wondered about the description. "Isn't she just some sort of local fertility deity, with all those breasts. Our goddess can feed the world. Her bounty overflows. She's the opposite of hungry."

"Breasts?" Viv laughed scornfully. "Have you ever seen any breasts? They're not breasts, they're bull testicles.

Lylly started. "Jesus Christ. What?"

"Not evil, you say? Not hungry? Think of all the bulls that had to be sacrificed just to cover the goddess head to toe front and back with all those testicle sacks."

Lylly looked at the statue with new eyes. It seemed that Viv was right.

"No idea why Bruno makes the connection between Ishtar and her but this horror's also got Sylvie's face."

Viv came closer. "I guess so. Why? What's the connection?"

"That exists only in Bruno's mind."

"You're probably right mate."

Lylly was standing off, giving the statue a longer appraisal.

"Looks like she's had a special coat made," he said. "She's gone down to the Ephesus equivalent of Savile Row and said bespoke me a coat festooned with as many bulls bollocks as you can fit on."

"It was Art who found out about all this shit," Viv continued. "I had no idea what was going on when we came here. I thought what the fuck, mate, just like you. But I had no idea. But

Art got into it and pinned it down. Look closely. There are no nipples. And aren't they all a little small for breasts anyway?

"Usually if you've got a fertility goddess and want to show she can feed the world you give her huge outsize breasts. Think of the Venus of Willendorf, or Rubens's Hera creating the Milky Way. These definitely aren't in that league. So no nipples and the wrong size. These are scrotal sacks, mate. Bull scrotums.

"And that makes her not a welcoming, embracing, feeding the world goddess, it makes her a hungry, greedy, rapacious and unforgiving goddess. Art didn't find out much about exactly what the Babylonians got up to worshipping this horrible thing, maybe nobody knows, but I don't think it was good."

"But this is just a statue," Lylly insisted. "They're not from real bulls." Lylly was surprised to find himself defending the goddess and her worshippers.

"I don't think that would satisfy the real Ishtar, mate. Art did find a website that suggested for the goddess's rites they had priestesses who they covered in bull's testicles like this in her honour. Or they put on a coat maybe, like you said. A coat of many bollocks. Or they might have had plain statues they covered to the same effect. And this and the originals in Babylon and Ephesus or wherever are just representations of the actual performances. But hey, it's still all bad shit."

"Babylon?" Lylly said. "You said this goddess was Babylonian?"

"Yes defo. That's her home town. Somehow it spread from Babylon to Ephesus. Maybe Alexander the Great and the successors brought her back with the conquests. Or she came on the Silk Road. Who knows, mate, but she made the trip. Then the Greeks and Roman tarted her up and toned her down into Artemis and Diana."

Something was nagging at Lylly's mind, but he couldn't pin it down.

"I think this was their sacred area," Viv said. "Art and I had no idea what it was when we found it. It was a mystery but we dismissed it as not relevant to our mission, as it didn't seem a threat to Stahl. Now I know what it is. And I am sickened."

"I think they used to watch," Lylly said, pointing to the benches.

He told her how they'd learned that Bruno had an inner circle of twenty-one followers whose activities the rest of the commune didn't know about, and if they did, didn't like.

"We were told by a member of the commune that Bruno's twenty-one followers, the inner circle known as the 'Perfects', always consisted of ten men and eleven women. Which with Bruno made up his magic twenty-two."

"Well mate I think they used to come here to practice."

As long as no one was forced, they could "practice" all they liked, Lylly thought. But with all he knew and had learnt about Bruno Ludo and his mad, sadistic and deranged world he didn't think consent was one of the options. Pi-rape-frames and now the hungry and pitiless Babylonian goddess Ishtar as well. The more they thought they understood Bruno the more helical depths they found, corkscrewing deep into depravity. It looked like Bruno wasn't faking the bits of Christianity he used, he just added in the aspects he wanted. Particularly the notion of Jesus as sacrifice. Druids, the old religion, Christianity, and Ishtar. The one thing they all seemed to have in common was the centrality of sacrifice. The only part of his pan-religious bedrock that didn't involve sacrifice was the mathematical symbol pi. Yet for all Lylly, or anyone knew, pi might involve sacrifice too. He wouldn't put it past Bruno to entangle sacrifice into it somehow. It was becoming apparent that Bruno thought that sacrifice was integral to grasping the keys to the universe.

He remembered the three-foot stump he had seen on the patio which also had Sylvie's face on it. The one that was now face-down in the stream. He wondered if that had been cut from the same tree as this effigy? He assumed it had.

Lylly had a closer look at the sculpture. The roughness of the cuts seemed to chime with the idea of an aggressive and hungry deity.

"I think this was carved with a chainsaw," he said.

He ran his hand over the surface. Attacking the wood in that way seemed more appropriate to the subject than delicately chiselling and tapping it with a mallet and chisel. The outcome would be much quicker too.

"I reckon you're right mate. They probably couldn't get her impatient spirit out of the wood quick enough."

The ripping intrusive noise of the saw coupled to the greater speed with which she would emerge from the tree trunk seemed so much more suitable to the kind of deity they now thought she was.

"The way things are created goes hand in hand with the spirit of the end result doesn't it."

"Yeah mate, it's a kind of cause and effect."

Lylly shivered. The hair on the back of his neck stood up in an instinct of ancient caution. He didn't want to imagine what had been going on here in this grove in the name of this saw-cut horror-deity. Then the nagging feeling about Babylon clicked into place inside Lylly's mind.

"Babylon, ancient Babylon, it's now in Iraq, isn't it?"

"I think it is, why?"

"Bruno was stationed in Iraq for a while."

He told her about the rumour that something had happened to Bruno while he was in Iraq.

"Supposedly he came back different."

"You think maybe he met this lady there?" She pointed to the statue.

"God knows. It's possible. He must have come across her somewhere."

"Sure. More likely in her homeland than anywhere?"

Lylly's mind was reeling. It had all seemed relatively simple all those weeks ago when he'd entered the tunnel and found Merci Stahl hanging there. Human sacrifice and strange intimidating goddesses were the last things he would have thought of to explain it all. Especially when he discovered that Alain Stahl was an arms dealer. Lylly knew his train of thought had been predictable. He is an arms dealer: he will have enemies: they might target his wife as a threat to him: simple.

But it wasn't simple. And even when he subsequently learned that Merci Stahl's daughter was in a commune, possibly brainwashed, he'd thought that it was sad, of course, and even if he wanted to help and do something about it, he still thought it was unrelated to the main problem. He never suspected that the real focus, the real danger, came not from Alain Stahl's business dealings but from the connections and plight of his step-daughter.

It was all too easy to be predictable. And the hardest thing was to think outside the box and follow the unpredictable. And that was hard because you often imagined you were being original in your thinking and imagining the unpredictable when in reality you were being just as predictable as everyone else. It was hard and it was human. But Lylly thought he'd made it harder than it need have been.

True, finding Merci Stahl pinned to the tunnel wall had strongly suggested the story of Andromeda to him. But that story belonged to the wrong mythology. A more comfortable mythology perhaps. One where there were heroes and the good people prevailed, with help from the gods. He didn't know, but he suspected that in Ishtar's mythology there were no heroes and the gods never helped anyone.

Admittedly Lylly wasn't alone in this massively erroneously conclusive train of thought and its consequences. Viv and her partner Art, the presumed experienced and professionally efficient Israeli agents, had also dismissed the commune and its leader as innocuous, if strange, and definitely not a threat to Alain Stahl. And they too had initially thought the kidnapping of Merci Stahl was somehow directly connected to Alain Stahl, his business and his potential enemies. They too had taken an assumption and worked back from there and made the facts fit.

Cause and effect was like water flowing downhill. It took the obvious and predictable route. But the actions of humans were not like that. And it was dangerous to make the assumption that they were. And Lylly had been guilty of that. It wasn't sexism, that wasn't it, he could spare himself that accusation. But if you took three people, an arms dealer, his wife and her daughter, you made assumptions, everyone did, and it would be surely fair enough to assume it was the arms dealer who might be the target of desperate and dangerous people. You'd never think the most exposed, at risk and therefore most problematic of the three was the step-daughter.

Yet there was one positive thing that Lylly had done. He could give himself that. And that was insisting – against Frank Koggs's better judgment – on tracking down the rock-climbers and getting to the bottom of their story.

If they hadn't found Rochdale and his partner they would never have got hold of the phone number of their paymaster. And in turn would never have met and talked to the two presumed Israeli agents. And it was because Viv via her drone had witnessed the kidnapping of Merci Stahl that the pieces began to fall in place and they all began to realise that the bad guys here were not some phantom enemies of Alain Stahl but the leader of this exotic commune, Bruno Ludo.

The tracking down of Rochdale and his mate changed the equation. It changed the direction of the water flowing downhill. It put them at last on the right track.

But even so Lylly didn't feel he could take any credit from that. It was just one reasonable decision taken among so many bad ones. And now even though they knew everything, especially in the presence of this monstrous deity, and could now see the chain of events that ultimately led them here, and thought they could at last understand and explain everything, Bruno was still out there ahead of them. In the end understanding didn't help you win. With Bruno gone and Sylvie with him, they were no nearer any solution. They were back to square one with more snakes than ladders.

Lylly suddenly felt deflated. They were no nearer to any real understanding of where Bruno might have gone. They were beginning to find out plenty about Bruno's past but nothing at all about his present. How do you hide twenty-two people? And a young girl who might be desperately dissembling for her life?

Viv looked at his expression. She strode over to him and pressed his face between the fingers of both hands and kissed him.

"Can we find a sandbank, do you think mate?" she said.

Lylly laughed.

They didn't find a sandbank, but what they did find, they decided, was good for them both. For a while for Lylly it drove away the dark thoughts and dispelled the pitiless hunger that the statue of Ishtar had engendered in his mind.

Later when they went their separate ways she said, "I got your number. I'll keep it. You never know," and smiled.

"Mate," he said.

32

IT WAS NOW SIX DAYS since Sylvie Stahl had been taken. At lunchtime Donna came back from Brest.

Neither she nor Koggs had nothing useful to report. There were snippets of new information but nothing that helped them understand where Bruno Ludo might be hiding.

"All we got was this rumour about Iraq. No details. Even if they knew something the S.O.Bs weren't talking," Koggs said. "Should've known they'd close ranks. I'd've done the same."

He'd thought he'd get the same reception at the barracks in Marseille as he'd received in Lyon, but had travelled there that day all the same.

"So I guess we're in the hands of the ministry now."

One thing that had emerged from Donna's conversations with Bruno's former fellow academics in Brest was the confirmation that Bruno Ludovico did definitely have a half brother or some kind of relation who might be, or was probably, German. Also Bruno's name was not originally Ludovico. His patronymic was Neuville. His father was Patrice Neuville, a customs official. One former colleague claimed Bruno had changed his surname to Ludovico – his mother's name - as soon as his father died, which was while Bruno was still a teenager. And his father's death had been something of a "cause celebre" according to the lecturer.

But beyond that the academics couldn't say much about Bruno Ludovico's background. And nothing at all about his career after he left the college. As to why he left, all she heard was that there were rumours of strange beliefs which led to even stranger actions, and perhaps dead cats and a fixation with the π symbol. But they already knew that.

In concert with Merci – because he thought together their French might be up to it – Lylly searched the internet for anything they could find on both Bruno Ludovico and Patrice Neuville and the 'cause celebre'.

All they got on Ludovico were several of the papers he had authored while at the university. Lylly felt he ought to try to read them but couldn't face it. In any case they all seemed to be on rediscovering or factually pinning down aspects of the religious practices of the old gods, Druids and others.

One paper on the Druids had the subtitle <Were The Romans Right?>. A second was titled <Babylon - The Origin Of All Gods?>. A third was <The Silk Road - Highway Of Goods And Gods?>. Bruno obviously liked questions in his titles. In the end Lylly agreed with Merci that reading the Asterix comics would get them closer to Bruno's whereabouts than wading through his academic writings.

As regards Patrice Neuville, things were more interesting, though if anything less useful.

It had been a 'cause celebre' as the lecturer had claimed. Bruno's father had been a customs officer, most latterly at the customs station on the Eurostar terminal at Paris Nord rail station. He had been there since not long after the Channel Tunnel opened. One afternoon he had not turned up for the night shift and had not been seen since. Bruno himself had been at school at the time on the day.

"Interesting, but not particularly useful," Merci said.

Lylly agreed.

It seemed it was immediately after his father's disappearance, and assumed death, that Bruno had changed his name. He'd been taken in by a foster family and had completed his schooling. He'd then become an academic, and they more-or-less knew his career from there.

It was around two-thirty in the morning that same night that Camo Lylly suddenly sat up in bed and switched on the bedside light. In a semi-dreaming state his part sleeping, part waking mind had put two and two together and came up with three and a half. But even an ill-fitting and precarious three and a half was better than the zero they had.

He didn't tell anyone. It might be nothing, no more than a weird coincidence. As soon as light came he set off by himself in his car. He told no one where he was going.

He headed for the hotel overlooking the entrance to the Gorge du Verdon. When he got there he managed to peek over the receptionist's shoulder as she ran through the bookings in the computer as he pretended to be unsure as which day he wanted to stay. He looked ahead. It was as he hoped. The booking he was looking for was in two days' time. He booked himself in for the same day.

On his way back he called in at a Briconaut diy megastore to buy the necessary equipment.

In the evening Frank Koggs attempted to pull together what they knew over dinner. Which was not much. There was Donna's information about a possible half-brother who might be German. And there was Koggs's evidence, no more than a rumour, about something that had happened to Bruno in Iraq. Koggs was still angry about the reception he'd received from his fellow military men.

"They don't care what the bastard's done, just so long as it don't stain the unit's good name. And the only way it don't stain the unit's reputation is if it don't get out and no one knows about it. So it don't get out. So even if they know all about anything bad he's done when he was in the unit they're not going to publicise it, and they're not going to tell. Even a fellow soldier gets the stone wall. If I had personal or longstanding contacts with 'em, it'd be different, they'd know they could trust me and they'd tell me. But I don't."

So now, the colonel said, as for finding Bruno, "Sorry but we got to wait for the police to do their job. The ministry will let me know as soon as." He shrugged as if to say that was that.

Merci stared at him then turned and walked out of the dining room, slamming the door.

Lylly understood. Her action was unfair, of course. But he

knew she blamed Koggs for Sylvie's recapture. She did not blame him for Alain's death in any way. There was nothing he could have done about that. But calling for the reinforcements from Gap had been a terrible mistake. But Koggs knew that. Which was why, Lylly knew, he was trying to find Bruno now, instead of abandoning the job and taking on new work. He wanted to undo what he had done. Koggs would be hurting more than any of them, even Merci in a way. He just didn't show it.

Next day Lylly was due to head for the gorge hotel. As before he didn't tell anyone. Maybe in a way he didn't want his idea to be laughed at.

He put all his hiking equipment in the car. He wanted it to look like he was trekking the GR4 long-distance path. He stowed his two trekking poles as well, unscrewed into their three sections and with the normal hiking tips in place, and hid the Seecamp .32 back in its hiding place inside the spare wheel. The special release key was in his pocket.

Even though he left early, so as not to have to answer any questions, there was no need to be there early, but he felt the need for his cover plan to seem as authentic as possible. So he set off in the car for the hotel. He was already wearing all his walking gear apart from his boots. He left the car in the hotel car park, changed into his boots, and descended into the gorge without first checking in to the hotel. He filled up his two one-litre water bottles at the hotel's outside tap.

He'd already checked his torch was working, and this time he also borrowed a back-up torch from the chateau household.

He came down through the trees to the water level. Then he ascended the steps to the first tunnel. He dug out his headtorch and walked through the tunnel.

When he came out the other side, instead of carrying on along the path to the next tunnel, he cut down through the trees, down the steep slope, and descended to the river. He spent some hours just sitting on a large rock in mid-stream. The Verdon river gurgled, wallowed and spluttered past the rock. He looked up and watched the vultures. Later he rejoined the path and passed through the second tunnel. Some time later he retraced his steps, went back through the tunnel and descended to the same large midstream rock again between the two tunnels. He sat there watching the vultures and thinking. Sometimes it all seemed to fall into place. Then other times it seemed farfetched and ridiculous.

Eventually towards the end of the afternoon he thought the time was right. He put his heavy pack on and ran up the slope the thirty metres from the water's edge to the path. He wanted to raise a sweat and get some dust and grime on his face and neck. Then he headed out of the gorge back up the slope towards the hotel. He wanted to arrive at the hotel looking like he'd been walking the trail all day.

"I have a reservation," he said at the check in desk at the hotel above the gorge.

He had a shower in his room, and changed into fresh clothes. Then around dinner time he waited till he thought the time was right.

In the dining room he saw him sitting alone at a table set for two. He asked the waiter to take him over to the same table.

"Hello Mr Kellner," he said. "Do you mind if I join you?"

33

LOUIS KELLNER LOOKED SURPRISED but immediately smiled and stood up, extending his hand.

"Of course," he said. "Camo Lylly it is very good to see you again."

Lylly shook Kellner's hand and sat down opposite him at the table.

"Which way are you headed?" Lylly asked agreeably. "Digne or Draguignan?"

"I am on my way north to the clinic in Digne," Kellner said. "It'll be a week or ten days there, then back here again. I'm not sure though. Sometimes I have to go direct and avoid stopping the night. And you? Which way are you going?"

Lylly thought he was talking too much. He couldn't quite put his finger on why. Kellner was clearly surprised to see him, but there was something else, something underlying Kellner's normally smooth manner that indicated a certain amount of flustered unsettledness.

"Me?" he responded. "I'm heading back the other way on GR4 than when we met last. I got to the Rhone. Took a break. Then thought I'd do the trail again, heading back the other way. Funnily enough I actually came through the long hidden tunnel this afternoon."

The unsettled look flashed across Kellner's face again.

"You must have heard what happened, what I found, when I went through the tunnel last time? In fact if you recall it was at your suggestion I went through the tunnel that day." Lylly almost used the word "insistence" which would have been more accurate but let it go; "suggestion" would do for now.

"Yes of course. Did I really? That was fortuitous. How terrible. It was all over the local news. The poor woman, pinned up like that naked. In fact I'd be fascinated to hear all about it from yourself. I don't think the authorities have got to the bottom of it yet?"

Got you, Lylly thought. The fact that it was him who'd discovered Merci Stahl pinned to the wall had not been publicised. Nor had anything been published about the position Merci Stahl was in when she was found. This was at the express request of the police. And Lylly had obeyed that request. Yet Louis Kellner knew all about it. He hoped he sounded calm as he carried on, but inside his heart was accelerating like a rollercoaster on the downhill section.

"Sorry, no idea about that. I've been away." He tried to sound not particularly interested.

Lylly wondered if Kellner would bring up the gunfight at the Stahl chateau, which wasn't far away at all, and which also had been 'all over the local news'. And he couldn't pretend he hadn't heard about the search for Bruno Ludovico since that was all over the national news.

Before he spoke Lylly reminded himself that if he had been out of the area as he claimed he would most likely know nothing about the gunfight at the Stahl chateau and the death of Alain Stahl. He might have seen something about the hunt for Bruno Ludovico on the national news but wouldn't have thought it had any significance or any connection to the woman in the tunnel.

"But yes of course, I'll tell you what happened."

So he did. It was part true. All the stuff about the tunnel and the discovery of Merci Stahl he related as it really happened. But he said nothing of finding out who she was and the job as a shepherd-bodyguard. He just said the last time he had seen her was when she was loaded into the rescue helicopter outside the tunnel. He noted how Kellner tried to feign astonishment when Lylly descried how he'd found "the woman" and how she was pinned in a star-shape to the wall. But Lylly wasn't convinced.

He did say that he had been interviewed by the police – that was most likely anyway. But then he implied he had returned to the gorge and had carried on his trek to the Rhone. He hinted he had stayed with friends in the Rhone valley (without making it a definite claim) then had decided to retrace his steps along GR4 and so had ended up at the hotel again.

"Absolutely fascinating," Kellner said. "Did you wonder why? What had happened? How did the woman get there? Terrible."

"Of course I wondered. It was the most bizarre thing I've ever seen. As to the why and wherefore I've no idea. I don't think that part made the news or perhaps I'd have seen something about it."

"No. No I don't think it did. I think I would have seen it. Most odd. It was good then you came along when you did I think."

Lylly glanced at him but it seemed that Kellner had said this without any hint of irony.

"As I recall it was only down to you I did go that way. I had no idea it existed till you told me."

That seemed to throw Kellner for the final time. He didn't want to talk about it any more it seemed. Maybe he realised he'd made a mistake. He hurried through the rest of his dinner then abruptly stood up.

"So good to meet you again, Camo. But I'm up and away early in the morning – I have to get on the road at six." He smiled in a kind of apology. "A lot of paperwork to do before I have appointments with clients."

He extended his hand as Lylly also stood up. Lylly shook it.

"And remember. If you need any 'work' done –" he put a stress on the word "--You know who to call and where to find me." He turned and left the dining room. Lylly sat down again, pondering his next move and how it would go.

34

AT FIVE-FORTY-FIVE THE NEXT morning Lylly stood in his hiking gear and boots next to his car boot in the car park at the rear of the hotel. He had already checked out and paid his bill the night before. His backpack with the necessary equipment was already on his back. Even at that early hour it was fully light in midsummer.

He looked around, then opened the boot. Carefully and surreptitiously he deflated all the air in the spare tyre and used the special tool to click open the Seecamp's hiding place. He took the gun and put it in a pocket.

He had already noticed Kellner's black Mercedes A-Class saloon parked on the edge of the car park by a thick fig tree. Lylly disappeared behind the tree and sat on a rock to wait.

At exactly six o'clock Louis Kellner emerged from the back door of the hotel. He was dressed in a smart charcoal business suit with black lace-up shoes with a delicate silky shine. He was carrying an overnight case and a briefcase. He clicked open the Mercedes boot with the key fob. He placed the case and briefcase inside the boot and closed the lid. He had just opened the driver's door when Lylly stepped out from hiding behind the tree and pushed his .32 into the side of Kellner's neck.

"We're going for a little walk," Lylly said in a low voice, almost a whisper. "Then we're going to have a talk. Come as you are."

It seemed to Lylly that in some deep meta-conscious way Louis Kellner had been expecting this to happen, or something like it. He didn't say anything or try to scream or look like he was contemplating making a run for it, or pondering whether to attempt to shift or fight off Lylly's weapon. He just stood there immobile and silent.

"Head downhill," Lylly said.

He shifted the gun to the side of Kellner's midriff and walked alongside him. There was no one about, and even if anyone had seen them they would have thought nothing of it, except maybe the two men were getting a little intimate with each other, but hey, who said they couldn't?

It was still a surprise to Lylly that Kellner didn't try to protest or seek to evade his instructions. In a strange way, unlike Hamlet's mother he was protesting too little. Nevertheless, they proceeded down the trail to the river level and up into the first tunnel.

All Kellner said as they climbed up the steps to the tunnel portal was "I'm not dressed for a hike."

"You'll do," Lylly said.

In this way they penetrated deep into the gorge. And so they came, eventually, to the place that Lylly wanted to take him. The entrance to the long hidden, forbidden tunnel. And he wanted him to see what was in there.

As they entered the tunnel Lylly suddenly stepped behind Kellner and took his neck from behind with both hands in the vicelike angular twisting grip he'd been taught by the Dog Island instructor in the Legion. Kellner grunted and fell unconscious in a few seconds. Lylly took both feet and dragged him on his back fifty yards into the tunnel.

He stopped at the point where the light from his headtorch showed four neat holes had been bored into the rock of the tunnel wall. It was the place where Merci Stahl had been pinned to the wall as a human sacrifice.

Lylly lowered his backpack to the ground and took out the tools he needed. He'd found everything he needed at the Briconaut diy megastore. None of it was as fancy or as expensive looking as the original climbing versions, but these construction versions would do the same job. First he took a hammer and tapped four expansion bolts into the four holes. Then he rotated the heads with a spanner so the sheaths of the bolts tightened against the holes. He tested them. They were rock solid. Then he tied four short lengths of climbing rope through the eyerings on the head of each expansion bolt.

Then he untied Kellner's shoes and took them off. Then he lifted up the unconscious form of Louis Kellner and leaned him against the wall between the bolts, with two bolts on either side of him. Then he stretched out Kellner's arms and legs and tied them to the short lengths of climbing rope.

Louis Kellner was now pinned and spread-eagled against the tunnel wall exactly as Merci Stahl had been some weeks before when Lylly had found her.

Lylly took Kellner's shoes and walked to the tunnel opening. On one side of the flat area by the tunnel mouth was the top of a huge scree that dropped all the way down to the river. This was the outfall of the tons of rock and debris extracted when digging the tunnel. It was made up of big boulders, small rocks and various sizes of gravel and a mass of rock dust and debris.

He drew his arm back and was going to throw the shoes down the scree. Then, a little surprised at himself, he lowered his arm, then descended twenty metres down the middle of the scree and placed the shoes together on a prominent rock. He made sure they were secure and wouldn't fall any further. Then he climbed back up the scree to the top and went back in the tunnel and waited for Kellner to wake up. It didn't take long.

Kellner woke and immediately realised where he was and the position he was in.

"No!" he said and pulled against the restraining ropes with both arms, but strangely he didn't seem surprised.

Lylly watched him with casual interest. Kellner wasn't going anywhere.

"You're Bruno Ludovico's half-brother, aren't you?" Lylly said.

Kellner looked first as if he would try to deny it. But he gave it up and just sighed instead.

"Not only are you related to him, you know everything about him. Including his little peccadillos, especially his desire for and fascination with human sacrifice."

Kellner looked panic stricken, as though his inner being had been exposed and all the world could see inside, and see inside for what he was, and judged him, and found him wanting.

"And not only that, you deliberately tried to send me into this hidden tunnel that day, didn't you? That's because you knew exactly what I'd find here. But let's be charitable. You sent me in here because you wanted to save her life."

Kellner didn't argue. He didn't say anything, but gave a tiny nod.

"But how did you know?" Kellner wanted enlightenment. "What made you come and find me?"

"Your first name is Louis – which I'd imagine is not that common in Germany, especially compared with the German form Ludwig. Bruno's mother's name is Ludovico. It took me too long to get it, I admit it. But Ludovico while a relatively common Italian surname is also the Latin for Louis, give or take an inflection.

"It just seemed too big a coincidence. Louis and Ludovico, two names both meaning the same. Louis, Luigi, Ludwig, Luis, Ludovico, Ludovicus, they're all Louis. And on top of that was the fact that you deliberately sent me into the tunnel to find Merci Stahl. You knew she would be in there, pinned up."

"I did not know that," Kellner persisted. "I—"

"I think you knew all right," Lylly interrupted. "You mentioned it last night. No one but me and the police knew that. And if not actually knowing, you suspected it was highly likely. You know how Bruno operates. You know all about Bruno's fascination with human sacrifice as well as his weird reverence for pi. You knew she'd be bound to be pinned like that. He probably says Ishtar tells him to do it.

"You admitted as much last night at dinner before you realised your mistake and rushed off. You knew stuff you shouldn't know. Any road, you know she'd be in there, left there to die by Bruno. As close to the ancestors as he can get in these parts."

"Yes, yes," Kellner insisted, suddenly changing tack. "I knew.

I knew it would be horrible. He's insane. I wanted to rescue her. He comes to my surgery sometimes for check ups. He told me in great detail what he was planning. The who and the where and the how. And the day. He said he was going to take advantage of the chaos and disruptions on the day of the military exercise."

"Did he tell you why? Why Merci Stahl?" Lylly hoped Kellner might be able to give him an insight into Bruno's mind. Or at least bolster his suspicions.

Kellner heaved a sigh. "Bruno has created a religion. He believes there are certain keys to the universe that he is the first to discern. He is certain that certain old religions, or aspects of them, hold lost truths. Including--"

"Human sacrifice?"

"Yes that. It had to be the mother, otherwise there is no insight to the universe. He believes you have to break the connection between mother and daughter. He believes spiritual benefits are divinely given to the one that breaks that bond. I wanted to stop him. I told you."

It was good to have his suspicions finally confirmed, Lylly thought.

"How about pi?"

"That too. His beliefs combine the low and the elevated. The base and the intellectual. I don't know how it works but he believes that human sacrifice combined with pi will somehow raise him to a higher plane."

"What about Ishtar? What's she got on him?"

Kellner reacted with sharply indrawn breath and shook his head. "Bad," he said.

Lylly told Kellner about the effigy he had found in the secret grove beyond the commune.

"I did not know about that place. But you're right," Kellner said. "She talks to him."

Kellner said that Ishtar appeared to Bruno while he was stationed with the French Army in Iraq.

"She spoke to him in a dream. But he said it wasn't a dream.

He says he was awake and she came to him. A vision then. She tells him what to do ever since that time."

"Strange bedfellows," Lylly mused, trying to see the connection between all the strands. But couldn't.

Kellner sighed. "You can let me go, now."

"Yet, it was still a huge gamble," Lylly said. "Wasn't it? You might have got me interested in taking the tunnel route instead of going the long way round. But you'd have no idea whether I would or did actually take the tunnel. For all you knew I could have changed my mind at the entrance and backed off.

"What was your back up plan then? What was your plan B? Did you have one? Were you going to rescue her yourself? I don't think so. You're too scared to act openly against Bruno. What's he got on you?"

Kellner didn't reply. Lylly guessed that attempting to aim Lylly in the direction of the tunnel had been the limit of his desire or ability to thwart Bruno's plans. He understood that Kellner could in no way countenance Bruno becoming aware that he, Kellner, had been indirectly responsible for Merci Stahl's rescue.

Lylly sat down on the ground in front of Kellner. He placed his head torch to one side of them and angled it upwards between them and then delved in his backpack and dug out the other torch. He placed that on the ground on the other side of them, also angled upwards. Now each could see the other without being blinded.

"Give me the background," Lylly said. Connect it up."

Kellner sighed deeply. Lylly had a feeling he wanted to talk.

"My mother was Gabriella Ludovica. She was also Bruno's mother. Bruno is two years older than me. She had Bruno with Neuville before she met my father Klaus Kellner. She and Neuville met on holiday in Rome. He was a cruel man. He beat her. He left her as soon as the child was born and took the baby back with him to France. She did not know where they went.

"When I was born she wanted to give me a name that would remind her of the boy she lost, the son she had borne who she would never see again. She couldn't guarantee I would end up with the same surname as her, if she married. But I would always have the Ludovico first name, Louis. She wanted my name to be the French version not Ludwig in recognition of the fact the father was French."

"And you went looking for Bruno didn't you?"

Kellner hesitated. "Yes. Yes. I sought him out. Before she died my mother asked me to find him. I followed him to Brittany. I was surprised and pleased that he had taken my mother's surname. But I fell under his spell. I tried to break away. But could not. Bruno is very powerful, very compelling, very charismatic. He can be astonishing to listen to. Very convincing. It sickens me, but I became a follower, one of the Perfects."

"Then how did you escape? How did you get away?" Lylly couldn't see Bruno voluntarily letting followers go.

"Who said I got away?"

It took a while before Lylly realised what Kellner was saying. Then he got it. Kellner had become one of the Perfects, perhaps the only member of the Perfects who operated outside the commune. There must be something advantageous in that arrangement for Bruno.

"You know, don't you, that Bruno killed his father?"

For some reason that had never occurred to Lylly.

"Yes," Kellner continued. "That is one thing I am not sorry about. He was an evil man."

"And Bruno isn't?"

"Not then perhaps, as a teenager. He hit him with a garden spade and buried him by night under the flagstones of his patio. Then went to school. He told me he thought it was probable that his father was only unconscious and not yet dead, badly hurt maybe but still alive when he buried him. He laughed about it."

"So where is Bruno now?"

That was it, Lylly thought. That's what it's all come down to. This was the question that mattered. Only this now, in the dark in this hidden tunnel. Everything that had happened came down to this.

Kellner was silent. In a way Lylly took this more as a refusal to answer than an inability to say from not knowing. Kellner knew.

"All right. Fair enough. Didn't think you'd tell me. Enough said. Time to go," Lylly said, reaching for his backpack and standing up.

"Tell you what. I'll leave a water bottle by your feet. You should get to the point where it becomes the centre of your world. In the only universe you've got."

He took out a one and a half litre plastic bottle of mineral water from his backpack. He wiped it with a wet wipe to remove any fingerprints and placed the bottle upright between Kellner's outstretched feet.

Strangely, it was the wiping of the fingerprints that seemed to finally bring home to Kellner that his situation was dire and Lylly was serious.

Kellner screamed. It was both desperate and incredulous at the same time, as though he could not believe what was happening to him. His chest heaved as he inhaled and then let out another huge scream.

"That's fine by me, make as much noise as you like. No one'll hear you. Maybe it's one of the reasons Bruno chose here. Maybe this is as good as it gets for getting as close to the ancestors as possible too? But who the fuck knows. But by all means carry on. It'll probably tire you out quicker. And certainly make you thirstier. You as a medical man should know that."

Lylly shuffled on his backpack. He took his walking poles.

"So long," he said and started walking back to the tunnel entrance. He flicked the headtorch on to illuminate the floor in front of him. Then he stopped.

"Strange, isn't it," he said. "I was glad to meet you. I thought you were a good man. Well, live and learn." He turned and walked on.

Kellner screamed again. And again.

It was as Lylly was just nearing the light at the end of the tunnel fifty metres away that he heard Kellner say something different. It was a faint whisper.

"Spain," he said. That's what it sounded like. Then again it could have been "Pain."

Lylly turned and walked slowly back to the spreadeagled form pinned to the wall. He stood in front of Kellner and leaned on a walking pole. He shone his headtorch directly at him. Kellner tried to shy and turn his head away and closed his eyes. Lylly reached down and took a drink from the water bottle. Kellner was breathing heavily, his chest heaving with the effort.

"Sorry, didn't hear you," Lylly said. "'Pain' was it?"

Kellner carried on with the heaving breaths for a moment. Then suddenly fell silent. There was total silence in the tunnel. This is it, Lylly thought. This is why we're here. He realised they were both holding their breath.

"He's in Spain," Kellner hissed finally, letting his breath out with a huge sigh. He sagged down as far as he could go against the restraining ropes.

35

"THE DESFILADERO. HE'S HIDING in the Desfiladero." At last Louis Kellner's fear of being left hanging in the dark tunnel overcame his fear of his half-brother.

"Desfiladero? That just means 'defile' in English. I need more than that. Which Desfiladero? Where? I know several 'desfiladeros'."

"That's what it's called," Kellner panted. "It's the Desfiladero de Despeñaperros. They just call it the Desfiladero. The 'Defile' as you say."

"Despeñaperros? Ok. What's there?" Lylly asked. He knew the name. Everyone in the Legion knew that name. "Apart from the site of Navas de Tolosa."

But Kellner looked blank at the reference.

"It's a battle. But what's there for Bruno?"

Lylly cut Kellner free. He collapsed on the floor. He was panting and sobbing. Lylly had one of his walking poles ready, now with the knife attached. While Kellner lay on the tunnel floor sobbing and panting Lylly removed the ropes and expansion bolts from the wall. He stowed them in his backpack.

Listening to him Lylly detected a feeling of outraged innocence emanating from Kellner. As though this was all a supreme injustice.

"I tried to save her," he panted. "I wanted to stop it. I sent you in after her."

"Not enough," Lylly said. "I might have changed my mind and you had no back up plan. She would have died."

He saw Kellner about to reach for the water bottle and picked it up out of his reach.

"Please," Kellner said.

"Not yet. What's in the Desfiladero de Despeñaperros?" Lylly repeated for the third time, impatient, ready to string Kellner up again. "What's there for Bruno to hide in?"

Kellner sighed and nodded, breathless, as though he was trying to help, but yet couldn't.

In fact Lylly did know where the area was. Lylly knew it was a remote area, now a national park, on the border between Castile and Andalusia, set in the rugged rolling sierras in the wild country of south-central Spain where the terrain opened up and plunged down suddenly from the three thousand foot high Sierra Madrona range at its eastern edge into a deep and strange canyon. This defile – a gash in the earth's surface - was centred on where the Rio Despeñaperros coming in from the north had chiselled vertically down into the sierra and through to the other side.

"There's some old buildings there. Ruins. Maybe repaired, I don't know. Right at the bottom. A convent," Kellner said.

Between sobs and heavy breaths and pleading for water from Kellner and threats from Lylly he learned that deep towards the bottom of the Desfiladero de Despeñaperros gash there was an old ruined monastery or convent, Kellner didn't know which, with a farm complex and outbuildings and haciendas that had been abandoned long ago.

Now it had been taken over and occupied by an unofficial and unrecognised Christian sect that called themselves the Maria Magdalenas, or just the Magdas, who derived their modus operandi, their total being and rationale from the unjust treatment they perceived that history and the early Christian fathers had meted out to Mary Magdalene, who they, the Magdas, considered to be the first disciple.

"The leader, always known as the Maria, owes Bruno some kind of debt. I do not know what. He has gone there. She will give him sanctuary. All of them."

"Good enough," Lylly said. He laid the two-thirds full water bottle by Kellner's feet. He donned his backpack and set off for the tunnel mouth. Behind him he heard Kellner greedily gulping the water.

"If you want your shoes," he called back, "They're down on the scree by the entrance that falls down to the river. It won't be nice but you can get them all right." Then he left him.

It took Lylly scarcely an hour to return to his car at the hotel car park. He ran most of the way.

He drove back to the Stahl chateau. He saw Kogg's helicopter was still on the tennis courts. In the hall he looked through the double doors and saw all the principals were sitting round the table in the breakfast room: Merci, Koggs, Donna and Todd.

He stood in the doorway, still wearing his hiking gear and boots.

"Going somewhere son?" Koggs said. "Good idea. Wondered where you were. Get some space. Find peace. Can the mental crap."

"He's in Spain," Lylly said.

36

THAT DAY IN THE LATE MORNING, on the ninth day since Sylvie had been taken, they had their final conference at the Stahl chateau seated round the dining table.

They'd all been looking up the Desfiladero de Despeñaperros on various map apps on tablets and laptops as soon as Lylly mentioned it.

They discovered the Despeñaperros Defile is a natural wonder of Spain. It lies 160 miles south of Madrid near and between the towns of La Carolina in the south and Almuradiel to the north. The old main road to the south from Madrid used to snake through it, dropping nearly a thousand metres down in three kilometres to the stream at the bottom from the small town of Santa Elena before climbing and winding the same height up the other side. Wild and empty uncultivated country stretched away up the slopes and terraces. Best access down into the defile seemed to be via several tracks and b-roads from Santa Elena on the edge of the drop on the south side.

Somewhere in this jagged depression in the earth was the old convent.

The search for information on the Desfiladero de Despeñaperros came after Lylly told his story.

He started the tale way back on his first attempt to walk the GR4 trail. How he'd approached the Gorge de Verdon a day out of Castellane and spent the night in the hotel overlooking the gorge entrance. What he'd originally assumed was a chance meeting with a German surgeon named Louis Kellner in a crowded hotel restaurant he now knew was not random, he told them. The surgeon had deliberately sought out the only person in the hotel who seemed to be hiking into the gorge on the morrow.

"His first name is Louis," Lylly said.

There were blank looks round the table at this. So what the looks said, you've told us that already?

"Bruno's full surname is Ludovico," Lylly explained. "The Latin for Louis is Ludovicus."

That got them. Lylly had their full focus.

"Louis and Ludovico. The same name. It seemed too big a coincidence to me. And we knew that Bruno had a German half-brother, thanks to Donna's enquiries at Brest. But it didn't hit me at first, obviously. It took a long while for it to sink in."

"None of us got it, son," Koggs growled.

Lylly related how he suddenly hit on the coincidence in the two names in the early hours of the morning two days previously.

"I didn't dare say anything to you," he said. "Sorry Merci. I thought it couldn't be true. We were desperate and I may have been clutching at straws. I had no idea. But I had to check it out."

He said it was only talking to Kellner over dinner the previous night that he finally became convinced he was on the right lines.

"He was so shifty. At first too breezy and talkative, as though I was a surprise and unwelcome revisit, a shocking embodiment and manifestation of a guilty conscience. He made a verbal slip, indicating he knew something there was no way he should have known, then suddenly he couldn't get away from me quick enough. I think that was because he knew Merci hadn't died, but didn't know for certain if I was the one who had rescued her. It wasn't in the news. It all got too confusing for him and he wanted out. I don't think he wanted to talk about it or even think about it anymore. Bruno scares the shit out of him."

"You realise you'd be under arrest now if you'd been wrong?" Koggs said. "You'd be facing a charge and a trial and maybe a lengthy jail sentence for assault and battery on an innocent person. Maybe attempted murder."

"That did occur to me. My word against his. There were no

witnesses. But in any case the more I thought about it the more it seemed that he had definitely tried to direct me into the hidden tunnel. He had wanted to thwart Bruno but didn't know how. Or maybe in reality just half-thwart him. Bruno is a fearsome man. His sincere belief in quasi-religious mumbo-jumbo plus military training is a bad combo – as we know to our cost."

He saw Merci nodding at that.

"And I don't think Kellner dared do much against him. Maybe in this instance for Louis Kellner his Hippocratic oath finally overcame his fear of Bruno. So I was just the half-best available, least worst option. Maybe it all occurred to him the moment he saw my hiking boots. Either way it was a chance meeting he could use, or make use of to a certain extent, with no risk of any comeback on him from Bruno. And in the end if I didn't take the long tunnel, he could console his conscience with the thought that at least he'd tried.

"And of course obviously he never knew about the Israeli agents and their drone. Nor the rockclimbers they paid to watch the tunnel.

"I think his entire world revolves round Bruno Ludo. Trying to steer me into the hidden tunnel was the best – and only thing - he was prepared to do. He could do no more than that. I don't think we ought to judge him harshly, really."

"How d'you get him to talk?" Donna asked. "You go on a little hike together?" indicating his outfit.

"Ah. Yes," Lylly said. "In a way."

He told them about ambushing Kellner in the car park and forcing him to trek at gunpoint into the tunnel dressed only in his business suit and smart shiny-black street shoes.

He told them how he'd strung Kellner up in exactly the same way and in exactly the same place as Merci had been left. He heard Merci draw in a rapid breath and watched her place a hand over her mouth.

"He admitted everything. The Louis-Ludovico connection. The fact that they are half-brothers. The story of his and Bruno's mum. And the fact that he is the only member of Bruno's 'Perfects' who's allowed to operate outside the group. I got the whole story."

Lylly was beginning to think of Bruno's Perfects as the 'Prefects', just like the woman in the commune said. They seemed exactly like a bunch of mindless school enforcers making everyone else abide by rules they did not adhere to themselves. But he thought if he switched to 'Prefects' it would only confuse Todd and the others.

"But what about this hideaway place in Spain?" Todd said. "How d'yer get him to tell you about that? Ain't that betraying his bro Bruno just a tad too much? Especially seeing as how he wouldn't dare do anything independent to harm him, just send you into the tunnel? Telling you where his bro is will really harm him."

Lylly could understand why the ex-military members of Koggs's team wanted to know the precise details.

"I'd strung him up and pinned him to the wall. I'd also thrown his shoes away. I even wiped my fingerprints off the water bottle I teased him with. Then I left him there. Started walking out the tunnel. I don't think you can remain conscious in that position for long. It's a kind of crucifixion and your chest and lungs are under tremendous pressure. He probably knew all about that. If he was going get free he knew he was going to have to call me back before he lost consciousness."

Lylly had wondered at the time what he'd do if Kellner hadn't called him back. He realised he didn't really know.

"I heard him say something as I got to the tunnel mouth, so went back. But in fact I think it was the wiping of the fingerprints off the bottle that did it. It showed him I was covering my tracks for the subsequent murder investigation, when at some point his body would be found."

Donna laughed and Todd clapped him on the back.

"You knew about this Defile place already?" She asked him.

"Of it, yes. But not that it was a place to hide. There was a battle there."

"Oh yeah?" Todd cried. "Now you're talking."

"Yes. The battle of Las Navas de Tolosa in 1212, which was

a turning point in the Reconquista, which as you know–" but he didn't care if they didn't "–was the retaking of Spain by the Christians from the Moors. Famously a shepherd led the Christian army by secret ways through the Defile to surprise and defeat the Saracen army. The victory opened up the whole of Moorish Andalucia to imminent conquest."

"Cool," Todd said.

"I made him tell me about the place in Spain. About the hiding place in the Despeñaperros. The "Desfiladero" as he called it. And the "Defile" sounds right in English too for Bruno to be hiding in, doesn't it?"

There were nods round the table. Bruno seemed to defile everything he touched.

"So I cut him loose and left him."

"You think he might've been bullshitting you?" Koggs asked. "Saying anything just to get out of there."

Lylly had thought of that. "I think it's real. I think if you'd been there you'd agree."

Lylly thought in a way Kellner wanted the information to be known. He wanted Bruno to be caught, or at least his actions stopped. He just didn't want it coming back on him. Just in case.

Koggs seemed satisfied. He nodded then gently thumped both fists down on the table top.

"Right. Good work son. Now we go on down there and pull her out."

"First thing we do," colonel Koggs said as the principals gathered round the table after a short break. "Is relocate."

They needed to make a main base in a strategic location in the Despeñaperros area. Koggs was going to bring the whole of his team there.

"Sorry Merci," he responded as Merci Stahl wondered why they couldn't just go in immediately and rescue her daughter.

"We got to check it out first. We got to find out what he's got. If he's as good as he thinks he is he'll be expecting us. Or the police. We got to find out everything we can before we go in. It's the only way. Probably take a couple of days."

As well as researching the Desfiladero in the break they'd also found out quite a lot about the Magdalena sect.

"It's real deal Christian," Donna reported. "No underground ancestors, sacrifice, Babylon or pi shit. Just not recognised by the Vatican. Too left field. But maybe they got a point."

Donna related how the sect focussed on the perceived wrong doings history and the early Church had done to Mary Magdalene.

"They reckon the Church obliterated her. Purely because she's a woman. They couldn't have the first disciple being female."

None of the internet sources of course revealed why there was a debt owed by the head of the order to Bruno Ludo, nor why she might let him hide there. But they just took that as a given. They had to assume that Bruno and his 'Perfects' were hiding out somewhere in the sect's complex of buildings. They'd know more when they set up an observation post.

Another issue they discussed was when and what to tell the French police. Lylly found himself in two minds over this. They – and the Spanish police who they were bound to hand the problem over to – would have much better resources even than Koggs could lay his hands on. They'd be able to block ingress and egress to the whole area. They would then isolate the convent and start negotiations.

There were considerable risks though with letting the police action take its course. It could take days, even weeks, for the negotiations to reach a successful conclusion. And there was also the very real risk that Bruno would go down fighting rather than surrender. And even the possibility that the whole group would suicide themselves rather than be captured, including a presumably reluctant Sylvie.

"Remember Waco," Donna said.

The Americans nodded, but Lylly didn't get the reference.

"A wacko sect in Waco, Texas," Donna explained. "FBI surrounded the place. Negotiations stalled. Negotiations led to a fifty-day siege. Eventually they stormed the place, made mistakes. A fire started somehow. Got hold. A bloodbath."

Her inference being, Lylly guessed, that they would only hand it over to the authorities if their own rescue attempt failed. And the last thing they wanted was failed negotiations that led to a siege. Negotiations were good when they worked, but could be a disaster if they failed. And the trouble with involving the authorities was that there would always be negotiations. It was their automatic fallback position.

The instincts of the Koggs group were leaning towards the immediate rapid extraction as soon as they saw the lie of the land. It had worked before, admittedly when they also had surprise on their side. And they thought it would work again, even though they now knew that Bruno and his Perfects were heavily armed. And would be expecting them.

After some discussion Koggs decided they would only call in the police and hand the problem over to them if, on inspection, it appeared that getting Sylvie Stahl out, extracting her again, might be too difficult for Koggs's teams. Merci Stahl accepted that reality. Koggs knew that a failed extraction, and deaths on either or both sides, would at the least mean his licence to operate in the EU would be removed. But Lylly reckoned he was so desperate to make up for his initial mistake he was prepared to take that risk.

After a little more discussion their plans were made. They identified a large hotel on the main road near La Carolina a little way south of the Desfiladero. It had an advantage in that it didn't lie on the brink of the Desfiladero – Santa Elena was closer – which meant that any possible spies that Bruno might have out might not look as far away from the Defile as La Carolina. They would leave immediately and all make their own way there and rendezvous there in a day's time, the next evening, after a night stop on the road. They would all be in La Carolina on the tenth day since Sylvie Stahl had been recaptured.

Frank Koggs's entire group of twenty people would make their way from the Stahl chateau and the remainder from Marseille to the La Carolina rendezvous by road traveling in the company white vans and black SUVs. Koggs himself would fly the company chopper there. He offered Lylly and Merci a lift.

Lylly declined. He preferred to take his own car. Though Koggs now seemed to be including him in his team he might need his independence again – after all he had needed the car when he decided to return to the gorge without telling anyone and intercept Louis Kellner. Merci Stahl surprised him by asking if he minded if she travelled with him.

Koggs's secretariat in the office back in Paris made all the bookings and ensured Koggs had the necessary permissions to take the helicopter into Spain and land in the field next to the hotel's car park.

They set off immediately after lunch. Merci left the chateau in the hands of the permanent staff.

37

ONCE AGAIN CAMO LYLLY was heading across the Spanish plain, across the arid, burnt and ancient lands of Castile-La Mancha province south of Madrid. Merci Stahl was alongside him in the car.

They'd all left the chateau immediately after lunch. And for a while it seemed the vehicles were travelling in a connected line. But while Koggs's vehicles headed for Castellane and then north to Digne before seeking to join the motorway system, Lylly headed west on the old roads to Moustiers, past the abode of the now harmless de-fanged Bozonian commune, then on to Riez and Greoux-les-Bains before joining the same A51 motorway. It was the route he knew from his recent trek along the GR4 trail and he thought Merci might prefer it.

Once on the motorway they were all heading in the same direction – towards the Spanish frontier south of Perpignan. The route they all took to get there didn't really matter. All that mattered was they all should reach the rendezvous hotel at La Carolina by five in the afternoon of the following day. They all agreed in any case that the vehicles should drive well apart even if they were on the same road. It looked less of a convoy, and so of less interest to any observer. It could be, for all they knew, that Bruno had posted watchers along the road. They didn't want to take even that remote chance that they would stand out and be spotted. Even though Bruno Ludo must surely have felt safe and unfindable in his Spanish redoubt, they now knew enough about him to know he would be very very careful.

"I ain't going to underestimate the bastard again," Koggs said. "So keep well separate. Different roads if you can."

Once they hit the motorway Lylly increased speed. There

were no hold ups. They crossed the border into Spain and well after dark that night they stopped in a roadhouse hotel on the Zaragoza ringroad. He knew the Spanish road system well, and once over the border he'd headed inland to avoid the traffic crush and chaos on the Mediterranean coast.

They took separate rooms. But late in the night something woke Lylly. He was instantly awake. Silently he reached for the hiking pole he had assembled and which lay on the floor by the bed, with the fighting knife attached. He too would never underestimate Bruno or take him lightly again. He heard a light but insistent tapping on his door. He went to the door and checked through the spyhole. He opened the door. Merci Stahl stood on the threshold.

"Hold me," she said.

Next day Camo Lylly and Merci Stahl drove south.

On the evening of the tenth day after Sylvie Stahl's recapture, after dinner the whole of the operational arm of Frank Koggs's security company SteadyState Secure met round the large long table in the hotel conference room in La Carolina. Camo Lylly and Merci Stahl were also in attendance.

They had detailed plans of the area as well as map apps. After various options were discussed Koggs decided a recce team of three would descend into the Defile at dawn the following morning.

After his success in finding where Bruno was hiding, Koggs now treated Lylly as much more of a professional. And it was Koggs who suggested that the recce team should consist of Lylly, Donna and Todd. Which was good, Lylly thought, because he'd decided he was going in anyway before or after Koggs's team, and as part of it or not, whether Koggs liked it or not.

Once the recce team reported back they would decide what their next options were. One of the prerequisites for the forward team was to find the best place to set up an observation point.

Lylly offered the use of his Mazda for the team of three to descend the first part of the way into the Desfiladero. It was a standard run-of-the mill small SUV, one of hundreds of thousands on the road. He felt, and most of the others agreed, that neither the company white vans nor their black Mercedes SUVs would be as anonymous. Lylly knew that some of the team, especially ones who had not had first hand experience of Bruno's capabilities, thought this was being over-cautious.

"Who's gonna notice a goddam black SUV?" one of them asked.

Bruno for one, Lylly thought.

"We just cannot underestimate him," Lylly said. "You think you're good, ex-special forces or whatever the hell you are, and you can just go down there openly and brazenly with a dogshit pile of drones overhead and sort the bastard out because he's no match for you. Well you can't. He holds all the cards. And that's that. We do this first incursion in my car or we don't do it at all."

There was uproar round the table. He noticed Donna and Todd grinning at him.

"Look," Lylly carried on in an attempt to mollify the opposition. "At some point we're going to have to leave the vehicle, probably it'll have to be along a track or even by the side of the road, and go ahead on foot. Which is more suspicious, a small white SUV with Spanish plates whose occupants might be having a picnic, or some sodding great black SUV or white van both with French plates lurking abandoned in the bushes?"

"Enough," Koggs growled. "You go in Camo's car. After that we'll see."

Given that it would be daylight when the recce would take place it was also agreed the three of them would all wear hiking gear. The large scale maps showed plenty of hiking trails in the area. What they absolutely did not want to do was wear anything which carried the company logo. Nor anything that in any way resembled a military uniform or a paramilitary uniform. Nor did they want to wear the same hiking gear. It was best if they all looked slightly different.

So just before dawn on the eleventh day they met by Camo's car in the hotel car park. Camo had on his desert camouflage combat trousers which already looked what they were, army surplus, plus a faded blue polo shirt and a fawn sleeveless vest. Todd wore blue jeans and a washed-out white tee-shirt.

"I know what I said about jeans before," he said. "But I guess it looks amateurish enough to be real. I can live with that kind of look."

Donna appeared in a fetching pair of tight red cycling shorts that seemed to stick to every curve, with her socks folded down over the top of her boots.

"Time to get me a tourist tan on my legs," she said.

Above the shorts she was wearing an olive drab very light very thin anorak style jacket over a white tee-shirt. It almost seemed to Lylly to be made out of silk, but must surely be some kind of polyester. Lylly thought the shorts and the anorak were perfect. Donna pushed her ponytail through the back of her baseball cap. Todd went bareheaded and Lylly wore a floppy white sunhat. Donna carried a large scale map that showed the hiking trails. All three carried sunglasses, water bottles and had walking poles. They were ubiquitous and they'd agreed it would be conspicuous if they didn't have them. Lylly's poles were his usual modified disguised stabbing weapons. The fighting knife was in his backpack.

"We're hiking tourists on the hiking trail to hell," Todd said as they drove out of the car park and headed north to Santa Elena and the Defile.

On the other side of the small town the road ran steeply down just as the sun broke over the ridge tops. A series of hairpin bends took the old A4 main road down into the depths. A junction with a smaller b-road appeared on the right and they took that. The road carried on downwards. It bent round, then between, a pair of the huge concrete legs that carried the new road on an elevated viaduct over this section of the Desfiladero. Lylly had looked at the maps and knew the new road almost ignored the presence of the Defile. The new road stayed high up, far above the deep cleft, and was carried across the space on soaring viaducts and then delved into deep tunnels punched through the obstructing sierra ridges to keep its constant level, immune to the landscape as motorway standards required, and maintain the pretence that there was nothing but flat land around and below. Over to their left the viaduct's consecutive pairs of concrete legs strode across the valley.

Donna in the passenger seat with the map announced there was a hiking trail coming up which crossed the road, which would allow them to make their way through shrubby trees and undergrowth to the area down by the river where they suspected the convent might lie. They need to find a place to park and leave the car.

It turned out where the trail crossed the road, coming in from the higher ground on their right and continuing across the road and then downhill towards the river on their left, there was a large parking area on the right. It was also the place where the civil engineers and road menders stored gravel to mend potholes and resurface the road. Three large piles of gravel stood like vast molehills at the back of the parking area. Lylly parked the car facing out between two of the gravel piles. Without a word they collected their gear, shuffled on their backpacks, made final adjustments to their poles and hats and set off across the road and into the trees.

It was similar in a way Lylly reckoned to the terrain up on the GR4 trail in Provence, where he had started his trek so many weeks before. A well-worn trail hugged the contour on a slope which dropped away to their right. The steep defile slope came down to their path from the left. Trees and shrubs obscured much of their view as they peered forward, and sideways to the right, looking for any sign of buildings or ruins, or cultivation and habitation of any kind.

After an hour Donna cautioned them that there might be traps, or at least alarms, on the trail if they were approaching the convent.

"I guess it's a public footpath," she said "So he ain't going to take the risk of injuring joe public and causing a ruckus. But it's Bruno." She shrugged as if to say they just couldn't be too careful.

Lylly wondered what kind of alarms there could possibly

be that might alert Bruno to approaching visitors, but nevertheless they continued on a little more cautiously than they had done hitherto.

Once they stopped for a drink and an energy bar. Then they carried on through the trees, with the path descending slowly across the contours all the time.

After an hour and half on the trail they could see they were approaching a rocky bluff with sheer sides ahead which stood clear above the trees. Only a few scrubby trees clung to the steep arid sides round the base. The path came right up to the bluff and curved to the right round its base. And as they followed the rock and turned again to the left as the bluff ended, the trees dropped momentarily away and a vista opened up ahead of them.

They stopped and looked. Ahead and to their right the ground dropped away from the path and then began to flatten out. They had reached the bottom of the Defile. The Rio Despeñaperros ran through steep banks through the middle of the narrow but surprisingly flat valley. On the floodplain on either side of the river in the long narrow fields there were crops growing. Lylly recognised potatoes and corn among a myriad of other food species he had no idea about. They could see figures, mostly women but a few men too, working in the fields. It looked like hard labour.

They looked up, above the thin flat fields to the far side of the narrow valley. That side of the Defile was far steeper and rockier. There were cliffs in many places.

"We ain't coming down that side without equipment," Todd said.

Which was true, Lylly thought, and that meant there was no way they could get Sylvie Stahl out that way. While they could definitely set up an observation post on the cliffs on the other side of the valley, it was this side of the valley that was going to be only option for both the extraction and the escape.

Far in the distance was another monstrous concrete centipede, where the vast supporting legs for another huge viaduct, capped by the underside of the highway, like a modern Stonehenge, strode across the valley. The road above then disappeared in a black entry to a tunnel in the cliffs.

But it was what was below the steep cliffs on the far side of the defile on the other side of the river that most held their focus.

38

ON THE FAR SIDE of the valley three bluffs or hillocks stood out, seemingly separate from but close to the cliffside above. On the biggest of the three bluffs stood a large stone, brick and render amber-coloured building. More than anything it resembled an early medieval castle on top of its small hillock, which was known as a motte. Many of the motte mounds in those old motte-and-bailey castles were man-made. But these three humps which strode across the far side of the valley floor like three giant molehills were definitely natural. In places they could see the exposed rock on the steep sides.

A substantial access road approached the building from their right as they looked across the valley. Lylly realised this main access drive must branch off the road at some point, perhaps not far beyond where they had left the car. They would have to find it before they returned to the hotel.

Though still ruinous in places, Lylly could see new work on the walls and especially on the roof that indicated the building was weathertight, and smoke rising from several huge chimney stacks along the red tile roofline told them that the building was also tenanted. This then was the old convent, now the home of the unrecognised Maria Magdalena order.

They could see a wide track, walled throughout its length on both sides by stone, an old road perhaps, erupting out of a pair of massive gates at the front of the convent, which then descended towards them in straight sections and hairpin bends down the motte to the level of the fields.

Looking on, they realised that in fact what they were seeing was a series of three craggy hillocks in a line standing out, and separate from, the line of the cliffs. The convent building stood on the furthest right and tallest of the three mottes. They descended in height from the first one on the right as they looked to the last one on the left. And on the top of each mound a building of some kind had been built, with bridges connecting them between the mounds. The diminishing height of the mottes meant that the third building from where they looked was on a rise not much higher than the surrounding fields.

It seemed the convent and its outbuildings were all in a line, connected by a single well-made brick and stone paved road, bridges and several subsidiary walkways. Lylly counted three substantial stone buildings, each on top of a motte, plus an unknown number of sheds and storerooms, all connected by bridges, and strung out along the bottom of the valley, each on its own high ground below the cliffs.

Though the mottes and the buildings which stood atop them were disconnected, the road between them which linked them together was not. To avoid descending from one bluff and ascending to the next, the main road or paved track between the three bluff buildings had been built up, raised on bridges made entirely of stone, so the road level could be maintained throughout the whole complex, from the convent on the first motte to the third and last building on the last motte in the distance.

They could also see that the main driveway, accessing the main building from the right, split as it approached the front of the building. One strand carried on to the front of the building while the other strand dropped down to the level of the fields and ran along the base of the three knolls.

"Looks like the road goes independently to each of the three buildings," Donna said and pointed. "Looks like the bridges carry foot traffic between the buildings while the service road at the bottom at valley level carries vehicles and heavier traffic."

Each of the buildings was connected to the road below by a zigzagging track.

They could see that the second of the two bridges was longer and was built on several archways, while the first one contained a single large arch. And judging by the fresh unweathered colour of the stones, the double-arched bridge had been recently repaired.

"I guess Bruno's in one of those two buildings beyond the convent," Todd said. "I'd go for the end one." He waved his hand up and down as though he was following the coiled backbone of a serpent and stopped after three ups and downs.

The third and last building from where they looked was different to the previous two in that it was single storey, while still being a large and substantial building under a striking red-tiled roof. It was painted white, in contrast to the amber rendering on the other two buildings. It looked to be in good order and was not ruinous to any degree. It was possible Lylly thought that the third building had been in constant use and maintained while the other two buildings had been allowed to decay.

Lylly thought the third building might be a hacienda, which was a kind of farmhouse characteristic of Spain. In the old days when the convent was still a convent the hacienda would be where the farmer and the farm hands and their families would live. It would also be the place where the cows and the flocks of sheep and goats would live in the winter months. When the convent was extant it would have tried to be as self-sufficient as possible in not just food but in repair and other necessary artisan skills, and all the vital pottery making and mending skills such a large collection of buildings required. These artisans too would all have lived and worked in the hacienda. Which in turn required it to be a very large and substantial building.

If the third building was the old hacienda then it looked plenty big enough to house the twenty-three people that Bruno would have arrived on site with.

Donna took off her backpack and dug out a large Canon digital camera and several lenses. She began taking a series of shots with the various lenses, both panoramas and close-ups.

"Until we know which building Bruno's in we're going to have to put the OP maybe somewhere midway between the buildings," Camo said. "Then when we confirm which building it is, we can go closer to it. Still on the cliff tops of course. But I agree the end building looks like the best bet."

"There's nothing beyond it. So more of an escape route out the back there and into the wild if they get cornered," Donna said. "I'd go for that one."

"If he gets to have a choice," Todd said.

Donna looked up from the camera's viewfinder. She kind of squinted across the valley at the third building. She let the camera go. It hung on the strap suspended from her neck. She dug in an anorak pocket and came out with a compact pair of 10 x 50 binoculars.

"Oh yeah," she said as she trained the binoculars on the third building. She handed the binoculars to Todd.

"At the back," she said.

Todd inspected the building through the binoculars. He bunched a hand into a fist and waved it up and down a few times.

"Got him," he said.

He handed the binoculars to Lylly.

Lylly focused the lenses on the back of the large hacienda building. The access bridge and track from the second building approached the front of the hacienda building where there was a set of double doors, then the track split and ran along both sides to the rear. From this viewpoint he couldn't see whether there was a car park at the rear. But just jutting into view at the far gable end of the hacienda was the bumper and rear two feet of a camper-van.

"I agree," Lylly said. "He's there."

He pointed to the section of high cliffs directly above the third building. "So that's where the OP goes."

The two men waited while Donna continued taking more photos. Lylly noticed that the hiking trail split at this point, at the base of the bluff they were standing under. The main trail seemed to carry on in the direction they had been heading, along and parallel to the river. The map showed this trail eventually emerged from the Defile many miles away to the north on the far slopes of the Sierra

Madrona, after it joined an ancient packhorse trial and trade route it crossed the river on an ancient medieval stone bridge.

The other smaller track headed away at right angles from the larger path directly down from the bluff where they were standing towards the river. They could see it snaking through the cultivated fields until it crossed the river on a small stone footbridge, continued up the other side and joined the main convent access road on the lowest hairpin, which had descended to that point in straights and hairpins from the convent building.

Further away the second and third buildings also appeared to have tracks running across the fields to the river, where they crossed on small ancient arched bridges and intercepted the hiking trail they were on somewhere ahead out of sight.

If these field-crossing tracks were the only access routes into the convent complex from this side of the valley, Lylly realised, it was as nearly unusable as descending down the cliffs. It looked like they'd have to come along the convent's main access track after all.

They were also going to have to continue along the hiking trail they were on to see if it, or any tracks leading off it, led them any closer to the third building.

"We're going to have to carry on along here to see how close we can get to the third building; and then when we're back at the car we'll need to trace where that main access road hits the tarmac."

He pointed across the valley to the access road approaching the convent. The others agreed.

"So this trail first I guess," Todd said.

They all took a drink, shuffled on their backpacks and continued along the trail. It carried on through low trees, and shortly after leaving the rocky bluff the trail dropped down to the level of the fields. They were glad the trees shielded them from any searching eyes examining this trail for any intruders.

"I reckon the trees are hiding us good," Todd said.

Donna estimated that the third building and the low bluff it was built on were situated about a hundred yards beyond the second building, which in turn was fifty beyond the convent. That meant the whole of the convent complex of three buildings and the hillocks they were on occupied a space about three hundred yards long.

And after a few hundred yards from where they had restarted their trek from the bluff they came to a small junction in the trail. It was a replica in a way of the T-junction at the bluff. Their hiking trail carried on under the trees at the edge of the fields. But a new trail at ninety degrees to the hiking trail turned away in the direction of the second building. Carrying on another hundred yards they came to another trail snaking away into the field. This one aimed for the third building. They could see it too hopped over the river in a small arched stone bridge like the other two paths. It appeared to issue into the third building's car park at the back of the building.

Also at this point, looking across the fields and the river to the line of the three buildings they were far enough along to see directly into the car park behind the third building. In the car park were a large number of vehicles. Among them were two minibuses and three vans and several SUVs. Plus a few small saloons and ancient-looking pick-ups.

They stopped and turned back. They had seen all they had come to see along this trail. They returned to Lylly's car.

Once they were in the car, instead of turning left, back the way they had come, Lylly turned right, to carry on further along the road. They followed hairpins and less abrupt bends, still descending. Eventually the road bottomed out. They were at the low point of the Defile.

Ahead they could see a small humpbacked stone bridge carrying the road over the river. Lylly drove to it and stopped the car on the apex of the arch. Over the parapet he watched the water ooze silently along over underwater green weeds slowly in its bed below the bridge.

Immediately on the other side of the bridge and the river on the left hand side of the road were a pair of massive wrought iron gates. The gates were closed and were suspended from sturdy rectilinear pillars constructed from large amber-coloured stones. Lylly parked in front of the gates. Beyond the gates a wide stony track disappeared over a low brow into trees.

A sign was fixed to the right hand gate pillar. It read MARIA MAGDALENAS and underneath it in smaller letters, the English equivalent: MARY MAGDALENES. Nothing else.

They'd seen enough. It was nearly noon. They were nearly halfway through the eleventh day since Sylvie Stahl's retaking. Lylly turned the car and they headed back to La Carolina to report.

39

LYLLY HIT THE INTERNET. He had an idea. It might be the best way forward. He opened up his laptop and found the website dedicated to the Maria Magdalenas sorority. After a while he found the information he was looking for.

He was in his room. Through the window he could see the hotel car park where Koggs was organising the rota for the observation point they were going to set up immediately that afternoon. It would be sited undercover in the undergrowth on the cliff top above the third building, the presumed hacienda. It would be manned twenty-four hours a day with two observers a time. It looked like a good position. The only difficulty was it would take a great deal of time to trek across the Defile terrain to it, where only a portion of the route would be along hiking trails. Koggs told Merci that if things went according to plan he hoped to have enough information about Bruno Ludo's setup, situation and movements to allow an extraction in two days' time.

You could tell Koggs had done this kind of thing before, Lylly thought as he looked out of the window. That was because Koggs was handing out old-fashioned Nokia phones to each person. These came from a time way before smartphones were even dreamt of. They couldn't do anything but make phonecalls. Even texting was a cumbersome rigmarole using the dialling buttons that had three letters on each button. But they had a single overwhelming advantage over any smartphone yet produced. And that was, once fully charged the battery would retain power for a fortnight or even longer before requiring a recharge. There was only one number pre-programmed into the phones, and that was Koggs's central company smartphone, which would always be either on Koggs person or in the hands of the duty operative in charge if Koggs wasn't available.

When they returned from their dawn patrol Lylly, Donna and Todd had reported to Koggs and the rest of his operatives in the conference room. Koggs didn't believe in some kind of top-down hierarchy. He thought it best if all his operatives heard any new information at the same time.

Donna had printed out multiple copies of all the shots she had taken of the convent, perspectives of the other two buildings, the cliffs behind, the fields in front, the bluff from where they taken their first view of the convent, the three tracks and bridges they'd found across the fields, and the third building especially and the car park at the year of the third building and the vehicles in it. Koggs had decided not to send a drone up to take more shots.

"Reckon it's deadly quiet in that valley," he told the group round the table. "I know deep valleys have a spooky sound-deadening quality, and there's a chance someone'll hear the drone. Ain't going to risk it."

It would be a serious giveaway and would immediately alert Bruno that there might be potential opponents in the area.

When the first teams had gone off to set up the OP Lylly sought Franks Koggs out.

Lylly knew that Koggs had far more respect for his ideas and the way he wanted to do things since he had successfully identified the way to discover Bruno's whereabouts. Now Koggs listened patiently to Lylly's idea.

They were alone in the conference room. After Lylly finished speaking Koggs got to his feet and walked to the large picture window at the end of the room. It overlooked the Sierra Madrona in the distance.

"It's real dangerous," Koggs said, talking to the window, so Lylly only heard the words over Koggs's shoulder. "You'll be on your own. No help. We'll be too far away to get to you in time if it goes belly up."

"I know that," Lylly said. "But I reckon it's the only way we can get this done as fast as possible. The setup here isn't as favourable as it was at the Bozonian place. Where are your teams going to come in from? The track across the river from the bluff? It's maybe half a mile of open country, just potatoes and cabbages to hide under. If Bruno's got infra red and night sights he'll literally see you coming half a mile off. And with you silhouetted on the crown of a bridge he wouldn't need 'em."

Koggs turned back to face Lylly.

"But you know what? I was going to suggest this myself." He grinned at Lylly. "Couldn't ask you to take it on. But I kind of hoped you'd come up with the idea yourself."

Lylly laughed. "So we do it?"

"One good thing about those red devil masks Todd told me you got to wear at Moustiers. Bruno ain't going to know your face, if you run into him over there. Todd said you also put on some kind of Speedy Gonzales act too. So Bruno ain't going to recognise your voice neither. And if I recall you were wearing some of the company outfits on both occasions? So that's good too. Only thing. He might recognise your walking pole. So dump that."

"So we do it?" Lylly repeated.

"We do it."

Lylly's idea was that the best way of getting Sylvie out safely and as quickly as possible was to have a man inside the convent complex. In a way he envisaged it as a variation on Bruno's skilful attacks on the Stahl chateau and the Gap chalet. Koggs's men would attack the hacienda from a safe distance, probably from two different directions, making as much noise and uproar as they could muster. They also needed a man inside to tell them if the hacienda building contained only Bruno's company and no innocent bystanders. Only if it were just full of Bruno's people would the attack go ahead. It would be a diversion, because the apparent attack would result in all Bruno's men responding and engaging in the defence. That would give Lylly a chance to go in, find Sylvia, and bring her out.

While both Koggs and Lylly had agreed on the principle of

the plan, the details needed pinning down. Koggs called in Donna and Todd. Between the four of them they came up with a detailed plan.

It was all possible because what Lylly had found on the website was that the Maria Magdalena sorority welcomed novices. As long as they paid, of course, Lylly noticed in a deeply hidden note on the website. Actually that seemed fair enough he thought, since the convent was providing board and lodging for the novices. Apparently novices could be both men and women. The initial training course for novices was two weeks. Both sexes would be instructed into the story of Mary Magdalene and the full miserable catalogue as they saw it of the injustices history and the church had inflicted on her. After further instruction and training, women could be allowed to make a start on becoming full members of the sorority. Men could not become members. But armed with their new knowledge men were expected to take the message out into the wider world. In this way the Maria Magdalenas intended to create a ripple effect across society and eventually undo all the historical wrongs and let the true story emerge. According to the website the novices were housed in the second building along from the convent. That was the building adjacent to the hacienda.

Lylly's plan was to immediately enter the convent as a novice. He would turn up that same evening in his hiking clothes and backpack, claiming he had hiked there specifically to take part on the novice learning process.

Lylly would have a Nokia phone with him. Just in case he had to relinquish such worldly unnecessaries to undergo novice training, he asked Donna to get another Nokia placed that night in a safe spot under the stone footbridge over the river which carried the track from the second building across the fields to the hiking trail and further on to the rocky knoll on the other side of the valley. He also asked her to put his .32 there and a pair of night viewers.

At the moment they were all hoping the attack and the extraction could take place at the earliest in two days' time on the night after next, and at the latest on the night after that, on the third day from Lylly entering the convent. They intended then that the extraction would take place on either the thirteenth or the fourteenth day since Sylvie had been taken.

It would happen at night. There was nothing they could do about the state of the moon. They no longer had time to wait till that was right.

Lylly went to find Merci Stahl to tell her the plan.

40

AT AROUND SIX IN the early evening later that same day, the eleventh day, Camo Lylly arrived at the entrance way to the former convent that was now the house of the Maria Magdalena sorority. He was tired and dusty. He looked like a pilgrim. At least he hoped he did. Much of the tiredness was not faked. It had been a long day and he'd been up since dawn when he went out with Donna and Todd to spy out the land.

To create some plausibility he had started hiking towards the convent at least two hours by foot away from it. Todd dropped him off in Santa Elena, in a back road away from public view.

Todd stood with him at the tailgate of the SUV as Lylly retrieved his belongings. Hat and full backpack, water bottles, map, one walking pole.

"You need that?" Todd questioned. "You're only hiking two hours."

Lylly had debated that himself. He felt the urge to be as authentic as possible. Nearly all long-distance hikers these days used walking poles, usually two, sometimes one. To have none at all would have raised, if not suspicions, at least a question. And of course its main attraction for Camo was that it was a disguised weapon. He discounted the risk of Bruno Ludo remembering it if he were to see it, though he was well aware that Frank Koggs had specifically warned him that Bruno recognising it was a real possibility. He recalled that Bruno had spent a lot of the time at their two previous meetings trying to hypnotise him by boring into his eyes behind the red devil mask with his astonishing husky eyes and hadn't seemed to be looking at the pole. And in any case once he arrived at the convent the pole would spend nearly all its time dismantled in or attached to Lylly's backpack.

"Yeah I'll take it," he said.

Todd shook his hand and said, "See you soon muchacho. We'll come and get ya when you call."

Camo Lylly set off down a hiking trail that descended into the Despeñaperros Defile. The trail ran through spindly trees and sharp bushes. It seemed relatively untrodden. The thorny undergrowth occasionally snagged his combat trousers and he was glad he wasn't bare-legged as Donna had been on the hike that morning. Was it only this morning, he thought, slightly surprised. Things were moving fast now. They had to.

The path descended into the Desfiladero. Some of the way down it merged with the road when a crag or small bluff obstructed the route and prevented any other easy way forward. Eventually he came to the bottom of the Defile. He crossed the road bridge over the Rio Despeñaperros and immediately came to the large double wrought iron gates on the left hand side. The black letters MARIA MAGDALENAS and MARY MAGDALENES stood out on the white painted wooden board fixed to the gate railings. The gates were closed, as they had been in the morning when he had first seen them. Closed, but not locked, he noted. There was an iron balance-latch just next to the white board. He pressed down on the latch. That raised its end from the groove in the other gate. He pushed against the right hand gate. It moved inwards away from him easily and without squeaking. He passed through and closed it behind him.

On the mile-long approach drive from the wrought iron gates to the convent entrance porch Lylly mentally prepared himself and his story. He also dismantled his walking pole and stowed it under straps down the side of his backpack. His story was that he had started trekking along back roads and hiking trails a month before, taking his time. He had started from beyond Granada, he would claim, from the summit of Mulhacén, the highest peak in the Sierra Nevada mountains which overlooked Granada from the southeast, and whose melting snow, it was said, fed the waters of the palace of the Alhambra itself.

Much to his surprise, around halfway along the driveway, when he rounded a curve where the drive hugged the steeply ragged side of the defile he saw two hikers ahead of him. They had stopped in the middle of the drive and were consulting a map and taking turns drinking from a water bottle. They heard his boot steps as he approached and turned to greet him.

He could see they were two women. One seemed young, barely out of her teens, perhaps twenty. The other seemed older and more mature, maybe in her late thirties, perhaps even forty.

"Hello," the younger one said. "Are you wanting to be a novice too?"

She had an accent that Lylly thought might be Flemish or Dutch. Startling really, Lylly thought, that in the middle of Spain strangers immediately resorted to English as the most likely common language.

"Hope to be," Lylly said. "Yes. What about you?"

"Yes we too," the elder woman said. Then added unnecessarily. "We are Netherlanders. I am Tilde. This is my god-daughter Else."

"I'm Camo," Lylly said. "English."

They walked on together and began to tell each other their back stories. The elder woman Tilde related how she was a lifelong Christian, but like "All of us" as she put it, "I gave no thought to Mary Magdalene." Apparently it was Else who put her on to her and the dastardly doings of the Church fathers.

Lylly admitted that he wasn't a Christian, far from it, he said. But he was fascinated by the story of Mary Magdalene, and specifically if it was true that she had been the First Disciple, and had been the victim of a historical cover up and deliberate distortion of the facts, purely because she was a woman.

"I'm a sucker for backing the underdog," he said, actually with considerable truth. "Male or female," he said with a grin in Else's direction. "I hate all official wisdoms and rigid handed-down traditionalism. If this story is true about Magdalene I want to hear all about it. And if I think it holds water I'm happy to tell all my family and friends about it. I think that's the point of allowing men in here, isn't it?"

To Lylly's considerable surprise what he had just said was very close to the truth.

Young Else was evidently a crusader for women, especially forgotten or unjustly overlooked women. That was why she was here, she said. Unlike her god-mother she wasn't a strong Christian either, but wanted to know the story.

"Maria Magdalena was a woman," she said, "And that is more important than her Christianity. The early Church was Roman, very patriarchal. They just could not allow a woman to be important. We will change that."

Her godmother frowned, then smiled.

The more he thought about it Lylly was glad to have their company. Three pilgrims arriving together simultaneously was far better than him arriving on his own.

They carried on. Now they could see the convent ahead. Facing them was an outer perimeter wall. It was rendered and painted an amber colour. The wall was topped with semicircular red tiles. In places a few tiles were missing. There were large double wooden doors set in the centre of the wall as they came up to it. When fully opened the two doors would have revealed an entrance-way wide enough to take a horsed carriage. A port was set in the right hand door. It was propped open by an amber coloured stone.

Lylly went first. He ducked slightly and stepped over the threshold into the courtyard beyond that was fully enclosed by a wall on three sides and by the bulk of the convent on the fourth wall straight ahead. It was open to the sky. His new companions followed.

Ahead of them on the far side of the courtyard was a roofed porch in brick and tile which originally would have provided wet-weather cover for the passengers of an entire carriage to alight and enter the convent's main entrance. They grouped together under the porch. They stood before a large black pitched wooden door studded with bolt heads and reinforced with bands of iron.

Lylly wondered whether they were supposed to knock, or whether the modernisation and rescue of the building had involved the installation of some kind of electric doorbell or even some modern electronic address system. But he doubted it.

Else spotted an iron handle protruding from the wall by the right hand side of the door. She grabbed it and pulled. Through the door a bell could be heard ringing dully in the distance.

They waited, smiling expectantly at each other. Lylly took off his hat and stowed it in his backpack.

Then they heard noises from the other side of the door. Locks being turned and bolts being extracted. The door was pulled open inwards. After being opened a foot or a so they saw a pair of tiny delicate hands and arms insert themselves in the gap, place themselves against the door and proceed to heave and push it fully open.

An impossibly thin woman in her fifties stood in the doorway.

Lylly was just about to introduce himself and his companions in Spanish when she beat him to it.

"Hey come in you guys," she said. "Great to have you here."

41

THE WELCOME AT THE FRONT DOOR was astonishing and slightly disconcerting for Lylly. For no particular reason he'd expected the denizens of the convent to be dour and unfriendly, strict and self-denying, cold and unwelcoming. And maybe rigidly old-fashioned and backwards looking. He didn't think they'd really welcome men either. He discovered right from the start he was wrong on all counts and they were none of these.

The impossibly thin woman who opened the door and welcomed them in was Lana, she said. She was Irish. She ushered them into the large reception hall. While still ruinous and tatty to a degree, repairs and remedial work were taking place. Long planks supported on two trestle tables provided a platform for two women to repair and patch the walls in places. They were hacking off sections of rotten plaster with brick hammers and pry-bars. The debris fell onto a series of dustsheets laid along the edge of the floor. Further along the platform a third woman was applying fresh plaster to the exposed stonework. The way she skilfully scooped dabs of plaster from her hawk board and made broad confident sweeps with the plastering trowel showed she either knew what she was doing or had long experience in the art.

All three women turned and welcomed the new arrivals in variously accented English as they stood in the hall.

"Back to work scallywags," Lana joshed the women. "So far your repairs look worse than the previous ruin."

The women laughed, but nevertheless returned to their tasks. It all seemed bright and gentle to Lylly, and very good-natured.

"You're welcome in the main building here any time," Lana said. "And of course the chapel for daily services and readings is in this building. But your place of eating, sleeping, learning and all your daily activities is in another building. So please follow me. And oh yes, I'm afraid we do not allow mobile phones, nor laptops nor tablets here. Not at your neophyte level anyway," Lana added with a superior twinkle in her eye. "For the duration of your stay this is and should be the focus of your stay. In that case perhaps you could deposit anything like that you have in the lockers."

She pointed to the other wall of the reception hall where there was a long stack of metal lockers, exactly the same as the left-luggage lockers at a train or bus station.

The only piece of convent communications contraband Lylly had was his Koggs-issued Nokia. He'd expected this. Perhaps it was a state of mind. If your prime focus is on the activities of the 1st century you might not want to be reminded of the trappings of the 21st century. Or maybe, on the other hand, it was just the first demonstration of control. Once you're in our building you are fully under our control. Maybe a combination of both. And I bet, he thought with his usual cynicism, that the hierarchy here has ready access to mobile phones, computers, and the internet. Authority was the same everywhere. It wouldn't be do as I do, but do as I say.

Lylly dug out his phone and placed it in a locker. He removed the locker key and put it in a pocket. The two Netherlander women did the same with their much more modern smartphones. It looked like they too expected it. None of them possessed a tablet or a laptop.

Lana then led them through a long passage that exited the far end of the reception hall and travelled all the way down the valley side of the convent building. Various doors and sub-corridors led away at right angles, but all the doors were shut and Lylly couldn't see into the rooms beyond.

Eventually Lana opened a door ahead of them and they emerged into a smaller replica of the main entrance hall. They were at the back of the main building. They passed through the large back door and stood out under the evening sun on a terrace surfaced with brick and tiles. From his reconnaissance early that same morning Lylly recognised they were at the back end of the first knoll. A low wall surrounded the terrace on both sides. Ahead there was a gap in the terrace wall. This was the entry to the first bridge.

Lana led them on and across the bridge, which was covered with red bricks and tiles like the terrace, towards the second building.

Waiting in the entrance of the second building was another woman, younger.

Lylly noticed that the tiled track from the bridge to the second building split up and made a path round both sides of the building. Which meant you could access the second bridge and the third building without having to pass all the way indoors through the second building.

"Hello. Welcome. You are welcome," the younger woman said. "I'm Grazyna."

She had an east European accent, Lylly thought, possibly Ukrainian or Polish.

"If you go with Grazyna," Lana said to the two Dutch women. "I'll take the young man."

Inside the entrance hall of the building there were two exits. One route led off from the left of the hall and the other from the right. Lana led Lylly towards the left-hand route, while Grazyna took the Netherlanders through the right hand door.

"We don't have men and women living together," Lana said by way of explanation. "We have separate sleeping quarters. Everything else of course you'll do together; eating, recreation, seminars. It's just sleeping that's in separate dormitories. This is the men's."

Lana opened a wide door to reveal a large long room with two lines of beds running down the sides.

"Seminary and refectory are beyond." She pointed to a door at the far end of the dormitory. "Choose any bed you like."

Thinking rapidly, Lylly chose the bed nearest to the door they'd just entered by.

Lana pointed to another door, splitting the row of beds on

the right hand side.

"That goes to the washing and bathroom facilities."

Lylly went over to have a look. It was a large space with two rows of basins, with shower and WC cubicles. At least they had doors, he thought. He'd seen plenty of campsites with worse facilities.

"I'm afraid you're on your own," Lana said as he returned to the dormitory. "We do get men, sure like you now wanting to hear our message, but given our mission we do tend to receive more women than men. The two women next door for example will find there are three women already in the women's dormitory. Drop your stuff, and I'll show you the rest."

Lylly dumped his backpack on the bed. He followed Lana down the aisle between the beds to the door at the end.

She opened the far door and they went through into a large well-lit space that took up the entire gable end of the second building. It was a full-height room, reaching up to the exposed beams and rafters above.

The Netherlanders with three more women and Grazyna were already in the room.

The floorspace was split into two. Half of it contained a kitchen area and four rows of long tables with benches either side. The other half seemed to be the seminary-cum-teaching space. There were desks and chairs there, and shelves with books lined the walls. A lectern stood at the end. There was a slim book on each desk. It looked like the same book. Lylly walked to the nearest desk and looked at the cover. *The Gospel of Mary* it said. Lylly had never heard of that one. It wasn't in the Bible the last time he looked.

The entire space was lit by a series of large windows set into the gable wall. There was another door, directly accessing the outside set between the windows.

"What's the next building?" Lylly asked. He pointed through the window to the bridge and the low white building beyond it.

"That's our farm building. It's known as a hacienda in Spanish. It's where we keep all our farm machinery and where the animals live in winter."

"I'd like to see the animals," Else said.

"Yes darling I'm sure. But they are all out in the fields at the moment. I'm sure you'll get a chance. But in any case the hacienda is out of bounds. The machinery in there is much too dangerous, I'm afraid. Nor do we want to be the object of any dreadful legal action in case of injury."

Ah, Lylly thought, that's how they're playing it. They were stopping access to the hacienda by pretending it was dangerous. If women could be patronising, Lana had just done it. Matronising? He could have pointed out that machinery that wasn't working could hardly be dangerous, but didn't bother. He wasn't there to question the rules, just to ignore them.

"You do your own cooking," Lana said. "You'll find everything you need in the refrigerators and cupboards over there."

"Guests usually find the best way is to pair up and cook for the others, in a daily rota," Grazyna said.

"In which case Tilde and I will cook for everyone this evening," Else said.

"Well we'll leave you to yourselves just now," Lana said. "You're welcome to wander about and come into the main building, go into the chapel, explore, whatever you wish. Just remember that the farmhouse building over there is out of bounds for the moment.

"Then first instruction is at 9.30 tomorrow morning, with the Maria herself. It would be useful if you all read the *book*--" she stressed the word as though there was only one book, and pointed to the volume on the nearest desk "—before first instruction. Our Mary gospel is taken from the Berlin Codex plus additions from the Oxyrhynchus papyrus. And you'll learn all about that. Notice particularly the contempt that Peter and Andrew have for Mary purely because she's a woman, and Mary's willingness to disagree with them and her insistence on standing up for herself. Also interesting is that Levi-Matthew defends her. There were a few good men even then." She smiled disarmingly at Lylly.

"Of course it is unfortunately true and a cold fact," Lana

carried on, picking the scab of a deeply-cut sore, "that throughout history women have often found themselves in need of defence and protection. But you will learn more about Mary and her life and times and what we call 'the erasure' in due course. Prepare yourselves."

That should be interesting, Lylly thought. Pity I most likely won't be there to hear it.

"Then we'll tell you our story and you can tell us yours, or as much of it you want to," Lana said. She smiled at them all then turned and left the room.

42

CAMO LYLLY KNEW HE HAD to go exploring that same night. There was a hurry now and his time wasn't really his own. They were in a race to contact Sylvie and bring her out before she had either begun to regress or Bruno had tired of her. Apart from that he needed to go out anyway some time during the night to retrieve the phone and his .32 that Donna would have had hidden under the bridge.

Lylly went out just after half past one in the morning. First job was to retrieve the .32 and the phone and see if Koggs or Donna had left any messages on it.

He left the dormitory then went out the second building's front door then circled back round the side till he was facing the top of the zigzagging road which ran from the building down the side of the knoll to the fields below, heading for its footbridge over the river and its junction with the hiking trail on the far side of the valley half a mile away.

There was a half moon in the sky and a luminous splash of stars overhead. This gave sufficient light to proceed carefully, without the need for a torch. There was the constant zizzle sound of cicadas forming a backdrop to the night.

He and Donna had agreed the phone and .32 would be hidden under the second bridge, not the third. They'd thought if placed under the third bridge it would involve Lylly approaching too closely to the third building from a direction that was expected to be watched. They didn't yet know what night-seeing capabilities Bruno and the twenty-one had, so until they had a better idea it was wise not to approach the third building until they wanted to.

He followed the path as it hairpinned down the hill to the

fields below. At the bottom the path joined the main unmetalled service road which ran along the base of the knolls, between them and the fields, before feeding into the car park at the rear of the third building. Lylly crossed over the road and entered the narrow path that ran through the fields. The field on his right was growing maize, with the corn spears over two metres high. This was just what Lylly needed, since the tall rows of maize shielded him from anyone scanning the fields from the windows or the roof of the third building.

The path ahead of him ran dead straight through the fields. Within a quarter mile he came to the arched stone footbridge over the Despeñaperros river. He had agreed with Donna that the items would be placed under the bridge on the far side of the river. This was to avoid Donna or anyone she sent to place the items being silhouetted on the bridge apex or extrados. The same applied to Lylly of course if he had to cross the bridge to retrieve the items. But they'd felt that Lylly would be arriving on the bridge later and there would be fewer spying eyes then.

Fewer spying eyes or not, Lylly took no risks in being silhouetted on the bridge by ducking down and crouching behind the parapet as he crossed the bridge. At the far side he dropped down the bank to water level, then ascended until he was under the initial stone springers and voussoirs as they launched the arch above from the solid base in the skewback set deep into the earth and bedrock. In the centre of the underside of the bridge by the stone base he found a small backpack. Inside was a Nokia phone, his .32, a couple of torches, a length of rope and a set of night-vision goggles.

There were two numbers programmed into the phone. One said OP, the other said K. There was one message on the phone. This was from K. It said:

<OP in place north cliffs above 3. Essential no action tonight. Eyes on only. Extraction poss tomorrow night subject to report>

Armed with the night goggles Lylly felt more capable of spying out the third building. He had originally planned to survey the building during daylight the next day. He'd felt he could more innocently stroll about and explore the area during the day. If spotted at night it would raise the alarm. That was, of course assuming he would not be recognised when and as he approached the third building. He was pretty certain the devil mask and his desperado impression had made him unknowable and unrecognisable to the members of the Perfects, especially Bruno and Heidi. But there was just the question of the hiking pole, as Frank Koggs had suggested. To be certain, he would dismantle the pole and stow it in the backpack during daylight hours.

But now, armed with the goggles he thought he would do both, take a look at the building now at night as well as during daylight the next day. He also thought it would be useful to have some new knowledge to be able to give Koggs a situation report as soon as possible. He sent a quick text to the OP number informing them he would be out this same night assessing the options and defence capabilities of the third building. He knew that from their observation point on the cliff top they'd be wearing night goggles too and at some point would no doubt see him as he moved around the area. He only hoped no one else would see him. But he thought the risk was worth taking.

He wondered about the best approach options. He thought the brick paved track over the connecting bridge from the second building to the hacienda's front door would be under observation at all times. As would the service road below the knolls that eventually fed into the car park at the rear of the third building and its back door. That meant both those approach routes were out. That left two options. The third path across the fields via the third arched footbridge; or a wider approach along the hiking trail, then cutting back either directly through the fields or along any path that might lie there, leading into the far end of the car park behind the hacienda.

He looked at his watch. It was just past two am. He decided to follow the hiking trail till he was well clear of the car park, then cut back to it. He reckoned it would take an hour. That would put him in the third building's car park around three am. He set off on the path from the bridge through the fields towards the hiking trail.

Fifteen minutes careful march brought him to the tee-junction. This was the one they called the second tee-junction, the one that linked the second building's path across the fields to the hiking trail. Lylly turned right.

A quarter mile along the hiking trail brought him to the third tee-junction. He stopped to look around. A path led away to the right down through the fields towards the third arched stone bridge and the service road below the third building. Lylly ignored that option and carried on along the trail.

A mile later on Lylly was well beyond the third building and past its car park. He had left the cultivated fields behind too. The hiking trail was making its way through thick woods. As far as he could tell in the moonlight and with the goggles the woods seemed to stretch all the way back to the car park.

He stopped because something caught his eye on a tree by the trail. There was a length of ribbon hanging from a low branch on a tree to the right of the trail. He couldn't tell, but he suspected the ribbon was red. Various bells were ringing in his mind. He knew that in Spain hunters tied ribbons – usually red - on trees by the side of roads and trails to help them locate animal traps they'd laid. The ribbon said in the woods directly in from this point there is a trap. Every trap a hunter laid would be so marked. They had to mark their whereabouts with reference to nearby roads and paths, otherwise they'd never find them again.

So far, so normal. But this was the first ribbon Lylly had seen. If this was a hunting area the woods would be festooned with such trap indicators. There hadn't been any. Yet the ribbon was an indicator of something. Lylly passed into the woods next to the tree with the ribbon. It was as he suspected. There were indications that a path had been made there. Certain slender tree branches had been pruned back. The undergrowth with all its snagging brambles and other path-inhibitors had been cleared.

There was definitely a path here, Lylly thought, and it was

heading in the general direction of the car park at the back of the third building. He followed it through the trees.

As he ducked and weaved along the path, two things struck him. One was a heartfelt relief that the trees would provide excellent cover and would shield him against being spotted, even by an observer wearing night-vision goggles. The other thing that struck him was to wonder that if this path did indeed end up by leading into the back of the car park, then how on earth did it cross the river? The nearest of the three footbridges was at least a mile away.

Lylly found the answer to that question a quarter mile later as he emerged from the trees and stepped into the open on the river bank.

A double rope and pulley wheel system had been slung across the river. The pulleys were anchored by wires and chains to stout trees on both banks of the river. Then a circuit of rope reached between the pulleys. Each of the two ropes had been attached by a secondary rope to a small rowing boat. You could step into a rowing boat and pull yourself across the river by hauling on the overhead rope attached to it. It didn't matter if both boats were on the same bank. You just hauled on the rope at the pulley to bring a boat back to your side.

Which was exactly what Lylly did, since both boats were on the far bank. He pulled one of the boats over to his side of the river. He stepped in it and pulled himself across to the other side. The pulleys were well oiled and made no noise.

It was in midstream that he realised that this route marked by a ribbon and this way of crossing the river was very likely the secret escape route for the inhabitants of the third building.

He left the boat and the riverbank and carried on through the trees on the far side. In less than another quarter mile he became aware that the trees ended up ahead and there was some kind of open space. He halted under the last trees. He was right at the back edge of the broad car park at the back of the third building. Beside him another short length of ribbon was hanging from the nearest tree.

He put the night-goggles on and looked around. The car park was half full with vehicles. There were camper-vans, a minibus, a white van, several SUVs and some saloon cars. Ahead the back of the hacienda had a set of high and wide double barndoors in the centre of the gable wall. Either side of the doors was a double window. And a third single window was in position above the doors, probably, Lylly realised, in the roof space. The double windows on the right as Lylly looked had an opening casement, which was now fully open.

Lylly reckoned that he could move from vehicle to vehicle across the car park without being seen. This might even give him a chance to look through the windows either side of the doors. And that, he thought would be enough. It would all in all be a good night's work. It meant the next morning he could concentrate on the other sides of the building. He checked his watch again. It was quarter past three.

He entered the car park and hid behind the first camper-van. He dodged from there diagonally across to the minibus. Then to an SUV, then finally to a point behind the second camper-van. From there it was less than ten metres across open space to the gable wall. He covered the ground in a crouch and stood behind the stout double doors. He pressed his ear against the wood and listened. There was no sound.

He crossed over to the windows on the left. He had a feeling he might see better through the glass without the goggles on. He took them off and put them in his backpack. He crouched under the window, then slowly raised his head. It was a bedroom. There was a single bed against one wall, with a bedside cupboard beside it. A table lamp was on top of it and was switched on. There was a table and chair against another wall. There was no one in the room. The bed was empty but the bedclothes were thrown back, as though the occupant had recently left.

He ducked down again and crossed the building to the other set of windows. The large casement window stood open. The room inside was pitch black. He heard no sound coming from inside and thought the room was most likely as empty as the one on the other side had been.

Lylly thought he could easily step over the threshold and enter the room without making a sound. His decision that he'd already done enough for one night was abandoned. It was too good an opportunity to find out more. He laid the backpack down. He dug out the Fairbairn-Sykes knife from the backpack and attached it to the pole. He took his .32 and his hiking pole and stepped over the low window frame and into the room.

43

HE HEARD VOICES WHISPERING from the far side of the large deep room. He froze. He could neither advance nor retreat without alerting the speakers.

"Heidi. Enough. I've had enough. Please leave me be. Please"

He thought it might be Sylvie's voice. She was pleading and sobbing.

"You do not get a choice girl. Now roll over and present."

"Bruno won't like it."

"You are wrong. He loves the idea. He likes to watch. But he's not going to know, is he? Because we're not going to tell him, are we?"

Lylly stood still. Eventually he realised he had no option. He clicked back the slide on the Seecamp.

With incredible speed as though attuned to any possible threat, Heidi leapt out of the bed, alerted by the alien sound. Behind her Sylvie clicked on the bedside lamp and sat up. The lamp threw a low amber light across the room.

Heidi stood naked facing him with her back to the bed. She half-crouched with her legs apart, well-balanced, ready for action. Then Heidi darted down to a pile of clothes by the side of the bed and came up with a black leather belt with a sheathed knife hanging from it. She withdrew the knife and threw the belt and sheath aside. In her hand was a long thin stabbing dagger with a nine inch blade. It was a classic stiletto, designed to penetrate the body easily with minimum force and cause maximum damage to the subcutaneous organs.

Lylly couldn't help noticing in the gloomy light of the bedside lamp that next to the pile of Heidi's clothes was a collection of sex equipment. There was Heidi's massive silver and black leather dildo, various vibrators and tubes of lubricant, plus some other things he didn't have time to recognise. Toys seemed an inappropriate and irrelevant word. These were all deadly serious. They must be the first items she put in her travel bag, he thought, never going anywhere without them.

Heidi noticed the direction of his glance and grinned at him.

It didn't seem that Heidi recognised him. The devil mask and the bandit impression at the commune had been sufficient to fool her. He was just some unwelcome intruder who needed to be removed with violence. He presumed she also thought she was protecting Sylvie. Even if Sylvie didn't want the kind of protection she was offering.

"I don't think you will use that, will you?" she said looking at the gun in his hand. "Do that and wake up twenty-one people? Have you enough ammo for all of them? I don't think so. It is not going to happen."

She was right. Lylly pocketed the gun. He grasped the hiking pole with both hands.

It was strange and disconcerting to fight a completely naked woman, Lylly realised. Things moved off-puttingly when you needed everything to be still to maintain focus. Heidi was slim and athletic with long stringy muscles, fast and very powerful. She circled round away from the bed into greater space, moving with lithe grace, confidently flaunting her nakedness, certain it was having a disconcerting effect on Lylly.

Lylly could see Heidi thought she held all the cards. She knew Lylly couldn't make any noise. He wondered momentarily why she didn't call for help and rouse the building, then realised that she felt she didn't need any help. She wanted to take him down on her own without any assistance from anyone else. Was there also an element of wanting to teach Lylly a lesson? Thinking he could brazenly steal into her bedroom and disrupt her activities? And threaten her woman?

Perhaps also he wondered whether what Sylvie had whispered rang true, that Heidi didn't want Bruno to know she was in Sylvie's room about to have forced sex with her. Maybe things had moved on considerably since the time they were both raping Sylvie simultaneously on the pi-frame. Perhaps now Bruno claimed exclusive rights. It made sense to Lylly. If she didn't fear Bruno she might want to compete with him.

Heidi moved in front of the bedroom door, reached back behind her and flicked the lock, such was her confidence in not wanting to be disturbed while she dealt with the intruder. She kept circling, angling her body one way then the other. She opened her legs and thrust her hairless depilated pudendum towards him in a mock sexual act while grinning in ironic lust. Lylly tried not to look. It was a diversion he guessed would often work. He kept watching her feet. He began to realise the depth of the danger he was in. This woman knew all the moves. Her leopard-like movements grew in fluidity and confidence. She was waiting for the most opportune moment to strike.

They circled each other warily. From his training in the Legion Lylly knew that two of the keys to fighting someone armed with a club or knife when you yourself were unarmed or armed to a lesser degree are the physical and the metaphysical. The physical is pretty obvious. Look at the weapon, the size of the opponent, the ground conditions, the space around the fighting area, even what clothes they're wearing to see how much freedom of movement they have.

The metaphysical elements are more ephemeral, less concrete but more important. They include assessing the skill of the opponent, apparent and real, checking commitment, balance, aggression, momentum. How much is bluster and how much is real. All fighting to some degree carries a certain amount of bluster. Everyone unless they're a pure bully, no matter how well trained they are, prefers not fighting if they don't have to. They all prefer shouting to fighting. Shouting carried no risk, fighting carries a hundred per cent risk.

Some unarmed combat experts said never take your eyes off

your opponent's eyes. Others say watch his hands. Camo's Dog Island instructor Hernan back in Melilla said that was nonsense.

"You must ignore the hands. What you must do above all else *ingles* is watch the feet."

Camo watched his opponent's feet. At the exact moment when the moving woman was most unbalanced with her own momentum as one sideways crouching stride melded into the next, Camo charged. He parried the knife with the shaft of the hiking pole and hit her with his full one hundred and fifty pound weight at fourteen feet per second in her chest with his upper arm and shoulder. Pumping his legs Camo inexorably shifted Heidi backwards off her feet and slammed her against the solid stone wall. As Heidi's breath was forcibly expelled from her lungs by the impact Camo banged the back of her head against the wall twice. As she dropped to the ground, stunned, Camo stepped back. He grasped the walking pole tightly but did not raise it up to strike. He found he was somehow reluctant to commit to the coup de grace, the killing stab with the pole.

It was a mistake. In that fractional hesitation Heidi recovered. She sprang to her feet, driving the stiletto up in a vicious arc aimed at his groin as she did so. It was fortunate that Lylly leapt back as she rose up. The blade missed. Heidi grinned. It seemed as if she had realised she had underestimated Lylly, but was now over that and was ready, better prepared for phase two. Heidi began to circle the room again with her back to the wall. Lylly turned constantly to keep his eyes on her.

But there was one thing she hadn't taken into account. She still underestimated the walking pole. She thought Lylly's main and only real weapons were the .32, his superior weight and his fists. She thought the walking pole was still only a pole. Remarkably, Lylly realised, that because Heidi didn't expect to see a knife attached to a hiking pole, she didn't actually see it, even though she glanced at it several times. Without the .32 she was confident that Lylly carried no threat that couldn't be outmatched by a skilful opponent comfortable in the use of a stiletto.

Lylly took instant advantage of Heidi's overconfidence. As Heidi planted her feet and made her first serious lunge with the knife in phase two, Lylly stepped back and aside and immediately counter-thrust the pole forward gripped tightly in both hands and stabbed Heidi firmly through the front right-centre of her neck. The blade severed key arteries, cleaved apart two neck vertebrae and cut major nerve roots, instantly and almost completely paralysing Heidi, as well as ruining, ravaging and obliterating her vocal cords. She fell to the floor, dropped the knife and tried to hold her neck with both hands. She was making a desperate gurgling sound.

Lylly had seen it before, but he was still astonished how quickly major neck trauma resulted in rapid death. Soon there was a massive pool of blood round Heidi's head and neck and she was gone.

He didn't know how much noise they'd been making. They must have been making some, but immersed in the action he had no awareness of the noise his fight with Heidi had made. But then again maybe the other members of the Perfects were used to loud, strange and probably nasty noises coming from Sylvie's room and were used to ignoring it.

Now he realised he had only an instant to make a choice. He could leave immediately by the way he came in. On his own, without Sylvie, he was confident he could get clear away without pursuit or serious risk. But what if he could also take Sylvie with him? If she would come.

Lylly seized the moment.

"We need to get out of here," he said.

He extended his hand to Sylvie. She was still sitting up in bed, her eyes wide with shock.

"Get some clothes on. Fast."

44

THIS WAS THE CRUNCH point. Everything now depended on how much Sylvie wanted to get away from Bruno and the Perfects and how much she recognised it was now or never.

Had she ever imagined this moment in her mind? And even if she had, would she be able to act on it and release the shackles, break out of the brutal iron maiden that Bruno had thrown round her mind, and flee from a situation she might have despaired of ever getting out of? Lylly held his breath.

There was another thing, even if Sylvie agreed to go on the run with him now, and they managed to escape from the building. They would be on their own. There would be no help waiting, no reinforcements, no back-up.

He was aware that Frank Koggs had more-or-less ordered that there would be no extraction attempt on the first night, this night, because of the underlying reality that they knew nothing. Lylly was supposed to be on a fact-finding mission. He was supposed to find out as much as he could and report back. Only with the information he supplied could they make a full and proper assessment of what a successful extraction would require.

Yet Lylly had jumped the gun, extended his brief, changed the plan. And sure every military leader and planner who ever lived would respect that. This was war and the first casualty of war is the carefully laid plan. But there was no escaping the consequences: if you changed the plan you were on your own.

His only hope was that the observation point on the cliff top above the convent complex was both in place and alert. When he and Sylvie emerged from the back of the third building and ran for cover in the trees, he hoped that the two members of the team at the OP would see them, recognise them, and get a message over to Koggs. What would Koggs do then? Lylly had no idea.

But Sylvie was willing and recognised the opportunity. Lylly wasn't sure if she recognised him from his two visits to the commune, but it seemed that Sylvie did want to leave. She began to throw on some clothes as rapidly as she could. They were committed now. He only hoped the OP would see them.

Lylly heard a noise from the door. He saw the door handle move as someone outside tried to open the door and found it locked. There was a single muffled but powerful thump as though the person was kicking the door.

Then the door flew back, splintered round the lock, and Bruno Ludo walked in to the room.

"I told you never lock the door against your master," he said then looked around.

He took in the scene with impressive and impassive rapidity. The naked Heidi lying dead in a pool of her own blood. Sylvie lacing up the second of her trainers. Lylly standing by the open window, ready to hoist Sylvie through and away. If he was disappointed to see his chief lieutenant Heidi dead on the floor he didn't show it.

Then Bruno's eyes widened to the full blue circle and he smiled. Lylly realised with a shock that Bruno recognised him. Perhaps it was the pole after all, as Frank Koggs had forecast. Or something else. Maybe when you try to hypnotise someone you remember their eyes. Or it might be something in Lylly's body language, movement or posture that gave him away. But whatever it was Lylly knew that the looming struggle with Bruno was going to be personal. Bruno was out for revenge.

"Eet ees meester Speedy," Bruno said in a fair imitation of Lylly's desperado act. "Weeth thee vairy darngerous steek. You no leeve 'ere alive."

Bruno's sole item of clothing was a white bathrobe. There was a large blue H on the breast pocket. He might have stolen it from an upmarket hotel, Lylly thought fleetingly.

Bruno spotted Heidi's stiletto lying next to her body and

dived down to the floor and picked it up. Then now armed he began to circle round the room, looking for an opening to attack. Lylly crouched correspondingly, with the hiking pole outstretched in front of him.

Also unlike Heidi Bruno recognised the danger represented by the walking pole straight away. He concentrated on it, never taking his eyes off it. He feinted to the left, and Lylly matched the feint with the pole, but Bruno leapt up like a centre forward meeting a cross to head into the top corner, and with the same complete mastery of muscle and limb as an Olympic gymnast, extended his bare feet in mid-air and with all his weight kicked Lylly on the right forearm and the left upper arm with both feet.

It was so sudden and skilful that Lylly didn't have time to react. Lylly's arms went numb almost instantaneously as Bruno's feet hit the pinchpoints in his arms and he dropped the pole. He had no choice. As he reached down to pick it up again, Bruno kicked it away.

Now he grinned at Lylly. "Where ees meester Speedy when you need heem, eh greengo?"

For the first time since entering the room Lylly realised he was out of his depth. Bruno was better than him at this. For all his training, Lylly recognised that much of his confidence in unarmed combat came from his proficiency with the hiking pole. With it removed from his grasp, Lylly was far less confident that he could take Bruno down. In fact he was beginning to realise he might be lucky to get out of the room alive.

Lylly tried to needle Bruno into careless action.

"Ishtar says she's going back to Babylon. Says you and your Prefects are a waste of space." He was chucking everything in he could think of to disconcert Bruno and make him overreact, to make him make a mistake.

He saw Bruno's eyes harden and the gleam diminish. There was an element of surprise there too, as though something very personal had been exposed, dragged out of its hiding place in the dark and now hung wriggling in the unaccustomed light.

"We chopped her up and burnt her by the way. Burnt very nicely. All she was good for really."

That got to him. Bruno let out an involuntary wounded gasp, but the insult did not make him rush into a reckless attack. He was too experienced, too good, to fall for that. The two men carried on circling. Lylly saw his attempt to provoke Bruno into mindless rage had failed. He also knew that time favoured Bruno more than him. There were twenty followers somewhere on the other side of the door that Bruno could call on.

Lylly finally thought he had no choice but to resort to his .32. He reached towards the pocket to pull it out. At that same moment Bruno leapt in the air and hit him again with both feet in his midriff, knocking Lylly backwards off balance. As he fought to remain upright he slipped on the edge of the pool of blood that had squirted out in vast quantities from Heidi's neck. His heels went from under him and he fell flat on his back.

In an instant Bruno was kneeling astride him, pinning his arms at the shoulder. Heidi's stiletto was in his right hand.

"Ishtar the great, the inexorable, is with me," Bruno whispered in his normal voice. "Now I theenk," he said, reverting to his Speedy Gonzales impression, "That thee tongue ees reemove first."

Lylly was leaping and bucking, but he couldn't shake Bruno off. Bruno now leaned forward and gripped Lylly's throat with his left hand. He began to alter his grip on the stiletto to cut and slice through Lylly's left cheek to get to his tongue. His eyes were lit up in triumph, revelling in his double revenge for the contempt of Ishtar and the lack of respect in the bandit impression, and delighted now with the prospect of the wreck he was going to make of Lylly's face.

"Bruno," Sylvie said. "

He turned to look at her in surprise as though he had forgotten she was in the room. His surprise deepened into disbelief and froze him into immobility when he saw that Sylvie was holding the hiking pole in both hands with the knife point aimed straight at him.

"Be gone," she said and stabbed him through the left eye

with the hiking pole as he turned his head towards her and opened his mouth to utter a word of command.

"You hurt me," she said. "You used me."

Sylvie's stroke was shaky and unprofessional, but it was enough. The seven inch blade cut Bruno's eye in two, and passed through the retina, sheared through the back of the eye socket and into the brain behind. She pushed as hard as she could as far as the blade would go.

"Be gone," she said again, as if to reinforce herself and exorcise his malevolent spirit from her being.

Then she let go of the pole and slumped to her knees. She was sobbing uncontrollably.

Bruno collapsed to the floor on his left side without a sound. Blood gushed for a moment from his eye socket and drool fell from his open mouth. He drummed his feet on the floor in a residual fit then lay still.

Lylly pushed him away and got to his feet. He was panting hard. They'd got lucky. Either Bruno had totally disregarded Sylvie and dismissed her as a threat, or his own attempt to infuriate Bruno to the point of sidetracking him had worked. Such was his anger at Lylly's scorn of Ishtar he had completely forgotten about Sylvie. Lylly didn't want to think about which one was more likely, but considering how tactically skilful and masterful Bruno was, both mistakes were foolish and arrogant.

Sylvie had stopped sobbing. She sat on the bed looking down at Bruno with shock on her face as though she couldn't believe she was responsible not only for his death but for the damage she had done to his once handsome face.

Lylly went over and sat next to her. He put an arm round her shoulders and held her tight.

"This time we really do have to go," he said.

She looked at him wildly, then seemed to focus. She nodded.

He picked up the end of the hiking pole and extracted it from Bruno's brain and eye socket. He also took Heidi's stiletto.

He almost pushed Sylvie through the open window. Then

he scrambled out after her. He picked up his backpack. He grabbed her hand. He guided her down the service road from the car park at the rear of the building to the fields below. They ran.

45

THEY HAD JUST REACHED the path through the fields below the hacienda when the lights came on in the building behind them. He thought he heard a shout or a cry coming from Sylvie's room.

It wasn't till they reached the small arched stone footbridge that Lylly stopped running and looked back. That was when he realised they were being followed. In fact they weren't just being followed, they were being chased. Bands of lights were heading down the path towards them. The beams of several torches seemed to be already approaching the edge of the fields.

He grabbed Sylvie's hand again and ran on down the other side of the bridge. He was heading for the hiking trail on the far edge of the fields. The trail he had been following a few hours before, the same one he had been on the previous morning with Donna and Todd.

They were gaining. Lylly could see the torch beams more clearly now. He tried to accelerate. Sylvie was panting hard. It began to occur to Lylly that they wouldn't escape along the hiking trail to the road before they were caught. And he was going to have to make a stand somewhere. He couldn't tell whether all the remaining twenty of Bruno's Perfects were chasing, or whether some had stayed behind. Either way he was going to be seriously outnumbered when he did stop and turn to face them. He had the .32 and he had the pole. He handed the stiletto to Sylvie.

"Do as much damage as you can," he said. "Don't make it easy for them." She nodded.

They reached the tee-junction where the path from the fields intercepted the hiking trail. He turned left onto the trail. They were heading now for the second tee-junction, followed by the bluff where the first tee—junction was. And after that it was another stretch to the road.

But what would happen when they reached the road? The pursuers weren't likely to give up just because they'd reached tarmac. Lylly stopped. They were both panting heavily. He dug out his Nokia phone. Rapidly he sent a text to the K number asking for help. But he knew they would be caught by their pursuers well before Koggs could raise a rescue party and send it down into the Defile.

And anyway would Koggs dare send a rescue party when he had no information to work with? Lylly didn't know. Lylly thought if it were him in Koggs's shoes then he would send a party into the Defile to attempt a rescue. But Lylly knew he was confusing reality with wishful thinking. Maybe Koggs would attempt to steer a middle way. He'd send a small investigative scouting group to have a look and report back. But would they have orders to engage if necessary? Lylly stopped chewing on it. There was no point. He had no idea what Koggs would do.

They ran on again. They came to the second tee-junction. They sped on.

Almost in confirmation of the hopelessness of their situation, he could now see torch beams penetrating through the fields along the path down from the first building. It was very likely that group would reach the first tee-junction, the one under the bluff, before Lylly and Sylvie. Then they would be trapped between the pursuers who had chased after them directly from the third building, and this new group. It was going to be close. He took Sylvie's hand again.

"Run," he said.

They ran. And they did get to the bluff first. Lylly stopped again. He could see that if they carried on running they would be caught in less than a hundred metres. It would be out in the open, on the path. They had to try something different.

He pushed his way through the scrubby trees at the very base of the bluff. He put on the night goggles again and tightened the strap.

"We're going to climb here," he said. "See if you can get up onto my back."

It was the only way they could both get up the cliff in the time available. He'd have to carry her, and she'd be riding piggy-back.

Lylly crouched down while Sylvie got up onto his back. She didn't hesitate. She seemed to trust Lylly implicitly. Lylly thought she knew who he was. She was there both times when Lylly did his desperado bandit act with Bruno. Perhaps she remembered. If he got a chance he'd ask her.

"Grip tightly round my neck," he said.

He stood up and looked at how to make a start on the cliff. He found the place and began to climb.

He wouldn't have done it without the night vision goggles. The eerie green light showed him where he could place his feet and where he could grip with his hands. Without the goggles he could not see the right places in the dark. He couldn't have climbed up and they would have had to make their stand on the ground at the base of the cliff. It wouldn't have been much of a stand.

About fifteen metres up there was a small ledge, cutting back into the rockface. Lylly climbed onto it and knelt to ease Sylvie off his back. Then he remained in that position for a moment, panting. They both stood there on the ledge. They were both too tired to go any further, too tired to even think about looking to go further.

The torchlights now clustered on the hiking trail outside the ring of trees at the base of the bluff. They pressed themselves against the rockface to avoid being highlighted by the beams. Lylly took the goggles off to avoid being light-blinded by a torch beam as the figures below waved their lights around.

"This'll have to do," Lylly said.

46

LYLLY PUT THE NIGHT-VISION goggles back on. He wanted to be able to see what the Perfects tried next and what direction it would come from.

He knew that much depended on whether the Perfects wanted to capture them or kill them. If kill them, then that was simple. All they'd have to do, if they had night-vision goggles, was stand off some way from the bluff and pick them off with rifles. There would be nothing that Lylly would be able to do about that. There was nowhere to hide on the ledge. If it was capture they wanted then they'd have to climb up to the ledge and pull them down. Lylly thought he should be able to interfere with that. But again, a lot depended on how they attempted the capture. If they had marksmen standing off to cover them while other members of the Perfects climbed up, then Lylly couldn't do much about that either. But if they just tried to swarm up without plan or thought, then Lylly could do them some serious damage. Enough to make them think again, at least, and come up with a better plan. And anything that took time was gold dust. It seemed a lot now depended on whether they had night-vision capability.

Lylly hoped that Bruno and Heidi had very much been the brains of the outfit and without them they wouldn't be so good at making effective plans.

He was right. As soon as the first crowd of torchbearers arrived at the base of the bluff they nearly all crashed through the trees and attempted to climb up the cliff in hot pursuit. The ones that remained at the base couldn't shoot at Lylly or Sylvie for fear of hitting their fellow Perfects climbing up the cliff face. Lylly was able to do considerable damage to arms and faces and hands, cutting and slashing with the hiking pole before they abandoned the idea. Eventually they all clustered at the base of the bluff in conference.

What next? Lylly thought. He wasn't worried about food or water. He hoped it couldn't be too long before Koggs's rescue party arrived. If it was coming. But however long or short it was there would still be plenty of time for the twenty members of the Perfects to kill or capture them.

The way the Perfects attempted to swarm up the cliff and pull them down told Lylly the Perfects were indeed fighting like Aztecs. That meant they wanted to capture not kill them. Isolated as he and Sylvie were on the cliff edge it would have been the easiest thing in the world for one of the Perfects to move away to the right distance and shoot them. The fact that none of them did this told him either that they couldn't see them from a distance in the dark, or that their intention was capture not kill.

That gave him a certain amount of hope. He reckoned that by stabbing down from their high point with pole and stiletto he and Sylvie could prevent anyone climbing up to grab them. However the hope was diminished to a large degree though by the fact that the Aztecs always fought to capture not kill because they needed their captives alive so they could be taken for immediate sacrifice on the steps of the great pyramid of Tenochtitlan.

He looked at his watch. It was nearing five am. He thought sunrise might be in another hour and a half or two hours.

Lylly was wondering whether it was time to make a noise. He still had his Seecamp in his pocket. Several shots would rouse the occupants of the convent, especially if this was not a hunting area and shots were unusual in the vicinity. On the other hand he still didn't know what the deal was between Bruno's Perfects and the Maria Magdalenas. They had handed over the hacienda to Bruno, certainly, but had they also given the Perfects licence to hunt people and kill or capture them? And anyway did the arrangement still apply if Bruno was dead? Lylly thought it might not.

While they waited for the next attack, or for the Perfects to try something different, Lylly filled Sylvie in on the background.

He didn't know what she knew, or even what she remembered. He couldn't imagine what it was like to go through everything she had experienced over the last two years in her short life.

He told her all about the attempted human sacrifice of her mother by Bruno. That really shocked her. He told her how he had come along and found her mother and released her. He told the story of the horse ride and the attempted shooting of Merci, and the dead horse. Then the agreement with Frank Koggs that he would use his company people and expertise to extract her from the commune. Then came the successful extraction.

But then he told of the masterstroke by Bruno that resulted in her recapture. He saw that Sylvie, utterly quiet, now had tears rolling down her cheeks.

"Go on," she said. "Tell me everything. How did you find me?"

He told her the strange story of Bruno's half-brother, the successful plastic surgeon. And his half-hearted attempt to use Lylly to thwart Bruno. He didn't tell her anything about his torture of Louis Kellner to extract the information about Bruno's whereabouts. He just said Louis told them where Bruno was.

"Then you came and got me out," she said. She smiled through the tears.

"Yes," he said. But thought frying pan and fire.

Below them the Perfects regrouped for another more coordinated and sophisticated attempt to swarm the ledge. Lylly looked across to where Sylvie prepared herself to challenge the attackers. He knew that Sylvie was physically exhausted and emotionally shattered. She wouldn't be able to do much in the way of wielding the stiletto to prevent the attackers scaling the cliff and scrambling onto the ledge if the attacks kept coming. Not only that she'd had no training and wouldn't be particularly adept at handling the knife. The hiking pole was far better suited to this kind of work. She would try her hardest, Lylly knew that. But he also knew he would have to be extra vigilant and come to her aid if it looked like she was being overwhelmed.

Now two of the Perfects tried to climb up at the very far edges of the ledge simultaneously. This was a clear effort to split Lylly and Sylvie up in their defence of their position on the ledge. The climber at her end of the ledge even managed to grab Sylvie's ankle from below before her scream alerted Lylly and he leapt across and stabbed the man's wrist. He too screamed and fell back to the base of the cliff. The attacks ceased for the moment.

Lylly was pretty sure he hadn't killed anyone. Yet. As far as he could tell he'd stabbed fingers and hands, wrists, forearms and shoulders. Nasty but not deadly. He wondered how long that would last. He also wondered if he did kill someone, more by accident than design, whether the Perfects would then give up their attempts to capture them, and would just bear off, wait till they could see, and shoot them from a distance.

For the time being the attempts to scale the cliff and capture them continued. There would be an attempt, either coordinated or just random. And Lylly, with growing confidence and considerable assistance from Sylvie with the stiletto, managed to beat the attack off. Then there would be silence for a while. Then another attack would come.

Lylly knew that this couldn't go on. Both he and Sylvie were close to exhaustion. He or she, or both of them would make a mistake, and that would be it.

For some reason Lylly thought it would be better when daylight came. He had no reason for thinking this. It was just an instinct. Things would always be better when daylight came. But he also couldn't help thinking that when light came he and Sylvie could be seen and so could be shot.

Another attack came. More thrusting with the pole, more stabbing with the stiletto. The attackers retreated. Lylly's biggest fear now was the Perfects would find some way of protecting their hands and arms as they attempted to grab him and Sylvie; some way of preventing the successful fending-off stabbing. Perhaps they'd sent, or would send when it dawned on them, people back to the hacienda to bring up the necessary armour. Bin lids or boxes would be very effective. The armour didn't even have to be metal or wood, strong thick plastic would do, even cardboard if they had enough layers.

Then the next expected attack didn't come. Instead one moment there was massed torchlight in a group below them, then next there were separate and scattered torch beams disappearing at speed back down the hiking trail in different directions.

Lylly thought he heard shouting coming out of the woods below. Was it more of them? Then overhead came the clatter of a helicopter. Its heavy searchlight was fixing the trees with light.

Then below them was only blackness and silence. Then a voice split the silence.

"You going to stay up there till daylight?" It was a woman's voice.

"You need help get down?" A man's voice.

Lylly recognised them both.

47

"THE OP SAW YOU BOTH running from the building down the road into the fields. They sent a message over saying you and Sylvie were out, but the followers were in hot pursuit," Donna said. "We assumed then that Bruno was leading the chase. I reckoned you were making for the bluff." She smiled, "That's what I'd've done. Make a stand there. But it didn't look like you'd make it. Frank put a drone up with infra-red and we could see."

It was a debriefing session in the hotel in La Carolina. Donna and Todd at the head of most of Koggs's hands had brought Lylly and Sylvie out of the Defile and back to the hotel.

"So I sent a team out tout-de-suite," Koggs said.

"Good thing. Thanks, both," Lylly said.

He knew that if Koggs hadn't responded to the emergency by sending in his full team, he and Sylvie would probably now be dead or captured. More likely, Sylvie would be captured and he would be dead. It was a brave move on Koggs's part. He'd acted on no more information than the fuzzy hotspot infra-red images received from a drone camera. Lylly's respect for Koggs's decision-making climbed a big notch.

"We came as quick as we could. But I knew you were already being attacked," Donna said. She'd led the team in to the Defile.

"We started making a ruckus on the trail in the woods as we got close. Make them think there were more of us than them. We expected there might be some shooting. Knives. Maybe some hand-to-hand. We were ready for that. But they just dispersed and melted away.

"Guess that happens when there's no real leadership. We didn't know till you told us he wasn't there, but without Bruno they were kind of lost. No plan. And Frank got the chopper out overhead with the searchlight going. Looking like it was the police."

"But what the hell?" Koggs said. He was angry. "I sent you a text. No extraction the first night. Eyes only. We just didn't know enough at that stage. Then next thing I get a message from the OP saying they'd seen you and the girl on the run. And the gang is on your tail. Then I get your message saying you're holed up and need help and rescue. How come? What would you have done if I thought it was too dangerous to send my people in? Way too many unknowns. We should've done it my way."

"Should we?" Lylly responded. "What exactly was your plan Colonel? Shoot the place up? Create a racket. Cause chaos. Get everyone milling about. The headless chicken approach? And somehow that would give me or another one of your teams a chance to get in and spirit Sylvie away? What happened if the women in the convent got involved? What happened if the noise brought them all out to see what was going on? And they got in the firing line? What happened if the Magdas called the police at the sound of the first shot? Or Bruno and the Perfects started taking hostages? He stays calm and doesn't become a headless chicken? Where's your plan then?"

"He's right, boss," Donna said.

"I saw a chance to get Sylvie out. And took it. There was minimum noise and commotion. It was a risk, I agree. But it worked. More-or-less."

He didn't add: and I got rid of the two most dangerous opponents, but he could see they thought it too.

"He's right, boss," Donna said again. "And only two deaths. Far as we know."

And with no murder weapon found with the bodies, and with the Perfects dispersed and on the run, the deaths could be put down to infighting in Bruno's band. In fact it might be a good assumption that the Perfects themselves thought that Bruno and Heidi had fought over access to Sylvie and had killed each other. At which point Sylvie had slipped away through the open window, fleeing to a rendezvous with Lylly somewhere nearby, taking Heidi's stiletto the presumed murder weapon with her for defence. But none of the Perfects were around to elicit their opinion or their view of the matter.

Lylly had originally wanted to tell the full story to the Spanish police. He would also claim both Heidi's and Bruno's deaths had been at his hand, to avoid any further trauma for Sylvie. In self-defence of course, but his doing. But Koggs and Donna had persuaded him to let it lie and let the police assume the Perfects had fought amongst themselves. And let the fleeing Perfects continue to think that Bruno and Heidi might have killed each other. And if eventually any of the Perfects were arrested they'd pass on to the police the view that Bruno and Heidi had fought.

"It's neat," Koggs said.

"Long as it sticks," Donna said.

Koggs had been talking to a contact in the Spanish police and had learnt that the current head Maria of the Magdalenas was French. She claimed Bruno and his Perfects' use of the hacienda was down to blackmail rather than because he was a friend. He wasn't that, she said with a degree of loathing apparently. She'd called the police with all the commotion going on, and she was talking, trying to keep her sisterhood out of it, Koggs said.

It wasn't that she had owed Bruno a favour; she had let them use the hacienda because she had no choice. She never admitted what the blackmail was about and the police didn't push it. It was clear that she was glad that Bruno was dead and the blackmail had died with him. Koggs's contact said that the Maria had been in the French military and the supposition was she may have known or met Bruno during their time in the army when their units were billeted near each other or when they were on joint war games or exercises. Maybe Bruno had got something on her then. That was the assumption in any case, but no party any longer had any desire to follow it any further and find out what it was.

"What about Sylvie?" Lylly said. "I know she's with her mum now but we need to get her to the psych doc, rapido. I think she's good, but she's been through a hell of a lot."

"Already sorted," Koggs said. "Doc Siding was on the transatlantic plane this morning with her team, soon as I told her we got Sylvie. They'll make their way to the Gap chalet. I'm going to fly Merci and Sylvie in the chopper to Alicante and they'll get a flight to Nice, Turin or Geneva from there, whichever's first, with a two person escort. Company car and personnel will meet them and drive them to the chalet. The doc can assess her there. Talk more later."

Koggs left the room to get the chopper ready for his flight.

Sylvie was currently sleeping in a room in the hotel in La Carolina. As far as Lylly could tell she seemed to be glad to be out. She was still crying a lot. He hoped she was crying in a kind of relief because it was all over.

Lylly heard the noise of a helicopter firing up its engine. He went upstairs to talk to Merci Stahl. And to say goodbye.

As he watched Koggs's chopper climb into the bright hot and still July midday air and whisk Merci and Sylvie Stahl away to the east from the Desfiladero de Despeñaperro, Lylly suddenly felt empty, deflated, worn out. He didn't have a sense of victory. He had no sense of successful completion or of a job well done. He knew he needed sleep, but that was just part of it. It was this lifestyle that was exhausting him. It wasn't the obvious, the threat to his own life and limb, such as occurred throughout the recent two days. It was more the constant worry about the well-being of other people. Above all, Lylly was tired of the responsibility. He wanted to stop caring.

"I need to sleep," he said, but he didn't think that would be enough.

48

NEXT MORNING HE FELT slightly better. But he knew there was a deep problem and didn't know how to shift it.

They held a post-operation meeting in the hotel conference room. All the members of Koggs's teams were there. Many of them congratulated Lylly and clapped him on the back. But he didn't feel like the main character in a heroic saga. Instead he felt like an insignificant spear-carrier caught in a whirlwind of events beyond his understanding and doomed to carry out his orders.

Koggs himself had returned later the night before with the chopper from Alicante airport. He'd had contact with professor Siding and said she was installed in the Gap chalet and was already looking forward to working with Sylvie. As soon as they arrived she'd ask Merci to go back to her chateau, but thought she might be able to return very soon.

The main item under discussion was to decide if they needed to do anything more about the remains of Bruno's Perfects. There would be twenty of them in all, some in urgent need of medical attention. It was agreed that when Koggs's teams had collided with them below Lylly's bluff, they seemed to have split up and dispersed into the landscape. With the head Maria at the convent calling in the police, the Perfects had no safe house any longer. With Bruno dead they couldn't go back to the third building, the hacienda. They were a proscribed and hunted group throughout Europe for their attack on the Stahl chateau and chalet and the killing of Alain Stahl.

Bruno Ludo had been the unifying and guiding force within the group. With him gone the unity and cohesion of the group was bound to wither. Some, the ones that needed him most, would indeed cling on to the memory of Bruno and perhaps try to keep the group going. Others, over whom Bruno had less hold would begin to go their own way.

It remained to be seen, if there was a Bruno-rump forming, whether they would attempt to continue his agenda. In which case would that mean there would still be a threat against Sylvie Stahl and her mother? And if so what should they do about that?

For once Lylly and Koggs were agreed. They both felt that the danger to Merci and Sylvie Stahl had passed. If there was a Bruno-rump forming then it was more likely they would create their own agenda, depending on the whims of the leadership group, rather than blindly continue the remnants of Bruno's personal agenda. They agreed that Bruno's fixation with Sylvie Stahl had been deeply personal. And would most likely not be passed on to any remaining members of the Perfects.

Regarding the job-lot package of Bruno's religious peccadilloes, the men and women round the conference table thought that only Bruno had sufficient knowledge and experience to put such an unlikely and bloodthirsty combination together. They thought it was unlikely that anyone would be causing havoc anywhere or seeking human sacrifice in the name of the ancient Druids or Ishtar of the Babylonians.

"We'll watch and listen," Frank Koggs said. "Follow the news. Keep contact channels open. But I reckon it's over."

Lylly agreed.

They were all in the hotel parking area later in the morning after they'd come out of the final winding-up conference and checked out. They were dispersing by car in various directions, to Paris and Marseille. Koggs himself was driving back to the Stahl chateau, then up to the Gap chalet to confer with professor Siding. He told Lylly he didn't want to fly the chopper up. He'd delegated that to one of the team.

"Road trip sometimes is the best way to wind down," he said. "Often take me an automobile home whenever a job's done. Gets me ready for the next contract."

Koggs wanted to talk contracts with Camo Lylly but he could see that Lylly had had enough and needed to think things through. Though he wanted Lylly to join his organisation, he knew it wasn't the right time. He didn't now offer him a permanent job in the company. The time might come, but it wasn't yet. He hadn't yet told Lylly that his ad hoc on the hoof decision to get Sylvie out as soon as he saw her worked better than his own plan would likely have done. But he would tell him in time. His organisation needed someone who could take unpredictable decisions and then make them work. He had shown Lylly that he was angry with him for changing the plan, for putting Koggs in the situation where he had to make an instant decision based on no information. But anger or not he knew Lylly had made the right call. Koggs had great respect for the fact that Lylly had disagreed strongly with him afterwards about the plan and hadn't apologised or backed down.

"I ain't saying goodbye," Koggs said, extending his hand to Lylly. "I got your number. I'll call when you're ready."

The last to leave were Donna and Todd. They were sharing an SUV on the long road back to their office HQ in Paris.

Donna came over to Lylly as he was standing by his car door. He hadn't yet decided which direction he would go in, or to what destination. Most likely he would go home to his apartment in Antequera in the south. He didn't want to look further ahead than that. She handed him a company card. It had two phone numbers handwritten on the back.

"Mine and Todd's," she said. "You need anything, call."

She patted his arm above the elbow, then grinned and turned away. Todd waved in salute from the driver's seat of their car.

Lylly watched their vehicle disappear to the north. He stood for a while by the roadside waiting for something, but he didn't know what.

EPILOGUE

49

CAMO LYLLY EASED THE BACKPACK off his shoulders and pulled out one of his water bottles.

He was on a long-distance trail again. This time he was heading south. It was over a year, fifteen months, since he'd had to interrupt his walk along GR4 when he found Merci Stahl pinned to the tunnel wall. Now he was trekking on a more rugged trail across bigger mountains. This time it was along the GR5 trail, the big one across the High Alps. He was heading south across the mountains to Nice, hugging the Swiss and Italian borders all the way. He'd started on the southern shore of lake Geneva in the last week of August. Now it was mid-September and he'd been on the trail for three weeks as it hugged the Italian border heading south. He was still a week away from Nice.

He'd walked with other people several times for several days, as they headed along the trail, but always left them to go his own way. He preferred to be on his own. It was good to walk and it was good to talk, but sometimes it was good just to walk.

He stayed in official high-pasture trailside gites, in dilapidated mountain huts and roofless shepherd bothies. Other nights he slept in his tent, alone except for the sounds of the night. Then occasionally when the trail came down from the high ground and passed through Alpine towns and villages he checked into a hotel, finding the attraction of a hot meal and comfortable bed too strong.

There were other nights too which stayed in his memory more. This was when he didn't put up the tent but instead lay out under the stars in his sleeping bag, insulation mat and waterproof bivvy bag and watched meteors speed across the night sky. It was those nights that helped mend him most.

In places the trail passed through land frequently disputed across the ages. The new trail followed old military supply lines and packhorse trails. The mountains, while themselves not particularly in contention, had provided access throughout history to what lay beyond, to areas that had been much fought over and invaded, by way of easy passes through the mountains.

The high ground was monitored and the passes blocked by fortifications dug deep into the rock or perched on crags and clifftops. Blockhouses, gun emplacements, ouvrages, casemates and embrasures, even whole garrisons, had been built in prominent positions overlooking the high passes to make the passage of the mountains uncertain for the invader. For days the GR5 trail coincided with the original supply routes to these strongpoints. In some cases, Lylly was well aware, the derelict but intact ouvrages and casemates belonged not to France but to the extinct nation of Savoy which had fortified the passes against the growing and ambitious encroachments of France. They were successful only for a while.

Lylly evidenced the depth of time involved in the militarisation of the mountains, where he noticed the fortifications turned from stone blocks to concrete. One night Lylly pitched his tent outside one of the most recent of these more modern works. It was a blockhouse dug deep into and under the base of a cliff, dominating a bend in the trail which could be swept by the field of fire from the deep slits in its concrete façade. He knew this was a fortification built under the Maginot programme to stop an intrusion from Italy by Mussolini's Fascisti in the lead-in to the Second World War.

In a way Lylly found this evidence of old struggle comforting. The fact that these massive and expensive works were all abandoned, ruined and unused was after all a sign of progress.

Around this time, for a while, a big pyramid shaped mountain that towered above all its neighbouring peaks was a constant companion on his left hand side. He knew it was Monte Viso. It was a few days after leaving Monte Viso behind that the trail made a huge jump in climate and vegetation as it made the crossing into Provence.

Now, a week north of Nice, Lylly made the same traverse. When he ascended the steep climb up to the high ridge of the Pas de la Cavale, between Larche and St Etienne de Tinee, he crossed over into Provence.

He came up to the line of the ridge, and as his head was first raised above the parapet of the col he was assailed by a wave of smells, of herbs and flowers, and shrubs and perfumed vegetation, but most of all by the clean smell of lavender. The ridge marked the northern edge of the Alpes de Provence, the transition between the higher but greener Savoy Alps and the lower but more rugged Provencale Alps.

Camo eased the backpack off his shoulders and pulled out one of his water bottles. He found a convenient rock and sat down on the apex of the col on the doorstep of Provence.

Perhaps it was the smells. But Lylly thought it was more likely it was the aggressive vegetation. He was hit by the full force of the reminder of the similar smells and the same snaggy uncharitable vegetation at the Stahl's ranch, the chateau in the wild land west of Castellane, deep in Provence.

There, then, at the northern edge of Provence he wanted to see Merci and Sylvie Stahl again. It was time. Now at last he was ready.

He hadn't seen them for a year. He had been avoiding them. They'd texted him but he hadn't replied. Merci had left voice messages but he hadn't responded. He wanted to be alone for a while. He wanted to work through everything that had happened. Not least he wanted to come to terms with the fact that he had killed one person and been responsible for the death of the other. It felt like he was the killer of both of them, both Heidi and Bruno. He had killed them for no greater reason than they would have killed him.

It should have been enough. But for a long while it wasn't. He wasn't sure he wanted a life where such things were not only possible they were not even uncommon. But now he was content. He hadn't become accustomed to it. He just accepted it. If he had become an agent for other people's deaths, then so be it. He now fully realised he was good at it. And he could live with that.

Lylly sat on a rock by the trail slowly sipping from the water bottle. He looked at the map. He was in the high mountains above the small town of St Etienne-de-Tinee. He could get a taxi from there.

He shrugged the heavy pack back onto his shoulders. He planted the two walking poles firmly into the ground and set off at pace downhill.

It took an hour on foot to descend to the town, then another two and a half hours by road to reach the gates of the Stahl chateau and the beginning of the red road. He asked the taxi driver to drop him off at the gates. He began walking along the four mile long red tarmac drive.

He came out of the trees into the broad parking area in front of the chateau. He stopped and looked around. Two women were playing tennis on the courts.

They played on without noticing him. Then the younger one looked up. Her mother's service whizzed past her while she made no effort to return it.

"It's Camo," she shouted, almost a laugh. "Camo!"

Her mother turned round to see. Then both women dropped their racquets and ran towards him with open arms.

Lylly stayed with the Stahls in their chateau for three weeks. First, a day after arriving he retrieved his car which he'd left in Nice when he organised his walk along the high trail.

He walked with Merci and Sylvie, sometimes together and sometimes separately, through the woods and on the mountain slopes. They talked a lot and Lylly listened. Sylvie talked of her time in the commune under Bruno's spell. She also spoke about the work that Doc Siding had done with her and it was clear she was deeply in her debt.

He'd called Professor Tess Siding quite a few times during Sylvie's recovery period. She told him she was astonished at the rapid speed of Sylvie's progress. Now Lylly too was amazed at how serenely normal Sylvie seemed. She was lively and bubbly, excited with the world, just like he might expect any happy confident woman in her late teens to be. As they talked he could find no grim echo or repository of the horrific ordeal she had experienced at the hands of Bruno Ludo and Heidi.

But maybe it was still all too early to be sure, he thought. He knew that Siding was still in touch with Sylvie and visited her regularly for check-ups. Lylly knew that he too would do the same. He would be there if she needed him.

There was one thing still nagging him. And that was the shooting incident with the dead horse. It had been an unfilled hole in his mind ever since he'd learnt what the pi-frames were for and met the representation of Ishtar of the Babylonians, and had discerned Bruno's obsession with human sacrifice. He hoped Sylvie might be able to help.

The two of them were hiking on a nearby hillside and had stopped to eat a sandwich.

"Why did Bruno try to shoot your mum?" He asked her. "What was that about? There was no ritual to it. No pi, no Ishtar. Was he in a hurry for some reason? Because it doesn't fit."

Sylvie was silent for a long while. She took in the view, then examined the backs of her hands. Eventually she spoke.

"You know what," she said. Her voice was still and quiet. "I was ok with it. I was ok with Bruno trying to sacrifice my mum. It seemed necessary to make the universe function. He said it would give us insights. Oh my." Tears came.

"That wasn't you," Camo said. "It wasn't you." He reached for one of her hands and held it between his two. "It was Bruno. It was all Bruno."

She smiled slightly and dried her eyes.

"I'm glad I killed him. I'm glad it was me. It was me who got rid of him. That makes it right." She was purposeful and spirited again. The darkness had passed.

During the days he spent with her Lylly was continually

amazed at Sylvie's strength and her powers of recovery. He doubted that he would have been such a successful survivor.

"But no you're absolutely right," Sylvie continued. "It wasn't Bruno. It was Heidi who took the shot at my mum. She did it without permission. She left the commune on her own and tried to shoot her. She told me it was because she wanted to be the one to take my mum's life-force, then I would be hers forever. It was horrible. But in my dream-state I accepted it. It seemed obvious and fitting and the only course of action that made sense.

"Bruno naturally was almost catatonic over it. I don't think he ever forgave her. They began to go their separate ways from then on. She was no longer the trusted lieutenant. I think Heidi might even have tried to get rid of Bruno. Challenge him somehow at some point and take over.

"I'm glad they're both gone. She was as bad as him in her own way. I'm not just saying that from my own point of view. The world's a better place without them."

"Do you think she could? Challenge him?"

"No. She would have failed. Bruno would have killed her."

They came down from the mountain. Lylly had no more questions.

On another day Camo and Sylvie walked along the arroyo. The watercourse was dry still in late September. He knew it would be quite a sight in winter, roaring and flashing, turbulent and impatient, laden with mud and debris when the rains came.

Sylvie was still talking to him about her time in the commune. But he knew it was all coming to an end. She was almost talked out and had nothing more to say about it. And he knew that was good. She could look forward instead of back. There was one last thing and it lit up her face as she recalled it.

He was astonished and delighted to learn that Sylvie had first begun to see through Bruno and fall away from her orbit round him when she heard Lylly's ludicrous Mexican bandit impression.

"It was hilarious," she said. "But I didn't dare laugh. He was on fire. He couldn't stand it. He took it as a slight, a personal affront. He was desperate to find out who you were. I had orders to ask my mom all about you and who you were. He was desperate to teach you a lesson. But I just thought it was funny. I'd never seen anyone disrespect Bruno in that way. I don't think Bruno had either. He said he was going to cut out your tongue."

She also saw a petty, cruel and mean side of Bruno for the first time.

"It set me thinking," she said. "It felt like I hadn't done that for ages."

Another time, on the tennis court, he was also delighted to hear that Sylvie was set to go to university in the autumn.

He already knew that after Doc Siding's work was done, Sylvie had returned to school. She was voracious. She rapidly caught up all the year she'd lost, the education she'd missed while in the commune. She started studying while she was still in the chalet, recovering under Doc Siding's gentle programme.

It gave her a new focus, the doc told Lylly when he checked up quietly in the early days, a while back. She couldn't get enough learning. She breezed through the exams. She was going to study English literature at Notre Dame college, which wasn't far south of professor Siding's department in Chicago. Which was also good, Lylly thought.

"I'm so glad," Lylly said. "But pity you didn't choose to do a proper subject like civil engineering."

She laughed then fired an unreturnable service at his weaker backhand side.

But Lylly was glad she was going to study English. It had been her quotation of Middleton's great line that had first told Doc Siding that Sylvie might fully recover. The realisation that the only benefit she gained from Bruno's bewitching minute was a poor one was crucial in her willingness to seek help to climb out of the deep well she was in. Then later the knowledge that the poor benefit of a bewitching minute was all there really was to the entire universe was the start on her road to regaining her individuality.

He and Merci were very comfortable together. They did not

make love, but both seemed to acknowledge that it could happen at any time now or in the future should either of them wish it.

Often they rode quadbikes up into the high meadows and followed the sheep and watched the dogs patrolling the outskirts of the flock, or sat by the stream.

He even played tennis, a lot, and found that both women could beat him.

50

THERE WAS ONE MORE THING he had to do to keep Sylvie safe. Bruno and Heidi might be dead and the Perfects dispersed, but there was a horror still out there that was created during Sylvie's time under Bruno's spell and its connection to her must be cut.

One day while still at the Stahl chateau Lylly took a day-trip west in his car. He found what he needed in the farm workshops and loaded the boot with a large cross-cut saw, a two-handed felling axe, a sledgehammer and four large steel wedges.

He didn't find a chainsaw. But then he wasn't looking for one. A chainsaw would make it too quick and definitely too techno. There was too much distance and separation, agnosticism and immunity inherent in the technology. What Lylly needed was something much more personal. It had to be a hands-on task with the appropriate tools from the right epoch. The fact they were steel not bronze only multiplied their impact. She needed to feel every rasp of the saw, every bite of the axe, every blow of the sledgehammer, and every prise of the wedge. Only then would she be vanquished and the connection to Sylvie severed.

He was going to do what he had told Bruno he had already done. He was going to destroy the effigy of Ishtar.

He didn't ask Merci or Sylvie to come with him. He thought they'd react badly to the depiction of Sylvie as the goddess Ishtar.

He arrived at the entrance to the commune. He assumed the place was carrying on now much as it had done before Bruno came, an eccentric but essentially harmless home for a cult. He saw that the B&B was still in operation and there was a stack of cars parked behind the big building. He crossed the bridge over the stream and parked with the other vehicles behind the B&B. He noticed that the big ball of mistletoe on the gable end had gone.

He took the axe, saw, wedges and sledgehammer and set off through the woods following the track by the side of the stream.

As before, he came to the point where the trail ended in a wall of trees. He crossed the stream by the stepping stones and came to the grove of Ishtar.

In the fifteen months since he had been in the clearing it looked as if no one else had found the place. The ground was undisturbed, and the pi-frames and the statue were untouched. The ad hoc benches still marked out the perimeter. Only the emergence of new growth underfoot showed that time had passed.

First thing he did was saw through the bases of the pi-frames near ground level and throw them down. That was the easy part. It also cleared the space round the statue so he could more easily set to work on it.

The statue of Ishtar was going to be more difficult. It had been a living tree before being cut down, truncated, and carved into the effigy of the goddess. The base still had all its roots embedded in the ground. In Bruno's savage world perhaps it had to be a living tree, he thought, to be fully invested with the spirit of Ishtar.

Lylly stood facing Ishtar. He felt her staring back at him implacably. It's you and me now, he thought. There's no one else. No one's coming to defend you. They ran away. You're out of time. He felt like a gladiator in the arena. He had all the skills and all the weapons to be victorious.

"It ends now," he told the image. "She is yours no more."

He began his attack.

First he cut the arms off at the shoulder with the saw. He chopped them and the snakes they held into small pieces with the axe. Then he thought he would use the saw to cut through the base of the stump and so topple it over. And he started on that. But there was something off. He hesitated. It didn't feel right. Then he got it. The saw wasn't destructive enough.

He abandoned the saw and took up the felling axe. Now he dug deep into the base of the stump with great swings and bites of the axe. Large chips flew out and up, rotating rapidly in the air like somersaulting gymnasts. He knew it would take longer this way than cutting it with the saw, but it felt much more the right thing to do. With the blows of the great axe Ishtar was being destroyed as well as toppled.

He knew it would take a long time. Gradually his strikes made a gash in the side of the tall stump. First he attacked the effigy on one side, then went to the other side and started a new cut from there. In time the two cuts converged.

Eventually there was only a slender strand of timber at its heart keeping the whole statue upright. Lylly stood back. He moved to stand directly in front of its face.

He raised the axe high over his head.

"Be gone," he shouted and brought the axe down directly into Ishtar's face.

The statue reeled and tilted back on itself under the blow. It hesitated for a moment as the supporting strand resisted the turning moment, but then the remaining wood sheared apart under the top-heavy weight and the effigy crashed to the ground.

He stood panting over the fallen statue with the axe head resting on the ground. That was the easy bit, he knew. Now he switched tools. He took out the four heavy steel wedges from his backpack. He gripped the sledgehammer. What he had to do was split the statue timber to break it up. Once split into smaller pieces he could then saw those pieces and so destroy the effigy completely.

It was long hard laborious work. He would drive a wedge into the wood with the sledgehammer. Then follow that by hammering in a second wedge alongside or parallel to the first. A crack in the timber formed, following the grain. Then he used a third and a fourth wedge to widen, extend and deepen the crack. Then he extracted the wedges and repeated the process. Eventually the crack extended the full length of the timber. With more wedges the crack reached all the way into the heart of the wood and out the other side and the statue fell apart lengthways into two pieces.

He then repeated the process on the first of the two pieces

and induced a longitudinal crack in that. That too eventually fell into two pieces. Then he attacked the other piece and so by mid-afternoon had four long pieces of wood. The statue had been split into four spars and was unrecognisable. The deity had no defences against the deadly steel.

With four pieces of wood much thinner in section he could now use the saw on them. He improvised a saw-horse by placing parts of one of the pi-frames on a bench at the perimeter of the grove. He fixed one of the four long pieces of the statue into place on the horse. With long slow sweeps of the saw he started to cut into the wood about two feet from one end, just where the quarter section of her head ended and the neck began. The repetitive see-saw seething donkey-cry of the saw blade completely overwhelmed and dominated the unheard disappearing shingle-sigh of the vanquished deity.

By the end of the day he had cut up all four parts of Ishtar's statue. The two-foot long pieces were small enough to throw into the river. Two by two he carried them to the bank of the stream and threw them into the deepest fastest flowing part of the water. He watched them float away.

He left the remainder of the tree, the base of the statue, untouched and still rooted into the ground. Without the presence of the sculpted deity above, it was now a harmless stump. He rapidly chopped away the protruding pieces of wood and smoothed the surface of the cut. In time the perimeter benches would collapse and rot away, but the stump would remain as the single strange sentinel and witness to the nightmare horrors that had once taken place here in the name of the goddess by the command of Bruno Ludo.

He hoped too that perhaps the tree wasn't completely dead and now relieved of the deathly and ominous burden of the statue, the trunk could push out new shoots, and new life might emerge into the light.

The grove of Ishtar was cleared. But it would still take many years for the spirit of the place to dissipate completely. And while Lylly felt thankful he had completed the task in daylight, he knew that without the locus of her statue Ishtar could not return. For the time being the goddess, damaged and diminished by Lylly's onslaught, had fled home to Babylon.

He made his way back to the chateau. He was tired but deeply satisfied. Any connection between Ishtar and Sylvie had been destroyed.

Where had he been, they asked? They'd missed him.

"Oh just spreading a bit of healthy atheism," he said. "Cleaning up some rubbish."

At the end of the three weeks Lylly was ready for whatever was going to happen next. Living with two fun-loving carefree women, who had come unscathed through the most spirit shattering experiences imaginable had taught him a big lesson. While his own philosophy had been: maybe today can be better than yesterday, Merci and Sylvie Stahl's was: tomorrow can be better than today, we'll make it so.

At the end of three weeks he was ready to leave. He was sure he would see them both again. But it didn't matter when.

He didn't go back to Larche or St Etienne to finish his walk. He felt he was done with walking for the time being. He didn't know what he was going to do but he thought it wouldn't involve walking.

He was heading home. But as he drove down the long red winding road leading away from the chateau he wondered if Viv, the agent from the unspecified country, was still in France. Well, he thought, there was only one way to find out.

MARK MOORE
Casita Galgo 2022
108,700 words

Printed in Great Britain
by Amazon